Anonymous

Report on the Administration of the Madras Presidency during the Year 1867-68

Anonymous

Report on the Administration of the Madras Presidency during the Year 1867-68

Reprint of the original, first published in 1868.

1st Edition 2022 | ISBN: 978-3-37504-822-8

Verlag (Publisher): Salzwasser Verlag GmbH, Zeilweg 44, 60439 Frankfurt, Deutschland
Vertretungsberechtigt (Authorized to represent): E. Roepke, Zeilweg 44, 60439 Frankfurt, Deutschland
Druck (Print): Books on Demand GmbH, In de Tarpen 42, 22848 Norderstedt, Deutschland

REPORT

ON THE

ADMINISTRATION

OF THE

MADRAS PRESIDENCY

DURING THE YEAR

1867-68.

Madras:

PRINTED BY H. MORGAN, AT THE FORT ST. GEORGE GAZETTE PRESS.

1868.

CONTENTS.

Section I.—EXECUTIVE GOVERNMENT.

Section II.—LEGISLATIVE.

Section III.—JUDICIAL.

Section IV.—REVENUE.

SECTION V.—PUBLIC WORKS.

SECTION VI.—MARINE.

Section VII.—FINANCIAL.

Section X.—EDUCATIONAL.

APPENDICES.

APPENDIX—I.

Legislative.

APPENDIX—II.

Judicial.

APPENDIX—III.

Revenue.

APPENDIX IV.

Public Works.

APPENDIX V.

MARINE.

APPENDIX VI.

FINANCIAL.

APPENDIX VII.

Political.

Travancore.

Cochin.

APPENDIX VIII.

Educational.

APPENDIX IX.

Miscellaneous.

Medical.

Municipality.

Observatory.

ANNUAL REPORT

ON THE

ADMINISTRATION OF THE MADRAS PRESIDENCY

DURING THE YEAR 1867-68.

SECTION I.—EXECUTIVE GOVERNMENT.

Retirement of Sir Thomas Pycroft, K.C.S.I.

ON the 29th October 1867, Sir Thomas Pycroft, K.C.S.I., having completed his term of office as a Member of Council, retired, after a service of thirty-eight years, a great portion of which was passed with high distinction in offices of the highest responsibility. He was succeeded by Mr. A. J. Arbuthnot, Chief Secretary to Government, and Provisional Member of Council.

Tours of H. E. the Governor.

2. His Excellency the Governor, in the month of June, visited the South Arcot District, and on the 17th of the following month left Madras on an extended tour through Cuddapah, Kurnool, and Bellary, the scene of the Madras Irrigation Company's operations. In September and October His Excellency visited the Districts of Trichinopoly and Madura, and in the month of February last spent three weeks in the Travancore State.

SECTION II.—LEGISLATIVE.

Additional Members.

3. The undermentioned gentlemen were appointed Additional Members of the Council for making Laws and Regulations, and took their seats on the dates specified opposite their names :—

Mr. Thomas Clarke—6th April 1867.

Mr. W. Reierson Arbuthnot—4th May 1867.

Mir Hoomayoon Jah Bahadur—15th November 1867.

The Honorable Messrs. J. B. Norton (Advocate General) and A. F. Brown, and Gajala Lutchmenarasu Chettigaru, were re-appointed Additional Members.

Acts passed by the Council.

4. The Council for making Laws and Regulations have during the year passed the following Acts :—

Act No. II of 1867, "An Act to repeal Section 37 of Regulation XIV of 1816, relating to Government Pleaders," which received the assent of the

Governor General on the 9th May, and took effect from the 1st July 1867. Under the provisions of the Madras Regulation, referred to in the title of this Act, the nomination of Government Pleaders in the different Courts of the Mofussil was vested in the Zillah Judges, and the appointments made by Government. The Act was passed to relieve the Judges from all connexion with these appointments, and to enable the Government to make such arrangements as they thought desirable for filling the post of Government Pleader.

Act No. III of 1867, "An Act to provide for the examination and settlement of claims against His Highness Prince Azeem Jah Bahadur," received the assent of the Governor General on the 1st June, and took effect on the 11th June 1867. Fifteen lacs of Rupees having been allotted for the settlement of claims against His Highness, this Act legalizes the proceedings of a Commissioner charged with investigating all claims laid before him, and gives him the powers of a Civil Court for examining witnesses, &c., and also provides that the creditors who may make their claims to the Commissioner shall abide absolutely by the award of the Government of Fort Saint George, on the report of the Commissioner.

Act No. IV of 1867, "An Act to repeal Madras Act I of 1863 (to enable Subordinate Magistrates of the second class to take cognizance of offences under Section 174 of the Indian Penal Code)," received the assent of the Governor General on the 10th June, and took effect from the 2nd July 1867. The Act repealed enabled the Subordinate Magistracy to punish disobedience to their summons, an offence the cognizance of which by the Penal Code was confined to the Higher Magistracy. The Imperial Act VIII of 1866, having given this power to all Magistrates, the Madras Act became superfluous and was repealed.

Act No. V of 1867, "An Act to repeal parts of certain Regulations and Acts relating to the offices of Hindoo and Mahomedan Law Officers," received the assent of the Governor General on the 21st June, and took effect from the 12th July 1867. This Act rescinds all such enactments affecting this Presidency as refer to the offices of Hindoo and Mahomedan Law Officers, these offices having been abolished by Act XI of 1864.

Act No. VI of 1867, "An Act to amend Act XII of 1851 (an Act for securing the Land Revenue of Madras)," received the assent of the Governor General on the 27th June, and took effect from the 1st July 1867. The object of this Act is to give the Collector of Madras the power of distraining and selling moveable property, by forcible entry, for the recovery of arrears of revenue due upon land situated within the town of Madras, as well as the power of selling the land itself in case of there being no other means of realizing the revenue. These powers are exercised by all the Collectors in the Mofussil under Madras Acts II of 1864 and VIII of 1865, and it was deemed expedient that the Collector of Madras should be invested with the same powers.

Act No. VII of 1867, "An Act to consolidate and amend the laws relating to the levy of Port dues and fees at Ports within the Presidency of Fort Saint George," received the assent of the Governor General on the 12th July, and took effect from the 2nd August 1867. In August 1866, a Bill was introduced into the Local Legislature, the object of which was simply to provide for the levy of Port dues, under Act XXII of 1855, in the port of Beypore and any other port to which the Act might hereafter be extended; but the Select Committee appointed to report on the Bill, recommended that, in place of the measure then before the Council, a single Act should be passed, applicable as well to ports in this Presidency, to which Act XXII of 1855 has already been extended, as to those to which it may hereafter be extended. The present Act, accordingly, repeals and re-enacts the provisions of the several enactments regulating Port dues in this Presidency, with such amendments as experience has shewn to be necessary or desirable.

Act No. VIII of 1867, "An Act to incorporate the Police of the Town of Madras with the General Police of the Madras Presidency; to extend the jurisdiction of the Town Police Magistrates; and to amend and consolidate the provisions of Act No. XIII of 1856 (for regulating the Police of the Towns of Calcutta, Madras, and Bombay), and of Act No. XLVIII of 1860 (to amend Act XIII of 1856)," received the assent of the Governor General on the 24th July, and took effect from the 1st September 1867. This Act amalgamates the Madras Town Police with the General Police of the Presidency in all respects, and gives the Town Police Magistrates the full powers of a Magistrate in cases in which the accused consents to their finally disposing of case.

Act No. IX of 1867, "An Act to amend the law relating to the appointment of Municipal Commissioners for the Town of Madras and the management of its Municipal affairs, and to make better provision for the Police, conservancy, and improvement of the said town, and to enable the said Commissioners to levy taxes, tolls, and rates therein," received the assent of the Governor General on the 5th September, and took effect from the 1st November 1867. This Act amends the former Municipal Act, and provides for the registration of births and deaths, the taking of a census, the levy of lighting and water rates (in expectation of the supply of Madras with water from the Red Hills), and other minor points; and it makes the President of the Commission solely responsible for the executive duties, and provides for the appointment of thirty-two unpaid Commissioners from eight divisions of Madras, in place of the former six Commissioners, of whom three were salaried and three unpaid.

5. The Legislative Returns, prepared according to the forms prescribed by the Calcutta Statistical Committee, will be found in the Appendix.

Statistical Committee's Returns.

Section III.—JUDICIAL.

GENERAL.

6. The Judicial work on Hill ranges has always given rise to some trouble. In 1862, the Revenue Officer, the Deputy Tahsildar and Sub-Magistrate of the Shevaroy Hills, was invested with the powers of a District Moonsiff, but it was found difficult to secure a qualified officer, and the jurisdiction has been re-transferred to the District Moonsiff of Salem, who visits the Hills four times a year (or oftener if necessary). The Judicial work on the Hills is very light.

Administration of justice on the Shevaroy Hills.

7. It has been found necessary to decide that District Moonsiffs shall not hereafter serve on Municipal Commissions, since the institution of suits against the Commissioners in the District Moonsiff's Courts was becoming not uncommon, and it was necessary to transfer the suits to other Courts, a course alike inconvenient to both parties.

Ineligibility of District Moonsiffs as Municipal Commissioners.

CIVIL JUSTICE.

8. The Principal Sudder Ameen who was temporarily appointed in 1866 to assist in clearing the heavy files of the Bellary Civil Court, having completed his work there, was, on the 1st July 1867, transferred to Vizagapatam, to assist in clearing the increasing files of the Civil Court at the latter station.

Vizagapatam Principal Sudder Ameen.

9. Certain Bankers, Merchants, and Sowcars of Bellary, having, through the Bank of Madras, prayed for the extension of Act V of 1866, for the summary procedure on Bills of Exchange, &c., to the Civil Court, the Government directed that the provisions of Sections 2 to 7 of the Act in question be applied to the Courts of the Civil Judge and of the Principal Sudder Ameen of the Zillah of Bellary.

Extension of Act V of 1866 to Bellary.

10. The majority of the local Judicial officers continue of opinion that the Whipping Act VI of 1864, has worked satisfactorily, and that the punishment of whipping has a certain deterrent effect in the prevention of crime.

Whipping Act.

11. At the close of 1866, there remained 62,844 Original Suits undecided, and during the year 1867, 1,63,727 were instituted, 2,054 were remanded or re-admitted, making a total of 2,28,625 (not including Suits received by transfer), being 4,115* less than the number of Suits in 1866.

Original Suits.

* Original Suits pending, instituted, and re-admitted.

1866	2,32,740
1867	2,28,625
Decrease	4,115

These 2,28,625 Suits came before the following Courts :—

Panchayets	509
Village Moonsiffs	50,783
District Moonsiffs in their ordinary jurisdiction...	89,401
District Moonsiffs under Madras Act IV of 1863	70,328
Cantonment Small Cause Courts...	1,870
Principal Sudder Ameens in their ordinary jurisdiction	2,182
Principal Sudder Ameens under Madras Act IV of 1863...	1,892
Subordinate Judges and Assistant Agents...	51
Civil Judges and Agents in their ordinary jurisdiction	1,207
Civil Judges and Agents under Act IV of 1863...	509
Judges of Small Cause Courts......	9,431
Judges in the exercise of the powers of a Principal Sudder Ameen.	462
	2,28,625

12. Of the number of Suits brought before the abovementioned Courts, 1,68,232 Suits, or 73½ per cent., were disposed of, and 60,393 remained undecided at the close of the year, being less by 1,664 and 2,451,* respectively, than the number determined and remaining unsettled in the previous year, though the number of Suits actually decided on the merits was slightly in excess of the number so decided in 1866.

Number of Original Suits disposed of.

The following table shews the several Courts of Judicature by whom the 1,68,232 Suits were disposed of :—

	Ordinary Suits.	Small Causes.	Total.
Panchayets	362	...	362
Village Moonsiffs	39,493	...	39,493
District Moonsiffs	48,283	64,932	1,13,215
Cantonment Small Cause Courts	...	1,815	1,815
Principal Sudder Ameens	993	1,776	2,769
Assistant Agents	42	...	42
Civil Judges and Agents...	686	464	1,150
Judges of Small Cause Courts...	...	9,064	9,064
Do. in the exercise of the powers of a Principal Sudder Ameen	322	...	322
	90,181	78,051	1,68,232

	Disposed of.	Pending.
* 1866	1,69,896	62,844
1867	1,68,232	60,393
Decrease ...	1,664	2,451

Original Suits how disposed of.

13. Of the Suits disposed of by the several Courts in their ordinary jurisdiction, 45,315, or 50 per cent., were decided on the merits in favor of plaintiffs; and 10,096, or 11 per cent., in favor of defendants; 10,414, or 12 per cent., were dismissed for default; 22,658, or 25 per cent., were adjusted or withdrawn; and 1,698, or 2 per cent., were disposed of in other ways. Of the small causes disposed of by District Moonsiffs and others under Madras Act IV of 1863, 37,892, or 56 per cent., were decreed on the merits for plaintiffs; and 8,868, or 13 per cent., for defendants; 3,735, or 6 per cent., were dismissed for default; 14,966, or 22 per cent., were adjusted or withdrawn; and 1,711, or 3 per cent., were otherwise disposed of.

Of those disposed of by Courts of Small Causes under Act XI of 1865, 5,559, or 61 per cent., were decreed on the merits for plaintiffs, and 632, or 7 per cent., for defendants; 431, or 6 per cent., were dismissed for default; and 2,442, or 26 per cent., were adjusted or withdrawn. Of those disposed of by the Cantonment Small Cause Courts, 1,045, or 57½ per cent., were decreed on the merits for plaintiffs; and 124, or 7 per cent., for defendants; 236, or 13 per cent., were dismissed for default, and 410, or 22½ per cent., were adjusted or withdrawn.

Duration of Suits.

14. The length of time during which Suits remained on the files of the Courts were on the average as follows :—

	Ordinary Suits.			Small Causes.		
	Y.	M.	D.	Y.	M.	D.
District Moonsiffs	1	...	5	...	1	22
Cantonment Small Cause Courts	...	...	...	...	...	14
Principal Sudder Ameens...	...	8	11	...	1	...
Assistant Agents	...	6	7	...	...	...
Civil Judges and Agents	...	11	25	...	1	18
Judges of the Small Cause Courts having powers of a Principal Sudder Ameen	...	6	27	...	...	20

Nature of Suits newly brought.

15. The Suits newly instituted during the year may be classified as follows :—

For rent and revenue derivable from land...	5,580
Lands	10,298
Real property, such as houses, &c.	4,169
Debts, wages...	1,41,879
Caste, religion, &c...	380
Indigo, Sugar, &c...	1,421

The value of the property in question in the Original Suits pending at the close of the year, amounted in all to 167,88,405 Rupees.

Appeals.

16. The Appeal Suits brought before the Courts subordinate to the High Court in the course of the year, together with those which were pending at the close of 1866 (but exclusive of those received by transfer), amounted in all to 12,358. Of these, 6,758 were disposed of as shewn below, and 5,600, of the value of Rupees 17,50,868, were left undetermined at the close of the year.

Appeals how disposed of.

17. 2,011, or 30 per cent., were decreed on the merits in favor of Appellants, and 3,721, or 55 per cent., for respondents; 394, or 6 per cent., were remanded to Lower Courts; 282, or 4 per cent., dismissed for default; 323, or 5 per cent., adjusted or withdrawn; and 27 were disposed of in other ways.

Duration of Appeals.

18. The average duration of Appeal Suits was one year and twenty-five days before the Civil Judges, one year and thirteen days before the Principal Sudder Ameens, one year two months and eighteen days before the Judges of Small Cause Courts vested with the power of a Principal Sudder Ameen.

74,578 applications for execution of decrees, and 1,69,900 petitions of a miscellaneous character, were also disposed of by the Lower Courts, and there remained undisposed of 13,653 of the former, and 3,671 of the latter.

High Court, Original Jurisdiction.

19. 84 Suits were pending at the commencement of, and 567 instituted during, the year under review on the Original Side of the High Court, making a total of 651. Of these, 219 were decided at the settlement of issues, and 150 on final disposal; 7 were dismissed for default, 5 were withdrawn with leave to bring fresh Suits, 103 absolutely, and 9 were disposed of in other ways, thus leaving 158 Suits pending on the 31st December 1867. There were also 6 cases disposed of during the year out of those remaining on the file of the late Supreme Court.

Appellate Jurisdiction.

20. At the close of 1866, there were pending before the High Court in its Appellate Jurisdiction, 31 Regular and 179 Special Appeals, and 115 Regular and 611 Special Appeals were received in 1867; altogether there was a total of 146 Regular and 790 Special Appeals pending and instituted. As compared with the previous year, there was an increase of 21 Regular and 45* Special Appeals in the number newly instituted; 79 Regular and 516 Special Appeals were disposed of, and there remained on the file, at the close of the year, 67 Regular and 274 Special Appeals.

	Regular.	Special.
* 1867	115	611
1866	94	566
Increase ...	21	45

Disposal of Appeals.

21. The following statement shews the manner in which the Appeal Suits were disposed of, viz. :—

	Regular.	Special.
Decrees confirmed	50	458
Do. amended	8	15
Do. reversed	13	18
Suits remanded	4	11
Appeals dismissed for default	2	10
Do. adjusted or withdrawn	1	4
Do. otherwise disposed of	1	0
	79	516

Duration of Appeals.

22. The average duration of Appeal Suits disposed of was three months and twenty-three days, and the total value of the Appeal Suits, pending at the close of the year, was Rupees 24,53,329-13-6.

Of the 294 Civil Petitions brought before the High Court 236 were disposed of as follows, viz. :—

Orders confirmed	166
Do. reversed	36
Dismissed for default	23
Otherwise disposed of	11
	236

51 cases were referred for the Judgment of the High Court, under Section 22, Act XI of 1865, and Section 28, Act XXIII of 1861. Of these, 45 were disposed of within the year.

CRIMINAL JUSTICE.

High Court. Criminal Petitions.

23. The High Court disposed of 207 of the Criminal Petitions brought before them, viz. :—

Dismissed after hearing without perusal of record	142
Orders or Sentences of Lower Courts confirmed after perusal of record	19
Sentences amended do.	17
Do. reversed do.	24
Otherwise disposed of without perusing the record	1
Do. after perusing the record...	2
Remanded	2

Sentences of death.

24. 78 trials, in which sentence of death was recorded by the Session Courts, were referred for the confirmation of the High Court, of which 75 were disposed of within the year as follows :—

Sentences confirmed	63
Modified or amended	10
Reversed	2

25. 67 references were made to the High Court under Section 434 of the Code of Criminal Procedure. The sentences or orders of the Lower Courts were reversed in 41, modified or amended in 9. In the remaining 17, there was no error on a point of law to justify the High Court's interference.

References.

26. Of 1,812 Calendars of Cases tried by the Session Courts, which were reviewed by the High Court, the records in 23 were called up, in 7 of which the sentences were confirmed; in 3 the sentences were quashed or reversed; and in 17 the sentences were modified or amended.

Review of proceedings of Lower Courts.

Of the other Calendars, the High Court, without perusing the records, quashed the sentences in 7 cases, and directed the Session Courts, under Section 402 of the Criminal Procedure Code, to pass fresh sentences; in 55 they remarked on certain irregularities and omissions; in 11 the sentences were altered after perusing the explanation submitted by the Session Courts, and the rest called for no remark.

In addition to the above, the High Court revised the Proceedings of the Session Courts passed upon Appeal or upon review of the Calendars of the Magistracy in 307 cases, and which were submitted in accordance with their Circular Order dated 5th March, 1867. In 14 of these cases, they had occasion to point out certain irregularities, and in 6 cases, the orders of the Session Courts were confirmed after perusal of the records. The others called for no notice.

27. During the year 1,32,386 offences of all kinds were committed, being 10·1 per cent. less than in 1866, and 6·8 per cent. less than the average of three years. In these cases, 273,689 persons were concerned. A comparative statement regarding these offences will be found, appended. 65·6 per cent. of cases reported were brought to trial, and 63·3 per cent. of the persons accused. While in 77·5 per cent. of the cases tried, convictions were obtained, 67·3 per cent. of the persons tried were convicted. 21·3 per cent. of lost property were recovered. 17·4 per cent. of cases went by default. One in 142 of the population appeared to answer a charge before a Court.

Summary of offences.

28. 75,311 offences punishable under the Penal Code, and involving 173,645 persons, were committed, being a decrease of cases of 4,103 as compared with 1866. 52·2 per cent. of cases and 52·3 per cent. of persons concerned were brought to trial. In 68·9 per cent. of the cases brought to trial, convictions were obtained; and of persons tried 56·1 per cent. were convicted. 21 per cent. of lost property were recovered.

Offences under the Penal Code.

29. Offences against the person shew 21,493 cases, against 20,909 in 1866. Of these, 53·3 per cent. of the cases and 51·3 per cent. of the persons concerned were tried; and in 63·6 per cent. of

Offences against the person.

the cases tried, convictions followed, 46·3 per cent. of persons being convicted. The large number of petty hurt and assault cases which fell through accounts for the low per-centage of convictions in these cases.

Murders.

30. During the year under report 222 murders were committed, being 20 less than in 1866. Convictions were obtained in 109 cases, or 49 per cent. In these cases, 534 persons were supposed to be concerned, and 472 of them (88·3 per cent.) were produced, of whom 180, or 38·1 per cent., were convicted; 94 were sentenced to death; 84 to transportation for life; and 2 were pronounced to be insane. 80 culpable homicides occurred, in 49 of which cases convictions were obtained. Each case on an average involved three persons. The proportion of cases of murder and culpable homicide taken together, in which convictions were obtained, was 52·3 per cent.

Attempts to commit suicide.

31. 245 attempts to commit suicide were reported, against 170 in 1866.

Causing Miscarriage and abandonment of offspring. Kidnapping and abduction. Rape.

32. 113 cases of causing miscarriage and abandonment of offspring were entered, in which 200 persons were concerned, but only 26 were punished in 19 cases. 33 persons were punished for kidnapping or abduction in 93 cases reported. 15 persons only were convicted of rape out of 84 charges, and only one person was convicted of prostitution of minors, 9 cases being entered.

Petty offences against the person.

33. There were 19,666 charges of hurt, assault, and wrongful restraint, 10,167 (51·6 per cent.) of which were tried. Half the persons complained against were tried, and of these 45·6 per cent. were convicted. 8,365 cases, involving 19,926 persons, were withdrawn or allowed to go by default.

Offences against property with violence.

34. Of offences against property with violence there were 8,632 cases, involving 19,224 persons. Of these, 5,198 persons were tried, and 3,181 (61·1 per cent.) convicted. The property lost was Rs. 5,85,802, of which Rs. 77,622, or 13·2 per cent., were recovered. There has been a great decrease in this class of offences as compared with 1866, amounting to 24·8 per cent.

Dacoities.

35. Dacoities have fallen to one-half nearly (52 per cent.) of the last year's numbers. This was to be expected in a year of sufficient plenty, occurring after one of great distress. The number was 533, and convictions were obtained in 130 cases—24·3 per cent. 145 cases arose in houses and villages, the rest in fields, highways, &c. Torchlight gang robberies fell to 65, against an annual average of 165 for the four past years, a decrease of 60·6 per cent. 27·7 per cent. were convicted. In dacoities, 534 persons, or 31·4 per cent., of 1,699 persons produced, were punished. 17·1 per cent. of property lost were recovered.

36. There were 812 cases of robbery, against 1,124 in 1866, shewing a decrease of 27·7 per cent. In 24·1 per cent. of the cases reported convictions followed, and 46·7 per cent. of persons arrested were punished. Out of 23 cases of robbery by drugging (in five of which death followed) 9 convictions were obtained (39 per cent.), and 12 persons were sentenced out of 26 brought to trial.

Robbery.

37. There were 6,883 house-breaking cases, against 8,586 in 1866—a decrease of 19·8 per cent. 20·9 per cent. of cases reported were detected; and of 3,529 persons arrested 2,057, or 58·3 per cent., were convicted. Rupees 4,46,337 of property was lost, of which Rupees 55,366 (12·4 per cent.) was recovered. House-breaking cases in villages are very difficult to detect. In towns, 29·3 per cent. of cases were detected, (*i. e.*, prosecuted to conviction.) 68 per cent. of persons arrested were convicted, and 16 per cent. of property lost was recovered. In Madras Town, 31 per cent. of property was recovered. In 75·3 per cent. of all house-breaking cases the amount lost was less than 50 Rupees, and in 1,392 cases the amount was under 1 Rupee.

House-breaking.

38. There was a decrease of 9·9 per cent. in 1867 in the total number of offences against property without violence. 22,594 cases were reported, of which 19,602 came under the head of Theft. Convictions were obtained in 40·5 per cent. only of theft cases, which is a very poor average for this crime. Only 586 cases of criminal breach of trust were reported, of which 390 were brought to trial, resulting in the conviction of 240 persons. There were 436 cases of cheating—264 cases were tried, and 150 persons were punished. The very small number of cases reported under these two very common heads of offence leads to the conclusion that such offences are not accurately reported. These cases are not cognizable by the Police, and the statistics given are obtained from the Magisterial returns. 31·6 per cent. of property lost has been recovered in all offences against property without violence.

Offences against property without violence.

39. There was a slight decrease under the head Malicious offences against Property, 4,848 offences having been committed against 5,115 in the previous year. 50 per cent. of cases were brought to trial, and in 62·9 per cent. of these cases conviction was obtained. Out of Rupees 19,613 lost, only Rupees 652 were recovered. This is accounted for by the large amount lost under the heads of Mischief by Fire (Rupees 12,367), and Mischief to Animals (Rupees 2,958). 85·4 per cent. of all malicious offences against property were cases of petty mischief, and in 4,140 cases of this nature the average loss or damage did not amount to 1 Rupee per case.

Malicious offences against property.

40. 335 offences were reported under the head Forgery and offences against the currency. 344 were reported in 1866. 186 cases of forgery were reported, in which 405 persons were sup-

Forgery and offences against currency.

posed to be concerned. 362 persons were produced, of whom 116 only were committed to the Higher Courts, where 67 were convicted. Six cases were tried by the High Court, in which six persons were concerned. The whole were convicted and sentenced. The statistics of forgery thus presented cannot be supposed to afford any real indication of the actual state of this crime in the country. The offence is not primarily cognizable by the Police, and it is possible that a certain number of offences reported escape registry in the Magisterial returns. All cases finally disposed of are, of course, entered; but some in which the inquiry, owing to circumstances (absconding of offender, &c.,) remains incomplete, may perhaps be omitted. Only 11 cases of counterfeiting, or altering coin, were brought forward, and in only one of these was conviction obtained. 129 cases of uttering or possessing counterfeit coin were reported. 156 persons were concerned, of whom 136 were produced, and 68 convicted in 60 cases. 50 per cent. of persons were convicted to every 100 offences against the currency. Only five cases of fraud relating to stamps, and three cases of offences relating to trade and property marks, were reported throughout the Presidency.

Contempts and offences against public justice.

41. The number of contempts and offences against public justice has increased from 2,950 in 1866 to 3,522 in 1867. The increase was mainly under the head of Contempt of Legal Process or Orders, of which there were 2,204 cases against 1,660 in the previous year. In 2,156 cases 4,869 persons were produced, of whom 4,055 were punished. 270 cases of perjury were brought forward, of which 189 were committed to the Higher Courts,where 131 persons were convicted out of 226 tried. Only 107 cases of false charge were brought forward (the offence is constant), and 56 persons were punished. There were 56 cases of negligent escape, in which 45 persons were found guilty against 86 cases and 83 persons in 1866, shewing increased vigilance of custody. 139 cases of insult, or causing interruption to a public servant sitting in a judicial proceeding, occurred under Section 228 of the Penal Code. 162 persons were punished, of whom 11 were imprisoned for periods of one month or under, and 151 were fined in sums averaging about 8 Rupees. 82 per cent. of these cases occurred in Sub-Magistrates' Courts.

Miscellaneous.

42. 13,887 offences were reported under miscellaneous heads, of which 53·2 per cent. were brought to trial. 61·7 per cent. of these cases were proved, and 55·2 per cent. of persons were punished. There were 257 cases of rioting, in which 2,522 persons were said to be concerned, 1,233 of whom were punished in 239 cases brought before the Courts. Out of 8,333 complaints of criminal trespass, involving charges against 24,334 persons, 2,041 cases (24·5 per cent.) only were prosecuted to conviction, and 4,482 persons were punished. 4,134 cases, or one-half, were allowed to go by default.

Four cases of bigamy brought forward were not proved. 133 cases of adultery, under Section 497, were brought forward, in which 159 persons were produced for trial, of whom 14 only were convicted and punished. This Section is but rarely brought into action, and then chiefly by the lower classes of natives as a channel for vindictiveness.

43. There were 57,075 offences against Special Laws, shewing a considerable decrease as compared with the three previous years, which averaged 62,186. 83·3 per cent. of cases, and 82·4 per cent. of persons concerned, were brought to trial. Convictions were obtained in 84·6 per cent. of cases tried; and of persons tried, 79·6 per cent. were punished. 13·7 per cent. of cases went by default. 41·3 per cent. of property lost was recovered.

Special Laws.

18 cases of trespass, &c., by European British subjects were charged, in which 12 persons were punished. There were 233 offences against the Railway Act, in which 285 persons were punished. 148 persons were convicted in 47 offences against the Merchant Seamen's Act. In 1866 there was the same number of offences, but only 98 persons were punished. The number of contempts of Courts, &c., under the Criminal Procedure Code, has fallen from 285 in 1866 to 58 in 1867. Only nine persons were bound over to keep the peace under the Criminal Procedure Code, and 96 persons (out of 136 produced) were required to furnish security for good behaviour as rogues or vagabonds under Chapter XIX., Criminal Procedure Code. Of these, 42 were committed to prison for various periods in default of security. In 1866, 215 persons were bound over to give security, of whom 183 were imprisoned in default. The Courts become more and more chary of exercising the wide powers given under this chapter.

44. 8,841 offences were reported under the Madras Town Police Act, against 12,065 in 1866. The decrease has been caused partly by lowered prices, partly by the substitution of Act VIII of 1867 (which came into operation on the 1st September) for Act XIII of 1856. All offences against property, whether petty or otherwise, are now tried under the Penal Code. There has also been a considerable decrease under the heads of Assault and Miscellaneous offences, such as nuisances, breaches of Police and Street Regulations, &c. The Town Police Magistrates disposed of 5,923 cases, in 4,388 of which (74 per cent.) convictions were obtained. 9,183 persons were produced, of whom 6,604, or 71·9 per cent., were convicted. During the last two years there has been a marked decrease in the number of persons produced before Magistrates for petty breaches of Street Regulations, &c.

Madras Town Police Act.

45. There has been a decrease of offences against the Revenue Laws. 2,001 were reported, against 2,319 in 1866. The decrease is under the head of Salt Laws. Breaches of the Salt Laws fell

Offences against Revenue Laws.

from 1,126 cases in 1866 to 468 cases in 1867. Breaches of the Stamp Act increased from 57 to 106. Abkarry cases increased from 1,136 cases in 1866 to 1,427 cases in 1867. Convictions were obtained in 82 per cent. of cases reported, and 82·8 per cent. of persons arrested were convicted.

Cases tried by Heads of Villages.

46. There has been a considerable decrease in the number of cases disposed of by Heads of Villages. Out of 27,031 offences, 23,018 were disposed of, against 36,229 offences and 30,400 disposed of in 1866. The decrease under the head of Petty Theft may be accounted for by the comparative cheapness of food, but there is also a decrease of nearly 23 per cent. under the head of Petty Assault, which is not so easily accounted for. Excluding the famine year 1866, a progressive increase is visible over former years in the number of cases disposed of by Heads of Villages. 74 per cent. of all cases resulted in conviction, against 70·6 per cent. in 1866.

Cases by Officers commanding Cantonments.

47. 36 cases were disposed of under Section 84 of the Articles of War, in which 64 persons were produced and punished. Two were imprisoned, 56 fined, three flogged, and three simply admonished.

Cases Summarily disposed of.

48. 37,558 cases under the Penal Code were summarily disposed of by Magistrates, against 39,523 in 1866. The difference has been caused by the decrease of crime, for a larger proportion of cases tried have been adjudicated by the Lower Courts. 19·5 per cent. of all cases summarily tried under the Penal Code were disposed of by Magistrates with full powers, 19·2 per cent. by Subordinate Magistrates of the first class, and the remainder, or 61·1 per cent., by Subordinate Magistrates of the second class. 56 per cent. of persons tried were convicted. The average varies little with Magistrates of different classes, but Magistrates with full powers convicted the smallest proportion. This differs from the results of former years, in which Subordinate Magistrates of the second class convicted the smallest proportion of persons brought to trial. 219 cases of robbery were disposed of by Magistrates with full powers, against 183 in 1866.

Cases under Special Laws tried by Magistrates.

49. The progressive decrease in the number of cases under Special Laws, disposed of by Stipendiary Magistrates, continues in the year under review. There were 24,519 cases tried, against 25,270 in 1866. The decrease since 1864 amounts to 26·7 per cent. 47,933 persons were tried, of whom 38,518, or 80·3 per cent., were convicted. The decrease in the number of cases disposed of is entirely under the head of Magistrates with full powers. The number of cases disposed of by Subordinate Magistrates of the first and second class has increased. The difference under the former head has arisen from the smaller number of cases disposed of by the Madras Town Police Magistrates.

Heads of Villages summarily determined 23,018 cases, in which 34,544 persons were tried, of whom 27,203, or 78·7 per cent., were convicted.

85,095 cases in all were summarily disposed of by Magistrates and Heads of Villages, shewing a decrease of 10·6 per cent. as compared with 1866. 169,658 persons were charged, of whom 114,596, or 67·5 per cent., were convicted.

Preliminary enquiries.

50. Magistrates of all classes held preliminary inquiry into 2,688 cases, of which 1,774, or 66 per cent., were committed to the Higher Courts. 6,513 persons were produced for inquiry, of whom 3,801 (58·4 per cent.) were committed for trial. There has been a decrease of 26·2 per cent. in the total number of committable cases inquired into, as compared with 1866. This is attributable to the decrease of grave crime. There has been increased action on the part of the higher classes of Magistrates. Magistrates with full powers held inquiry into 14·2 per cent. of the cases, against 12 per cent. in 1866. First class Subordinate Magistrates inquired into 16·2 per cent. of the total cases, against 13·4 per cent. in 1866. The remaining cases (69·5 per cent.) were inquired into by second class Sub-Magistrates, against 74·5 per cent. in 1866. Of cases actually committed, 17·4 per cent. were by Magistrates with full powers; 15·6 per cent. by Subordinate Magistrates, first class; and 66·8 per cent. by Subordinate Magistrates, second class.

Cases tried by higher Courts.

51. 1,819 cases were tried by the higher Courts. Of 3,834 persons tried, 2,207, or 57·5 per cent., were convicted. This is a slight falling off from the last year, in which 60·3 per cent. were convicted. The average of the past five years is 57 per cent. Diminution of grave crime has caused a decrease in the number of cases tried. 57·1 per cent. of persons tried by Principal Sudder Ameens, and 56·5 per cent. of persons tried by Session Courts were convicted. Before the High Court, 75·3 per cent. of persons tried were convicted.

Punishments.

52. 119,549 persons were punished in 1867, against 134,378 in 1866—a decrease of 11 per cent. An increase, however, is exhibited over the year 1865. The intervention of a year of great scarcity, and consequent crime, has disturbed progressive calculations.

Death.

53. 96 persons were sentenced to death—94 for murder, one for abetment of murder, and one for dacoity with murder.

Transportation.

54. There has been a very striking decrease in the number of persons sentenced to transportation. Only 186 have been so sentenced, against 537 in 1866 (a decrease of 65·4 per cent.), and against an average of 525 in the four last years. The number of persons transported for murder has increased from 77 in 1866 to 84 in 1867. The decrease is chiefly under the heads of Dacoity and House-breaking. Only 48 persons have been

transported for dacoity, against 299 in 1866, and seven persons have been transported for house-breaking, against 42 in the previous year. The marked difference affords a very satisfactory illustration of a decrease in gravity of the circumstances of offence, far more than corresponding with the decrease in actual number of crimes committed. Six persons have been transported for theft, one for cheating, two for forgery, and one for giving false evidence.

Imprisonment.

55. 49,403 persons were sentenced to imprisonment, shewing a decrease of 24·6 per cent. from the famine year 1866, but an increase over the years antecedent. The decrease is distributed throughout the different terms of imprisonment.

Whipping.

56. Only 3,307 persons have been whipped, against 6,078 in 1866—a decrease of nearly one-half. There is also some decrease from the number (3,986) whipped in 1865, the year after the present Act came into operation. The per-centage of persons whipped shews that this punishment has been somewhat more sparingly awarded during the past year. 27 dacoits and robbers were whipped. The rest were principally house-breakers and thieves. 16 persons were flogged in the town of Madras for offences against Port Regulation and Boat Rules, and 463 persons for offences against the Madras Town Police Act. 1,027 persons were flogged under this last head in 1866, but there were grain riots in that year.

Persons fined.

57. 66,557 persons were fined, against 62,123 in 1866. The total amount levied was Rupees 3,08,464, against 2,96,204 in 1866. In the famine year fines were less, and other punishments more.

The following is a comparative summary of all Criminal Judicial proceedings against persons from 1864 to 1867 :—

	1867.	1866.	1865.	1864.
Total number of persons arrested and proceeded against ...	173,485	188,854	175,219	176,694
N. B.—Proportion of persons proceeded against to population, one in...	142	128	136	138
Acquitted and Discharged.				
Under Penal Code	39,920	43,305	40,647	51,783
Do. Special Laws	16,762	18,119	18,238	17,620
Total discharged, &c...	56,682	61,424	58,885	69,403
Per-centage of persons discharged to persons proceeded against	32·6	32·5	33·6	39·2

Convicted and Sentenced.

To death...	96	91	101	105
„ transportation	186	537	495	616
„ imprisonment	49,403	65,549	46,329	37,432
„ whipping	2,932	6,078	3,986	2,530
„ fine...	63,823	62,123	67,966	69,005
„ other punishments, (security for good behaviour, maintenance of orders, &c.) ...	363	...	...	...
Total convicted...	116,803	134,378	118,877	109,688
Per-centage of persons convicted to persons proceeded against...	67·3	69·4	66·3	60·7

The number of persons proceeded against has decreased. There is a very slight decrease in the per-centage of convictions as compared with 1866, but an increase as compared with previous years. The ratio for 1867 is 67·3 per cent. 60·2 per cent. was the ratio in England in 1862.

Prevalence of crime according to locality.

58. The Comparative Return of Offences against the Penal Code for 1867 shews that murder was most rife in Vizagapatam. Attempts at suicide were most frequent in Vizagapatam, Cuddapah, and North Arcot. Bellary has most robberies. Dacoity was most prevalent in Bellary, North Arcot, South Arcot, and Madura. Tanjore suffers far more from burglary than any other district. Cases of ordinary mischief predominate in Salem. Bellary has most cases of arson. Cuddapah, North Arcot, Tanjore, and Salem shew most forgeries. North Arcot and Tinnevelly head the list in cases of perjury, while rioting is most prevalent in Tanjore, Madura, Tinnevelly, and Salem.

Castes of offenders.

59. The Return of Castes of Convicted Offenders against the Indian Penal Code shews that out of 180 murderers 44 were persons of the Mudali, Naidu, and Chetty castes; 46 were Páriahs and other low castes. 10 Christians, 2 Mussulmans, and 4 Moplays and Lubbays committed murder. Out of 117 persons convicted of attempt at suicide, 47 were of the Naidu and Mudali castes, and 23 were low caste persons. In petty cases, of causing hurt, the Naidus and Chetties largely preponderate, as also in petty assault. Robberies and dacoities are chiefly committed by Pariahs, Koravers, and wandering tribes and low castes. Only 24 Mussulmans have been convicted in these crimes out of a total of 880 persons. Naidus and Mudalis contribute 99. Pariahs, hill and wandering tribes and other low castes are the principal house-breakers; but here again Naidus, Mudalis, &c., contribute 20 per cent. of the

whole. They also figure largely in theft, accompanied by Pariahs, Koravers, Moravers, and other low castes. 701 Mussulmans committed theft out of a total of 12,930 persons convicted. Out of 67 forgers, 11 were Brahmins, and 31 Naidus and Mudalis. Five East Indians committed forgery. The fabricators of false evidence are chiefly Naidus, Mudalis, and low castes. Out of a total of 51,047 convicted offenders, 30 were Europeans, one of whom committed murder, and 23 were guilty of acts of petty violence. There were 50 East Indians, 23 of whom committed offences against property. 1,953 were Brahmins, chiefly concerned in petty cases. 16,549, or 32 per cent., of the whole number were Naidus, Mudalis, &c. Pariahs and low castes furnished 27 per cent. Only 2,646 Mussulmans (5 per cent. of the whole) were convicted of offences chiefly under petty heads.

POLICE.

Total strength of Police.

60. The total strength of the Madras Constabulary, (inclusive of the Madras Town Police,) stood as follows on the 31st March 1868:—

Inspector General and supervising Staff	6
Commissioner and Deputy Commissioners, Madras Town ...	3
District Superintendents	21
Assistant Superintendents	21
Inspectors	498
Constabulary of all ranks	24,418
	24,967

On the 1st September 1867, the Madras Town Police were incorporated with the General Police of the Madras Presidency under the operation of Act VIII of 1867. By this Act the Police of the Town of Madras were brought under the provisions of Act XXIV of 1859, and became subject to the control of the Inspector General. The change has worked satisfactorily, in securing co-operation with Mofussil Districts and greater exactitude of system.

The Kurnool Mounted Police, consisting of two Inspectors and fifty-six men, (the remaining portion of the old Rissalah of Irregular Horse,) were disbanded during the year. In their place, one Inspector and forty-five men have been added to the Foot Police Force in that District.

Sanctioned Establishment.

61. The full sanctioned establishment is 25,790 of all ranks. The force was, therefore, 3·4 per cent. below strength. At the close of the official year 1866-67, the force was only 1·6 per cent. below strength. The general rise of wages, the extension of the Railway and Irrigation Works, and other causes, operated to increase the difficulty of obtaining eligible recruits for the Police.

62. The following statement shews the distribution of the force in rural parts and in towns, the number of men employed on Revenue Preventive Service and in Guarding Jails :—

Distribution.

General Police duty, including Treasure Escorts, Guards, &c.

Rural Police	18,960
Municipal Police, Madras Town	1,129
„ other Towns	1,799
	21,888

State Services.

Revenue—Salt Preventive Establishment	1,610
„ Land Customs	154
	1,764
Jail Guards	1,315
	3,079

Exclusive of purely State services, the proportion of Police to the inhabitants was one to 1,127. In rural parts the proportion was one to 1,224, and in towns one to 500. The proportion of Police to area was one to 5·6 square-miles.

63. 461 Local Watchers were employed for the protection of unhealthy ghauts, and for the performance of duty in certain wild parts of the country, where no ordinary Village Police exists. The sum of Rupees 22,510, formerly debited to the Police Department, in supplementary payment of the Village Watch in South Arcot, has been re-transferred to the Revenue Department, by order of Government.

Local and Village Police.

64. The cost of the Police was as follows :—

Financial Statement.

Wages and Allowances	Rs.	33,36,569
Clothing and Accoutrements	„	3,23,680
Miscellaneous Charges	„	1,04,400
	„	37,64,649
Add Village Watchers	„	35,927
	Total Rs.	38,00,576

Of the above sum Rupees 2,90,197 are debitable to purely State services, as follows :—

Salt Preventive Establishment	Rs.	1,38,734
Land Customs „	„	15,840
	„	1,54,574
Jail Guards	„	1,35,623
	Total Rs.	2,90,197

The actual cost of the Police Proper, exclusive of State services, was Rupees 34,74,452, being Rupees 158-11-9 per Policeman, and 2¼ Annas per head of the population. Of the above sum, Rupees 2,85,599 were contributed by Municipalities.

Madras Marine Police.

65. The Madras City Marine Police is a self-supporting force. Its cost for the official year 1867-68 was Rupees 28,915. The amount collected in fees from boat-owners, under Act XXVIII of 1858, was Rupees 32,258, leaving a balance of Rupees 3,343 to be credited to Government. A Marine Policeman accompanies every cargo boat, the boat-owner paying a fee of 3 Annas for each trip. Under this system the loss of property is very rare. The collections, in 1866-67, amounted to Rupees 28,009 only. The increase of Rupees 15·2 per cent. indicates the increased activity of trade during the past year.

Municipal Police.

66. Municipal Police have been established in forty-one towns (Madras city not included). The working is, on the whole, satisfactory. The State finances have been relieved to the extent of Rupees 2,85,599, under the head of Police Charge.

Superannuation Fund.

67. The Madras Town Police Superannuation Fund, amounting to Rupees 82,819-10-5, was amalgamated, on the 1st September 1867, with the Mofussil Police Fund. Exclusive of this sum, the income of the Mofussil Fund, during 1867-68, amounted to Rupees 1,16,961. The balance of the amalgamated funds, remaining on the 31st March 1868, was Rupees 8,19,710-1-5.

Internal Economy.

68. The progressive decrease, which had hitherto taken place year by year in the number of casualties, has been interrupted by an increase during the year under review. There were 3,863 casualties, or 15·6 per cent., of the whole force, against 3,342 (14 per cent.) in 1866. The increase lies under the heads Dismissed, Discharged, and Resigned, deaths having been fewer. This is partly accounted for by the number of men of the old Talook establishment, who are now becoming fairly worn out and superannuated, and who are discharged with the gratuity to which seven years' service in the new force entitles them. Another cause of increase has been the necessity of reforming the force in the Kurnool District, which from inefficient supervision had fallen into a state of some disorder.

The casualties of the whole force, during the year, have not been entirely replaced. The strength of the force (exclusive of Madras Town) on 31st March 1867 was 23,850, and on 31st March 1868, 23,616. 1,922 men were dismissed or discharged, against 1,453 in 1866; and 1,632 resigned, against 1,395 in the preceding year. Desertions are, of course, rare, as two months' notice gives freedom from service. A Police force must always be liable to considerable fluctuation, but it may be hoped that a greater degree of stability than heretofore will yet be attained. Resignations were most numerous in Vizagapatam, Kurnool, North Arcot, Tinnevelly, and Coimbatore. In Tinnevelly, the great demand for labor in Ceylon, and the consequent high rate of wages elsewhere, operate unfavorably upon the maintenance of the Police force at present rates of salaries, while in Coimbatore, the unpopularity of service on the Neilgherry Hills greatly increases the number of resignations. Madras Town shews the smallest per-centage (6·6) of casualties. This old established force is the most stable. South Malabar stands next, with 9·2 per cent.

There is a most satisfactory decrease in the death-rate, which is only 12·5 per thousand, against twenty per 1,000 in 1866. It seems remarkable that the death-rate in Jeypore is only 10·5 per 1,000, while Ganjam, with its traditionally pestilential Hill Maliahs, shews a death-rate of 9·6 per 1,000 only; both these districts being considerably below the general average. The highest rate of mortality is in the Kistna District, viz., 24·6 per 1,000. It is difficult to account for this, although parts of the district are very feverish. The death-rate in Vizagapatam is 16·2, and in Godavery 15·1 per 1,000. The death-rate for the whole Northern Range is 15·9 per 1,000, and for the Western Range 14·1 per 1,000. These are the two most unhealthy ranges. The death-rate in Malabar is 24·3 per 1,000, nearly equal to Kistna. The mortality rate in Madras Town was only six per 1,000. 44·3 per cent. of the whole force were treated in Hospital, against 42·5 per cent. in 1866. The Northern and Western Ranges shew the largest per-centages, viz., 65·4 and 53·1, respectively. The Southern Range is healthiest, shewing only 28·4 per cent. Madras Town shews a still lower per-centage of 22·6, but this is only for nine months of the year. Since, however, in Madras every Policeman off duty for a single day from sickness is treated in Hospital, while from outlying rural parts only severe cases are sent in for treatment, it will be evident that the Madras City Police enjoy a far higher condition of health than their Mofussil brethren.

Fines and Punishments.

69. There is some difficulty in the matter of punishing Police for minor breaches of discipline. The power to fine is given by law, and it is extensively worked. 11,578 Policemen were fined during the year, and a sum of Rupees 14,322 was mulcted from them. A system of punishment, by according black marks, leading ultimately (should bad conduct be persisted in) to reduction or dismissal, has been devised, but it requires care and trouble to ensure successful working.

Convictions of Police Constables.

70. 381 Police officers were convicted by Magistrates, and twenty-six by higher Courts, an increase, in the total number, of ten upon 1866, when, however, forty-two were higher Court convictions. In 1865, 407 were convicted by Magistrates, and twenty-six by Courts. Thirty-

four men were punished for assault and criminal force, and twenty-eight for causing grievous and other hurt. These mainly arose from the innate craving of an Indian Police to compel disclosures when they have the real criminals in custody. Fifty-eight Policemen were punished for extortion and bribery; thirty-nine for negligently permitting escape.

Education.

71. Out of 23,616 men, 14,327, or 60·6 per cent., can read and write. This shews a slight improvement on previous years. Out of 2,776 Head and Deputy Constables, (Station House Officers,) only 110 are now illiterate. These are bequests from the old Talook Peon establishment. Progress is being made in teaching illiterate men to read and write. Twenty-nine men have been taught to read and write in Canara during the year. The Southern and Western Ranges are the best off for educated men. In Nellore and the Ceded Districts it is exceedingly difficult to obtain educated recruits. Only forty per cent. can read and write in these districts, and in Cuddapah the number falls so low as thirty-six per cent. Tanjore has the largest proportion of educated men, but this fact does not seem to exercise a satisfactory influence on the criminal statistics of the district. Probably an educated Police has there to grapple with educated crime. The number of Police Officers who have passed the General Test Examination is ninety-seven, against sixty-seven in the preceding year. The Madras Town Police (lately incorporated) are not included in the statement of Education. The necessary information has not yet been obtained.

Instruction.

72. The important point of instruction has been carefully attended to, and with improved results as compared with former years. 5,193 men, or twenty-two per cent. of the force, received instruction in the District Schools, of whom 2,304 passed the prescribed test of their rank. Eighty Police officers passed the Special Test Examination. The largest number of men were instructed in the Northern Range. A great majority of Station House Officers have now passed the prescribed examination.

Castes and Races.

73. Out of 453 Inspectors 119 are Europeans and East Indians to 334 Natives. In Madras Town the Inspectors are almost exclusively Europeans or East Indians. There are 109 Brahmins, twelve Native Christians, and twenty-four Mahomedans in this grade. The Brahmin element predominates in the Central Range, and Bellary has a larger number of this caste (sixteen out of thirty-one Inspectors) than any other district. The Constabulary numbers 24,120 men, of whom 163 only are Europeans and East Indians. 7,284, or thirty per cent., are Mahomedans. The Central Range (comprising the Ceded Districts) has an unduly large proportion (forty-seven per cent.) of this class, which is being gradually reduced by restricted enlistment.

74. 28,551 Warrants were issued against 30,641 persons, and 281,308 Summons were issued to be served on 284,203 persons. The difference between the number of processes and the number of persons, shews that separate processes are not invariably issued for each person. There has been a marked decrease in the total number of Warrants issued, but the number of Summonses has slightly increased as compared with 1866. A satisfactory decrease continues to appear in the number of Warrants issued in minor cases, the less stringent process by Summons having doubtless been more frequently used. One in 103 of the population has been compelled to appear before a Court in connection with these minor cases during 1867, against one in 109 during 1866.

Warrants, Summons, and Miscellaneous Processes.

Minor Cases.

75. 10,115 convicts were guarded in the various Central and District Jails by 1,486 Policemen, at a cost of Rupees 1,65,366. Forty-eight convicts escaped from these Jails, of whom twenty-eight were re-captured. The difficult and anxious duty of guarding the convicts in the Hill Jails has been well performed by the District Superintendent of Coimbatore.

Convicts guarded in Jails and escaped.

16,833 convicts were guarded in Subsidiary Jails. Fifty-five prisoners escaped, of whom thirty-seven were re-captured. The average duration of imprisonment of these short-sentenced convicts was 10·14 days. 196 prisoners escaped from Police custody, of whom 141 were re-captured. Of the total of 299 prisoners escaped during the year, 206, or 69 per cent., were re-captured.

Subsidiary Jails.

Escaped from other custody.

76. The important work of constructing Station Houses and Huts was steadily pushed on during the year. 533 Huts and eighty-nine Station Houses were added to the previously existing accommodation, and five Police Hospitals were also built. The total sum expended on new buildings was Rupees 70,695.

Hutting and building.

77. 7,608 accidental deaths were reported, against 6,981 in 1866. 1,290 persons (of whom sixty-two per cent. were females) committed suicide. 6,680 fires occurred, 32,416 houses were burnt, and property was destroyed to the value of Rupees 7,18,031. In these fires 156 lives were lost.

Accidental deaths, Suicides; Fires.

78. The value of Salt stolen was Rupees 786 only, against Rupees 2,804 in 1866. Only 294 cases of theft occurred, against 690 in the preceding year. 366 persons were arrested, of whom 272, or 74·3 per cent., were convicted. Under the directions of the Board of Revenue better arrangements are being made for the security of platforms and for the better housing of the men, but much still remains to be done.

Salt Preventive duty.

The list of offences during the past three years stand as follows:—

	No. of Cases.
1865	386
1866	690
1867	294

Considerable fluctuation appears. The scarcity of 1866 may have increased the number in that year. Doubtless some cases occur without being brought to light. The duty is beset with temptation, but, on the whole, the salt is efficiently guarded.

79. 46,628 persons are borne on the suspected lists, against 40,601 in 1866. The increase points to improved knowledge of the criminal population, though it is probable that, by close local inquiry, some of the names formerly registered might be eliminated without detriment. There is a tendency, on the part of the Police, to keep a person who has once committed an offence on the suspected list for ever. Out of 46,628 persons, 36,976 were males, and 9,652 females. They are classified as follows:—

Known depredators and suspected persons.

Known depredators	12,531
Receivers of stolen property	1,883
Suspected persons	16,796
Wandering gangs	11,601
Prostitutes	3,817
	46,628

80. Coming after a famine year the season was one of greatly reduced prices, although (the Northern Range excepted) they stood higher than the average of five years preceding 1866. In various localities considerable pressure of scarcity was still felt. Diminution of crime might, however, have been anticipated, and the result has exceeded anticipation. But notwithstanding a large decrease of crime, the ratio of detection is slightly lower than in 1866, though higher than the average of four years past. In a time of scarcity people are more reckless in the manner of committing offences, and hence detection is facilitated. The per-centage of conviction to arrests has improved, and the recovery of property is somewhat less than in 1866, but equal to the average of four years past. On the whole, it has not been a year of progress in detection.

Season and Prices.

81. The following abstract shews the total of all offences committed during the year in the prevention and detection of which the Police are concerned. 55,116 cases were reported, against 62,556 in the previous year, shewing a decrease of 11·9 per cent., and as the

Offences.

cases in Madras Town were not shewn in previous years, the real decrease is 13·6 per cent. 55·7 per cent. of cases were detected against 57·7 per cent. in 1866. 73·1 per cent. of persons arrested were convicted, against 72·7 per cent. in 1866, and 21·2 per cent. of property was recovered, against 25·2 per cent. in the previous year. The averages of four years past were 49·7 per cent., 68 per cent., and 21·4 per cent., respectively.

	ABSTRACT OF ALL OFFENCES.								
	CASES.			PERSONS.			PROPERTY.		
	Reported.	Detected.	Per cent.	Arrested and proceeded against.	Convicted.	Per cent.	Lost.	Recovered.	Per cent.
Madras Town	1,112	493	44·3	922	602	65·2	54,507	13,967	25·6
Northern Range... ...	9,200	5,066	55	18,048	13,019	72·1	1,56,593	37,799	24·1
Central do. ...	19,985	10,897	54·5	26,062	19,279	73·9	3,51,430	66,455	18·9
Southern do. ...	15,189	8,244	54·2	20,528	14,718	71·7	3,55,499	70,184	19·7
Western do. ...	9,630	6,032	62·6	13,865	10,465	75·4	1,55,286	40,166	25·8
Total...	55,116	30,782	55·7	79,420	58,083	73·1	10,73,315	2,28,571	21·2
Compare									
* 1866	62,556	36,097	57·7	94,345	68,634	72·7	12,12,107	3,05,705	25·2
* 1865	49,353	25,179	51	72,558	50,940	70·2	8,73,243	1,67,577	19·1
* 1864	49,302	21,715	44	67,271	42,965	63·8	10,14,762	2,15,377	21·2
* 1863	35,650	15,044	42·2	45,449	27,815	61·2	9,06,819	1,69,848	18·8
Average...	49,215	24,508	49·7	69,905	47,588	68	10,01,732	2,14,626	21·4

Neilgherry Hill Police.

82. Considerable difficulty is experienced in maintaining the Police force on the Neilgherry Hills in an efficient and satisfactory condition. The rates of hill batta, now given, do not compensate for the dearness of provisions, and for the discomforts of the climate. Consequently resignations are frequent. The Superintendent of Police, Coimbatore District, has, however, by assiduous care and attention managed to keep up the force to a good working standard.

Police in Hill Tracts, &c.

83. In certain tracts the difficulties of Police working are greatly augmented by the isolated and unhealthy conditions of the country. Such are the Hill Maliahs of Ganjam, the Sowrah Hill country and the Gudum Hills in Vizagapatam, the Jeypore District, the Rumpah Hill country of Godavery District, the Hill talooks, Collegal and Suttiamungalum, of Coimbatore and Wynaad in Malabar. But in all these places the work has been carried on with determined energy, notwithstanding the ravages of climate. In the Khond Hill Maliahs of Ganjam, the work of civilization slowly but steadily progresses, and it is believed that Meriah human

* These do not include the offences of the Madras Town.

sacrifices have entirely ceased. There has been no symptom of disaffection to Government since the repression of the last disturbance, in the beginning of 1866. Lieutenant Pickance, the officer immediately in charge of these Hill tracts, has remained at his post doing valuable service. The Hill Maliahs have also been visited and inspected by Captain Tennant, Deputy Inspector General, (in attendance on the Agent to the Governor,) and Captain Lys, the Superintendent. The reserve force at Baliguda has been effectively housed by the exertions of Lieutenant Pickance. The Superintendent writes, "The Khonds seem to be contented, and have been quiet as regards their conduct to Government officials. Among themselves, unfortunately, there have been tribal feuds. A serious combat took place in May 1867, between some villages near Koomaricoopa—four persons were killed. The Udayaghiri Sub-Magistrate and a party of Police were soon on the spot, but had great difficulty in separating the combatants, thirty-seven men were subsequently convicted by the Agent of culpable homicide.

The force in the Godavery District has also suffered cruelly from malignant fever during the year. Captain Davies, the Superintendent of South Malabar, writes, regarding the Wynaad country, "The Police administration of Wynaad, (the greater part of the talook is under this district,) has been as usual a difficult and up-hill work. In the Goodaloor Division, where the Inspector and men are partially hutted, and a Civil Dispensary (benefits of which institution it is impossible to over-estimate) established, the working of the Police has been satisfactory; their shew of work in detection is very fair, and men are settling down to remain there. Much, however, is still required to make the men comfortable." The vital importance of close attention to the comfort and health of the men is here strongly illustrated.

European Vagrancy.

84. The evil of European vagrancy seems to be on the increase, and many officers loudly call for the assistance of legislative action in this matter.

JAILS.

Admission and disposal of Prisoners.

85. The daily average number of prisoners confined in the Mofussil Jails, during the year, was 9,668, being 140 less than that of the year 1866-67. On the 1st April 1867, the number was 9,999, which fell to 9,662 by the 31st March 1868. During the year the Penitentiary at Madras was placed under the general supervision of the Inspector General of Jails, and the population of that prison brings the daily average number of prisoners up to 10,159. The location of gangs on the sites of the Central Jails in course of construction at Vellore, Trichinopoly, and Cannanore, the completion of the Central Jail at Coimbatore, the progress of the buildings at the Rajahmundry Central Jail, and the augmentation of the strength of the gang at the Lawrence Asylum Works Jail, afforded the means of relieving the most crowded Jails to the extent of upwards of 1,800 men during the year.

86. The health of the prisoners may be favorably contrasted with that of former years. In 1866-67, there were 1,134 deaths in hospital, being 11·56 per cent. upon the daily average strength. During the year under review there were 410 deaths in hospital, being 4·24 per cent. upon the daily average strength, and if the Madras Penitentiary be included, the per-centage will be 4·15. In 1866-67, the per-centage of admissions to strength was 123·49, and that of deaths to admissions 9·36. In 1867-68, the per-centage of admissions to strength was 96·13, and that of deaths to admissions 4·41. Subjoined is a table shewing the per-centage of deaths to daily average strength for the last ten years :—

Health of Prisoners.

Years.	Per-centage of deaths to daily average strength.
1858-59	7·3
1859-60	8·2
1860-61	6·7
1861-62	9·30
1862-63	8·94
1863-64	10·99
1864-65	12·70
1865-66	11·26
1866-67	11·56
1867-68	4·24

There were only fifteen admissions from cholera, and twenty-eight from small-pox during the year, and only six of the former and nine of the latter class of cases proved fatal. The comparatively good health of the Jail population may be ascribed, in a considerable degree, to the absence of epidemic disease, but it is also due in a great measure to other causes. The ventilation of most Jails has been much improved, and there has been little crowding compared to what there was in former years. The new and liberal scale of diet has had time to tell. The clothing in several prisons is of a better quality than it used to be, and great care has been devoted by Superintendents to all matters connected with sanitation. The personal cleanliness of the prisoners is better attended to. The buildings, yards, and precincts of the Jails are kept scrupulously clean, and much attention is paid to conservancy arrangements. Although neither cholera, small-pox, fever, nor Jail diarrhœa appeared in an epidemic form in any prison during the past year, this immunity did not extend to many towns and districts in which Jails are situated. For example, fever was very prevalent in the town and district of Rajahmundry. At Kurnool, cholera was epidemic in the town, and the Native Regiment stationed there suffered markedly from fever. At Mangalore and in South Canara the mortality is reported to have been great. In the town of Nellore, cholera, small-pox, and fever were epidemic. At Calicut and in the district of Malabar generally, small-pox was very prevalent, 12,000 cases having been officially reported. Epidemic cholera also shewed itself at Salem. It is not, therefore, too much to say that the exemption of the Jails from some of the epidemic diseases above specified, has been due in no small degree to improved management and cleanliness. In twenty-four of the thirty-six Jails the death-rate has diminished, and in most instances to a considerable extent. In three Jails it has remained the same, and in nine it has increased.

The nine Jails in which the rate of mortality has increased are those at Guindy, Tranquebar, Guntoor, Trichinopoly, Tanjore, Neddiwuttum, Paumben, Cannanore Fort, and Mangalore.

The Jails at Guindy and at Guntoor do not call for any remark.

None of the remaining Jails were crowded during the year, with the exception of that at Tranquebar, but the daily average number was ninety less than it was during the preceding year. Out of the nine men who died, three were received from Tanjore in a very bad state of health.

At Trichinopoly, almost all the able-bodied men were transferred to the site of the Central Jail, leaving few remaining, except the sickly and delicate.

The Jail at Nediwuttum is exposed to the full force of the south-west monsoon. The rains are very heavy, and fogs and mist being of frequent occurrence, the climate is trying for men from the plains. Twenty-four were sent away for change, of whom two died. Out of the eight deaths, five were from dysentery, two from diarrhœa, two from anasarca, and one from bronchitis.

At Mangalore, the health of the prisoners was good, except during the first three months of the monsoon. The officer in medical charge attributes the mortality in some degree to exposure to the weather while the convicts were employed extramurally, but he also states that the population of Mangalore and of the district generally were unhealthy, and the mortality was unusually large during those months.

At Tanjore, the health of the Jail, if judged by the number of admissions into hospital, viz., sixty-one, would seem to have been good, but the death-rate is very high. Out of twenty deaths, ten were from diarrhœa, four from dysentery, two from cholera, two from small-pox, one from disease of the lungs, and one from atrophy. This Jail is a hired building, within the town of Tanjore, surrounded by other buildings, and badly situated. A new Jail has been sanctioned.

The gang stationed on the works of the Cannanore Central Jail shewed a very high rate, upwards of ten and a half per cent., the number (daily average) being 256, and the deaths twenty-seven. The temporary Jail was first occupied in April 1867, and the prisoners were tolerably healthy until August, when diarrhœa, rheumatism, and scurvy, became prevalent. Of the twenty-seven deaths, nine are recorded as from rheumatism, three from dysentery, four from diarrhœa, two from anasarca, two from dropsy, two from disease of the lungs, one from dyspepsia, one from atrophy, one from wound, and two from ulcers. Early in October further medical advice was called for, and the medical officer separated a number (fifty-two) of the men, as suffering from scurvy. He is of opinion that the deaths attributed to rheumatism were really from scurvy. The Jail has not been crowded, but it is much exposed to the weather, the monsoon was very violent, and the convicts were prevented from going out to labor. The diet scale was pronounced ample. There seems strong reason for supposing that there was an epidemic of scurvy, which was not recognized by the medical officer in charge, but this does not appear to have been introduced from the Jails from which the men were drafted.

87. There were 8,513 convicts released during the year, exclusive of those from the Madras Penitentiary. Of that number, 7,831 convicts are reported to have been released in the same state of health as when admitted, viz., 7,728 in good health, seventy-five in indifferent health, and twenty-eight in bad health. 372 were released in an improved, and 310 in an inferior state of health.

Health on admission and release.

88. For some time, during the construction of the Central Jail at Coimbatore, the Superintendent had in force a system under which convicts of good character were employed to superintend the labor of their fellow convicts, to have charge of the wards and cells, and look after their cleanliness, the state of the bedding, &c., to superintend the cooking, and generally perform the duties of warders. These men wore a brass badge, were released from their fetters, and were exempted from Jail punishments, being, however, liable to immediate reduction from their offices of trust, when they again become liable to Jail punishments.

Convict Warders.

The system was found to work well, and arrangements are now being made for the introduction of a similar plan into all Central Jails ; where the number of paid warders will be reduced in proportion to the employment of convicts. At the same time measures are in process of completion for introducing a system of gradual remission of sentences as a reward for good conduct and industry. The system will be based upon an allotment of marks for conduct and work performed, and will be combined with a classification of the prisoners based on conduct in Jail.

89. The conduct of the prisoners has been generally reported as good upon the whole, but the punishments have been numerous. No serious offences were committed, with the exception of an assault upon the Keeper of the European Prison by life-convict George Baker, and an outbreak at the Vellore Fort Jail, which was immediately put down, and the offenders punished. There were a number of minor offences at the Central Jails of Rajahmundry and Cannanore during the early part of the year, but the conduct of the prisoners subsequently improved. A considerable

Conduct of Prisoners.

proportion of the punishments at Rajahmundry were for breaches of conservancy rules, and want of cleanliness.

Previous Convictions.

90. Of 11,814 Adult Convicts admitted into the Mofussil Jails during the year, 845 had been previously convicted, viz.:—

Second convictions	615
Third do.	169
Fourth do.	42
More than four times	19

Of ninety-three Juvenile Convicts received into the same Jails, eleven had been previously convicted, viz.:—

Second convictions	9
Third do.	2

Out of 1,755 Adult Convicts admitted into the Penitentiary at Madras, 479 were old offenders, viz.:—

Second convictions	243
Third do.	76
Fourth do.	82
More than four times	78

Of 119 Juvenile Convicts admitted into the Penitentiary forty-three had been previously convicted, viz.:—

Second convictions	28
Third do.	12
More than four times	3

The great majority of the convicts in the Penitentiary have been sentenced by the Police Magistrates for short periods, and many of them have been committed very frequently. In the Mofussil Jails the per-centage of re-committals to admissions was of Adults 7·16, of Juveniles 11·82. In the Madras Penitentiary, of Adults 27·29, of Juveniles 36·13.

Education.

91. 12·52 per cent. of the prison population in 1867-68 were able to read and write, 5·38 per cent. could read, and 81·72 per cent. were entirely ignorant. The rate in the different Jails is extremely unequal. The Southern Jails are far in advance of those in the Northern and Central Districts.

The only Northern Jail, where there is a large proportion of educated prisoners, is at Guntoor, where the per-centage was 36·07. In the European Prison twenty-four out of twenty-five men in confinement during the year were able to read and write, and the remaining man was able to read.

Pardons.

92. Twenty-two pardons were granted, viz., two to State prisoners from Malabar, four on account of dangerous illness, seven for services rendered, one by His Excellency the Commander-in-Chief, and eight to persons who had been convicted of dacoity for a grain riot in the Wynaad, whose sentences the Government thought might properly be reduced.

93. There were forty-one escapes, and six attempts to escape. Thirty persons were re-apprehended. Twenty-six of the escapes were from temporary Jails.

Escapes.

94. The extramural labor of the convicts was principally given to the Department of Public Works for the construction of the new Jails, and for employment upon roads and other public works. Gangs were occasionally placed at the disposal of the Municipal Commissioners at the undermentioned towns, viz., Vizagapatam, Rajahmundry, Masulipatam, Nellore, Kurnool, Bellary, Cuddapah, Salem, Cuddalore, Tanjore, Tinnevelly, Cochin, Mangalore, Paulghaut, and Coimbatore, and at some Jails the available surplus labor was hired by private individuals. The prisoners not employed beyond Jail precincts were engaged in menial offices, in gardening, and in manufactures. The amount realized in cash was Rupees 25,553-12-4, and the value of labor not paid for is estimated at Rupees 1,61,075-4-11.

Employment of Prisoners.

95. Manufactures are carried on in the Jails specified below,* but not to any extent, except at the Central Jails at Rajahmundry, Coimbatore, and Salem, and at the District Jails of Mangalore, Chingleput, Cuddalore, Bellary, the Madras Penitentiary, and the European Prison. The prisoners in the Central Jails at Coimbatore and Rajahmundry make all their own clothing, blankets included, and a large quantity has been supplied to other Jails. It is expected that, before long, all Jails within the respective Circles of these Central Prisons will be so supplied. At Bellary the clothing and blankets are made in the Jail, and at Salem, Chingleput, Cuddapah, and Cuddalore the clothing is made.

Manufactures.

96. The cost of the Jails, exclusive of guards and buildings, was Rupees 7,49,977-7-1, of which Rupees 4,83,969-4-8 were for food, inclusive of extra diet to sick. The average cost per prisoner was Rupees 76-6-7, all charges included. The average cost of food for each Native prisoner was Rupees 49-2-7, and that of clothing Rupees 3-15-9. The diet of each European prisoner cost Rs. 171-1-1, and his clothing Rs. 27-9-9.

Expenses.

97. A barrack for boys, situated within a distinct compartment, has been completed at the Coimbatore Central Jail, and one of the same description at the Rajahmundry Central Jail is nearly ready. Similar buildings have been sanctioned at the Central Jails now in

Juveniles.

* Vizagapatam.
Rajahmundry (Central).
Nellore.
Kurnool.
Bellary.
Cuddapah.
Vellore Fort.
Chittoor.
Salem (Central).
Chingleput.
Cuddalore.
Tranquebar.
Tanjore.
Tellicherry.
Mangalore.
Coimbatore (Central).
Coimbatore District.
Paumben.
European Prison.
Madras Penitentiary.

course of construction at Vellore, Trichinopoly, and Cannanore, and also at the District Jail which is being built at Calicut. At the Salem Jail there are separate wards for sleeping in, but no distinct yard or compartment. In the new Jail at Madura there is a ward for boys, but no distinct compartment. The number of juvenile offenders is small. On the 31st March 1867, there were fifty-two boys and five girls in the Mofussil jails, which was rather more than the general average, owing to the famine during the preceding year. During 1867-68, there were ninety-three admissions, and on the 31st March 1868 only forty-six boys and one girl were remaining.

Education of Juveniles.

98. In six Jails instruction in reading and writing was given to boys confined, and in four others some trade instruction was given; but the numbers are too small and fluctuating, and the sentences generally too short to admit of a regular system of instruction, unless juvenile offenders could be collected in a few centres, where systematic arrangements could be made.

The number of female juvenile convicts is extremely small.

Subsidiary Jails.

99. The condition of the Subsidiary Jails has been under careful investigation during the past year. The Committee appointed in April 1867 has furnished very complete reports on the condition of the class of Jails in ten Districts,* and has submitted to Government proposals to meet the requirements of these provinces. The whole question of the cost involved in providing adequate accommodation for short sentenced prisoners has been submitted to the Government of India, and is under consideration.

REGISTRATION OF ASSURANCES.

Number of Registrations.

100. The total number of registrations during the year was 1,08,931, against 1,00,425 during the eleven months which constituted the official year 1866-67. By a comparison of the monthly averages during the two years, the total average decrease in 1867-68 is twelve. Of the total number of registrations, 97,172 instruments refer to immoveable property, and are divided as follows:—

Compulsory	78,129
Optional	19,043

The number of registrations of miscellaneous documents in Book VI, amounted to 11,759.

---

* Madras. Salem. North Arcot. South Canara. South Arcot. Madura. Coimbatore. Nellore. Cuddapah. Vizagapatam.

101. The value of the transactions registered has been calculated, for the first time this year, on the principle which regulates the value in the table of fees. The total value of the instruments registered in Book I, was Rupees 3,92,53,170, and in Book VI, Rupees 77,68,266, amounting together to Rupees 4,70,21,436.

Value of transactions registered.

102. The number of registrations, on the payment of a penalty, was 174, against 236 last year: Rupees 1,597 were paid as penalties.

Penalties.

103. The number of instruments specially registered, which fell last year from 12,715 to 7,964, has risen during the year to 10,392, although there has been no change in the table of fees.

Special Registration.

104. The number of cases in which registration was refused was 1,026. Appeals to Registrars were preferred in 222 cases, in thirty-three of which registration was ordered, and in 189 it was refused. The number of instruments registered under the orders of the Registrars was seventeen, and under the orders of Courts 215.

Refusals to register.

105. The number of sealed covers deposited during the year was eleven. The number of Wills presented open was 133, and authority to adopt, one. Eight sealed covers were opened on the death of the depositors, and all contained Wills executed by Hindoos.

Wills, Codicils, and Authorities to adopt.

106. There has been a large increase in the registration of memoranda of decrees affecting immoveable property, the number of registrations in Book V this year having been 19,812, against 13,142 in last year.

Registration of Memoranda of Decrees affecting immoveable property.

107. The number of memoranda of decrees affecting registered instruments has risen from sixty to 194.

Memoranda of Decrees.

108. There were ninety instruments, accompanied by translations, presented this year, for registration in a language not understood by the Registering Officer.

Translations.

109. The number of searches was 1,138, and of copies and extracts granted 2,541.

Searches, Copies, and Extracts.

110. Five prosecutions were instituted during the year under Section 95. In two of these the parties concerned were convicted and punished. In one the parties concerned were acquitted, and two cases remained undisposed of.

Prosecutions.

111. The number of registrations in Books I and VI, in the different classes of Offices, was as follows:—

Registrations in different classes of Offices.

Offices.	Book I.	Book VI.
Registrar General	116	...
Do. of Madras	3,262	410
21 Mofussil Registrars	307	42
294 Sub-Registry Offices	93,482	11,307
Total ...	97,167	11,759

Registrations and Collections in each District.

112. The following table represents the number of registrations and collections in each district during the years 1866-67 and 1867-68 :—

Districts.	Registrations in Books I and VI.		Collections.					
	1866-67.	1867-68.	1866-67.			1867-68.		
			RS.	A.	P.	RS.	A.	P.
I Class.								
Tanjore	9,164	9,094	23,252	0	0	25,726	0	0
Tinnevelly	11,119	14,550	25,425	4	0	36,081	0	0
Tranquebar	5,392	6,110	14,208	12	0	19,648	10	0
Calicut	12,566	13,558	27,787	0	0	31,742	0	0
II Class.								
Godavery	4,892	5,025	11,462	4	0	13,902	4	0
Salem	4,102	4,260	8,564	0	0	10,655	0	0
Madura	7,109	8,486	17,104	4	0	21,403	12	0
Trichinopoly...	5,125	4,878	11,917	0	0	10,917	0	0
Coimbatore	4,794	4,929	10,262	12	0	10,519	4	0
Tellicherry	6,447	6,782	14,448	8	0	16,504	0	0
South Arcot	3,423	3,201	7,307	12	0	7,458	12	0
South Canara	3,914	4,845	13,500	12	0	16,583	0	0
North Arcot	3,397	3,151	7,482	8	0	8,174	0	0
III Class.								
Vizagapatam	2,297	2,192	6,145	8	0	5,882	8	0
Bellary	2,661	3,061	7,036	0	0	7,753	0	0
Madras	3,074	3,672	9,578	8	0	11,112	8	0
Kurnool	1,781	1,758	4,293	3	0	4,057	4	0
Chingleput	2,520	2,677	5,470	4	0	6,196	8	0
Ganjam	2,265	1,680	5,153	0	0	4,790	4	0
Kistna	1,540	1,610	4,062	4	0	4,780	4	0
Cuddapah	1,526	1,791	3,843	12	0	3,737	12	0
Nellore	1,235	1,505	3,510	0	0	4,313	8	0
General Registry Office	82	116	1,557	12	0	2,443	12	0
Total ...	1,00,425	1,08,931	2,41,873	15	0	2,84,331	14	0

Abolition of Sub-Registry Offices.

113. During the year the Sub-Registry Offices at the following stations were abolished :—

Kurnool District.
Peapully.

Tinnevelly District.
Wattrap.

Trichinopoly District.
Rajendrapatam.

Salem District.
Shevaroy Hills.

The name and station of the Sub-Registry Office of Pattamaday, in Tinnevelly, were changed to Shermadevi, and certain changes were made from the 1st April 1867 in the limits of the Districts and Sub-Districts of Tanjore and Tranquebar, in consequence of certain changes in the arrangement of the Revenue Divisions of these districts.

Financial position of the Department.

114. The following abstract shews the financial results of registration during the year. The collections amounted to Rupees 2,84,381-5-0, but as in this Presidency the fees collected in one month are remitted to the treasury on the 1st of the following month, the department has, as usual, been credited with only the sum actually paid in during the

year, which amounted to somewhat less than the collections, viz., Rs. 2,80,772-2-0. The total cost of the department, including the value of all articles received from the Stationery Office and the Mint without cash payment, was Rupees 2,22,527-2-10, leaving a surplus of Rupees 58,244-15-2 on the year. This amount, added to the surplus of last year, entirely clears off the deficit with which the working of the department was attended from the 1st January 1865 to the 30th April 1866, and leaves a clear balance of Rupees 3,969-3-1.*

Receipts.	RS.	A.	P.	Expenditure.	RS.	A.	P.
Remitted to the Treasury as per Appendix IV.	2,80,772	2	0	Salaries of Registrar General, Registrar of Madras, and 21 Mofussil Registrars.	51,013	2	6
Deduct cost of the Department ...	2,22,527	2	10	Commission paid to Deputy Registrar General, Registrars of Madras, Ganjam, and Tranquebar, and 294 Sub-Registrars	1,24,965	6	8
Balance in favor of the Department	58,244	15	2	Establishments of Registrar General, Registrars of Madras, and 21 Mofussil Registrars	18,642	0	9
				Contingent expenditure of Registrar General and Registrar of Madras ...	598	12	0
				House-rent of General Registry Office and Registry Office of Tranquebar ...	1,680	0	0
				Furniture	5,352	3	2
				Service Postage	45	15	6
				Travelling bills of Registrar General and his establishment	1,896	15	0
				Binding of Registers and Indexes ...	173	0	2
				Carriage of Registers and Indexes ...	1,708	9	0
				Refunds of fees	2	0	0
				Total Cash Expenditure ...	2,06,078	0	4
				Estimated value of articles supplied without payment.			
				Paper for Registers and Indexes ...	15,396	14	0
				Stationery and packing materials ...	618	4	6
				62 Seals	434	0	0
				Grand Total ...	2,22,527	2	10

115. During the year the Registrar General made two tours—one extending over a period of three months, and the other of five weeks, and inspected seven Registry Offices, of which one had been visited by him before, and ninety-eight Sub-Registry Offices, of which five had been previously visited. Five of these Sub-Registry Offices were abolished

Inspection.

* Year.	Deficit. RS.	A.	P.	Year.	Surplus. RS.	A.	P.
1864-65	43,770	9	8	1866-67	23,300	5	6
1865-66	33,805	7	11	1867-68	58,244	15	2
Total...	77,576	1	7	Total ...	81,545	4	8
				Deduct deficit ...	77,576	1	7
				Balance to the credit of the Department ...	3,969	3	1

during his inspection. His remarks on the result of his inspection are as follows:—

"I found the Registry Offices of South Arcot, Tranquebar, and Trichinopoly in a satisfactory condition, those of Tanjore, Madura, and Salem, in tolerable order, and that of Tinnevelly in an unsatisfactory state. The general result of my inspection of the ninety-eight Sub-Registry Offices above referred to is shewn below. These tours, extending as they did over the whole of the Tamul Districts, except Coimbatore and portions of Madura and Trichinopoly, gave me opportunities of visiting a number of very important Offices, including, among others, those of nearly all the Special Sub-Registrars, who have been appointed during the last two years. The Offices of the Special Sub-Registrars were, with a few exceptions, in excellent order, and as a general rule the Offices of the official Sub-Registrars were in a more efficient condition than those of the same class in the Telugu Districts, to which my attention has been hitherto mainly directed. Notwithstanding, however, that the blunders committed in these Offices were fewer in number and less gross in kind than those previously noticed, I found abuses prevalent in some of them, which did not exist in the Telugu Offices. No Registration Office can be considered in an efficient condition, unless, as a general rule, an instrument, admitted to registration, is returned on the same or the following day. In small Offices, this can of course always be done without any difficulty, but I found that in some of the large Offices, the copying of instruments had always been and still was considerably in arrears, involving in some instances a delay of fifteen or twenty days in the returning of instruments. In consequence of this pernicious practice the parties had got into the habit of going away to their villages and leaving their instruments unclaimed for weeks and even months together, and in some Offices there was a large collection of instruments which had accumulated in this manner. I endeavoured to check the first of these evils by instituting a monthly Return of instruments uncopied, and by directing that the payment of commission should be suspended until the work of the month had been completed. It has been shewn elsewhere that the arrears under this head are now almost nominal. A reduction in the number of instruments already lying unclaimed cannot be so readily effected, as under the present rules the parties, who leave them unclaimed, are not subject to any penalty for doing so, as they are in the other Presidencies, and an Officer who has once allowed instruments to accumulate on his hands cannot readily get rid of them again, but a considerable improvement has been effected in some Offices since the inspection. Another abuse, which was much more common in the Tamul than in the Telugu Districts, was the laxity which had been allowed to creep into the preparation and transmission of the monthly copies of the Indexes. In many Offices, particularly in the Tinnevelly District, the preparation of these copies had been allowed to fall many months in arrears. In these cases also the payment of the commission bills has been suspended until all arrears are brought up."

Districts.	Highly credit-able.	Satis-factory.	Toler-able.	Unsatis-factory.	Dis-graceful.
Chingleput ...	...	1	5	1	...
North Arcot ...	1	2	3	...	1
South Arcot ...	3	4	6	1	...
Tanjore	3	3	3	1	...
Tranquebar ...	2	4	1	1	...
Tinnevelly ...	2	3	10	4	...
Madura	1	3	6	3	...
Trichinopoly ...	...	3	...	1	...
Salem	2	5	8	1	...
Total ...	14	28	42	13	1

Section IV.—REVENUE.

116. The year commenced hopefully, but ended gloomily. The copious north-east monsoon of 1866 was followed by a fair south-west monsoon in 1867; but the subsequent north-east monsoon was scanty everywhere, and failed almost entirely in many districts. The season was accordingly unfavorable to agriculture in Coimbatore and South Arcot, more unfavorable still in Tanjore, Madura, Salem, Nellore, and Cuddapah, and absolutely disastrous in Madras and North Arcot. Before the close of the year, serious cause was seen for apprehending famine in South Arcot, Salem, Madras, North Arcot, Nellore, Cuddapah, and Bellary, and vigorous measures were taken to prepare for the emergency and relieve existing distress. In the Northern districts* the season was good, and on the Western Coast, and in the Kistna and Trichinopoly districts, it seems to have been fair on the whole.

Season.

117. The public health was about the average. Cholera decreased all over the Presidency, but small-pox was virulent, and fever was more widely spread and more deadly than usual. Cattle disease was prevalent, and, combined with want of pasturage and water, caused heavy losses. Tinnevelly, Vizagapatam, and the districts on the Western Coast were decidedly healthy.

Public Health.

118. At the quinquennial census taken on the 1st March 1867, the population of the Presidency, exclusive of the town of Madras, was found to be 26,089,052.† The population of the town of Madras has never been accurately reckoned, but it is supposed to be about 450,000.

Population.

119. The steady increase in the prices of staple articles of consumption was checked in the year under report for the first time since 1860-61. In consequence of the plentiful harvests at the end of 1866-67, they declined below the rates of 1864-65.

Prices.

120. In consequence of the demand for labor excited by Railways in progress, and by favorable agricultural prospects, as well as of the cheapness of food, emigration diminished throughout the Presidency, and ceased altogether in many districts.

Emigration.

121. Statements B. and C. in the Appendix shew the receipts and charges for the last five years. Every item in the former statement, with the exception, of course, of Income Tax, exhibits an increase when compared with 1866-67. The proportion which the charges bear to the receipts is one per cent. less than that of last year.

Net Revenue.

---

* Ganjam, Vizagapatam, Kurnool, and Godavery.

†

Hindoos ...	24,172,822
Mahomedans ...	1,502,134
Christians ...	414,096
	26,089,052

To facilitate the comparison of receipts with charges an abstract statement, Appendix D, is given, which shews the proportion borne by the one to the other for the last five years. The amount collected by coercive processes was Rupees 1,03,679.

Area under cultivation.

122. The area under cultivation increased by acres 353,286, or two per cent., but the assessment thereon decreased by Rupees 2,12,391. This was the result chiefly of the want of rain, which in many places necessitated the relinquishment of attempts to cultivate highly assessed irrigated lands. The principal increase of area took place in Bellary, Trichinopoly, Madura, and the Godavery, and the principal decrease in assessment in North Arcot and Cuddapah, where the season was unfavorable, and in Kurnool where the new settlement rates were introduced.

Land Revenue.

123. The total amount of Land Revenue collections was £4,239,705. As compared with those for the preceding twelve months they increased by Rupees 14,67,487 in ten districts, and decreased by Rupees 8,33,852 in nine districts. The greater part of the increase is shewn in Bellary, where the collection of kists for 1866-67 had been deferred on account of the famine; in Tinnevelly, where the dues were more punctually collected; and in Ganjam, where the comparison is made with a period when the state of the district required that large remissions should be given. The greater part of the decrease is to be ascribed to the character of the season in Madras, North Arcot, and South Arcot.

Abkarry.

124. The Abkarry collections amounted to £506,741. Comparing them with the collections for the preceding twelve months, there was an increase in every district except Cuddapah, where it was found necessary to grant large remissions to the contractors, whose receipts were seriously affected by the depression of agriculture.

Income Tax.

125. Rupees 215 was collected on account of arrears of Income Tax.

License Tax.

126. The License Tax, though, as was anticipated, unpopular, was collected without much difficulty. The total sum thus realized was £80,714, being £12,114 more than was expected.

Sea Customs.

127. The Sea Customs Revenue amounted to £237,194, or £41,497 more than in the preceding twelve months, and was higher than it has been since 1860-61. More extensive trading operations, combined with the enhancement of duty on the export of grain, produced an increase in the revenue everywhere except in the Kistna, South Canara, and Malabar Districts, where there was a small decrease. In Madras, a large exportation of Indigo occasioned a material portion of the increase. Particulars are given in Statement E. in the Appendix.

A statement* of the declared value of imports and exports during the last twelve years, and an analysis† of the principal articles of trade during 1867-68 will also be found in the Appendix.

Comparing eleven months of 1867-68 with 1866-67, it appears that the most important increase in imports took place in Cotton, Piece-goods, Paddy, Metals, Railway Stores, and Spices, and the largest decrease in Twist, Rice, Wheat, Grain of sorts, and Seeds. In exports the largest increase was in Cocoanuts, Coffee, Cotton-Wool, Indigo, Oils, Seeds, and Spices, and the largest decrease in Rice, Grain of sorts, and Sugars.

Statement H. shews the quantity and value of the export trade in Coffee, Cotton, Indigo, and other important staples for three years. Taking eleven-twelfths of the collections for 1867-68, it appears that there is an increase in the quantity of every article except Sugars, and in the value of every article except Sugars and Rice.

Cotton cultivation.

128. The area of land under cotton varied but slightly. It increased in Kurnool and Bellary, the great cotton-producing districts; but it decreased in most of the other districts. The increase altogether was only 65,533 acres.

Statement I. shews the area cultivated with cotton and exports in cotton-wool for the last ten years.

Bullion.

129. The export and import of bullion continued to diminish. The excess of the imports over exports was Rupees 11,37,895, or less than it has been for the last twelve years.‡

Land Customs.

130. The Land Customs increased by Rupees 40,335.

Salt.

131. There was an increase of Rupees 4,65,979 in the revenue from salt, but compared with twelve-elevenths of 1866-67, there was a decrease of Rupees 4,86,024.§ The sales also, though larger than during the eleven months of 1866-67, are nearly eight per cent. smaller than twelve-elevenths of the sales for that year, but the decrease in sales for home consumption is very trifling. The decrease of two lacs of maunds in the sales for inland consumption is accounted for by the fact that salt began to find its way into Central India by rail from Bombay, and that the demand in the Nizam's territories was slack, the market being overstocked. The decrease of three and a half lacs in sales for exportation seems to be due to ordinary and not exceptional causes. The exports had been unusually large in 1864-65 and the two following years.

Stamps.

132. The Stamp revenue increased when compared with twelve-elevenths of that for 1866-67 by Rupees 4,54,835. This was due in great measure to the new Stamp Act, which was introduced on the 1st May 1867.

* Appendix F.
† Appendix K.
‡ Appendix G.
§ Appendix L.

133. The receipts and expenditure in connection with the District Road Fund are shewn in Statement M. The effect of the Road Cess Act has been to increase the income by ninety-three per cent. The expenditure has also increased.

Local Funds.

134. The District Printing Presses turned out work valued at Rupees 1,88,745, at a cost of Rupees 54,856, or including interest at five per cent. on the estimated value of plant, Rupees 59,405. The cash receipts for work done for private individuals, and on account of subscriptions to District Gazettes were Rupees 24,288.

District Presses.

135. Experiments were continued in introducing exotic plants. Carolina paddy was successful in Salem, but the results were doubtful elsewhere. Ohio and Shiraz tobacco gave favorable results in the Godavery District. Carob beans, French honey-suckle, Pinus Maritima, and Indian Corn were also tried in different parts of the Presidency with varying success.

Experimental cultivation.

136. Five ruined tanks and one ruined channel, capable when in repair of irrigating 138 acres, have been given up to cultivators. The nature of the season prevented the number of applications for such tanks from being so large as was to be expected.

Ruined Tanks.

137. Thirty acres of waste land were sold in Ganjam for Rupees 297, fifty-six on the Shevaroy Hills for Rupees 135, and 307 on the Neilgherries for Rupees 5,898.

Sale of Waste Lands.

138. In the Madras District 1,242 acres were planted with Casuarinas, and 668 acres were given to applicants under the Tope Rules. In the Tinnevelly District ordinary planting operations were prosecuted with vigour. In other parts of the Presidency little was done by Revenue officials in the way of raising plantations.

Plantations.

139. The annual Cattle Show at Adanki, in Nellore, held on the 21st and 22nd January 1868, was a decided success, and an agricultural and industrial exhibition, held at Palghaut in November, was even more successful than that held at Calicut in February 1867.

District Exhibitions.

140. Veterinary Surgeon Thacker is still engaged in his labors for the repression of cattle disease, and is understood to be compiling a Manual on the subject. General directions as to segregation and common remedies have been published in every District Gazette. Directly anout-break occurs in any district, particulars are telegraphed to Mr. Thacker, and he prescribes the treatment to be adopted, or proceeds to the spot as occasion requires. The agriculturalists are beginning to have great confidence in his system.

Cattle disease.

141. The experimental system of registering deaths was placed on a more satisfactory footing during the year. A separate establishment was sanctioned for the work, and the registration of births as well as deaths was ordered. The returns are in future to be submitted direct to the Sanitary Commissioner.

Registration of Deaths.

142. The Revenue Settlement Department conducted field operations in Kurnool, Cuddapah, Godavery, Nellore, and Kistna Districts. The total area demarcated was 598 square-miles, and that classified 1,196 square-miles. In Kurnool District field operations are completed, eighty-two more villages having been brought under the settlement. In Kurnool proper thirty-four villages remain to be settled. The settlement of the Salem District has been completed. The only point remaining for decision is commutation rate, which is now under the consideration of Government. The total expenditure for the year was Rupees 2,35,763, including Rupees 41,858 paid to the Collectors of Tinnevelly and Nellore for the establishments working under them.

Revenue Settlement.

143. Revenue Survey operations were carried on in the districts noted.* 900 villages, containing 2,306 square-miles, were surveyed; 912 villages, containing 2,089 square-miles, were mapped; and the maps of 632 villages, containing 2,613 square-miles, were lithographed. The mapping of 801 villages (2,634 square-miles) was in progress at the end of the year. The Survey in Kistna, Salem, and Nellore, was completed, and the employés were draughted to other districts. Work on the Neilgherries has progressed satisfactorily. In Madras, Ganjam, and Coimbatore boundary demarcation of 563 villages (858 square-miles), and field demarcation of 331 villages (435 square-miles) were completed.

Revenue Survey.

The total expenditure for Survey and Demarcation is Rupees 5,92,502, as against Rupees 5,29,468-9-5 for last year.

144. The principal work done by the Inam Commission this year has been the settlement of certain classes of rent-free tenures, which had been previously overlooked in the Districts of Godavery, Kistna, and Madras. The permanent addition to the annual revenue in the nine years during which the Commission has been at work is 9½ lacs of Rupees, while the total cost up to the present time does not exceed 11 lacs.

Inam Commission.

145. The charges under this head for the year were Rupees 2,72,840, and the receipts Rupees 4,24,184; but owing to a decrease in the value of timber in stock on March 31st, 1868, the net profit

Forests.

* Coimbatore.
(Neilgherry Hills.)
Salem.
Kurnool.
Cuddapah.
Kistna.
Tinnevelly.
Nellore.
Madras.
Ganjam.
Malabar (Wynaad).

was only Rupees 67,624. The operations of the department have been satisfactory. Improvements have been introduced in the system of conservancy, and attention has been paid to the formation and plantation of fuel reserves. A new lease on favorable terms for ninety-nine years has been obtained of the valuable teak forests belonging to the Colingode Nambudry in South Malabar.

Chinchona.

146. The past year has been somewhat unfavorable to Chinchona cultivation, owing to the comparative failure of the two monsoons. The average monthly increase by propagation is less than last year, there being no demand for plants, except for the requirements of the Government plantations. This is owing to the gratuitous distribution of Chinchona seed, of which more than 100 ounces have been given away, a quantity capable of producing 2,000,000 plants. A new and valuable variety of C. Calisaya has been introduced, and is reported to be doing well. The total number of plants on 31st March 1868, was 2,353,370 against 1,926,044 for last year. Mr. Broughton has obtained highly satisfactory results from the analysis of the different species of barks. He has also been fortunate in discovering, in districts near the Neilgherries, certain economic products of great importance in reference to the question of alkaloid manufacture in this country.

SECTION V.—PUBLIC WORKS.

147. Inclusive of private contributions, the Public Works grant for the past official year was Rupees 84,17,519, against an aggregate outlay of Rupees 79,88,374, classified as follows :— *Allotment and Expenditure.*

	Grant.	Outlay.
	RS.	RS.
New Works	43,51,965	40,41,172
Repairs	23,98,277	22,26,861
Tools and Plant	81,277	91,141
Establishments	16,40,000	16,29,200
	84,71,519	79,88,374

148. Excluding advances to Civil Officers, the expenditure on works fell short of the allotment by Rupees 4,82,209, but was in excess of the outlay in the preceding year by Rupees 16,39,600. *Expenditure contrasted with allotment and with outlay in previous year.*

149. Rates of labor had a tendency to rise in the districts comprised in the 2nd, 3rd, 6th, and 8th Divisions. *Rates of labor.*

150. The usual detailed statements of expenditure will be found in the Appendix, and the following are a few particulars of the progress made on the more important works which were on hand. ** Detailed statements of expenditure and progress made on important works.*

151. Four wash-houses were built for the European Regiment at Bellary, and two others were in progress, with an expenditure of Rupees 13,192. A blacksmith's forge, and workshops for collar-makers, carpenters, and armourers, were completed at a total cost of Rupees 18,118, of which Rupees 6,961 were spent in 1867-68. In connection with the project for the drainage of the European Infantry Barracks, a sum of Rupees 6,364 was appropriated to the preparation of materials, and to the completion of 2,860 running feet of drain. Of the six Staff Serjeants' quarters at Bellary, four were enlarged and improved, and out-offices provided at a cost of Rupees 7,535. The construction of a Canteen for the use of the Artillery was in progress, and Rupees 5,953 were laid out on the erection of the walls, and the preparation of the roofing, which is now ready to be put up. Satisfactory progress was made with the project for improving the water-supply to the Cantonment of Bellary, Rupees 11,806 having been laid out on the earthwork and stone revetment, and on the construction of the necessary masonry works. A camel shed at Bellary and another at Sultanpore were built at a cost of Rupees 20,299, and the erection of two additional sheds at the latter station was in progress. *Military buildings at Bellary.*

152. The Roman Catholic place of worship at Bellary, and the building for the performance of Divine worship at Ramandroog, were completed during the year, with an outlay of Rupees 2,269; *Churches at Bellary and Ramandroog.*

and Rupees 7,266 were spent on the construction of a Protestant place of worship at Bellary, which is now very near completion.

153. A sum of Rupees 6,694 was spent on the provision of a Fives and Racket Court in Fort St. George. The side walls were raised to their full height, the gallery was roofed in, and the centre wall built to a height of five feet. A swimming bath was built at a total cost of Rupees 5,321, of which Rupees 4,510 represent the outlay in 1867-68. Alterations and additions were made to the Office of the Controller of Military Accounts, at a cost of Rupees 36,499, for the purpose of providing accommodation for the Examiners of Ordnance and Commissariat Accounts.

Military buildings in Fort St. George.

154. Rupees 16,951 were appropriated to the drainage of the Native Infantry Lines at Perambore. The main and street drains were complete; three tanks were turfed; a well for flushing the drains was sunk in the lines of the right wing, and another was commenced in those of the left wing.

Improving the drainage of the Perambore Lines.

155. A new female hospital was under construction at St. Thomas' Mount, and Rupees 16,993 were spent on completing the brick work, laying the flooring of the lower story, and building the walls of the upper story to a height of twelve feet. The construction of twenty-four family quarters was also in progress. Twenty quarters were nearly completed; four others were commenced, and good progress was made with the formation of roads and drains. The year's outlay amounted to Rupees 32,238.

New Female Hospital and Family Quarters at St. Thomas' Mount.

156. A sum of Rupees 2,62,829 was spent on the Race Course Barracks at Bangalore. One block of barracks for the Artillery was completed, and four blocks were sub-divided for the Serjeants' Mess, School, and Recreation rooms. Four blocks of married quarters; quarters for the Serjeant Major and Quarter Master Serjeant, two bowling and skittle alleys, two harness-rooms, gun-shed, sick stables, and forge were also completed. For the Cavalry, quarters were provided for the Paymaster Serjeant, Saddler Serjeant, and Instructor of Musketry. Stables, forge, and seven saddle-rooms were constructed, and good progress was made with the Armourer's shop and Regimental workshops. The female ward of the European Hospital, two separate wards with kitchens, and the Medical Subordinates' quarters were nearly completed, and the construction of the male pavilions and administrative rooms was on hand.

Bangalore Race Course Barracks.

157. In connection with the Infantry Barracks at Bangalore, two additional blocks were completed, and extra Provost cells were built at a cost of Rupees 19,440.

Infantry Barracks.

158. A sum of Rupees 72,572 was spent on the Ulsoor Water Supply Project, which will soon be sufficiently advanced for trial. Pipes were laid to the cisterns on the Race Course; stand-pipes were fixed, and the setting up of a second pump for raising water to the filter was nearly completed.

Ulsoor Water Supply Project.

159. Good progress was made with the Lawrence Asylum buildings, on which the year's expenditure amounted to Rupees 1,02,887. The sites of the buildings were excavated, and the foundations and basement of the Boys' Asylum, as well as the road approach and workshop, were nearly completed. The longitudinal and cross walls on the north and west sides were partly raised, and those of the cook-rooms were built to their full height. Seven blocks of Police lines and a temporary Jail, to accommodate 500 convicts, were finished, as also servants' quarters, hospital, water channels, and other minor works.

Lawrence Asylum at Ootacamund.

160. The married quarters at Cannanore were completed during the year, with an outlay of Rupees 20,585. Considerable progress was made with the construction of the Artillery Barracks, one range of which was finished, as also the out-houses of two ranges, and of the Apothecary's quarters at a cost of Rupees 41,597.

Married quarters and Artillery Barracks at Cannanore.

161. Quarters for the Commissariat Serjeant at Bellary were provided at a total cost of Rupees 5,073, of which Rupees 1,059 were spent in 1867-68. The alterations to the criminal side of the Grand Jail at Madras, to adapt it as a Commissariat Store, were finished, with the exception of the raising of the floor and the formation of sidings to the tramway leading to the beach. Rupees 16,356 were spent upon this work, and on completing the alterations and additions to the Commissariat Arrack and Porter Depôt at the Presidency. At Bangalore, a sum of Rupees 16,020 was appropriated to the construction of a Bakery. The building was roofed in, and the chimney carried to its full height. The construction of a Commissariat godown at Cannanore was in progress, Rupees 10,519 having been spent on the erection of the walls, three-fourths of which were completed.

Buildings for the Commissariat Department at Bellary, Presidency, Bangalore, and Cannanore.

162. The shed for ambulance carts attached to the Arsenal at Bellary, upon which Rupees 4,334 were spent in 1866-67, was completed during the year with a further outlay of Rupees 121. Of the eighteen blocks of quarters proposed to be provided for the Warrant and Non-Commissioned Officers employed in the Arsenal of Fort St. George, twelve were completed; the foundation of three others were commenced, and materials were under collection for the remainder. The year's expenditure amounted to Rupees 60,767. A sum of Rupees 20,940 was applied to the completion of the Reserve Powder Magazine at St. Thomas'

Buildings for the Ordnance Department at Bellary, St. Thomas' Mount, Presidency, and Cannanore.

Mount, and of a range of quarters for the Overseers attached to the Gun Powder Manufactory at Madras. Fair progress was made with the construction of a Grand Powder Magazine at Cannanore, Rupees 7,023 having been appropriated during the year to the completion of the roof, and to the plastering of the building, compound wall, and guard-room.

CIVIL BUILDINGS.

Central Jails at Rajahmundry.

163. Rupees 49,065 were spent on the Central Jail at Rajahmundry in completing four radial blocks of cells, three workshops, three barracks, a central ward, six sides of the enclosure wall, a portion of the inner palisading, one well, six towers, jailer's quarters, hospital, juvenile workshop, female wards, and hospital for contagious diseases. Good progress was made with the other parts of the building and with the construction of a large latrine.

Vellore.

164. In connection with the Central Jail at Vellore, a sum of Rupees 64,267 was expended during the year. The foundations of seven radial wards, hospital, stores, and solitary cells were laid, and the outer wall was raised seven and a half feet. The walls of two radial wards were built to their full height, and those of another to a height of ten feet. The superstructure of the hospital, the walls of a block for stores, and two division walls were completed, as also the inner palisading and three sides of the outer palisading.

Salem.

165. At the Salem Central Jail, separate wards were provided for female prisoners, and a new hospital, Jailer's quarters, and two additional work sheds were under construction, with an outlay of Rupees 10,346.

Trichinopoly.

166. Good progress was made with the Central Jail at Trichinopoly, upon which the expenditure amounted to Rupees 1,13,767. The enclosure wall, hospital, guard-room, two ranges of cook-rooms, a male ward and a brick well with cistern for bathing were completed. An approach was made to the Jail from the main road, and a row of trees was planted all round the building.

Coimbatore.

167. The Central Jail at Coimbatore, upon which Rupees 47,655 were spent in 1867-68, was completed throughout at a total cost of Rupees 3,76,338.

Cannanore.

168. On the Central Jail at Cannanore, Rupees 72,460 were spent in completing the roof of the hospital and out-offices, as well as the masonry of one range of wards, and the basement of another. The construction of a dead-house and of the compound walls was also on hand.

169. With the exception of the surface drains and palisading, which are in progress, the District Jail at Vizagapatam was completed during the year with an expenditure of Rupees 16,144. Jails at Vizagapatam.

170. At the Jail at Berhampore, Rupees 9,406 were laid out in completing the compound wall, hospital, privies, cook-rooms, and dead-house. The construction of a prison-ward and two solitary cells was also on hand. Berhampore.

171. The improvements to the Jail at Guntoor, upon which Rupees 5,150 were spent, progressed favorably. The surrounding walls were fully built, and the interior new structures raised to an average height of seven feet. Guntoor.

172. Various improvements were carried out to the Jail at Bellary, at a cost of Rupees 10,393. New guard-rooms, condemned cells, and an office were provided; the roof of the Jail hospital was renewed, and materials collected for the extension of the Jail compound. Bellary.

173. The enclosure wall on the west side of the Penitentiary at Madras was completed during the year with a expenditure of Rupees 900. Penitentiary at Madras.

174. Two latrines and a dead-house were built in connection with the Jail at Cuddalore, and a wall to enclose the new buildings was raised to a height of seven feet, at a cost of Rupees 6,562. Jails at Cuddalore.

175. An expenditure of Rupees 24,638 was incurred in laying the foundations and building the walls of the Civil Jail at Ootacamund, and in providing guard, office, and record-rooms. Ootacamund.

176. In connection with the new District Jail at Calicut, a sum of Rupees 36,409 was expended. The roofing of the eastern ward was completed; three other wards were in progress, and the walls of the female hospital were raised to their full height. Calicut.

177. The new District Jail at Madura was completed during the year, with an outlay of Rupees 61,750. Madura.

178. The construction of a Talook Cutcherry and Subsidiary Jail at Trivellore was commenced, and the foundations and basement were completed at a cost of Rupees 6,000. Talook Cutcherries and Subsidiary Jails at Trivellore, Madras District.

179. A new privy, hospital shed, and a cook-house were added to the Talook Cutcherry at Ponnairy, and good progress was made with the erection of two wards for male and two for female prisoners. The year's expenditure was Rupees 3,597. Ponnairy, Madras District.

180. The new Small Cause and Principal Sudder Ameen's Court house at Madura, upon which Rupees 9,799 were spent up to 31st March 1867, was completed during the year, with a further outlay of Rupees 17,700. Small Cause Court at Madura.

181. In connection with the new Lunatic Asylum at Madras, the Superintendent's quarters and eight cottages were nearly completed, eleven other cottages were begun, and roads formed within the compound. The erection of additional wards to the Leper Hospital was commenced, and the walls were raised to the height of twelve feet. Segmental gutters in brick masonry were constructed all round the General Hospital buildings, and main drains were laid leading from three points to the Cooum river. The aggregate outlay upon these works during the year was Rupees 45,226.

Hospitals at the Presidency.

182. An additional shed was built in connection with the Public Works Workshops at Chepauk, at a cost of Rupees 11,711.

Public Works Stores at Madras.

183. The alterations and improvements to the Madras Medical College, upon which Rupees 43,200 were spent up to 31st March 1867, were completed in 1867-68, with a further expenditure of Rupees 8,390.

Madras Medical College.

184. Good progress was made with the erection of the new Church at Ootacamund, upon which Rupees 13,480 were spent from Imperial Funds, and Rupees 15,481 from private contributions. The masonry work of the nave, chancel, and transepts was completed, and the walls of the tower were raised to a height of forty-eight feet.

Church at Ootacamund.

AGRICULTURAL.

185. An expenditure of Rupees 15,468 was incurred in strengthening the apron of the Godavery anicut. Two anicuts were under construction across the Manimuthanaddy river in the South Arcot District. One of these, which was commenced in 1866-67, was nearly finished with an outlay of Rupees 2,078; upon the other, a sum of Rupees 27,022 was expended, and about two-thirds of the work were completed. At the south branch of the Lower Coleroon Anicut, Rupees 47,170 were appropriated to the completion of the bridge, which was begun in the previous year, and to the extension of the sluice aprons, and the construction of a rear retaining wall and an additional apron.

Godavery, Manimuthanaddy, and Lower Coleroon Anicuts.

186. A sum of Rupees 30,568 was expended on improvements to the supply channel of the Narraindavakerra tank, and on the restoration of the Goottoor, Pauthacotacheroo, and Yerrabomanahully tanks. The first two of these works were half completed. A breach in the bund of the third work was closed, and a large quantity of materials collected. The revetment of the last mentioned tank was re-built, a new sluice was provided, and about 700 yards of the bund were repaired and improved.

Tanks in the Bellary District.

187. The Somareddypully tank was restored and placed in thorough order at a cost of Rupees 6,230, and Rupees 7,355 were spent on raising the bund of the Gunjanapally Mallapah tank to an

Cuddapah District.

uniform level, and on erecting a calingulah and sluice and renewing the stone revetment.

188 In the Nellore District, an outlay of Rupees 8,000 was incurred on the excavation of a channel from the Vencatagherry river to the Chennur tank, which is now very nearly completed. The rough stone revetment of the Nellore tank, which was commenced in 1865-66, was satisfactorily completed during the past year with an expenditure of Rupees 4,119.

Nellore District.

189. A new calingulah was provided to the Cauverypauk tank at an expense of Rupees 6,000.

North Arcot District.

Irrigation works in the Godavery District.

190. Several masonry works were under construction on the Akeed canal. A flood calingulah was raised at Chinnakapaveram up to the level of the crown, and another was provided at a spot one and a half miles lower down the canal, at a cost of Rupees 17,045.

Akeed Canal.

191. A sum of Rupees 25,715 was appropriated to the excavation of the earthwork for four miles of the Samulcottah canal, and to the completion of the piers and abutments of eighteen bridges.

Samulcottah Canal.

192. In connection with the works for the cross drainage of the Ellore high level canal, Rupees 25,451 were spent on completing three outlets, two under-tunnels, and several small inlets.

Ellore Canal.

Irrigation works in the Kistna District.

193. The widening of the main canal from Bezoarah to Kunkipaud progressed favorably, no less than 272,000 cubic yards of earthwork having been completed. The Poolairoo channel was widened as far as the rapids at Bodlapaund, and the construction of the Weyoor calingulah was commenced, all under an outlay of Rupees 43,014.

Channels in the Masulipatam section of the Kistna Delta.

194. On the project for widening the head of the Masulipatam canal, Rupees 7,741 were spent in completing 36,000 cubic yards of earthwork, and in the purchase of some houses which require to be removed.

Head of Masulipatam Canal.

195. The east side irrigation channel of the Bunder canal was completed at a cost of Rupees 12,845. On the west side irrigation channel an outlay of Rupees 14,502 was incurred, but the progress of the work was retarded owing to failures on the part of the contractor.

Irrigation channels of the Bunder Canal.

Side channels from Doogeralla to Nizampatam.

196. About 135,000 cubic yards of earthwork for the side channels, from Doogeralla to Nizampatam, were excavated, and several masonry works commenced with an expenditure of Rs. 19,097

Locks at Doogeralla and Jaggerlamudy.

197. The construction of two locks at Doogeralla and Jaggerlamudy was in progress, and Rupees 16,927 were spent on building the chamber walls to a height of four feet, and completing the inverts.

Commamoor Channel.

198. Rupees 51,293 were laid out on the Commamoor channel, chiefly in widening the channel itself, and raising bunds in connection with the various outlets; the main drainage of the Rampairoo swamp was completed, and the extension of the drainage from Cadava Coodoor to the creek was commenced.

Western Bank Channel.

199. Fair progress was made with the widening of the Western Bank channel, Rupees 15,844 having been expended in excavating about 158,000 cubic yards of earth and completing all the necessary masonry works.

Main Canal near Seetanagram.

200. An outlay of Rupees 14,346 was incurred on the enlargement of the main canal near Seetanagram, in the excavation of 114,000 cubic yards of earth. The effect in increasing the discharge is said to be highly satisfactory.

Survapully Channel in the Nellore District.

201. The sanctioned improvements to the Survapully channel were actively prosecuted during the year, with an expenditure of Rupees 57,168. Three and a half miles of the Iduguly branch channel, and half a mile of the Welluru, one mile of the Ipuru, and three miles of the Survapully branch channels were excavated, on an average, to one-third of their ultimate section. The Iduguly branch head sluice, and the regulating sluice at the Iduguly tank were completed, and the foundations of and the escape for the Survapully reservoir were laid.

Venkiah Calwah Channel in the Cuddapah District.

202. In the Cuddapah District Rupees 6,100 were applied to the excavation of a new head, and the construction of a regulating sluice dyke to the Venkiah Calwah channel.

Madras Water Supply Project.

203. The works connected with the Madras Water Supply Project were vigorously carried on during the year, Rupees 2,83,902 having been expended on the construction of masonry works, excavation of channels, and strengthening of tank bunds.

Bungaroo Channel banks and Nagalapooram Tank Supply Channel, Madras District.

204. Various portions of the Bungaroo channel banks were revetted with stone at a cost of Rupees 7,523, and Rupees 3,380 were laid out on the excavation of a new head to the Nagalapooram tank supply channel, and on the construction of a regulating sluice.

205. The widening of the Cheyaur channel from Mookoor to Pooroosay was completed with an expenditure of Rupees 17,911. The first four miles of the Alliabad channel were widened, supply channels leading to four important tanks were excavated, and a bridge was built at a place where the main channel crosses a district road, at an aggregate cost of Rupees 30,437.

Cheyaur and Alliabad Channels, North Arcot.

206. A new channel was cut from the Cauveripauk tank to the Mahendravady channel, and the latter was improved, and a flood calingulah provided in connection with the Palar Anicut project at an expense of Rupees 15,740.

Channel from the Cauveripauk Tank to the Mahendravady Channel, North Arcot.

207. A sum of Rupees 26,977 was appropriated to the Pombay channel from the Pooniar anicut. The works in the first five miles were completed, and those in the remaining seven were more than half finished. The Ragavien channel, leading from the same anicut, was improved, and the Amoor branch channel re-opened with an outlay of Rs. 8,830.

Channels from the Pooniar Anicut, South Arcot.

The foundations of the north wing of the Cauvery dam, and seventy-nine feet of the retaining wall were raised five and a half and four feet respectively, and a large quantity of materials was collected for the Coodamurty and Arasalar dams. At the Veerasholen dam, the foundations of the portion in the Cauvery were raised to from three and a quarter to a quarter of a foot of the level of the apron, and the south wing was raised two feet above the foundations. The aggregate expenditure was Rupees 28,309.

About two-thirds of the works connected with the Wyacondan extension project were completed at a cost of Rupees 14,999. Ten surplus sluices were nearly finished on the north bank of the Coleroon with an outlay of Rupees 2,500. With the exception of the machinery for working the sluices, which is now under preparation, the estimate for providing surplus sluices in the Wyacondan channel was fully worked out, the expenditure during the year being Rupees 9,622. In connection with the Nunthyaur Anicut extension project, a sum of Rupees 13,950 was applied to the collection of materials and to the construction of sluices and tunnels, and the excavation of channels.

The west abutment, wing-walls, and the third and fourth piers of the aqueduct over the Vanipoothoor stream were completed, and a channel was excavated on the western side at a cost of Rupees 7,087.

COMMUNICATIONS.

208. An expenditure of Rupees 9,000 was incurred on the road from Aska to Pipplepunka, in completing the earthwork of twenty-one miles, the metalling and gravelling of fifteen miles, and the construction of several minor masonry works. On the road from Aska to Russelcondah, Rupees 12,000 were spent in finishing twenty-two miles of earthwork, clearing two and three quarters of a mile of jungle, gravelling sixteen and

Roads in Ganjam.

turfing seven miles of road, and building eleven bridges and a large number of culverts and road dams. The branch road from Ballepudra to Kurcholy was completed at a total cost of Rupees 29,749, of which Rupees 2,367 were spent during the year, and, with the exception of two bridges under construction, the sanctioned improvements to the road from Aska to the Ganjam port and salt pans were completed with an outlay of Rupees 5,341 during 1867-68.

Canal from Chilka Lake to Ganjam river.

209. Rupees 42,176 were laid out on the partial excavation of nineteen miles of the canal from the Chilka lake to the Ganjam river, and the dressing of seven and a half miles of the banks.

Roads in Vizagapatam.

210. The road from Vizagapatam to Cassepoor was metalled to the end of the 16th mile, and in portions between the 17th and 31st miles, and 129 minor masonry works were completed. Eighteen miles of the road from Vizianagram to Bowdara were completed; sixteen miles were metalled and gravelled, and eighty-three bridges and culverts were constructed. Trunk Road No. 6, from Chittavulsa to Chicacole, was completed from the 1st to the 10th, and from the 12th to the 28th mile. The earthwork of eleven and a half miles was finished, four miles were gravelled, four and a half miles of jungle cleared, three miles turfed, eleven miles of side drains excavated, and thirty-five bridges and culverts built. The aggregate outlay on these roads was Rupees 18,210.

Roads in Nellore.

211. Metalling was laid on more than one-half of the embanked road across the Musanur valley on Trunk Road No. 6, and the Pallivagoo, Munganoor, and Musanoor bridges were completed, while the foundations of the Oopelavagoo bridge were excavated at an expenditure of Rupees 11,002. The Pyderu bridge on this line was completed at a total cost of Rupees 24,204, of which Rupees 4,176 were spent during 1867-68.

Roads in Cuddapah and Bellary.

212. The 47th, 48th, and 49th miles of the road from Cuddapah to Bellary, in the Cuddapah District, and the portion between Kunchenhull and Goontacul, in the Bellary District, were metalled and gravelled, and a road dam, 240 feet in length, was built. On the road from Cuddapah to the Kurnool frontier several masonry works were built, and 4,220 lineal yards of road were metalled and gravelled. The total outlay on these lines was Rupees 15,606, of which Rupees 3,117 were appropriated from Income Tax funds.

Bridge over the Cooum Bar at the Presidency.

213. Good progress was made with the construction of the bridge over the Cooum bar, and the work will probably be completed in two or three months. Eight out of ten spans have been fitted with girders and covered in with planks overlaid with granite set in asphalte. The expenditure amounted to Rupees 1,03,774, of which Rupees 68,161 were appropriated from Income Tax funds.

214. Six miles of the road from Tripathy to Calastry, viâ the Railway Station, were formed, of which five miles were metalled. About nineteen miles of the road from Calastry to Naidoopett› on Trunk Road No. 6, and several masonry works were constructed. Materials were under collection for the further metalling of the road, and for the construction of culverts. On the road from Bungaroopett to Yaripett, several road dams and culverts were completed; the earthwork of about eighteen miles was laid, and materials were collected for additional masonry works. The outlay on these lines was Rupees 21,000.

Roads in North Arcot.

215. Two bridges on the road between Kullacoorchi and the Salem frontier, which were commenced in 1866-67, were completed during the year, and two others were under construction. A bridge of three arches was built across the Thumbipettah Oday, on the road from Cuddalore to the Salem frontier. The outlay on these bridges in 1867-68 amounted to Rupees 7,225.

Roads in South Arcot

216. A sum of Rupees 31,211, of which Rupees 1,211 were from Income Tax funds, was appropriated to the widening of the canal from Negapatam to Vedarniem, improving the slopes, and constructing several masonry works. Forty-three miles of the road from Trichinopoly to Trunk Road No. 9 were brought to completion during the year, with an outlay of Rupees 8,011, of which Rupees 1,011 were assigned from Income Tax funds. The road from Trichinopoly to Salem, viâ Torriore, was completed to within three and a half miles of the Salem frontier, with an expenditure of Rupees 10,188.

Roads and Canals in the Tanjore and Trichinopoly Districts.

217. Good progress was made with the Coonoor Ghaut trace, on which the outlay during the year amounted to Rupees 50,021. Twenty-four bridges and a large number of masonry works were completed, and several others were put in hand. About three-fourths of the entire length of the trace will shortly be open to cart traffic. The upper portion of the new Goodalore Ghaut, for upwards of two miles through the Chinchona plantations, was opened for cart traffic, and work in the lower sections was vigorously carried on with an outlay of Rupees 10,000. With the exception of three or four miles near Wellington, the whole of the road from Kotagherry, viâ Wellington, to the Coonoor Ghaut, upon which a large quantity of earth and masonry work was executed during the year, will shortly be opened for cart traffic. The expenditure amounted to Rupees 7,000. Rupees 11,000 were spent in opening to wheeled traffic eleven miles of the road from Ootacamund to the head of the Goodalore Ghaut, and in completing two bridges and sixty-two drains. From Pykarra to Neddivuttum, five miles of the road were opened to cart traffic, three miles to a width of fifteen feet, and a large number of bridges and drains were constructed. Eight miles of the southern portion of the

Roads in Coimbatore.

Burghoor Ghaut trace were nearly finished for cart traffic at an outlay of Rupees 8,027, during the year.

Roads and Ghauts in Malabar.

218. The Carcoor Ghaut was opened out to a width of seven yards, and several drains were built at an outlay of Rs. 22,960. On the road from Carcoor to Goodalore there was an expenditure of Rupees 16,273 in completing two miles near Nadakany, and in the construction of two bridges and sixteen culverts. On the road from Goodalore to Tippacaudoo, Rupees 4,960 were spent in widening the fourth mile, between Tippacaudoo and the Bedrahalla river, and in completing several minor masonry works. The Periah Ghaut was opened to full width for about three-fourths of its length, and revetments and retaining walls were built at the most dangerous parts, at a cost of Rupees 45,746. Improved traces were made for the Bowally road towards the Mysore frontier, and the earthwork was opened out to full width at an outlay of Rupees 1,640. On the Tambracherry Ghaut good progress was made with the earthwork and revetment, and the construction of several bridges was commenced. The expenditure amounted to Rupees 55,147. Rupees 5,743 were spent on the road between Luckady and Kulputty on earthwork and bridges, and the masonry of a bridge over the Koonuth river was nearly finished at a cost of Rupees 8,000. The construction of a bridge over the Kulputty river, on which Rupees 3,579 were spent, was much retarded, owing to a misunderstanding with the contractors. The whole of the earthwork of the road from Kulputty to Sultan's Battery, on which Rupees 18,088 were laid out, was completed to within three miles of Kulputty; materials were collected for the culverts, and the construction of two temporary bridges was undertaken. Rupees 9,706 were spent in completing the earthwork of the road from Sultan's Battery to the Mysore frontier, and on the collection of materials for the necessary masonry works. On the road from Manantoddy to the Coorg frontier, where the outlay was Rupees 10,327, the earthwork, excepting for about three-fourths of a mile, was open to full width, and materials were prepared for a number of temporary bridges. The earthwork of the Carcoor Ghaut and road, and much of the bridge work were completed, and the entire line was thrown open for traffic during the year with an outlay of Rupees 35,285, of which Rupees 2,736 were appropriated from Income Tax funds.

Roads in Canara.

219. Four large and ten small bridges and drains were completed on the road from Mangalore to Cannanore, viâ Vitla and Hoosdroog, and good progress was made with the construction of other masonry works. The expenditure was Rupees 14,322.

Roads in Madura and Tinnevelly.

220. On the road from Tirumungalum to the Coimbatore boundary, eleven miles of roadway were completed, the earthwork for a further distance of three and a quarter miles was thrown up, and seven small bridges were built with an expenditure of Rupees 22,662 from

Imperial, and Rupees 488 from Income Tax funds. An unfinished gap of two miles of the road from Madura to the Travancore country, immediately north of Satoor, was made and metalled; nearly five miles of roadway south of Palamcottah were constructed, and five old Irish bridges on other parts of the line were converted into tunnels with an outlay of Rupees 21,898, of which Rupees 3,114 were from Income Tax funds. Twenty-three miles of the road from Palamcottah to Tuticorin were completed and opened for traffic, and six additional miles were under construction. The whole of the piers and one of the abutments of the Nulla Mullay Oday bridge were built up to the springing line, and the foundations of the other abutment were partially laid with an expenditure of Rupees 21,197.

Paumbem Channel in the Madura District.

221. Progress was made in cutting off the inner angle of the reef channel at Paumbem, on which Rupees 5,450 were laid out in blasting 17,090 cubic feet of stone, and in removing 20,950 cubic feet of silt and gravel.

Expenditure from Local Funds.

222. The following is a statement of the allotment and expenditure from Local Funds by Officers of the Public Works Department. A list of the principal works undertaken from that source during the year 1867-68, is given in the Appendix :—

	Allotment.	Expenditure.
	RS.	RS.
New works	13,21,129	9,85,347
Repairs	3,82,419	3,35,510
Tools and Plant	3,081	2,393
Establishments	1,05,279	1,63,906
Total...	18,11,908	14,87,156

MADRAS RAILWAY.

South-West Line.

Number of Miles open.

223. The number of miles open for traffic upon this line remains the same as at the close of the last official year. Including the Bangalore branch, 492 miles have been worked during the year.

Train Service.

224. The train service has been carried out by two passenger trains daily, in each direction, over the whole length of line. In addition to these, other trains, both for passengers and goods, averaging four per diem in each direction, have been run on week days over longer or shorter portions of the line, according to the exigencies of the traffic.

Number of Passengers & Receipts.

225. The number of passengers throughout the year, and the receipts derived from them, have been as follows :—

Class.	Number of passengers.	Per-centage.	Receipts.	Per-centage.
			RS.	
First	9,521	·58	1,18,602	8·39
Second	61,729	3·79	1,37,285	9·71
Third	1,557,584	95·63	11,57,780	81·90
Total...	1,628,834	100	14,13,667	100

Average daily number of passengers.

226. The average daily number of passengers has been 4,450, or at the rate of 9·05 per mile of line.

Comparison of number of passengers and receipts with previous official year.

227. The official year 1866-67 consisted of eleven months only; but allowing for twelve months at the same average, the year 1867-68 exhibits an increase in the number of passengers of 155,891, and in the receipts of Rupees 58,079.

Tons of goods and receipts.

228. 279,931 tons of goods have been carried upon this line, and the receipts from this branch of traffic have been Rs. 24,05,239—shewing, as compared with the corresponding figures for 1866-67, a decrease of 11,950 tons, and of Rupees 1,931.

Rates and fares.

229. The rates in force for the conveyance of passengers and goods have been as follows :—

Passengers—First class, by day 18 pies per mile.
Do. by night 22 do.
Second class, by day 6 do. up to 31st Jan. 1868.
Do. do. 5 do. from 1st Feb. „
Do. by night 7 do. up to 31st Jan. „
Do. do. 12 do. from 1st Feb. „
Third class 3 do.

Goods—Special class 8 pies per ton per mile.
First class 12 do.
Second class 14 do.
Third class 16 do. up to 31st December 1867.
Do. 18 do. from 1st January 1868.
Fourth class 24 do.
Fifth class 36 do.

Special rates.

230. The following special rates have also been in force :—

Cotton, loose—from Bangalore and stations on that branch, raised from 30 to 36 pies per ton per mile.

Coffee—in full waggon loads of five tons, from Bangalore to Beypoor, 9 pies per ton per mile.

Salt—from Madras to Avenashy, 9 pies per ton per mile.

Sandal-wood—in the rough and roots, from Morapoor to stations on the Western Coast, 18 pies per ton per mile.

A drawback of 12½ per cent. was allowed as an experimental measure on the carriage of coir, cocoanuts, coperays, and pepper, in full waggon loads of not less than five tons, from any station west of Palghaut to Madras.

Chief items in Goods Traffic.

231. The chief items in the goods traffic have been the following :—

Up—from Madras.	*Down—to Madras.*
Salt.	Cotton.
Rice.	Coffee.
Jaggery.	Cocoanuts.
Raggy.	Betel-nuts.
Gram.	Potatoes.
Cloths.	Fruits.
Wine and beer.	Vegetables.

In several items, such as iron, timber, tamarinds, seeds, and tobacco, the traffic has been considerable in both directions.

Per-centage of working expenses.

232. The working expenses during the six months, from July to December 1867 inclusive, amounted to forty-six per cent. upon the total gross receipts of the line. They are composed as follows :—

	Per-centage on gross Receipts.
Permanent way	15·47
Locomotive Department	18·46
Traffic do.	8·40
Telegraph do.	·89
General charges	2·78
	46·00

Expenditure on Capital account.

233. The total expenditure on capital account up to 31st December 1867, was Rupees 6,35,14,769. The net profits for the half-year ended 31st December 1867 were Rupees 11,00,601, being at the rate of £3-9-2½ per cent. per annum.

Kuddulhoondy bridge.

234. The only large work in progress upon this line during the year 1867-68, has been the re-construction of the bridge across the Kuddulhoondy river, near the Beypoor terminus. The portion of the bridge across the northern channel of the river was finished during

1866-67; but owing to a peculiarity in the bed of the southern channel, it was found necessary to substitute iron cylinders for the piles which had been originally designed for the piers. The materials arrived only in October last, and the work is now making fair progress.

New terminal station and bridge across Cochrane's canal.

235. The new terminal station at Madras has been commenced during the past year, and the foundations are nearly completed. The iron girder bridge across Cochrane's canal, on the branch leading to the new station, has not yet been commenced. Materials are being collected.

Erode Junction.

236. At Erode, a junction has been effected with the Great Southern of India Railway.

Condition of Line.

237. The whole of the works upon the South-West Line have been maintained in good order during the year. The general condition of the line, and the results of the year's working, have been satisfactory and creditable to the executive management.

North-West Line.

Mileage open for Traffic.

238. No additional portion of the line has been opened during the year. Moodanoor, 153 miles from Arconum, is still the terminal station.

Train Service.

239. The train service has been carried out by one passenger train daily, in each direction, over the whole open line. Besides this, other trains, averaging four per diem in each direction, have been run on week days over various portions of the line, according to the state of the traffic.

Number of passengers & receipts.

240. The number of passengers throughout the year, and the receipts from them, have been as follows :—

Class.	Number of passengers.	Per-centage.	Receipts.	Per-centage.
			RS.	
First	875	·20	6,490	2·36
Second	5,210	1·17	8,774	3·19
Third	439,219	98·63	2,59,835	94·45
Total...	445,304	100	2,75,099	100

The average daily number of passengers has been 1,217, at the rate of 7·96 per mile of open line. The increase in the number of passengers over those carried in the previous year has been 82,806, while the receipts have been increased by Rupees 51,126.

241. During the past year 77,800 tons of goods have been carried on this line, the receipts therefrom being Rupees 6,70,971—being in excess of the corresponding figures for 1866-67 by 7,191 tons, and by Rupees 1,80,555.

Goods and receipts.

242. The rates charged for passengers and goods have been, throughout the year, the same as those charged on the South-West Line. The following special rates have been in force:—

Rates and fares.

For *Firewood*—for Mr. Barnett,* a rate of Annas 2-6 per mile per waggon from Coodoor to Moodanoor.

For *Cotton, loose*—36 pies per ton per mile.

243. The working expenses upon this line during the latter half of the year 1867, amounted to 40·47 per cent. of the gross traffic earnings—being composed as follows:—

Working expenses.

	Per-centage on gross earnings.
Permanent way	7·64
Locomotive Department	14·72
Traffic do.	6·57
Telegraph do.	·67
General charges	2·38
Hire of Rolling Stock from South-West Line...	8·49
	40·47

244. The total expenditure on capital account, up to the 31st December 1867, amounted to Rupees 1,93,21,238, and the net profits for the half-year ended 31st December 1867, were Rs. 2,80,014, being at the rate of £2-18-0 per cent. per annum.

Capital account and Profits.

245. The progress made during 1867-68, upon the portion of this line under construction, has not been thoroughly satisfactory; and it is now clear that the dates named in the Contract Agreements for the completion of the several sections will be considerably exceeded. The bridge over the Chittravutty river has been finished; and the portion of the line between Moodanoor, the present terminus, and Tadputry, a distance of thirty-two miles, is in a very advanced condition.

Progress of works.

The bridge over the Pennair river has made very slow progress, but the Contractor has now engaged to complete the masonry by the 31st December next; and in that case the opening of the line to Gooty may be confidently looked for before the end of 1869.

Between Gooty and Adoni the work is in a forward state, and after the line has been opened to the former place, the opening to the latter will probably

* The Company's Contractor on the unopened line beyond Moodanoor.

take place in as short a time as will allow of the permanent way being brought forward and laid down.

The completion of the line between Adoni and Raichoor, which will be the terminus of the Madras Railway in this direction, will depend chiefly on the progress made with the bridge over the Toongabudra river. This important work is now making fair progress, but it does not seem likely that the line will be opened to Raichoor before 1872.

GREAT SOUTHERN OF INDIA RAILWAY.

Miles open.

246. On the 1st of July 1867, an additional portion of the Erode extension from Caroor to Kudumudi, a distance of seventeen miles, was opened for traffic, and on the 1st of January 1868, a junction was effected at Erode with the South-West Line of the Madras Railway, making, in all, a distance of forty-one miles opened during the official year 1867-68. The number of miles now open for traffic is 168.

Train Service.

247. The train service has been carried out by one passenger train daily in each direction, over the whole open line. In addition to these, other trains, averaging two per diem in each direction, have been run on week days, over longer or shorter portions of the line, according to the state of the traffic.

Number of passengers and receipts.

248. The number of passengers throughout the year, and the receipts from them, have been as follows :—

Class.	Number of Passengers.	Per-centage.	Receipts.	Per-centage.
			RS.	
First	3,038	0·68	8,910	2·53
Second	* 1,634	0·36	2,702	0·77
Third	444,781	98·96	3,40,567	96·70
Total...	449,453	100	3,52,179	100

The average daily number of passengers has been 2,443, or at the rate of 16·76 per mile of open line. The decrease in the number of passengers over those carried in the previous year has been 28,007, while the receipts have been increased by Rupees 94,699.

Goods carried.

249. During the past year, 46,681 tons of goods have been carried on this line, the receipts therefrom being Rupees 1,82,359—shewing, as compared with the corresponding figures for 1866-67, a decrease of 23,114 tons, and Rupees 87,400.

* Second class fares were in force for only two months out of the twelve.

Fares and Rates.

250. The rates charged for passengers and goods have been as follows :—

	Class	Rate		Period
Passengers—	First class	12 pies per mile	...	Up to 31st December 1867.
	Second do.	5 "	...	
	First do.	18 "	...	From 1st January 1868 to 29th February 1868.
	Second do.	8 "	...	
	Third do.	5 "	...	
	First do.	18 "	...	From 1st March 1868.
	Second do.	5 "	...	
	Third do.	3 "	...	

	Class	Rate	Period
Goods—		1 Anna per ton per mile	Up to 31st December 1867.
	Gunpowder, Jewellery, &c.,	2 Annas per ton per mile	
	Special class	8 pies per ton per mile.	From 1st January 1868.
	First do.	12 do.	
	Second do.	14 do.	
	Third do.	18 do.	
	Fourth do.	24 do.	
	Fifth do.	36 do.	

Per-centage of working expenses.

251. The working expenses upon this line, during the latter half of the year 1867, amounted to 50·50 per cent. of the gross traffic earnings, being composed as follows :—

	Per-centage on gross earnings.
Permanent way	10·87
Locomotive Department	29·86
Traffic do. } Telegraph do. }	6·89
General charges	2·88
	50·50

Expenditure on Capital account and per-centage of profit.

252. The total expenditure on capital account up to the 31st December 1867, amounted to Rupees 1,27,23,313, and the net profits for the half-year ended 31st December 1867, were Rs. 1,57,525, being at the rate of £2-9-7 per cent. per annum.

Third class carriages.

253. The running of third class passenger carriages, which was discontinued on the 1st March 1867, was resumed on the 1st January 1868, and, since the 1st March 1868, the lowest fare has been reduced from five pies to three pies per mile. There can be little doubt that these changes will, in time, prove advantageous to the interests of the Company. The discontinuance of third class carriages, and the raising of the lowest fare, resulted in driving off the Railway twenty-five per cent. of its former passengers; but with the adoption of measures more suited to the

circumstances of the country, the recovery of the lost traffic, though probably a work of time, will be certain.

LIGHT RAILWAY BETWEEN ARCONUM AND CONJEVERAM.

Mileage open for traffic.

254. The Indian Tramway Company's short line of Light Railway has the same number of miles, nineteen, open for traffic as at the end of 1866-67.

Train Service.

255. The train service has been performed by two trains daily in each direction, and by additional trains to suit the requirements of the traffic.

Rates and fares.

256. The rates in force for passengers and goods have been as follows :—

Passengers—First class 24 pies per mile.
Second do. 6 do.
Third do. 4 do.

Goods—Special class 12 pies per ton per mile.
First do. 16 do.
Second do. 20 do.
Third do. 24 do.
Fourth do. 36 do.
Fifth do. 48 do.

Guaranteed dividend.

257. This line, which was completed in 1865, was originally constructed without a guarantee, but a minimum dividend of three per cent. on the paid up capital of £100,000 has lately been guaranteed. Full statistics regarding the traffic are not yet available.

Per-centage of working expenses.

258. During the half-year ended the 31st December 1867, the gross traffic receipts amounted to Rupees 21,312, and the working expenses to Rupees 18,488, or at the rate of 86·75 per cent. of the gross receipts.

Per-centage of profit.

259. No information is available as to the amount of capital actually expended; but taking the paid up capital of £100,000, the net profits, which came to Rupees 2,824 during the half-year, were at the rate of £0-11-3½ per cent. per annum.

Condition of work and management.

260. The line is constructed upon a gauge of three feet six inches, and the works have been maintained in good order during the past year. The traffic management seems also to have been satisfactory.

IRRIGATION AND CANAL COMPANY.

261. During the earlier part of the year the progress made was small; and, in the first six months, only in one or two divisions were the works fairly

re-started. Since that time, however, the works have made fair progress, and it is expected that the upper seventy-two miles of the Main Canal will be ready for the admission of water as soon as the river Tumbuddra will be able to afford a supply.

Estimates sanctioned.

262. At the beginning of the year the Government had sanctioned estimates, amounting to Rupees 80,41,215-8-6, (of which amount Rupees 249-8-3 was for revenue account, the remainder being for construction). These estimates provided for the construction of the Main Canal up to the end of the ninth section in the 178th mile, and also for the head works and anicut across the Tumbuddra at Sunkasala, the Somaisweram anicut across the Pennair at its entry into the Nellore District, for station buildings, and a few distribution works. There were sanctioned in 1867-68

Estimates sanctioned during the year.

estimates for Main Supply	Rs.	15,57,935
,, Distribution	,,	3,317
,, Buildings...	,,	5,433
		15,66,685

and for repairs, debitable to revenue, Rupees 355. A particular statement of the estimates is given in the Appendix. Below are shewn the original estimates of the cost of the various works, and, in juxtaposition, the estimates as they now stand. Those only in italics have been altered during the past year :—

Description of work.		Original Estimates.			Present Estimates.			Increase.		
		RS.	A.	P.	RS.	A.	P.	RS.	A.	P.
Kurnool Anicut		3,03,080	0	0	3,03,080	0	0	Abandoned.		
1 Mile of canal from Anicut		65,000	0	0	65,000	0	0	Do.		
Soonkasala Anicut and head works ...		1,25,000	0	0	4,27,052	0	0	3,02,052	0	0
1st Section, Main Canal, miles 18... ...		4,60,000	0	0	8,81,927	0	0	4,21,927	0	0
Hindry Aqueduct		1,45,000	0	0	2,46,029	8	0	1,01,029	8	0
2nd Section, Main Canal, miles 14... ...		5,34,000	0	0	18,00,150	0	0	12,66,150	0	0
3rd do. do. ,, 11... ...		1,88,500	0	0	9,58,000	0	0	7,69,500	0	0
4th do. do. ,, 17... ...		2,71,560	0	0	11,80,393	0	0	9,08,833	0	0
5th do. do. ,, 12... ...		2,50,003	5	4	7,05,345	0	3	4,55,341	10	11
6th do. do. ,, 19... ...		3,04,258	5	4	4,39,772	5	4	1,35,514	0	0
7th do. do. ,, 23... ...		2,34,893	5	4	4,74,453	5	4	2,39,560	0	0
8th do. do. ,, 28... ...		4,37,410	0	0	7,36,830	0	0	2,99,420	0	0
9th do. do. ,, 35... ...		8,02,811	0	0	9,45,837	0	0	1,43,026	0	0
10th do. do. ,, 8... ...		1,94,330	0	0	1,94,330	0	0	...	...	...
Distribution works		52,800	0	0	61,187	0	0	8,387	0	0
Buildings		78,765	14	1	99,688	9	11	20,922	11	10
Somaisweram Anicut...		1,41,357	1	7	1,71,727	1	7	30,370	0	0
Line of Telegraph		44,116	0	0	44,116	0	0	...	...	...
Revenue account		604	8	3	604	8	3	...	...	...
		46,33,489	7	11	97,85,522	6	8	51,02,032	14	9
Deduct retrenchment from										
Main Canal, 4th Section, Rs.	1,24,872									
Do. Building, do. ,,	2,395									
	1,27,267	...	...	...	1,27,267	0	0	1,27,267	0	0
		46,33,489	7	11	96,08,255	6	8	49,74,765	14	9

Expenditure.

263. The total expenditure on all accounts at the year's end was Rupees1,00,13,206, as shewn below :—

Construction, including special Superintendence and sundries				Rs.	68,46,047-14-6.		
Cost of the permanent Establishment—							
Controlling ... ... Rs.	7,52,249	7	1				
Executive ... ... „	14,53,408	1	4				
				„	22,05,657	8	5
Miscellaneous expenses				„	2,13,893	0	10
Store charges unadjusted				„	1,14,776	4	11
General plant in use on works				„	2,19,969	15	4
Revenue account				„	10,086	8	11
Stores				„	4,02,774	15	4
					1,00,13,206	4	3

The following description gives the state of the works during the year :—

Sunkasala anicut and head works.

264. The anicut* received no injury from the freshes of the year. The only work now in an unfinished state is the coping, which will probably be completed next year. The head and under-sluices continued in fair order, but the shutters of the latter are not efficient, and will need alteration and improvement; they are revolving shutters, working on a central verticle spindle or shaft.

1st Section, Main Canal, from head to 18th mile.

265. The work done here was not extensive, but the canal is capable of carrying more water than is at present needed. A revised estimate for its completion was prepared and submitted for sanction, but it was not approved, as it appeared to provide for a canal of less capacity than that originally sanctioned, and that capacity was by no means too great. Fair progress has been made in providing accommodation bridges for the villages near the canal. The expenditure during the year amounted to Rupees 56,300-9-0.†

2nd and 3rd Sections, Miles 18 to 43.

266. In the last year's report it was mentioned that serious breaches had occurred, and that the reformation of the embankments was found to be necessary before the canal could convey even a moderate supply. These works have been pushed forward with considerable energy, and it is expected that they will be finished before the time (June) for the admission of water. At any rate, the banks will be tried, and it is to be hoped that the measures adopted for remedying the defects of original construction will be found successful. Should this be the case, water can be sent down this year for about seventy-two miles, and no doubt some commencement

* Length of crest, 1,500 yards.
Coping finished for 1,300 „

† This includes Rs. 24,026-6-2 spent on clearing the canal.

of irrigation will be made below the 24th mile, to the country above which it has hitherto been confined. There will be only a commencement however. Even under the most favorable circumstances, the ryots will not be assured that water will be available until comparatively late in the season, and it will then be too late for them to alter the nature of the year's cultivation. If, however, a few acres here and there be irrigated in each village near the canal, it may be anticipated that the following year will, should the works be found efficient, see a marked increase in the area of land brought under irrigation. Expenditure of the year, Rupees 2,31,035-6-0.

267. The fourth section is almost complete, and also the fifth, the latter having been previously in an advanced condition. These are both likely to be ready by the time water can be brought down. The expenditure has been respectively Rupees 1,84,441-13-6 and Rupees 96,425-4-4.

4th and 5th Sections.

268. In the sixth section, which will be a still-water navigation with the exception of the upper six miles, no extension has been made, but labor which could be spared has been spent on the first six miles, at a cost of Rupees 25,480-0-4.

6th Section.

269. The seventh section has made little progress, from various causes, one being the want of Indian experience among the officers in charge. The masonry works, which are much behind, are being pushed on, and in another year this portion may be fit to receive water. Rupees 27,240-3-2 was expended on it.

7th Section.

270. The eighth section had, before work was suspended in 1865, made so much more rapid progress than the seventh, that it was thought advisable not to continue work on it until the seventh section was more advanced. Rupees 4,993-13-6 only was expended.

8th Section.

271. The ninth section will receive a supply from an anicut across the Kundar, into a tributary of which a large portion of the Tumbuddra water will flow from the surplus works at the 72nd mile. As, therefore, it can be brought into use independently of the seventh and eighth sections, the works have been gone on with as fast as the labor available would allow, and the upper portion has made very fair progress. The expenditure incurred in the year amounts to Rupees 95,255-4-4.

9th Section.

272. An anicut across the Pennair, near Adimapully, was designed and estimated for, but the plan was thought incapable of discharging extreme floods with safety, and was otherwise objectionable, and was disapproved by Government. This anicut was for the supply of the tenth section, which is the last to be completed under the supplemental contract of October 1866. It will

Anicut across the Pennair.

10th Section.

terminate near the Military Cantonment at Cuddapah. An estimate for its construction was sanctioned in January last, and the works are just being started. Expenditure, Rupees 2,356-11-1.

273. No progress has been made in the distribution works, but they have now been placed in charge of a special Engineer.

Distribution works.

274. The Right Honorable the Governor visited Bellary in July last, and inspected the line proposed for the Upper Bellary Canal project. In the absence of information as to the probable cost of the extension of this canal, as contemplated by the Company, and as to the necessity or advisability of carrying the upper part on the high level of the line chosen, no decision has been come to by Government.

Bellary Division investigations.

275. The Masoor site, on the Choardy, has been surveyed, and the estimates were nearly ready in March for submission to the Board of Directors. The estimates for the Luckawully site, on the Budra, had been prepared, but the surveys were still incomplete. The only other site under investigation is that on the Toonga, and the surveys of this will not be finished until about the end of another year. The Masoor site has been favorably reported upon, and it is probable that the construction of a reservoir there, by the restoration of an old native tank, will be found feasible and remunerative. The proposed reservoir would hold about 1,400 millions of cubic yards when full, but it is as yet doubtful whether the supply in ordinary years would exceed 700 to 800 millions.

Reservoir investigations.

276. The average labor employed on the Company's Canal works during this year, and also for the three preceding years, was as follows :—

Average labor employed on the Canal works.

	1864-65.	1865-66.	1866-67.	1867-68.
Coolies	16,707	6083·13	670·75	6473·55
Artificers	1,231	495·08	28·72	189·98
Carts	750	293·62	12·	178·08
Cattle...	1,966	675·40	31·75	438·19

These figures represent the average number of coolies, &c., employed daily during the year.

277. The mode of keeping the Irrigation Revenue Accounts is still undecided, although repeated references have been made to the Board of Directors.

Mode of Accounts.

278. The returns received from the Collector of Kurnool shew that, up to the 31st March, the total collections on account of irrigation amounted to Rupees 17,441-9-2,* and those of the year

Irrigation Revenue.

* In addition to this, Rupees 4,416-10-8 are due for Town water supply, but no credit has been given for it in the accounts furnished by the Collector of Kurnool.

to Rupees 6,942-8-5. The particulars of cultivation for the years 1866-67 and 1867-68 are subjoined :—

Description of Irrigation or Supply.	AREA.		Water rate.	Full demand.			Remissions.			Netadjusted balance of demand for supplies actually received.		
	Acres.	Decimals.										
			RS.	RS.	A.	P.	RS.	A.	P.	RS.	A.	P.
Cultivation of 1866-67.												
1st Crop	1,273	84	6	7,641	7	4	1,063	4	9	6,638	2	7
Do.	99	61	12	1,195	1	1	82	2	2	1,112	14	11
2nd Crop	12	26	6	73	9	0	......	...	...	73	9	0
Sugar-cane	5	45	12	65	5	0	......	...	...	65	5	0
Total...	1,390	66	......	8,975	6	5	1,085	6	11	7,889	15	6
Season 1867-68.												
1st Crop	1,042	38	6	6,254	4	10	17	1	7	6,237	3	3
Do.	66	57	12	799	3	1	222	10	6	576	8	7
2nd crop	14	68	6	88	1	4	......	...	...	88	1	4
Do.	11	75	12	141	0	0	......	...	...	141	0	0
Sugar-cane	3	45	6	20	11	2	......	...	...	20	11	2
Total...	1,138	83	......	7,308	4	5	239	12	1	7,063	8	4

Drafts by the Agent

279. The Company's Agent drew from the Government Treasury in India, during the year, Rupees 1,69,695-3-0, making a total from the commencement of Rupees 90,61,968-3-8. £130,000 was raised on loan in England, and Rupees 9,85,806-13-8 of this amount was remitted to the Agent in India.

Expenditure.

280. During the year Rupees 8,95,788-5-2 were expended in India, and the cash balance at the year's end was Rupees 4,00,322-8-9. The total expenditure in India, from the commencement, was Rupees 1,00,13,260-4-3, and in England, by the Board, exclusive of the value of those brought into the Indian accounts, Rupees 4,02,323. In addition to this, the Directors had to account for the balance of the loan of £130,000, raised in England, over the Rupees 9,85,806-13-8, remitted to India.

Audit.

281. The following is a summary of the state of audit of the expenditure incurred by the Company :—

	RS.	A.	P.
Amount drawn from Government up to 31st March 1867.	88,92,273	0	8
Do. during 1867-68	1,69,695	3	0
Amount remitted to the Agent by the Board during 1867-68...	9,85,806	13	8
Value of Stores supplied by the Board of Directors up to 31st March 1868	3,64,487	3	9
Amount under deposit on account of undischarged securities, &c., up to 31st March 1868	1,266	7	11
Agent's liabilities...	1,04,13,528	13	0

	RS.	A.	P.
Expenditure debited to permanent heads of charge in the accounts up to 31st March 1867, and passed by Government	80,00,188	1	9
Do. do. in the accounts from 1st April to 31st December 1867, and passed by Government	6,08,926	8	7
Do. do. in the accounts from 1st January to 31st March 1868, which are under audit in this office.	4,42,590	12	7
Do. under floating heads in the accounts up to 31st March 1868, but not yet debited to appropriate permanent heads of charge	2,11,488	14	8
Do. on general plant in use on works	2,19,969	15	4
Do. retrenched	1,27,267	0	0
Amount remaining to be accounted for by the Agent ...	8,03,097	8	1
	1,04,13,528	13	0

Extent of land made over to the Compy. from April 1867 to March 1868.

282. The extent of land made over to the Company's Chief Engineer by the Revenue authorities, during the year was—

Under Class A	Acres	588·27
„ B	„	234·98
„ C	„	11·82
„ D	„	1·71

And the total amount transferred with the amount of compensation paid are—

Class A	Acres	11,233·30
„ B	„	3,059·76
„ C	„	35·06
„ D	„	46·30
		14,374·42

	RS.	A.	P.
Compensation	64,079	2	4
Deduct for trees, &c.	2,956	11	5
Net amount paid...	61,122	6	11

for 5,712·20 acres while, for the rest of the land taken up, other lands were granted in exchange.

Section VI.—MARINE.

283. The Marine Department, during the past official year, has continued on the same footing as before; but the Superintendent having signified his wish to retire, the arrangements proposed will provide for the following establishment:—

Approaching change in the Department.

1	Master Attendant	Rs. 1,500
1	Deputy and Shipping Master	,, 800
1	First Assistant...	,, 400
1	Second do.	,, 300
1	Assistant for landing and shipping Government consignments	,, 300
	Per mensem	,, 3,300

284. Under the 5th clause of the 10th Section, the Merchant Shipping Act of 1867, the Government have issued rules forbidding vessels to proceed to the United Kingdom without a proper supply of lime juice, which has been inspected and certified to be of good quality by the Port and Marine Surgeon. The rules, however, only have force with regard to ships which left the United Kingdom after the 1st January 1868.

Lime juice for Merchant ships.

285. Under the same Imperial Act, rules have also been passed for the medical examination of seamen before engagement. This examination being, however, permissive, and not imperative, Commanders of vessels have not availed themselves of this mode of securing healthy seamen, preferring rather to run the risk of shipping a diseased man to paying the very moderate fee sanctioned as a remuneration to the examining Surgeon.

Medical examination of Seamen.

286. The only Marine Act passed during the year is No. VII of 1867, which came fully into operation on the 7th December last. It was introduced for the purpose of consolidating and amending the laws relative to the levy of port dues in this Presidency. Its principal features are—

New Port dues Act.

1st.—It groups the ports in two groups, Eastern and Western, comprising the ports on the East and West Coasts of the Madras Presidency.

2nd.—It abolishes the distinction between European and Native craft, and establishes three classes of vessels, each rateable in different degrees:—

(1.) Vessels, not being coasting vessels or coasting steamers, which are chargeable at all ports once in ninety days with the unit of due, whatever that may be.

(2.) Coasting vessels, not being steamers, chargeable once in sixty days at all ports with one-half of the unit rate.

(3.) Coasting steamers paying once in thirty days in the same group, irrespective of the ports entered, one and a half the highest rate levied in that group.

3rd.—It consolidates the various port funds into one fund, rendering the sums raised at one port available for outlay at another.

The maximum rate of dues leviable is three annas the ton, but this rate is levied only at four ports, at the thirteen others the rate being two annas.

The new rates are nearly double the former ones, but the funds have been largely drawn upon, and have decreased considerably during the past year. On the 1st April 1867, they stood in the aggregate at Rupees 2,41,358. On the 1st April 1868, they shewed a credit of only Rupees 1,83,713, being a diminution of Rupees 57,645, notwithstanding that a sum of nearly Rupees 24,000, the proceeds of flotsams and jetsams, had been transferred to them. The outlay at the Presidency has been particularly heavy, 60,000 Rupees having been sanctioned for pier repairs, and 30,000 Rupees for a Home for Sailors.

Overcrowding of Native Passenger craft.

287. Notwithstanding the penalties imposed for overcrowding Native passengers in small country craft, the evil still continues to a certain extent, and chiefly so in vessels bound from Ceylon northwards, and passing through the Paumben channels. During the year under review the masters and tindals of eight vessels have been fined under Act XXV of 1859, in sums amounting to Rupees 2,438, the cases having been heard in the Court at Ramnad.

Wrecks.

288. Several wrecks have occurred on the Coromandel Coast during the year, but only two that were not attributable to stress of weather. On the 18th June the U. S. Steam Frigate "Sacramento," Captain Collins, left Madras for Cocanada, and at 7-30 P. M., on the following day, ran ashore on a bank about sixteen miles south of Hope Island light, and two and a half miles off shore. Every assistance was rendered to the officers and crew by the Marine and other authorities at Cocanada, for which the United States Government expressed their thanks. No lives were lost, as the weather was fine, but a raft containing twenty-nine men and officers drifted out to sea, and was subsequently picked up by Captain J. J. Ballantine, of the B. I. S. N. Company's vessel "Arabia," who put back to Cocanada with the men, a service which was acknowledged by the United States Government by the presentation to him of a gold chronometer.

The only other vessel not driven ashore by stress of weather is the barque "Douglas," which was wrecked about six miles south of the "Sacramento," on the 13th September. This was occasioned by carelessness in heaving the lead. The Captain's certificate was suspended for a year.

The brig "Tar," having been much shaken in a gale, drifted ashore from her last anchor at Vizagapatam on the 13th May.

The other vessels lost were the "Eliza Bencke," of 983 tons, and the "Mercia," of 596 tons, which, with a native craft, were driven ashore in a cyclone on the morning of the 30th September at the port of Calingapatam; the Captain and thirteen men of the first named vessel having been drowned.

In the same cyclone the brig "Gallant Neill," at Vizagapatam, and a native craft of 112 tons at Poondy, were driven ashore and totally wrecked.

The wrecks of two or three vessels, among which were the "Lady Amherst" and "Michael Angelo," were washed upon the northern coast of Ramiaseram island, near Paumben, in the early part of 1868.

Examination of Masters and Mates.

289. The number of Masters and Mates who have obtained certificates of competency, during the year, are four and two respectively.

Coasting Steamers.

290. During the last half of the year under review, the number of coasting steamers has considerably diminished, in consequence of their services having been engaged for the Abyssinian expedition. The only lines left are those established under contract, viz., once a month by line between Calcutta and Bombay, and one between Madras and Rangoon.

Amended Boat Rules.

291. Revised Boat Rules have been brought into operation at most of the out-ports.

Weather.

292. The weather has been generally favorable, but very dry. Strong breezes have occasionally set in on our coasts, but there has been no continued bad weather, and the sea generally has been smooth. A cyclone struck the coast about Vizagapatam on the night of the 29th September, causing considerable damage to the shipping there and to the north; and on the setting in of the N. E. Monsoon, a heavy cyclone was experienced in the eastern and southern part of the bay, during which two or three vessels foundered, portions of the wreck of which drifted into Palks bay. On the 10th November, the "Blenheim," of $1,421\frac{57}{100}$ tons, which left Madras on the 18th October, arrived at Cocanada totally dismasted. A Maldive boat and a native vessel, the "Fyzel Careem," also put in there, during the same month, dismasted.

Reliefs.

293. The reliefs have not been heavy during the past year, but in consequence of this Government having been unable to procure the assistance of any vessels belonging to the State, it has been necessary to pay very highly for private ships for the purpose.

The ordinary reliefs of the season were principally effected by the Steamer "Dacca," of 1,659 tons, belonging to the B. I. S. N. Company, and the "Alnwick Castle," of 1,087 tons, the one under tow of the other. These vessels were engaged by the authorities at Calcutta: the first at $27\frac{1}{2}$ Rupees a ton per month, exclusive of coal, with an additional 8 Annas a ton for each day employed in towing; the latter at 15 Rupees a ton per month.

The following statement will give an idea of the very heavy expense necessarily incurred in engaging transports when Government have none of their own to fall back upon:—

The "Dacca" had 'tween deck accommodation for 164 Europeans, the "Alnwick Castle" for 401.

"Dacca's" hire per month	Rs. 45,622
Towing, twenty days	„ 16,590
Coals, at forty tons a day, at 27 Rupees	„ 21,600
"Alnwick Castle's" hire for one month	„ 16,305
	Rs. 1,00,117

The number of convicts sent to Port Blair, during the year, was 250 men and twelve women, in three parties.

Port Conservancy. Ganjam.

294. At Ganjam the bar of the river is shifting southward, and ships consequently have to bring up south of the former anchoring place.

Gopaulpore.

295. At Moonsoorcottah, henceforth to be called Gopaulpore, a road is being made from the godowns to the beach, which will much facilitate shipping operations.

Santopillay.

296. The lantern of the Santopillay Light-house, in the cyclone of the 29th September, was blown down and damaged to such an extent as to be useless. Another was sent from Madras, and the light again displayed on the 16th December last.

Bimlipatam.

297. The bar at Bimlipatam silted up during the dry weather, and had to be cut through, but during the cyclone of the 29th September, a large quantity of silt was brought down the river which, depositing at the mouth, formed the bar about 100 yards further to seaward. At the same time no less than thirty-four boats were swept out of the river and lost.

Cocanada and Coringa.

298. The new revolving light on Hope Island has not yet been fixed, it is, however, expected that, in a month or two, sufficient progress will have been made with the column to admit of the new lantern being raised to the position it is to occupy. Suitable buildings have been erected for the light-keepers, a great deal of discontent having prevailed among the men last year on the score of bad quarters. The silting up of the port continues, and the buoys will have to be placed a quarter of a mile further out. The channel leading into Coringa river is getting shallower and more intricate. A dredge has been at work at the mouth of this river for some time.

The amount of tonnage entering the port has been on the increase for the last four years. The native passenger traffic between Cocanada and the opposite coast continues to be brisk, 2,641 passengers having left, and 1,519 returned.

Ship building is still carried on to a great extent: three vessels are on the stocks, and several have been lengthened and repaired; and a number of cargo boats have also been built. There is now a superior class of native craft sailing out of this port, of from three to five hundred tons burthen, sheathed with zinc and yellow metal or copper, and commanded by intelligent natives, using sextants and chronometers, on salaries varying from 70 to 150 Rupees per mensem. They are principally from the Maldive Islands, and many hold certificates.

The new light at the port of Cocanada will not be used until the revolving one on Hope Island is put up.

299. At Masulipatam the depth in the river is still decreasing, and a mud bank has formed on the north side of the bar, which, however, has this advantage, that it renders the passage in very smooth. This bank is increasing to seaward. **Masulipatam.**

300. The pier, to which such objections existed when it was first brought into use, is now the principal point for the shipment and discharge of cargo; and already it is found that the wharfage is not sufficient for the traffic. Occasionally the quantity of cargo is so great that a dead lock ensues. **Madras.**

Considerable repairs were executed during the year, and it is hoped that, the error which occasioned the necessity for repair having been remedied, the pier will need no heavy repairs for many years. [A very few days after this was written, the pier received such damage as rendered it useless for traffic.]

The depths remain about the same as before, about twenty feet at the ladders. At the T head, however, the bank seems to have been permanently increased. Originally, the depth there was about twenty-six to twenty-seven feet, for the last two years it has been seldom more than twenty-one feet.

The boat system of the port is in a most unsatisfactory condition, for whenever a pressure of shipping operations occurs, the demand is invariably in excess of the supply.

To meet the difficulties thus experienced, a larger class of boats, holding from eight to fifteen tons, is now in course of introduction, and some iron boats of similar burthen have been obtained by a Company from England, while a revision of the boat rules is under the consideration of Government.

301. Little improvement has taken place in these channels during the year under review. The cutting away the angular point in the reef channel is still unfinished, after eight years' labor; and little has been done towards deepening the south channel to fourteen feet, the delay being attributed to want of convict labor. **Paumben.**

No vessels pass through drawing over eleven feet water, and very few indeed at that depth.

There is a slight increase in the number of vessels that have passed through; the figures being 2,180, of which sixty-two were steamers, against 1,861, during the previous year. The aggregate tonnage was 202,975.

Tuticorin.

302. There is great native passenger traffic between this port and Colombo. During the year, 135 vessels have been licensed, carrying 8,069 passengers; the number that returned being 9,907.

Cochin.

303. At Cochin the sea has made serious encroachments, and the new light-house was in great danger. The inroad, however, was checked by throwing stone into the breaches. Subsequently fears were entertained for the safety of the town of Cochin. The construction of groynes to guard against the inroad of the sea has been sanctioned by Government, and the work has been commenced under the direction of the Master Attendant.

The light-house was completed towards the close of 1867, and the new light exhibited on the 15th January last.

Two vessels proceeding to the Red Sea with pilgrims have been fined for infraction of Act XXI of 1858: the buggalow "Sadel Careem," Rupees 570, and the ship "Shelomith," Rupees 2,000.

Narrakal.

304. This place still maintains its character as a safe anchorage in the south-west monsoon. During the last monsoon thirty-eight vessels, aggregating 19,474 tons, visited it, against twenty-three vessels, of 15,499 tons, during the previous foul weather season.

All the coasting steamers now touch at this port during the south-west monsoon.

SECTION VII.—FINANCIAL.

305. The present financial review is, as in previous years, confined to the transactions appertaining to the Civil Department, the sums received and paid into the Civil Treasuries on account of the Military and Public Works Departments, as also on account of the Postal and Telegraph having been added at foot of the several statements appended, simply to exhibit, in one view, the whole of the monetary transactions of this Presidency.

The present review confined to the transactions of the Civil Department.

306. The total amount of revenue realised from all sources, from 1st April 1867 to 31st March 1868, was Rupees 7,10,42,000, or Rupees 24,83,000 below the estimated income. The total actual expenditure, during the same period, was Rupees 2,52,14,000, or Rupees 32,43,800, below the Budget provision.

Comparison of the Actuals with the Estimate for 1867-68.

Statement shewing the Estimated and Actual Income for 1867-68.

Heads of Receipts.	Estimated Income.	Actual Income.	Increase.	Decrease.	Per centage.
	RS.	RS.	RS.	RS.	
I.—Land Revenue	4,30,55,000	4,24,44,000	......	6,11,000	59·8
II.—Tributes and Contributions from Native States	34,46,000	34,46,000	......	......	4·8
III.—Forest	4,00,000	4,38,000	38,000	......	·6
IV.—Abkarry	56,50,000	50,65,000	......	5,85,000	7·1
V.—License Tax	6,00,000	8,13,000	2,13,000	......	1·1
VI.—Customs	20,78,000	25,19,000	4,41,000	......	3·5
VII.—Salt	1,24,00,000	1,09,38,000	......	14,62,000	15·4
VIII.—Opium	......	......	......	......	...
IX.—Stamps	40,05,000	35,37,000	......	4,68,000	5·
X.—Mint	1,31,000	44,000	......	87,000	·1
XI.—Post Office	......	......	......	......	...
XII.—Telegraph	......	......	......	......	...
XIII.—Law and Justice	7,35,000	7,37,000	2,000	......	1·
XIV.—Police	3,41,000	4,28,000	87,000	......	·6
XV.—Marine	32,000	30,000	......	2,000	...
XVI.—Education	48,000	62,000	14,000	......	·1
XVII.—Interest	1,34,000	1,38,000	4,000	......	·2
XVIII.—Miscellaneous	4,70,000	4,03,000	......	67,000	·6
Total, Civil Department...	7,35,25,000	7,10,42,000	......	24,83,000	100
Military Department	14,75,000	14,29,000	......	46,000	...
Public Works Department	2,03,600	3,98,600	1,95,000	......	...
Postal Department	5,42,700	5,97,000	54,300	......	...
Telegraph do.	2,86,500	2,80,700	......	5,800	...
Total Rupees...	7,60,32,800	7,37,47,300	......	22,85,500	...

Statement shewing the Estimated and the Actual Expenditure for 1867-68.

Heads of Charge.	Budget Grant.	Actual Expenditure.	Increase.	Decrease.	Percentage.
	RS.	RS.	RS.	RS.	
3.—Interest on Service Funds, &c.	9,74,000	7,45,000	......	2,29,000	3·
4.—Allowances, Refunds, and Drawbacks ...	1,96,000	2,09,000	13,000	......	·8
5.—Land Revenue	41,06,000	39,86,000	......	1,20,000	15·8
6.—Forest	2,73,000	2,59,000	......	14,000	1·
7.—Abkarry	2,17,000	2,16,000	......	1,000	·9
8.—Assessed Taxes	......	27,000	27,000	......	·1
9.—Customs	1,67,000	1,67,000	......	......	·7
10.—Salt	17,27,000	13,49,000	......	3,78,000	5·4
12.—Stamps	1,30,000	1,56,000	26,000	......	·6
13.—Mint	1,90,000	1,67,000	......	23,000	·7
16.—Allowances to District and Village Officers.	2,90,000	2,59,000	......	31,000	1·4
17.—Administration and Public Departments...	12,96,000	13,25,000	29,000	......	5·3
18.—Law and Justice	44,25,000	40,56,000	......	3,69,000	16·1
19.—Police	38,71,000	38,85,000	14,000	......	15·4
20.—Marine	2,26,000	2,35,000	9,000	......	·9
21.—Education	9,61,000	8,73,000	......	88,000	3·5
22.—Ecclesiastical	4,00,000	3,63,000	......	37,000	1·4
23.—Medical Services	6,06,000	6,63,000	57,000	......	2·6
24.—Stationery and Printing	3,63,000	3,74,000	11,000	......	1·5
25.—Political Agencies	99,800	1,14,000	14,200	......	·4
26.—Allowances and Assignments, &c.	47,25,000	30,97,000	......	16,28,000	12·3
27.—Miscellaneous	7,07,000	7,82,000	75,000	......	3·1
28.—Superannuation, &c	24,08,000	18,07,000	......	6,01,000	7·1
Total, Civil Department...	2,84,57,800	2,52,14,000	......	32,43,800	100·
Military Department	3,11,17,000	3,02,96,000	......	8,21,000	
Public Works Department	87,04,100	85,87,000	......	1,17,100	
Postal Department	6,29,000	6,87,000	58,000	......	
Telegraph Department	3,84,000	4,34,000	50,000	......	
Total Rupees...	6,92,91,900	6,52,18,000	......	40,73,900	

Variations between the actual Receipts and the Budget Estimate.

307. The following are the principal items under which the actuals fall below the estimate :—

I.—Land Revenue	Rs.	6,11,000
IV.—Abkarry	„	5,85,000
VII.—Salt	„	14,62,000
IX.—Stamps	„	4,68,000
X.—Mint	„	87,000
XVIII.—Miscellaneous	„	67,000

The decrease under "Land Revenue" is owing to the particularly unfavorable character of the season in the districts of Madras, North Arcot, Bellary, and Cuddapah, and that under "Abkarry," to the Farms having been resold at less favorable rates in some districts, in consequence of the failure of the original contractors' engagements. The sales of "Salt," and "Stamps," have not been so large as were anticipated when the Budget Estimate was prepared, while under "Mint," and "Miscellaneous," the decreases are owing, the first to copper coinage having been entirely suspended during the past official year, and the second to some of the petty sources of income not having yielded the estimated amounts.

The only items under which there has been any material increase are "Forest," "Customs," and "Police."* The value of timber supplied to

* III.—Forest	Rs.	38,000
VI.—Customs	„	4,41,000
XIV.—Police	„	87,000

Public Works and other Departments, during 1867-68, is Rupees 1,57,000, against Rupees 64,700 in 1866-67, while under "Customs," the increase is in consequence of the enhancement of the export duty on grain and a steady progress in the imports. Under "Police" the increase is owing to the more favorable working of the Municipal Act in some of the Mofussil Towns.

308. In the expenditure the actuals have exceeded the Budget grants chiefly under the heads—

Excess of actual charges above the Budget grants.

12.—Stamps	Rs. 26,000
17.—Administration and Public Departments	„ 29,000
23.—Medical Services	„ 57,000
27.—Miscellaneous	„ 75,000

The increase under "Stamps" is to be found in the item of discount on sales, for which the actuals amount to Rupees 1,19,000, against a provision of Rupees 93,000 : this increase, however, in the discount is not incommensurate with the increase under sales, as compared with the actuals of 1866-67. The increase under "Administration and Public Departments" is not very material, being caused chiefly by the item Official Postage, for which no provision was made in the original estimate. The excess under "Medical Services" is in consequence of the recent revision made in the salaries of the Officers of that Department, while under "Miscellaneous" the increase is to be found chiefly in the items of loss by exchange in transactions with the Home authorities and contributions to the Municipal funds.

309. Except under the heads noted at foot of page,* the decrease in the actuals on the Budget grants is not material. The savings under "Land Revenue," and "Salt," are caused, the first in consequence of the actuals for Collectors' establishments falling much below the Budget provision, and the second by the charges for the provision of salt having amounted only to Rupees 9,81,000, against a provision of Rupees 13,43,000, while the decrease under "Mint" arises from suspension of copper coinage. The payments on account of "Allowances to District and Village Officers," though falling below the Budget provision, exceed the actuals of the twelve months preceding 1867-68. Under "Law and Justice" the decrease is chiefly on account of the contemplated revision of Judicial establishments not having been as yet carried out, although increased provision was made for them in the Budget Estimate. The charges on account of "Education, Science, and Art," fall below the Budget provision, in consequence of the measures for

Decrease of actual charges below the Budget grants.

* 3.—Interest on Service Funds and other Accounts ..	Rs. 2,29,000
5.—Land Revenue	„ 1,20,000
10.—Salt	„ 3,78,000
13.—Mint	„ 23,000
16.—Allowances to District and Village Officers ...	„ 31,000
18.—Law and Justice	„ 3,09,000
21.—Education	„ 88,000
22.—Ecclesiastical	„ 37,000
26.—Allowances and Assignments, &c....	„ 16,28,000
28.—Superannuation, &c.	„ 6,01,000

putting the Educational establishments of this Presidency on a superior footing not having been carried out within the past official year. The provision under "Ecclesiastical" being according to the sanctioned scale, the decrease arises chiefly from savings on account of absence, &c. Under "Allowances and Assignments under Treaties and Engagements" a large saving will be observed, which is chiefly due to the provision made on account of Prince Azeem Jah Bahadoor's debts not having been utilised during the past official year, while the decreases under "Interest on Service Funds and other Accounts," and "Superannuation, Retired, and Compassionate Allowances" arise from the absorption of the Military Fund into the State receipts and charges.

On the whole, the financial results of the past year were not unfavorable, the total receipts of 1867-68 exceeding those of the previous twelve months; the slight increase in the expenditure under certain heads, during that period, is certainly not more than what the exigencies of the public service and improvements in the administration justly necessitate.

Comparison of cash balances for the past five years.

310. The actual cash balance on the 31st March 1868 amounted to Rupees 2,45,45,800, of which, however, Rupees 24,00,000 was in transit to Calcutta. The total amount remitted to other Presidencies, during 1867-68, including the above twenty-four lacs, was Rupees 1,55,50,000.*

The opening and closing cash balances in the several Treasuries for the last five official years are as follow:—

Years.	Cash Balance at the beginning of the year.	Cash Balance at the termination of the year.
	RS.	RS.
1863-64	3,77,81,700	3,17,78,000
1864-65	3,17,78,000	2,35,23,700
1865-66	2,35,23,700	2,55,90,700
1866-67	2,55,90,700	2,59,24,400
1867-68	2,59,24,400	2,45,45,800

Demand for small coins in the Mofussil.

311. There was a considerable demand for small coins in the provinces during the past year, the value of small silver sent amounting to Rupees 5,38,000, and shewing an increase of Rupees 2,39,000 over that sent in 1866-67. In copper there was a slight falling off, the quantity sent in 1867-68 being Rupees 94,350 against 1,03,300 in the previous year. No remittances of small silver and copper coins were made to other Presidencies during the year, except about 50,000 Rupees worth to Coorg, by the officer in charge of Her Majesty's Treasury, Bangalore. With the view

* Calcutta	Rs.	1,28,00,000
Bombay	,,	25,00,000
Coorg...	,,	2,50,000
		1,55,50,000

of reducing the large copper balance at the Bank of Madras, the Government, in August last, sanctioned as an experimental measure the sale by the Mint Master of a portion of that balance at a discount of half an anna in the rupee. The result of those sales has been a diminution in the amount of the copper at the Bank from twelve-and-a-half lacs on the 1st August 1867 to ten lacs on 1st April 1868, and it may, therefore, be said that two-and-a-half lacs have been added to the copper circulation in the course of eight months, which must be considered satisfactory.

Result of the transfer of certain Treasury balances to Branch Banks.

312. During the year under report the Government Treasury work at Cocanada, Bellary, Ootacamund, Calicut, Tuticorin, and Trichinopoly was transferred to Sub-Agencies of the Bank of Madras established there, the result of which has been to effect a saving of Rupees 739 per month, or Rupees 8,868 per annum, in the account establishments of five districts.* It was also arranged that the surplus Government balances at Cocanada, Bellary, and Calicut, should, whenever required, be brought to the credit of the Government cash balance in the accounts of the Madras Bank, on the understanding that the Accountant General refrained from drawing any bills upon such Mofussil Treasuries. This arrangement, while it has considerably relieved Government of the cost and delay in moving the surplus funds from those places down to Madras, at the same time utilises the cash balances, by placing them at the disposal of the Branch Bank for banking operations. The total Government cash balance in the hands of the Madras Bank and its branches on the 1st April was as follows :—

	RS.	A.	P.
Bank of Madras	44,56,972	6	11
Trichinopoly	3,60,161	0	8
Calicut	7,78,137	11	0
Bellary	7,02,197	9	0
Cocanada	6,54,428	14	8
Ootacamund	1,48,244	6	7
Tuticorin	45,530	12	9
Cochin	44,091	7	9
Total...	71,89,764	5	4

Transactions of the Bank of Madras.

313. A statement of the receipts and disbursements at the Madras Bank on Government account for the year under report will be found in the Appendix B.

Working of the new system of Accounts.

314. The result of the working of the new system of accounts has, on the whole, been very satisfactory. The dates on which the monthly Abstracts of Receipts and Disbursements for the year 1867-68

* Trichinopoly. Bellary. Ootacamund. Calicut. Cocanada.

were rendered to the Comptroller General of Accounts, Calcutta, are as follow :—

April 1867,	... ... Posted	4th June	1867.
May „	... ... „	6th July	„
June „	... ... „	5th August	„
July „	... ... „	4th September	„
August „	... ... „	8th October	„
September „	... ... „	6th November	„
October „	... ... „	7th December	„
November „	... ... „	8th January	1868
December „	... ... „	6th February	„
January 1868,	... ... „	7th March	„
February „	... ... „	3rd April	„

In each case the first P. and O. steamer of the month conveyed the abstract to Calcutta, being the earliest available means of remittance.

MINT.

Importation of bullion.

315. The circumstances unfavorable to the importation of bullion, which were reported on in the Administration Report for the year 1866-67, prevailed during the whole of the official year which has just closed, and a very small quantity of silver was accordingly received in the Mint. And as there happened to be a considerable quantity of copper coin on hand in the Bank of Madras, the coinage of that metal, during the year, was confined to 30,000 Rupees worth of one-eighth Anna pieces.

Silver Receipts.

316. The receipt of Silver into the Mint, and the value of the coin by weight delivered to the Bank of Madras, were as follow :—

	RS.	A.	P.	RS.	A.	P.
Balance in the Mint on the 1st April 1867				1,38,368	13	4
Received from Merchants... ...	1,48,120	3	8			
Uncurrent silver coins, &c., received for re-coinage	1,10,922	7	3			
Amount remaining in the Assay Office	131	12	8			
				2,59,174	7	7
				3,97,543	4	11
Weight of coin delivered to the Bank of Madras	3,47,733	1	0			
Silver used in making Seals, Medals, &c.	131	10	0			
	3,47,864	11	0			
Balance in the Mint on the 31st March 1868	49,897	11	2			
				3,97,762	6	2
Excess ...				219	1	3

317. The excess above exhibited is exclusive of silver in the dross, and is at the rate of 63 Rupees for each lac in value coined and remitted to the Bank of Madras. Excess of Silver.

318. The following is a statement of the number and value of each denomination of Silver and Copper pieces coined and remitted to the Bank :— Number and value of pieces coined.

	Pieces.	Value.		
		RS.	A.	P.
SILVER.				
Single Rupees	2,41,515	2,41,515	0	0
Half do.	19,444	9,722	0	0
Quarter do.	2,22,465	55,616	4	0
Double Annas	3,26,435	40,804	6	0
Total...	8,09,859	3,47,657	10	0
COPPER.				
One-eighth Annas	38,40,000	30,000	0	0
Grand Total...	46,49,859	3,77,657	10	0

319. The charges for seignorage and refinage on Silver bullion received for coinage, the gain on the coinage of Copper and on the sale of Copper scissel, the excess of Silver found in the different departments of the Mint, with the cash received for work done in the Mint for private parties, and charges for articles made for other public departments, in all amount to Rupees 81,682-13-5. The expenses of the Mint and of the Assay department, and the value of stores supplied to other public departments is Rupees 1,37,637-3-10, as shewn in the following statement :— Mint Receipts and Expenditure.

	RS.	A.	P.	RS.	A.	P.
RECEIPTS.						
Seignorage and refining charges on Silver Bullion	3,118	5	11			
Gain on Copper coins after deducting value of the Copper	18,428	10	11			
Gain on Copper scissel sold	5,363	0	4			
Excess of Silver found in the different departments	219	1	8			
Amount of cash received for work done for private parties, Acids, and Unserviceable articles sold..	12,756	9	9			
Amount value of articles made and supplied for other public departments, for which cash payments have not been received, as per Order of Government, No. 822, dated 19th December 1863.	41,797	1	8	81,682	13	5
DISBURSEMENTS.						
Mint Master's salary	21,000	0	0			
Mint Establishment	44,644	15	1			
Contingent servants	24,396	7	8			
Gram, straw, &c., and purchased articles	6,153	11	7			
Store articles including Copper	15,174	0	2			
Value of Coke and Iron, &c., supplied to the Commissariat department, Gun Carriage Manufactory, Department Public Works Workshops, &c.	2,376	7	5			
Assay Office Establishments	23,891	10	4	1,37,637	3	10

Cash receipts on Bills.

320. The total amount of cash received on Bills by the sale of Copper scissel, and for articles made and supplied to private parties is shewn in the following statement:—

RECEIPTS.	RS. A. P.	RS. A. P.
To Copper scissel sold at the Mint...	1,25,528 4 0	
To Iron castings and other articles for private parties, Nitric and Sulphuric Acids, and unserviceable articles sold	12,756 9 9	
To an old 6-H. P. portable steam engine and a steam boiler sold as per Orders of Government, Nos. 329 and 398, dated 19th July and 3rd September 1867	700 0 0	
		1,38,984 13 9
By Cash remitted to the Bank of Madras	1,38,077 9 2	
By Cash received in April for work done in March	907 4 7	
		1,38,984 13 9

Castings from the Mint Foundry.

321. The weight of castings from the Mint Foundry was—

For the Mint	Tons	27
For Public Departments	„	66
For Private Parties	„	12½
	Tons	105½

Coinage and Profits of the past ten years.

322. The following statement exhibits the Silver and Copper coinage, and profits of the past ten years:—

	Silver.		Copper.		Total of Silver and Copper pieces.	Total Value.	Profits.		
	Pieces.	Value.	Pieces.	Value.					
		RS.		RS.		RS.	RS.	A.	P.
1858-59	67,68,524	48,68,170	305,25,947	5,64,131	372,89,471	54,17,301	1,18,835	5	4
1859-60	110,78,847	56,61,623	654,68,832	9,02,992	765,47,679	65,64,615	2,76,093	10	2
1860-61	66,18,433	51,34,638	723,50,400	10,22,420	789,68,833	61,57,058	3,69,462	0	10
1861-62	60,59,977	43,99,069	709,49,760	10,76,750	770,09,737	54,75,819	4,26,556	7	5
1862-63	120,54,231	67,32,248	627,65,760	9,93,280	748,19,991	77,25,528	4,26,446	10	11
1863-64	160,06,926	127,76,705	953,21,280	17,69,630	1,113,28,206	145,46,335	8,40,639	9	7
1864-65	93,72,918	64,48,286	796,80,000	13,27,500	890,52,918	77,75,786	7,19,144	11	3
1865-66	55,05,318	54,49,646	541,01,760	9,56,440	596,07,078	64,06,086	5,04,937	7	11
1866-67	27,11 359	14,80,795	95,40,480	1,95,000	122,51,839	16,75,795	27,137	11	11
1867-68	8,09,859	3,47,658	38,40,000	30,000	46,49,859	3,77,658	..	..	..

PAPER CURRENCY.

Notes in circulation.

323. The transfer, towards the close of the last official year, of the Exchange department from the Bank of Madras to the Currency Office, had the effect of considerably reducing the nominal circulation, as the premium on the circulation which had been paid to the Bank having ceased, it was no longer an advantage to hold its reserve in notes, and consequently the stock held by the Bank has ever since been much smaller than it had been at any previous time.

The circulation has since been steadily rising, as will be seen by the following statement of the nominal and actual circulation on the last day of each month :—

	Notes in nominal circulation.					Stock held by			Notes in actual circulation.
	Madras.	Calicut.	Trichinopoly.	Vizagapatam.	Total.	Madras Bank and other Treasuries.	Commissioner, Madras.	Total.	
1867.	RS.	RS.	RS.	RS.	RS.	RS.	RS.	RS.	RS.
April ...	47,08,200	6,66,510	5,92,590	3,21,510	62,88,810	18,98,420	4,10,330	23,08,750	39,80,060
May ...	55,55,760	5,79,300	6,31,430	3,29,070	70,95,560	30,15,510	4,93,570	35,09,080	35,86,480
June ...	55,12,070	6,59,790	7,61,580	3,19,420	72,52,860	30,01,570	7,11,460	37,13,030	35,39,830
July	54,15,920	5,53,140	7,98,100	3,19,580	70,86,740	28,14,870	6,23,030	34,37,900	36,48,840
August.	55,19,870	6,87,410	4,31,120	3,13,110	69,51,510	28,00,330	4,23,580	32,23,910	37,27,600
Sept. ...	55,20,260	8,59,800	6,21,120	2,78,370	72,79,550	28,17,190	5,93,920	34,11,110	38,68,440
Oct. ...	54,96,240	9,97,770	8,46,640	3,03,390	76,46,040	26,96,040	6,12,240	33,08,280	43,37,760
Nov. ...	53,93,370	9,01,130	8,77,700	2,85,910	74,58,110	26,40,020	6,21,670	32,61,690	41,96,420
Dec. ...	55,19,150	5,79,710	8,95,650	2,58,250	72,52,760	21,62,320	3,97,840	25,60,660	46,92,100
1868.									
Jan. ...	57,42,630	6,94,080	10,76,980	3,40,370	78,54,060	33,36,180	4,79,000	38,15,180	40,38,880
Feb. ...	57,38,560	6,63,100	11,10,460	3,71,660	78,83,780	31,70,100	5,46,640	37,16,740	41,67,040
March...	56,31,890	5,69,660	11,36,910	3,62,540	77,01,000	26,60,490	5,31,400	31,91,890	45,09,110

324. The notes issued by the Exchange department in exchange for cash or other notes were Rupees 15,01,910, and the cash issued in exchange for notes was Rupees 28,01,890. The Exchange Department.

325. The number of notes issued and received by the several Circles in exchange for cash or other notes, during the year, is shewn below :— Notes issued and received.

	Notes issued.		Notes received.	
	No.	Value.	No.	Value.
Madras	94,298	88,79,560	97,548	79,65,870
Calicut	26,074	16,46,110	28,055	18,95,710
Trichinopoly	14,772	12,56,290	4,103	6,62,900
Vizagapatam	7,220	5,25,300	8,518	4,85,200
Total...	1,42,359	1,23,07,260	1,38,224	1,10,09,680

326. The receipt of Circle notes in the Head Office, Madras, were as follow :— Receipt of Circle Notes.

Calicut	Rs.	8,02,280
Trichinopoly	„	8,25,200
Vizagapatam	„	63,080
	Rs.	16,90,560

from which it is to be inferred that the notes of the Calicut and Trichinopoly Circles are largely availed of as a means of remittance to the Presidency; but periodical settlements are readily effected at a trifling expense through the medium of the Madras Bank and the Accountant General, the Bank finding the transfer of coin to the Madras Currency Office Treasury in exchange for a similar payment at Calicut, a convenient and economical mode of replenishing the Treasury of its branch there, and the Hoozoor Treasury at Trichinopoly being one that requires feeding periodically under the orders of the Accountant General.

Vizagapatam notes do not come to Madras in any considerable quantity, but in the event of their doing so, there would be facility for returning them through the branch of the Madras Bank at Bimlipatam.

Issuing and cashing of Notes by Government Treasuries.

327. Currency Notes have been issued freely at all Treasuries in the Provinces, in exchange for coin, and in payment of amounts due by Government, while notes have been freely cashed as far as funds were available. The results of these experiments follow:—

	Six months ending 30th June 1867.	Nine months ending 31st March 1868.
	Value Rs.	Value Rs.
Notes received by all Government Treasuries in exchange for silver	7,38,300	25,62,690
Notes received in payment of claims	9,83,340	16,48,090
Total...	17,21,640	42,10,780
Notes issued in exchange for silver	23,64,350	47,75,650
Notes issued in payment of claims	5,96,850	14,07,910
Total...	29,61,200	61,83,560

It will be observed that the demand for notes, in the Provinces, is greatly in excess of the notes presented for cash, but the Accountant General reported to Government, on the 19th October 1867, that no inconvenience had up to that time arisen from the accumulated coin paid into any Provincial Treasury by the public in exchange for notes.

Supply of new pattern Notes.

328. Notes of a new pattern, with their values printed in the four vernaculars, were introduced in June 1867, and are fast replacing those of the old pattern in the circulation.

The re-issue of the old pattern notes was stopped on the occurrence of a successful forgery of a ten-rupee note, which was not detected by the Cashiers of the Madras Bank. Several other forged notes were found in circulation, and were traced to the North Arcot district, but no clue was obtained to the forger.

Notes cancelled.

329. The notes withdrawn from circulation and cancelled during the year are shewn in the following statement :—

	No.	Value Rs.
Madras...	88,670	66,94,400
Calicut...	19,533	11,69,310
Trichinopoly	11,128	13,71,410
Vizagapatam...	8,532	7,03,830
	127,863	99,38,950

330. The investments in Government Securities, at the end of the year, were Rs. 30,28,580-10-6, composed as follow :— **Government Securities.**

	RS.	A.	P.
Madras...	27,28,403	15	9
Calicut	1,00,058	14	3
Trichinopoly...	1,00,058	14	3
Vizagapatam...	1,00,058	14	3
	30,28,580	10	6

331. The receipts and disbursements of the department during the past year, were as follow :— **Receipts and Disbursements.**

Receipts.

	RS.	A.	P.
Profit by interest calculated upon Government Securities of the Madras and other Circles	1,52,135	8	0

Disbursements.

	RS.	A.	P.	RS.	A.	P.
Salary of the Commissioner of Issue	3,000	0	0			
Do. Assistant do.	4,734	0	6			
Deputy Collectors in charge of Circle Offices...	3,528	13	0			
Establishment, including Circles	19,612	7	0			
Contingencies, do.	4,176	4	11			
Total cash payment...	35,051	9	5			
Cost of Note forms received from England during the year, including freight	6,160	2	0			
Work done at the Mint for the Currency Department for which no cash payment was made	1,066	15	4			
				42,278	10	9
Profit...				1,09,856	13	3

Section VIII.—POLITICAL.

332. The returns relating to the administration of the Travancore and Cochin States, which will be found in the Appendix, are drawn up, as usual, for the Malabar year which ended on 15th August last, but the present remarks are brought up to the close of the official year 1866-67.

The States of Travancore and Cochin.

Travancore.

333. A most important measure was passed during the year by His Highness the Maharajah, in a Regulation for establishing an improved system of Registration of Assurances. Registration, through public notaries, has long existed in Travancore, but in a manner open to serious objections and defects, which need not be dwelt upon here. The present measure is based upon the Act No. XX of 1866, for British India. By it, the registration is made compulsory of all deeds relating to immovable property, and to rights connected with the same. A separate machinery has been provided for carrying out the regulation, independent of the local revenue and other establishments, as this seemed essential for the success of the measure.

Civil Justice.

The introduction of the Statute of Limitation, alluded to in the last year's report, was referred for another year, to prevent hardship to litigants.

The work of the Civil Courts has again this year largely increased, mostly by the continued pressure into Court, of suits affected by the last named law.

The disposal of Appeals from the Zillah or District Courts, if taken as an index of the quality of work done, cannot be regarded as satisfactory, as only about one-half of the cases were confirmed on appeal.

There is no doubt that progress is being made in this branch, but the number of petitions still received by the Resident, against the proceedings of the Sudder and other Courts, indicates a want of full confidence on the part of the people, which possibly has been somewhat fostered by the introduction of legal technicalities from the British Indian Courts. In introducing persons from the British Service, with their better legal experience, it is necessary to guard against the old usages and prescriptive laws of Travancore being over-ridden by abstract principles of British law. The retention of a second Judge, who is generally well versed in the customs of the country, was found useful in this respect, and the time has not come for placing each of the District Courts under a single Judge, as the Government looked forward to in their Proceedings No. 38, dated 20th February 1866.

334. There continues to be improvement in the Criminal Courts, which are disposing of their work with increased speed. In the statement, however, of the graver cases, which are submitted by the District Courts for the confirmation of the Sudder Court, it appears that

Criminal Justice.

only one-fourth of the recommendations, amounting to twenty-nine, were confirmed, eighteen being modified, and four reversed. This shews either very defective judgment on the part of these Courts, or some caprice on the part of the Sudder Court in not paying deference to the decisions of the examining Courts. It is difficult to account for this altogether on the first supposition.

335. The Police under the Dewan's supervision is, upon the whole, active, but the large number of offences, which continue to be charged against the officials of this department, particularly those who are lowest paid, indicates a state far from efficient. Since the close of the Malabar year, the salaries have been increased by 15,000 Rupees per annum, but upon the old organization. Much more is still needed to improve the position and the *personnel* of this department. The pay of the Peons, as recently increased, is still only Rupees 4-7-0 a month, which is an insufficient salary to remove the temptations to the abuses of authority above alluded to.

Police.

336. These call for little special remark on the present occasion, except that their sanitary state has been well maintained. The mortality has been a trifle under four per cent. on the average daily numbers.

Jails.

337. This item of revenue amounted to Rupees 16,77,654, or about Rupees 37,000 above last year's amount. This mostly arose from the extension of cultivation.

Land Revenue.

It is to be regretted that nothing has been actually done about the re-assessment of garden lands, notwithstanding its having been in contemplation for the last seven or eight years or more, and all the principles upon which it should be conducted having been discussed with, and approved by, the Resident as far back as January 1866. His Highness the Maharajah is alive to the importance of the measure, which will bring in three lacs or more of annual revenue, which will be realised in a most unexceptionable way, by bringing under taxation trees which, according to the usages of Travancore, should have been assessed at the end of twelve years. It is now nearly thirty years since the last adjustment took place. The matter has been constantly and earnestly pressed upon the Dewan, and the delay in carrying out the measure may be said to have been a loss to the State of many lacs of rupees, which additional revenue could have been most usefully employed in accelerating, by years, the measures more recently carried out for the improvement of the several departments, by the increase of salaries and the grant of pensions, &c., &c.

An important measure, connected with the land tenures, was passed by His Highness the Maharajah in a Proclamation, defining the rights of Jenmies (or original proprietors) and their tenants. This solution of this long vexed question has been highly satisfactory, and is calculated to give certainty to the action of the Courts, and stability to the respective rights of the parties.

Customs.

338. The export trade continues to suffer depression. The value amounted to Rupees 42,60,000, of which more than half is in the products of the cocoa-palm. The duty amounted to Rupees 3,07,000, against Rupees 2,50,000 in the previous year. The increase of about half a lac of rupees is nominal, as the guaranteed amount of Customs was credited for two years, and a stricter comparison leaves a decrease of about Rupees 16,000. This is accounted for, mostly by the reduction of the exceptional duty on the areca-nuts to the ordinary export rate of duty, which must have a beneficial effect in removing many evil practices, and giving encouragement to the cultivation of this article. During the year, the exceptional duty on pepper was reduced from 15 Rupees to Rupees 9 a candy. Act III of 1861, provided for the levy of the former duty at British Cochin on behalf of these States. This has been so far repealed by Act II of 1868, as to substitute the lower duty, and to provide for any further reduction hereafter.

Salt.

339. The gross revenue is eight lacs of rupees, against about seven lacs in the previous year, and the net amount, after deducting the cost of foreign salt and other items of expenditure, is a little over five and a half lacs. The cost may be much reduced by the extension of the salt pans in the south, so as to greatly increase the home manufacture. The Sirkar has been losing about one lac of rupees yearly for a long time past, by being unable to supply the outlying talook of Shencottah with salt, owing to the line of road by the Puliaray pass being unfit for its transit. The Government has recently consented to an arrangement, by which the salt for that locality is allowed to pass through the Tinnevelly district; but as its transit through British India without payment of duty is illegal, the Government decided that the duty should, under the circumstances, be refunded. The necessity for this indulgence will, it is hoped, soon cease by the opening up the road in question.

The annual increase of revenue accruing from raising the selling price of salt to the standard in British India, is now about three to three and a half lacs of rupees.

Tobacco.

340. The tobacco revenue, amounting to Rupees 7,41,122, shews an increase of Rupees 6,000. In the consumption, there is a trifling increase.

The monopoly having given place to an import duty for the last five years, and the reduction in the latter having now had full effect, it seems desirable to take a brief review of the administration of this branch of the revenue, and, in doing so, it is unnecessary to dilate upon the evils of the former monopoly, and their aggravation on the abolition of the monopoly in 1851-52, in the neighbouring provinces of Canara and Malabar.

The former gross revenue from this source was about eleven and a half lacs of rupees, and the consumption 3,900 candies. In six or seven years, from the abolition of the monopoly in Canara and Malabar, the revenue fell to about eight and a half lacs of rupees, and the consumption in proportion. By the employment of stringent measures for the suppression of smuggling during the last five years of the monopoly, the revenue was brought up to the former standard of eleven and a half lacs of rupees, and the consumption to 4,376 candies.

On the substitution of the import duty in 1861-62, the consumption rapidly rose, till it now amounts to 7,218 candies in 1866-67, being an increase of not much less than about seventy per cent. The revenue, however, fell at once to nine and a quarter lacs, and subsequently, by reduction in the import duty, to about seven and a half lacs of rupees, its present standard. This, however, may be expected to rise gradually with the further increased consumption.

Forest.

341. The forest revenue is still very small (Rupees 41,000) compared with what might be easily realised by a better system, and the opening out of roads. The destruction of timber every year for a passing crop of paddy or other grain is enormous. A special officer has been appointed to check this waste, but the only effectual remedy for the evil is the absolute prohibition of all cultivation of this kind.

Coffee, Tea, and Chinchona.

342. There are three centres of coffee enterprise, Peermade in the north, Athreemulay, west of Travancore, and Asamboo in the south. The prospects in all are favorable, and happily there has been hitherto no trace of the borer or other destructive insect. The planters have, in almost all cases, been secured in their rights by the survey of their lands and the issue of title deeds.

Tea cultivation, judging from the results derived from the experimental gardens at Peermade, promises, if anything, to be still more successful. It has not, however, yet been taken up to any extent by planters.

The Chinchona experiment appears to be progressing favorably.

Education.

343. The senior branch of this department, under the able superintendence of Mr. J. Ross, M. A., has fulfilled the expectation entertained of it, though there is still much to be attained. This year, progress has so far been made that the scholars in this branch, one hundred in number, are candidates for the Matriculation examination. There are classes also for the higher examinations, and the necessity for another European Master is imperative, which will be a step towards the ultimate desideratum of the formation of a College department.

The General School, under Mr. Bensley's able management, has about 675 scholars, and a preparatory branch has been opened, which promises to be largely filled.

The Girls' School, under the Lady Superintendent who came out a year ago, has been completely reorganized, and has gained considerable reputation with the class of East Indians in particular.

The English District Schools continue to advance, and several of the Vernacular Schools, alluded to in the last report, have been opened. The appreciation of education in all its branches is felt and evidenced by the increasing demand for it.

Medical.

344. The Medical department keeps up its efficiency; three local hospitals were opened during the year, and other similar Institutions, for which the annual grant of His Highness the Maharajah of Rupees 20,000 provides, will follow.

The Vaccination branch continues to be efficiently superintended by Dr. Pulney Andy.

Military.

345. The Nair Brigade, which is a Militia force, has been somewhat improved in its position by a slight addition to the pay of the men, who, however, in most instances, supplement this by the occupation of land and other resources.

Observatory.

346. A small establishment is still kept up out of deference to the late Astronomer's representations in the cause of science, but with questionable utility, the native observers being without professional supervision.

Museum and Public Gardens.

347. These have kept up their attraction for the people. There were shows of flowers, fruit, and vegetables, in January 1867, and again towards the close of that year. The latter was a decided success.

Public Works.

348. The expenditure on public works continues at about five and a half lacs of rupees. Some check was experienced on the departure of the Engineer, Mr. Barton, to England on sick leave.

The expenditure on the Victoria Canal Works was nearly Rupees 81,000, bringing the total cost up to nearly six lacs.

The new public offices have considerably progressed, Rupees 93,293 having been expended upon the work during the year.

Progress has also been made with the Peermade Ghaut works, on which Rupees 31,500 were spent, besides some Rupees 40,000 on the bridge under construction over the Moondakayom river, at the foot of the ghaut. The work was unfortunately and unauthorizedly stopped by the new Engineer shortly after the transfer of a large body of laborers from the completed section of the Victoria Canal. It has since, however, been resumed with vigour.

A good cart or carriage road has been opened to near the foot of the Asamboo hills, which is one centre of coffee cultivation, at a total cost of nearly

Rupees 20,000, and other important roads have been constructed in South Travancore for opening up the country, and providing for the transit of traffic to the small local port of Colechel.

A large girder bridge, of eleven bays, is under construction over the Colitoray river, which is the only unbridged stream on the whole of the Southern Trunk Road. The outlay so far has been Rupees 46,000.

The repair and improvement of irrigation works in South Travancore have not progressed so satisfactorily as could have been desired during the year; but the attention of the Engineer is being directed to the subject. The appointment of the Assistant Engineer has proved a failure.

The Vurkally barrier project, alluded to last year, has not been entered upon by the Acting Engineer, but it will be commenced by Mr. Barton on his return.

349. The finances of the State preserve their wonted elasticity. The receipts were Rupees 44,82,000, while the disbursements were Rupees 43,60,000. Of the surplus, one and a quarter lac of rupees are in the salt revenue.

Finances.

350. His Highness the Rajah of Cochin paid a visit to the Maharajah in return for a visit which the latter paid on his way to Madras. This interchange of friendly visits, which has had no precedent in the present generation, is calculated to have a beneficial effect in promoting the common interests of both of these Native States.

Political.

The visit of His Excellency the Governor, being in return for the Maharajah's visit to Madras for the investiture of the Order of the Star of India, the reception of His Lordship by the Maharajah was made as cordial and magnificent as possible, and was perhaps unparalleled in the history of Travancore. Lord Napier's visit has given great encouragement to His Highness' administration, and tended to cement those feelings of loyalty and attachment which have long prevailed. The same may be said with regard to the Cochin State, where His Lordship met with a no less welcome reception.

His Highness' policy continues to be guided by the same enlightened principles as hitherto, and the Dewan, Sir T. Madava, has, as usual, been zealous and indefatigable. It cannot, however, be said that the efforts of the executive administration have been altogether judiciously applied to the best advantage of the State, for the long pending measure of the garden re-assessment, noticed more fully above, still rests on promises and assurances. Credit has in every report been given for measures of progress, many of which are of an important as well as of a popular character, but considering that Travancore is a province not larger than a good sized Collectorate of this Presidency, and the revenue less than that of several, the accomplishment of the measure might have been expected in the prolonged period alluded to.

COCHIN.

Civil Justice.

351. In the Judicial tribunals there has been a marked progress consequent on the measures before reported, as to the improvement of the *personnel* of the Appeal Court and each of the Zillah Courts. The enrolment of Pleaders, after being subjected to examination, has also here, as in Travancore, facilitated the work of the Courts.

The Courts have kept pace with the increase of work devolving upon them, and there has been greater expedition in the disposal of cases.

Taking the particulars of the Appeals in the several Courts, as indicating in a measure the quality of justice, the result appears, upon the whole, favorable.

Criminal Justice.

352. On the Criminal side there has been equal progress in the Courts. The jurisdiction of the Zillah Courts was considerably increased, and the Session Court, consisting of one of the Judges of the Appeal Court in rotation, for the re-trial of heinous cases, has been abolished. These cases are now referred to the Appeal Court, for their confirmation of the sentence recommended by the lower Courts, as in Travancore. Their disposal in this manner has proved satisfactory, and tended greatly to expedite justice, while the people are relieved from the inconvenience and hardship of the delay of a re-trial under the former system. Although the Appeal Court is as yet somewhat weak in its constitution, the tribunals in this State will compare not unfavorably with those in Travancore; but there remains much to be done here as well as in that State, to raise them to the standard that should be held in view.

Police.

353. Under the vigilant superintendence of the Dewan, the Police has somewhat improved in efficiency, and gang robberies, which were noticeable in last year's returns, have been greatly reduced and promptly dealt with.

Jails.

354. The improvements in the principal jails alluded to last year are in progress. They have, as usual, proved healthy, although densely crowded, with a minimum of ventilation. The ratio of mortality in the two Jails were one and a quarter and a little over four per cent. respectively.

Land Revenue.

355. The land revenue amounts to Rupees 5,90,000, or upwards of half the resources of the State, and is about Rupees 5,000 above last year's amount. The cultivation in the Trichoor lake has always been in a measure uncertain and affected by unfavorable seasons; the canal through the lake, recently completed, will tend to mitigate, though it will not remove, this evil.

Coffee.

356. About 8,000 acres have been taken up for coffee. Every year will now produce an increased revenue from this source.

357. The customs revenue actually collected by the Sirkar has been reduced to a mere trifle, but it falls back upon the annual guarantee of Government (Rupees 1,10,500) under the interportal arrangements. Customs.

358. The Salt revenue has nearly recovered from the lamentable falling off in the previous year. This branch will continue to require the Dewan's vigilant supervision, and the co-operation of the Malabar Collector is required to suppress the illicit manufacture for which there are such facilities on the backwaters. Salt.

359. The English School at Ernacollum continues to prosper under the assiduous care of Mr. A. F. Sealey, M.A. The Ernacollum school building premises, for which His Highness the Rajah has liberally granted the sum of Rupees 27,000, have considerably progressed. Education.

360. The Shoranoor bridge has now been opened. It has cost three and a quarter lacs of rupees. Funds will now be available to secure the services of a professional Engineer for this State, which have long been needed. Public Works.

The branch line from the Madras Railway to Cochin has been under survey for some time. It appears that Puttamby, instead of Shoranoor, is likely to be selected as the point of junction, though there is not yet any official announcement of this.

The Cochin Government not unnaturally feels no little disappointment at the Shoranoor bridge being thus rendered almost useless, though it was designed by British officers, and with the express view of carrying a railway, for a double line of which provision was made in the construction of the piers. An unconditional offer of the bridge was made to the Company for the purpose.

The Sirkar now regrets that the resources of the State have been taxed to so great an extent without contributing in any way to promote the project it was mainly intended to facilitate.

The Public Works expenditure amounted to Rupees 1,60,000, or fourteen per cent. of the total revenue of the State.

361. This port, with its still water, continues to be increasingly resorted to in the monsoon months. Narakel.

362. The resources of the State were Rupees 10,80,000, and the disbursements Rupees 10,27,500, leaving a surplus of about Rupees 52,500. Finances.

363. His Highness the Rajah's policy has been guided by increasingly enlightened views, while the executive administration has been ably, diligently, and faithfully conducted by the Dewan, Shun- Political.

goony Menon. There is every reason to hope that the progressive steps of reform now well instituted, will be followed up, and that this State will, ere long, compete with Travancore, even with the superior advantages of the latter.

CARNATIC.

364. The payments to Carnatic stipendiaries (including Jaghiredars) amounted, during the official year, 1867-68, to Rupees 6,43,030. This amount exceeds, by Rupees 72,530, the amount estimated in the Budget of 1867-68. The difference is accounted for by Nabob Khyre-u-Nissa Begum having drawn in that year a large sum of arrears, which had been accumulating from 1st December 1865 to 31st March 1867. On the death of the late Nabob of the Carnatic, Government entrusted to Her Highness, as the head of the Khás-Mahál department, a sum of Rupees 1,73,756 due to that department. A portion of this sum Her Highness ought to have distributed to the persons to whom it was due, but Her Highness neglected this obligation, till Government were compelled to direct that a certain portion* of Her Highness' stipend should be deducted till the amount due as above was accumulated. This having been done, the arrears are now being settled. The total amount recovered from Her Highness up to 31st March 1868 is Rupees 70,000. Of this about Rupees 54,000 have been settled by agreement between Her Highness and the claimants.

The number of persons receiving pensions on the 1st April 1868 was 1,210. The lapses by death, &c., in 1867-68, were fifty-seven persons, whose pensions amount in the aggregate to Rupees 10,835 per annum.

Bonuses to the amount of Rupees 49,497-10-0 were granted in commutation of 128 stipends, not exceeding Rupees ten per mensem, amounting to Rupees 5,790 per annum.

Petty claims against the estate of the late Nabob were settled to the amount of Rupees 9,558-4-0, and arrears of salary and pensions amounting to Rupees 6,413-0-6 were paid.

A Commissioner was appointed under Madras Act No. III. of 1867, and has been engaged in the settlement of the debts of His Highness Prince Azim Jah. It is expected that he will bring his operations to a close shortly after the end of the current year.

* Proceedings of Government, No. 151, dated 1st June 1867.

Section IX.—MILITARY.

365. The Straits' Settlements have been transferred to the control of the Imperial Government, but the withdrawal of the two Regiments of Madras Native Infantry, stationed there, has not yet been effected, in consequence of the non-arrival of the relieving corps which are to form the future Military force of the Settlements. The Batteries of Artillery, furnished from this Presidency, have been re-called, and the stores and other property of the Indian Government have been taken over at a valuation by the Imperial Government.

Withdrawal of Troops from Straits' Settlements.

366. By a re-distribution of the Artillery force, consequent on the withdrawal of the Batteries from the Straits, the strength, which hitherto consisted of—

Artillery Force.

Four Horse Artillery Batteries, eleven Field Batteries, and eleven Garrison Batteries, has been reduced by two Field Batteries, and two Garrison Batteries.

Three Batteries (Nos. 4, 5, and 6) of the 5th Brigade, Royal Artillery, destined for this Presidency from England, being surplus to its requirements, have been retained at Bombay, pending final orders of the Home Government.

The present reduced strength of Artillery is distributed as follows :—

	Horse Artillery.	Field Batteries.	Garrison Batteries.
Bangalore	1	2	0
Bellary	1	0	1
Cannanore	0	0	1
Fort Saint George...	0	0	1
Kamptee	1	1	1
Saint Thomas' Mount	0	2	1
Rangoon	0	0	2
Secunderabad	1	2	1*
Thyetmyo	0	1	0
Tonghoo	0	0	1
Trichinopoly	0	1	0

367. In connexion with the arrangements made for the despatch of a Military force from Bombay for field service in Abyssinia, the calls made on this Government for Troops, &c., were met to the following extent :—

Abyssinian Expedition.

Two Regiments of Native Infantry (12th and 17th) despatched, to be quartered at Poona and Kurrachee.

One Regiment Light Cavalry (1st) to be quartered at Poona.

Three Companies (G, H, and K) of Madras Sappers and Miners, for field service.

*With Heavy Field Battery attached.

Six Commissioned, three Warrant and seven Non-Commissioned Officers of the Commissariat Department for employment with the expedition.

Thirteen Officers for the Abyssinian Transport Corps.

Six do. as Field and Assistant Field Engineers.

Eight do. as additional, or 3rd Wing Subalterns, to Corps of Native Infantry on field service.

Transfer of 108th Foot to Bombay.

368. A European Regiment (Her Majesty's 108th Regiment) was also transferred to the Bombay Presidency without relief. It is now to be re-placed by another (Her Majesty's 45th Regiment) on its way from Abyssinia direct to this Presidency.

Troops for Hong-Kong.

369. Under instructions from the Government of India, a Regiment of Madras Infantry (the 29th) is being sent to Hong-Kong to garrison that colony.

Strength of the Army.

370. The following is the strength of the Army, European and Native, as it stood on the 31st March 1868 :—

Corps.	EUROPEANS.		NATIVES.	
	Officers.	Men.	Officers.	Men.
Her Majesty's British Forces.				
Cavalry	59	841	...	...
Royal Artillery...	196	2,671	...	* 271
Royal Engineers	70	10	...	...
Infantry	297	6,252	...	...
British Medical Staff	30	...	...	...
Total ...	652	9,774	...	...
Her Majesty's Indian Forces.				
Staff Corps, exclusive of those doing Regimental duty ...	423	...	...	...
Cavalry	80	9	48	1,443
Artillery	...	6	4	382
Sappers	20	54	20	1,271
Veterans	46	241	...	...
Infantry	505	54	642	27,602
Europeans, Unattached List, exclusive of those doing Regimental duty	242	...	...	...
Medical Officers, exclusive of those doing Regimental duty	134	...	...	...
Veterinary Surgeons, exclusive of those doing Regimental duty	4	...	...	...
Total ...	1,454	364	714	30,969
Grand total ...	2,106	10,138	714	30,969

Health of the British Troops.

371. The health returns of the British troops in Burmah not having been received for the last quarter, they are necessarily not reported upon for that period.

The health of the British Troops of the Madras Army, more especially in the third and fourth quarters of the period under observation has not been

* Store Lascars of Her Majesty's Indian Forces attached.

satisfactory, owing chiefly to the prevalence of fevers, bowel complaints, and hepatic affections, attributed to the effects of over-indulgence, arising from increased receipts of prize, bounty, and kit money, together with the extra 2*d.* per day. During the time under review, however, there has been great exemption from disease in any epidemic form.

Some movements of troops have been unavoidably carried out later in the season, than would otherwise have been desirable, but without any prejudicial results.

Immunity from Cholera.

372. The neighbourhood of stations occupied by troops have been generally free from cholera, and only a few sporadic cases occurred amongst the troops, with the exception of what, from the active and judicious measures pursued, proved to be only a slight outbreak of this disease, in a detachment of Volunteers for the 3rd Battalion 60th Rifles, on board the steam ship *Burmah*, from Calcutta. The disease made its appearance when they were off Cocanada, and four cases occurred on board, two of them fatal. To prevent the spread of the disease to the troops in Fort Saint George, the vessel on touching at Madras was ordered to Ennore, where the troops were landed. One fatal case occurred after disembarkation; but the men generally were in excellent health.

The total number of cases, during the year, was sixteen, and the number of deaths seven.

Small-pox.

373. This disease became more prevalent throughout the Presidency generally, towards the end of the year, and one or two cases occurred in the Royal Artillery and 91st Regiment at Kamptee. The whole number of cases was eighteen, and of deaths one.

General health.

374. The general health of the British Troops has greatly improved being 119·64 per thousand (of sick treated to strength) less than last year, and though there is a slight decrease (587 only) in the strength, there is a marked decrease in the ratio of sick in the Presidency and Burmah Circles—in the Mysore Circle there is also a decrease, while in the Hyderabad Circle (including Kamptee) there is a slight increase of 24·39 per thousand.

The following return shews the rate per thousand of sick to strength during the period :—

Circles.	1866-67. Sick treated to strength.	1867-68. Sick treated to strength.	Increase.	Decrease.
Presidency	1906·96	1578·84	......	328·12
Mysore	1151·88	1067·93	......	83·95
Hyderabad	1668·89	1693·28	24·39	......
Burmah	1699·85 (For 9 months.)	1381·43 (For 10 months.)	......	318·42
Average...	1543·26	1423·60	......	119·66

The mortality among British Troops, during the year, was at the rate of 20·43 per thousand—in the last year it was 21·70, shewing a decrease in the past year of 1·27 per thousand.

The following table shews the extent of sickness and mortality among Her Majesty's British Troops during the official year 1867-68 :—

Circles.	EUROPEANS.						
	Average strength.	Treated.	Died in Hospital from all causes.	Average daily sick.	Per-centage of		
					Treated to strength.	Deaths to strength.	Deaths to treated.
Presidency	1,947	3,074	38	160	157·88	1·95	1·23
Mysore	3,268	3,490	31	145	106·79	0·94	0·88
Hyderabad	3,469	5,874	97	227	169·38	2·79	1·65
Burmah (for ten months)	1,788	2,470	20	142	138·14	1·12	0·81
Total...	10,472	14,908	186	674	142·36	1·77	1·25

Decrease in strength of Europeans.

375. The decrease in the average strength of the British Troops during the past year is 587, occasioned by the temporary withdrawal of one Infantry Regiment from this Presidency.

Outstanding Retrenchments and Advances in the Pay Department.

376. Unadjusted retrenchments in the Pay Department, to the amount of Rupees 14,878, exist up to 31st March 1868, the annual expenditure being Rupees 2,52,00,000, the unadjusted advances to the same date may be estimated at Rupees 5,34,550.

Outstanding Retrenchments in Commissariat Department.

377. In the Commissariat Department the unadjusted retrenchments amounted, on 31st March 1868, to Rs. 11,083, the expenditure being Rs. 49,00,000.

Audit.

378. The audit is correct in all branches, and the compilations are rendered on the dates on which they are due.

Increases in expenditure.

379. The expenditure of Rupees 48,000 on the erection of new tiled huts for the 3rd Regiment Native Infantry at Royapooram, Madras, was sanctioned by Government in May 1867. Of this amount, Rupees 15,400 will be recovered from the men of the Regiment.

On the condemnation of the Native Infantry Lines at Vepery, Madras, Government sanctioned an outlay of Rupees 50,000 for the purchase of a suitable locality for new lines, and a grant of Rupees 20,000 to assist the corps in building the lines.

Compensation, to the amount of Rupees 3,220, has been disbursed to the 15th Regiment Native Infantry at Cannanore, to cover the difference in the value of tiled huts built by that corps, and the amount authorized by Regulation to be disbursed to the Regiment, on the price of their huts, on relief.

The additional expenditure consequent on the new Enlistment Act of 20th June 1867, amounted to Rupees 2,50,000.

In additional Presidency house-rent granted to Regimental Officers not provided with public quarters, obliged, by their duties, to reside in the Presidency Town, was absorbed Rupees 12,075.

Increase of pay to Non-Commissioned Officers and Soldiers of British Service, under the provisions of special War Office Circular of 6th August 1867, made applicable to India from 1st April 1867, cost Rupees 4,11,900.

Compensation in lieu of clothing and bedding to men re-engaged under the new Re-enlistment Act of 20th June 1867, reached the sum of Rupees 1,03,918.

The appointment of an Examiner of Military Officers in the Vernacular languages, caused an increase of Rupees 5,400.

Salaries of the Secretary and Office Establishment of the Military Fund, the assets of which have been transferred to Government, take up Rs. 17,651.

In adjustment of Bonus Compensation claims payable during the year, the Government of India, in the Military Department, authorised a special grant of Rupees 50,000.

Revised scale of pay and allowances to Warrant Officers of the Ordnance and Commissariat Department, caused increased expenditure of Rupees 26,018.

The several increases above enumerated, amount to Rupees 9,82,782.

Decreases.

380. By the abolition of the Pay Office, Northern Circle, from 30th April 1867, Rupees 11,982 was saved.

The discontinuance of the appointment of Personal Assistant to the Controller of Military Accounts, set free Rupees 5,400.

The appointment of Controller of Military Accounts on consolidated salary entailed a saving of Rupees 8,600.

These three decreases, amount to Rupees 25,982.

Estimates and expenditure.

381. The Budget estimate of the whole year 1867-68, exclusive of the cost of stores from England, amounted to Rupees 3,04,68,090.

The Regular Estimate of 1867-68, amounted to Rupees 3,14,97,870.

The actual expenditure of 1866-67, was Rupees 3,07,67,992.

Administrative Superintendence, British Medical Service.

382. In carrying out the re-organization of the administrative staff of the British and Indian Medical Services, the following stations have been assigned to the Circles of Medical Superintendence attached to the British Service :—

Presidency Circle.

Fort Saint George and Stations adjacent, Trichinopoly and Wellington in the Southern Division, and any Stations in the Northern District in which British Troops may be hereafter located.

Mysore Circle.

Bangalore, with the Stations in Malabar and the Ceded Districts.

Hyderabad Circle.

Secunderabad and Trimulgherry, with Kamptee and other Stations occupied by British Troops composing the Nagpore Force.

British Burmah Circle.

Rangoon, with the two frontier posts of Thyetmyo and Tonghoo.

Commissariat Commissioned Officers.

383. To provide for the duties of absentees on leave, from among the Commissioned grades of the Commissariat Department, without having recourse to the alternative of temporarily withdrawing for the purpose, and for indefinite periods, Officers holding Regimental and other substantive appointments, an addition of three Sub-Assistants Commissary General of the 3rd class has been made to the existing establishment of twenty-two Officers of the Department in this Presidency.

Victualling European Troops.

384. The price of all articles of food have fallen, and Commissariat contracts have been generally more favorable than in the previous year. Experiments have been sanctioned for feeding cattle and sheep for some time prior to slaughter, with the object of improving the meat ration of the Troops.

Government Bakery.

385. The Government Bakery at Madras now furnishes bread to all the Troops in the Division, the flour and soojee being ground and dressed by the machinery received from Europe. Two engines shortly expected from England will render the baking establishments at Bangalore and the Presidency complete.

Arrack.

386. The issue of Rum in lieu of Arrack to the European Troops commenced in the past year, and the change is reported to give satisfaction.

Public Cattle.

387. There has been a considerable reduction in the cost of keep of public cattle, consequent upon the fall in the prices of grain.

The mortality has not been so great among any of the different descriptions of public cattle as in the previous year.

Amrut Mahal.

388. The "Amrut Mahal" has made satisfactory progress. It numbered on the 31st January 1868, 6,175 head of cattle, against 4,594 on the 31st March 1867.

Manufacture of Gun Powder.

389. To meet a requisition from the Home Government, a Commissioned and a Warrant Officer of the Ordnance Department* were ordered to England, for instruction at Woolwich in the process of making the Boxer Ammunition for the Snider Rifle.

* Lieutenant-Colonel R. Cadell and Assistant Supervisor Thomas Lee, of the Arsenal, Fort Saint George.

Colonel Rowlandson, Superintendent of the Gun Powder Manufactory, has also been deputed to England for six months, to study the system of manufacture at Waltham Abbey.

Cantonment Act No. I of 1866, (Madras.)

390. Act No. I of 1866, (Madras,) to make provision for the administration of Military Cantonments in the Presidency of Fort Saint George, has been brought into effect from 31st March 1868 in the Cantonment of Poonamallee, having been previously introduced at Bellary, Cannanore, Trichinopoly, Wellington, and Saint Thomas' Mount. Act No. XXII of 1864, of the Government of India, having similar objects in view, has been extended to Kamptee, Secunderabad, Rangoon, Tonghoo, and Thyetmyo, being under the Civil Administration of that Government.

Banda and Kirwee Prize money.

391. The first and second distributions of the Banda and Kirwee prize money having been authorised, claims of individuals who served with the Saugor and Nurbudda Field Forces, having been investigated and verified, are in course of adjustment, shares not claimed in India having been remitted to England.

Health of the Native Army.

392. There has been a great improvement in the public health throughout the Madras Presidency during the official year 1867-68, and in this improvement the Native Army has fully shared, as will appear by the following details.

The average strength for the year was 27,220, the total number treated in Hospital 21,157, and the total of deaths 211. The corresponding numbers for the official year 1866-67 were as follows: average strength 27,403, total treated in Hospital 22,722, and total of deaths 336. It thus appears that the per-centage of treated to strength has fallen from 82·91 to 77·7; that of deaths to strength from 1·2 to 0·7; and that of deaths to treated from 1·4 to 0·9.

General immunity from Cholera.

393. There has been no general outbreak of cholera during the year, and although the disease has made its appearance from time to time, in different parts of the country, it has nowhere prevailed to any great extent, and has caused only eleven casualties in the whole Army during the year.

General immunity from Small-pox.

394. Although small-pox has been wide-spread, and very fatal among the general population throughout the Presidency, during nearly the whole of the period under review, only two deaths have occurred in the Native Army, a result which may be attributed to the success of the sanitary and prophylactic measures adopted for the protection of the Troops from epidemic and contagious diseases.

Diseases most prevalent.

395. The most prevalent diseases, during the year, have been fevers of the intermittent and remittent types, which have caused fifty-two casualties. The largest proportion of these was in Burmah and the Nagpore Division, and the smallest in the Presidency and Southern Divisions.

The following table affords more detailed information regarding the admissions and deaths in the several divisions of the Madras Native Army :—

Divisions.	Natives.						
	Average strength.	Treated.	Died in Hospital from all causes.	Average daily sick.	Per-centage of		
					Treated to strength.	Deaths to strength.	Deaths to treated.
Presidency	3,479	2,030	24	96	58·3	0·6	1·1
Southern	2,242	646	20	27	28·3	0·8	3·09
Mysore	5,908	4,529	43	159	76·6	0·7	0·9
Ceded Districts	3,080	1,976	18	85	64·1	0·5	0·9
Hyderabad Subsidiary Force..	2,689	3,466	14	91	128·8	0·5	0·4
Nagpore Force...	3,565	3,839	29	121	107·6	0·8	0·7
Northern	3,681	2,240	29	77	60·8	0·7	1·2
Pegu	2,576	2,431	34	122	94·3	1·3	1·39
Total...	27,220	21,157	211	778	77·7	0·7	0·9

Lock Hospitals.

396. The Returns of women treated in these Hospitals, during the past year, shew a decrease as compared with the year previous, the numbers being for the year 1866-67, 1,571, and for the year 1867-68, 1,217, the decrease being 354.

There has been, however, during the same period, a corresponding decrease in the number of admissions in the European Army of this Presidency from venereal diseases, the numbers being for 1866-67, 2,686, and for 1867-68, 2,276, the decrease amounting to 410.

The table appended shews the number of persons treated and died in Lock Hospitals during the year 1867-68 :—

	Bangalore.		Bellary.		Cannanore.		Kamptee.		Saint Thomas' Mount.		Secunderabad.		Trichinopoly.		Wellington.		Total.		Per-centage of deaths to treated.
	Treated.	Died.	Treated.	Died.	Treated.	Died.	Treated.	Died.	Treated.	Died.	Treated.	Died.	Treated.	Died.	Treated.	Died.	Treated.	Died.	
1867-68	289	3	178	0	96	0	117	3	9	0	269	0	110	0	62	0	1,217	6	0·49

Section X.—EDUCATIONAL.

397. The number of Colleges and Schools connected with the Educational Department at the close of the year was 1,687, with an attendance of 62,975 scholars; the corresponding numbers for the previous official year having been 1,386 and 51,118. These figures exhibit an increase of 301 schools and 11,857 pupils during the year under review; but the Director states that while the augmentation of pupils is accurately represented by the latter number, that of Colleges and Schools is in reality less than 301. This circumstance, it is explained, arises from the fact that in last year's report, an institution containing a College department for educating youths up to the B. A. standard, as well as a School department for conveying instruction up to the University Entrance course, was reckoned as a single institution; while now, in accordance with the Orders of the Government of India of the 11th December 1867, No. 1,252, the two departments are entered separately, and the institution is thus counted twice. The institutions treated in this manner are fourteen in number. The real increase, therefore, in the number of schools is 287. Normal Schools have been reckoned as single institutions in all cases. There is an apparent increase of nine Government institutions, but of these, six are given by the separation of departments just noticed; the remaining three being a Talook School in the District of Vizagapatam, and two elementary schools in the Gumsur Hills. The comparative non-extension of Government Schools under inspection, is in accordance with the policy laid down by Government. While the number of Government Schools has increased to a very trifling extent, the attendance at such schools has risen by 732; and this, notwithstanding the abolition of the junior classes in some of those schools.

Number of Schools and Pupils.

398. The following is a classification of the schools; 1st, with reference to the agency by which they are managed:—

Classification.

	Number of Schools.		Number of Pupils.	
	In 1866-67.	In 1867-68.	In 1866-67.	In 1867-68.
Government Schools	106	115	10,025	10,757
Schools supported by a rate, most of which received also grants-in-aid ...	95	107	2,802	3,441
Private Schools receiving grants-in-aid ...	784	835	30,893	37,785
Private Schools under simple inspection...	401	630	7,398	10,992
Total... ...	1,386	1,687	51,118	62,975

2nd, with reference to the standard of instruction imparted in them :—

	Number of Schools.		Number of Pupils.	
	In 1866-67.	In 1867-68.	In 1866-67.	In 1867-68.
First class Schools	31	47	8,030	9,192
Middle class Schools	280	391	17,976	23,089
Lower class Schools...	985	1,125	19,510	23,263
Girls' Schools	75	110	3,425	5,201
Normal Schools	11	10	1,619	1,685
Schools and Colleges for special or professional instruction	4	4	558	545
Total... ...	1,386	1,687	51,118	62,975

Of the number of schools entered in the above table under the heads of middle class and lower class schools, 9 of the former and 155 of the latter are mixed schools for boys and girls ; the number of girls attending these schools being 1,309.

Distribution of Pupils.

399. The following is a comparative statement of the distribution of the pupils under instruction at the close of the two past years, according to race and sex :—

	Number at the close of 1866-67.			Number at the close of 1867-68.		
	Boys.	Girls.	Total.	Boys.	Girls.	Total.
Europeans	413	192	605	365	172	537
East Indians	2,097	1,131	3,228	2,579	1,545	4,124
Native Christians	5,063	2,212	7,275	6,065	3,030	9,095
Hindoos	37,093	1,095	38,188	45,547	1,761	47,308
Mahomedans	1,814	8	1,822	1,909	2	1,911
Total... ...	46,480	4,638	51,118	56,465	6,510	62,975

The numbers studying different languages are as follows :—

Language.	English.	Greek.	Latin.	Sanscrit.	Hindustani.	Persian.	Uriya.	Telugu.	Tamil.	Malayalum.	Canarese.	Tulu.	German.
Number of pupils instructed in it	32,159	74	242	325	553	107	962	16,182	36,343	8,583	1,792	321	10

As many of the pupils study more than one language, the same youths enter the foregoing numbers twice or oftener.

400. The Inspecting agency employed at the close of the last two official years was as follows :— Inspecting agency.

	31st March 1867.	31st March 1868.
Inspectors of Schools	5	5
Deputy Inspectors of Schools	16	18
Inspecting Schoolmasters	9	10
Superintendent of Hill Schools..................	1	1
Total...	31	34

401. The aggregate expenditure was Rupees 8,43,397-14-6, distributed as shewn below :— Expenditure.

	RS.	A.	P.
Direction and its subsidiary charges...	34,110	8	5
Inspection and its subsidiary charges..	1,01,735	10	11
Instruction, including all educational expenditure not coming under "Direction," or "Inspection"	7,07,551	11	2

Of the last mentioned sum, Rupees 5,74,893-12-4 were disbursed from Imperial Funds, and Rupees 1,32,657-14-10 from Local Funds.

The expenditure may be further classified as follows :—

		RS.	A.	P.
Expenditure from Imperial Funds.	Direction	34,110	8	5
	Inspection	1,01,735	10	11
	Government Colleges and Schools	3,32,320	7	11
	Government Scholarships...	16,181	5	1
	Grants in aid of the current expenses of private schools	1,60,638	15	9
	Grant to the Madras School Book Society ...	2,000	0	0
	Public Instruction Press	1,863	10	0
	Preparation and purchase of school books ...	33,030	5	4
	Central Book Depôt	4,636	1	0
	University of Madras	24,222	15	1
Expenditure from the Educational Building Fund.	Building grants to Government Schools	70,414	2	8
	Building grants to Private Schools	7,421	6	0
School Fee Fund	Charges in Government Schools borne by school fees...	50,088	2	0
Subscriptions Donations, &c	Do. do. by donations and subscriptions	4,734	4	2
		8,43,397	14	6

	RS.	A.	P.			
Deduct University fees paid to the credit of Government	10,555	0	0			
School fees do.	8,467	0	1			
Proceeds of sale of books...	40,680	6	1			
				59,702	6	2
Net expenditure...				7,83,695	8	4

402. During the year under review certain changes were made in the rules of the University, relating to the fees for admission to the several Examinations in Arts, and which are to take effect from 1868-69. The fee for Matriculation has been raised from Rupees 5 to 8; that for the First Examination in Arts, from Rupees 10 to 15; and that for the B. A. Examination from Rupees 25 to 30.

University Examinations.

The subjoined statement exhibits the numerical results of the several examinations held by the University:—

	Number of Candidates examined.	Number of passed Candidates.		Total passed.
		From Government Institutions.	From Private Institutions.	
Matriculation Examination	1,069	128	210	338
First Examination in Arts	350	71	46	117
Bachelor of Arts Examination	24	13	1	14
Bachelor of Laws Examination	14	3	7	10

The new rule under which candidates at the Matriculation examination are required to secure one-third of the maximum marks in English, instead of one-fourth, as previously demanded, was brought into operation in 1867-68. The change might have been expected to reduce the number of candidates for the year; but such was not the effect, 1,069 candidates having presented themselves for examination in December 1867, against 895 in the previous year.

The progress of Anglo-Vernacular education in private schools, is shewn by 210 passed candidates proceeding from those institutions, while only 128 came from Government schools. The former number exceeds that for 1866-67 by forty-six, and the latter is less than the corresponding number for that year by fourteen. The falling off in regard to Government schools is ascribed to a greatly diminished number of matriculated students in the Provincial College at Combaconum; and on this point it is stated that, during the past year, the College has had for the first time a second year as well as a first year collegiate class, in consequence of which the Matriculation class was unable to obtain as large a share of attention from the senior teachers as fell to it in former years. The number of private schools which sent up successful candidates to the Matriculation examination of 1867-68, was forty-four against forty for 1866-67;

the steady increase shewn by the numbers for the former years, nineteen, twenty-nine, and forty, has consequently received a check most probably from the increase in the minimum in English.

While the majority of candidates for Matriculation came from private schools, the case is different in respect of candidates for the higher University Examinations; of those who passed the First Examination in Arts in 1867-68, seventy-one came from Government, and forty-six from private schools. Here there is a decided falling off on the part of the latter Institutions, as for 1866-67 the numbers stood at fifty-seven for Government, and fifty-nine for private schools. The total number of passed candidates at the First Arts test is only greater by one than that for the previous year.

The results of the Bachelor of Arts Examination for 1867-68 shew a slight improvement over those for 1866-67, the total number of Bachelors being greater by one, and one of the candidates for 1867-68 having secured a place in the first class, while nothing higher than a second class was obtained the previous year.

The Bachelor of Laws Examination was attended by fourteen candidates, of whom ten succeeded in passing, seven being placed in the second, and the rest in the third class. Up to the close of 1866-67, the graduates in Law numbered twenty-three; the addition of ten during the past year must, therefore, be regarded as a satisfactory result.

During the year under review, the Degree of Licentiate in Medicine and Surgery was conferred upon an ex-student of the Medical College, who claimed it under a Resolution passed by the Senate of the University in 1864. According to the Regulations now in force, the above degree has been replaced by that of Bachelor of Medicine and Master of Surgery.

The names of the Institutions which sent up successful Candidates to the several Examinations in Arts held during the year under review are given in the following tables:—

MATRICULATION EXAMINATION.

Government Institutions.	Number in both Classes.
Presidency College	30
Provincial College, Combaconum	13
Do. School, Bellary	7
Do. do. Calicut	11
Do. do. Mangalore	2
Zillah School, Berhampore	3
Do. Rajahmundry	2
Do. Salem	8
Do. Chittoor	12
Do. Madura	10

	Number in both Classes.
Zillah School, Cuddapah	3
Do. Kurnool	1
Madrissa-i-Azam	2
Normal School, Madras	8
Do. Trichinopoly	2
Do. Vizagapatam	4
Do. Vellore	1
Do. Cannanore	7
Anglo-Vernacular School, Mayaveram	1
Normal Class, Nursapur	1
	128

Private Institutions.

Doveton College...	8
Gospel Society's High School, Tanjore	11
Free Church Mission Institution, Madras	20
Saint Joseph's College, Negapatam	4
Anglo-Vernacular School, Sydapet	5
Hindu Anglo-Vernacular School, Coimbatore	4
Gospel Mission Seminary, Sullivan's Gardens	9
Patcheappah's Central Institution, Madras	13
Bishop Cotton's School, Bangalore	4
High School, Trevandrum	12
Wesleyan Mission School, Mysore	4
Do. do. Bangalore...	3
Church Mission Anglo-Vernacular School, Masulipatam... ...	4
Patcheappah's Branch School, Conjeveram	3
Military Male Orphan Asylum	2
High School, Bangalore	10
Wesleyan Mission School, Manargudy	2
Do. Institution, Royapettah	2
Saint Mary's Roman Catholic Seminary	4
London Mission Institution, Bangalore	5
Grammar School, Ootacamund	8
Government School, Hassan	3
Gospel Society's Anglo-Vernacular School, Vepery...	4
Saint Aloysius' School, Vizagapatam...	2
Church Mission School, Ellore	1
Wesleyan Mission School, Negapatam	1
London Mission School, Madras	6
Forest Hill, Kent, England	1
Gospel Mission Seminary, Vediarpuram	4

	Number in both Classes.
Anglo-Vernacular School, Royapettah	1
Church Mission Native English School, Palamcottah	6
Rate School, Palghaut	2
Hindu School, Vizagapatam	1
Bishop Corrie's Grammar School	4
Gospel Society's School, Trichinopoly	3
Hindu Anglo-Vernacular School, Tinnevelly	2
Lutheran Mission School, Tranquebar	2
Wardlaw Institution, Bellary	3
Saint Andrew's Parochial School, Bangalore	3
Native Education Institution, Bangalore	1
Free Church Mission School, Nellore	1
Wesleyan Mission High School, Trichinopoly	2
Chundrically Seminary...	2
Central School, Nursapur	1
Private tuition	17
	210

FIRST ARTS EXAMINATION.

Government Institutions.

Presidency College	29
Provincial College, Combaconum	18
Do. School, Bellary	5
Provincial School, Calicut	3
Zillah School, Rajahmundry	1
Do. Madura	2
Do. Salem	2
Normal School, Madras	7
Do. Trichinopoly	1
Do. Vellore	1
Do. Vizagapatam	1
Anglo-Vernacular School, Mayaveram	1
	71

Private Institutions.

Free Church Mission Institution, Madras...	9
Gospel Society's High School, Tanjore	4
Church Mission Anglo-Vernacular School, Masulipatam	3
Wesleyan Mission School, Bangalore	2
High School, Trevandrum	4
American Mission School, Madura	1
Bishop Corrie's Grammar School	1
High School, Bangalore	1

	Number in both Classes.
Wesleyan Mission School, Negapatam	1
Ootacamund Grammar School	1
Wesleyan Mission Institution, Royapettah	1
Gospel Society's High School, Trichinopoly	1
Rajah's Free School, Puducotta...	1
Church Mission Native English School, Palamcottah...	1
Gospel Mission Seminary, Sullivan's Gardens	4
Private tuition	11
	46

BACHELOR OF ARTS EXAMINATION.

Presidency College	12
Gospel Mission Seminary, Sullivan's Gardens	1
Private tuition	1
	14

The number of Candidates corresponding to each of the optional languages in the three examinations of the Faculty of Arts is shewn beneath :—

Languages.	Matriculation Examination.		First Arts Examination.		Bachelor of Arts Examination.	
	Examined.	Passed.	Examined.	Passed.	Examined.	Passed.
Greek	...	...	1	1	...	...
Latin	86	55	16	3	1	1
Sanscrit	10	1	3	2	...	...
Tamil	535	154	202	64	16	10
Telugu	203	64	59	24	7	3
Malayalum	98	31	35	11	...	...
Canarese	109	30	28	9	...	...
Hindustani	28	3	6	3	...	...

The several classes of the community to which the candidates belong are noted in the following table :—

Classes of the Community.	Matriculation Examination.		First Arts Examination.		Bachelor of Arts Examination.	
	Examined.	Passed.	Examined.	Passed.	Examined.	Passed.
Brahmins	539	172	203	67	9	8
Other Hindoos	312	70	77	25	12	4
East Indians	74	40	18	8	...	...
Europeans	49	28	11	4	1	1
Mahomedans	27	2	6	2	...	...
Native Christians ...	68	26	35	11	2	1

The expenditure of the University during 1867-68 was as follows:—

	RS.	A.	P.
Establishment	4,294	0	0
Examiners' fees...	15,750	0	0
Stationery	759	7	7
Printing charges	927	0	7
Furniture	9	0	0
Postage	984	10	0
Other contingencies	1,498	12	11
Total Rupees...	24,222	15	1

The amount of fees received from candidates was Rupees 10,555.

403. At the close of 1867 the lowest class of the Junior department was abolished in pursuance of the plan originally laid down, under which the College is ultimately to contain only Matriculated Students qualifying for the B. A. Degree.

Presidency College.

The increase in the numerical strength of the senior department, which, at the close of the official year, contained 104 students, against 85 in the preceding year, is satisfactory. Of the 104 College students, 46 belonged to the Town of Madras and the adjoining district of that name. The remaining 58 came from other districts, the largest numbers being from Malabar and Travancore, North Arcot, Salem, Ceylon, Bellary, and South Arcot. In the several University Examinations of 1867-68, the College may be said to have, on the whole, been successful; the number of passed candidates being eleven out of fourteen sent up for the B. A. Degree Examination, twenty-three out of twenty-eight for the First Examination in Arts, and twenty-nine out of fifty-eight for the Matriculation Examination. The results of the ordinary College Examinations were also generally satisfactory.

The new College building is expected to be finished early in 1869.

404. This institution, which was raised to its present grade at the beginning of 1867, will not send up its first set of candidates for the B. A. Degree until February 1869. The numerical strength of the senior department, or College proper, at the close of the year, was fifty-seven; it is worthy of notice that this number is equal to that of the senior department of the Presidency College for the year 1863-64. In the school department the number of pupils was 332. The results of the examination of the several classes were, as usual, very satisfactory.

Provincial College, Combaconum.

The Director notices in his report the liberality of a Hindu gentleman, Chandrapakasa Moopanar, formerly a pupil in the Combaconum Provincial School, in having invested a sum of money sufficient to endow two Scholarships of Rupees seven each per mensem, and to offer for competition an annual gold medal of the value of 100 Rupees. These benefactions, with the Beauchamp Medal and the Edward Bird Scholarship, constitute gratifying proofs of the interest taken in this institution by the inhabitants of the Tanjore District.

405. At the commencement of the Session, there were eight students in the Senior department, fifty in the Second, and sixty-three in the Junior department. Of the students in the senior department only one had completed the prescribed course at the close of the Session, and was awarded the diploma of the College. It should be remarked here that, with the issue of this Diploma, the privilege of granting Degrees of Medicine enjoyed by the College since 1852, has come to an end. Henceforward all students in the senior department must pass the University Examinations in order to obtain Degrees in Medicine and Surgery.

Medical College.

Of the students in the second department, forming the senior class, ten were found qualified for the grade of Assistant Apothecary; and of those in the Junior department twenty-two were passed as Hospital Assistants. The conduct of the students generally is reported to have been good.

406. The number of students in the Civil Engineering College at the close of the last Session was 102, of whom seven belonged to the first department, fifty-seven to the second department, and thirty-eight to the special department for Surveying and Drawing. None of the students of the first department had completed the prescribed period at the last annual examination; but one of them, a Military student, who was considered by the Principal to have made great progress in his studies, having been required to proceed to Abyssinia in September last, was given a special examination, on the results of which he was awarded a certificate as Assistant Engineer. Nineteen students of the second department passed as Talook Overseers, while the remaining six passed the minor test required for the Bengal Public Works Department. In the special department eleven pupils secured certificates for drawing, and eight, certificates for surveying. The results of the annual examinations were, on the whole, satisfactory; and the conduct of the students was generally good.

Civil Engineering College.

Attendance and expenditure in Government Colleges.

407. The subjoined statement exhibits the attendance and expenditure of the several Government Colleges, excluding the schools attached to them.

	General Education.			Special Education.		
Number of Institutions	4			3		
Number on the Rolls during 1867-68 (monthly average) ...	139			30		
Average daily attendance during 1867-68	122			23		
	RS.	A.	P.	RS.	A.	P.
Total expenditure from Imperial Funds	52,038	15	8	8,625	12	9
Total expenditure from Local Funds	4,280	4	2	250	0	0

408. The number of pupils in the three Government Provincial Schools at the close of the year is as follows :—

Govt. Schools of the higher class.

Provincial Schools.

	Number of pupils.
Bellary	294
Calicut	307
Mangalore	281
Total...	882

The report on the Provincial School at Bellary is satisfactory. In regard to the School at Calicut, the Director reports that, though it has advanced of late years, it has not made as much progress as was hoped for. The pronunciation of English in all the classes is stated to be very defective. In regard to the instruction in the vernacular languages also, which was unfavorably noticed in 1866-67, improvement is still called for. The Mangalore Provincial School is reported to have made as much progress during the year under review as the educational backwardness of the district and the weakness of the teaching staff would permit. At present instruction is imparted in this school up to the standard of the University Matriculation Examination, but it is hoped that by the beginning of 1869 it will be found practicable to establish a class for preparing students for the First Examination in Arts.

Zillah Schools.

409. Of the Zillah Schools,* those at Chittoor and Madura are as usual the most advanced, the former taking the lead in respect both of the number and the attainments of the pupils. The schools at Cuddalore, Berhampore, and Cuddapah have improved. The report on the school at Rajahmundry is very unsatisfactory; and this is attributed mainly to the existence of a species of feud between the master who was in charge of the school and some of his subordinates. The school has been placed in charge of another master. With respect to the school at Kurnool, the Director reports that, owing to the disadvantages arising from the backwardness of the district and the unhealthiness of the town, it will take some time before the school reaches the position it is intended to occupy.

* *Zillah Schools.*	Number of pupils.
Berhampore	235
Rajahmundry	201
Kurnool	91
Cuddapah	195
Cuddalore	212
Chittoor	365
Salem	321
Madura	282
Madrissa-i-Azam	307
Total...	2,209

The school at Salem is favorably reported upon. As regards the Madrissa-i-Azam, the report is not altogether favorable.

During the year under review, Pacheappah Mudaliar's Central Institution was placed in connexion with the Educational Department, and received various grants, amounting to about Rupees 558 per mensem. This school, which rests on the solid foundation of a tolerably large funded capital, and is under the management of a body of Trustees, is the most important Hindu Institution in the Presidency. The State aid now given to this Institution will not merely enable the Trustees to put it into thoroughly good working order, but will allow of their establishing new schools with the portion of their funds set free.

Private Institutions of the first class.

410. The Church Mission School at Masulipatam, the Free Church Mission Central Institution at Madras, and the Gospel Society's High School at Tanjore, are reported as standing the foremost among private schools of the first class in the educational divisions in which they are respectively located. The results of the University Examinations, in reference to the Candidates sent up from these institutions, as well as the results at the departmental inspections, bear ample testimony to the very efficient manner in which they are managed. The Gospel Society's Seminary at Sullivan's Gardens is also specially noticed by the Director. He states that "though this institution is professedly a theological one, the Principal, the Revd. Mr. Symonds, has felt it incumbent upon him to bring his students forward in secular as well as in religious studies, and his exertions have been marked with decided success. Beside a very creditable number of pupils who passed the First Arts and Matriculation tests last year, one student obtained the degree of Bachelor of Arts, being ranked in the second class." The Doveton Protestant College at Madras appears to have suffered during the year under review from the circumstance of several changes having been made in the staff of teachers. Of the five students of the College who presented themselves for the First Arts Test, the whole failed; but of the ten Matriculation Candidates sent up for examination, eight were successful. The other private schools of the first class under Government inspection do not call for any special notice.

Middle class schools.

411. The returns again exhibit a very considerable increase in the number of middle class schools, which, at the close of the past official year, numbered 391, with an attendance of 23,089 pupils. The increase in the number of schools, amounting to 111, is distributed over the sixteen districts noted at foot,* the greatest number of new schools

* South Canara. Malabar. Tinnevelly. Coimbatore. Trichinopoly. Tanjore. Salem. North Arcot. South Arcot. Madras. Nellore. Bellary. Kistna. Godavery. Vizagapatam. Ganjam.

being in the Godavery District, where twenty-three new middle class schools were either established or brought under inspection.

The number of Government Schools of the middle class, at the close of 1867-68, is sixty-nine, which is in excess of the number for the preceding year by only one. The Anglo-Vernacular Government Schools have all been favorably reported upon, and the reports on the Talook Schools are also, for the most part, satisfactory. In the last annual report, the backward state of the Talook Schools in Ganjam was made the subject of remark. It appears from the report now under review, that these schools have, with one exception, made decided progress in respect of both the attainments and the attendance of the pupils.

Of the newly opened middle class schools, one, an Anglo-Vernacular School, was established by the Rajah of Vencatagherry at Naidupett in the Nellore district, and the expenses are met by a small land-tax paid by the ryots in the Naidupett division. With the view of giving permanency to the Hindu School at Cocanada, the Rajah of Pittapore has munificently presented it with the handsome sum of Rupees 24,000, to be invested in Government Securities as an Endowment Fund. The Maharajah of Vizianagram, whose enlightened efforts to raise the standard of the Samastanum School, established by His Highness, were noticed in the last report, is stated now to be engaged in founding schools of an elementary character at different places in his Zemindary, and which, it is expected, will feed the Vizianagram Institution and assist it in taking the position which its founder desires it to occupy. The Zemindar of Bobbili and his Dewan are reported to take more interest than they previously did, in the school established by the former in that Zemindary.

Schools of the lower class.

412. The number of schools of the lower class connected with the department has risen from 985, with an attendance of 19,510 pupils, to 1,125, with an attendance of 23,263 pupils. Under the head of Girls' Schools, most of which may be classed as lower class schools, there has been an increase of 35 schools and 3,425 pupils. It appears that, besides the 110 schools for females, there are 164 schools with a mixed attendance, the girls therein numbering 1,309.

At the close of the year there were 721 schools under the operation of the scheme for improving indigenous schools on the payment-for-results plan, as first introduced into the Coimbatore District. Of these, 259 are in that district, 159 in Nellore, forty-three in Madura, thirty-nine in Cuddapah, and twelve in North Arcot.

Normal Scho[ol]

413. The Madras Normal School has not yet recovered the position which it held some years ago. The Normal classes are stated to have suffered, partly from certain changes made in the teach-

ing staff, which had the effect of depriving the students of a part of their instruction for a considerable portion of the year, and partly from the circumstance of the classes having been formed of youths who ought never to have been allowed to join them. The new Principal, however, who took charge of the institution towards the close of June 1867, has been using his best endeavours to bring it into a sound condition; and he has been aided by his Assistants; but time will be required before this important institution will regain the position which it formerly occupied. At the University Examinations in December 1867, only four Normal pupils, out of seventeen, passed the First Arts test, and five out of twenty-eight, the Matriculation examination; while out of six pupils who went up from the Practising School for the latter test, three were successful. With reference to the unsatisfactory results of the examinations, the Inspector quotes in his report the following remarks by the Principal:—"An educational institution constituted as this is, in which a fourth "or more of the time of every student is employed either in teaching or in "special duties, can scarcely hope to prove as successful in the examinations as "others, where the sole business of the students is to study the subjects required "for them. * * * Were it possible for the students to dispose of their work "in one continuous period of three or four months, and be left at liberty for the "remainder of the year to devote their whole attention to the subjects required "for the examinations, they would have a far better chance of success than at "present." The Inspector observes that this is a question of great importance.

The following remarks by the Principal, as to the increased interest which is evinced in the Criticism Lessons, which form a portion of the special work of the Normal classes, (viz., the practice and theory of teaching,) are deserving of notice:—

"The most important feature in the special work of the students was undoubtedly the Criticism Lessons. They excited far more interest, and were looked forward to with more eagerness than any part of their duties. They were usually appointed several days before the time for giving them, so that ample time was allowed for their preparation. The provision made in the time-table for the delivery of the lesson and the criticisms thereon was only an hour and a half, but it was always found necessary to exceed that time. Ordinarily, instead of finishing at five, the proceedings extended to half-past, and sometimes even so late as six. All the superior masters, and all the students, except those engaged in Practising Schools, were present, and the proceedings were conducted by the former in rotation, though each delivered his opinion of the lesson after the students' criticisms had been obtained. Every student present on the occasion, was afterwards required to record his remarks in a book provided for the purpose, which were subsequently examined by the master who presided."

The Inspector reports that the Students' Note Books, in which remarks are entered on the lessons of criticism, are more satisfactory than formerly. "The notes are fuller and better; and corrected for each lesson by the master "who presides on the occasion; the corrections applying as well to the language "as to the matter:" and he is of opinion that this part of the special work could not be done in a better way.

The progress of the Normal School at Cannanore is, on the whole, creditable.

The Normal School at Trichinopoly has been reported on very favorably, and that at Vellore appears to have done well.

Upon the whole, taking the practising branches of the Normal Schools into account, the results for 1867-68 are as follows :—Five students passed the First Arts Examination ; twenty-four, the Matriculation; twenty-five secured certificates of the fourth, and nineteen, certificates of the fifth grade ; and seventy-five took up appointments as teachers.

414. An examination of candidates for Teachers' Certificate was held at twenty-eight different stations in the beginning of August 1867 ; 581 Candidate Masters and twenty-six Candidate Mistresses underwent the test, 210 of the former and nine of the latter proving successful. While the number of candidate teachers was smaller by eighty-six than that for 1866-67, the number of passed candidates was larger by twenty-one ; this result may be considered satisfactory, so far as it indicates more careful preparation on the part of the candidates, but it is to be regretted that a more numerous body of female teachers did not come forward. The falling off in the number of Schoolmistresses attaches chiefly to Tinnevelly and Madras ; from the former district only seven came up against thirty-seven for the previous year, while the number of passed mistresses stands at 0 against 15.

Examination for Teachers' Certificate.

415. The number of schools supported by a rate under the provisions of the Madras Education Act, as entered in the returns of the year, is 107, which exceeds the number at the close of 1866-67 by twelve. Some of the schools, however, have since been closed. The reports as to the working of the Education Act continue to be far from favorable, especially in the case of schools established in rural villages. The school at Sydapett is particularly noticed as the best managed, and most successful of the Rate Schools. Its management reflects great credit upon the Commissioners, and especially upon the Honorary Secretary. The Rate Schools in Malabar and Canara have generally done well. Their success is due partly to their being above the class of village schools, and partly to their having as local Commissioners men of some intelligence.

Madras Education Act.

416. The number of aided colleges and schools rose from 879, with an attendance of 35,260 pupils, to 945, with an attendance of 40,525 pupils. The grant-in-aid expenditure for the official year, including scholarships, was Rupees 1,61,193-15-9. Of the aided institutions—

Grant-in-aid system.

6 were Colleges, with........	117	pupils.
19 were Schools of the higher class, with	5,312	„
310 were Schools of the middle class, with	16,888	„
509 were Schools of the lower class, with	13,006	„
97 were Female schools, with...	4,624	„
4 were Normal schools, with.............	578	„

The expenditure was distributed as follows :—

	RS.	A.	P.
Colleges	5,621	4	0
Schools of the higher class	50,187	0	1
Do. middle class	74,383	9	1
Do. lower class	18,041	10	8
Female schools	6,119	7	11
Normal schools	6,841	0	0

The average grants made to schools of the higher class amounted to Rupees 2,641-6-8 per school; those to middle class schools to Rupees 239-15-2 per school; and those to schools of the lower class to Rupees 35-7-2 per school; the average expenditure from all sources per school in each case having been as follows :—

	RS.	A.	P.
For schools of the higher class	9,575	1	8
Do. middle class	868	7	4
Do. lower class	125	12	3

The following observations by the Acting Inspector of Schools of the 1st Division, on the working of the grant-in-aid system, are deserving of notice :—

"The more the present system of salary grants becomes known, the more it seems to be appreciated by the people. No doubt the condition of many of the smaller schools is very unstable, and their permanence a matter of grave doubt, but I think we have advanced to some, perhaps very, small extent, in gaining the confidence of the people, by shewing them that we have only their advantage at heart. It has been my main desire to arouse their interest, and secure their confidence and co-operation, and with this view I have endeavoured to accommodate the present rules as far as possible to the circumstances of each case, without sacrificing their main objects, viz., efficient schools and efficient teachers; yet, however desirable it may be that the progress of education should be estimated by quality not quantity, still it has always struck me that the first step is to popularize our teaching, and when we have gained the sympathy of the people, and familiarized them with that teaching, allowing it to take hold upon their imagination, we shall then be able better to organize and systematize, and exact thorough efficiency. Government should demand a full return for the money given, but that return will be no less full, because it lingers."

Female Education.

417. It will be seen from the abstract statement given in paragraph 399 of this report, that at the close of the year there were 6,510 girls under instruction in schools connected with the Educational Department. The number of girls studying in schools unconnected with the department is stated to be 4,295, which, however, is exclusive of the number under instruction in Malabar and South Canara, for which districts no statistics are stated to be available. Of the whole number of girls, 108 are returned as Europeans, 291 as Eurasians, 2,420 as Native Christians, 1,365 as Hindus, and twenty-nine as Mahomedans; for eighty-two the nation or race is

not given. The instruction imparted in the schools is almost in all cases of a very elementary character; and in too many instances it is apprehended that the teaching is productive of no permanent effect beyond rendering the pupils better disposed toward female education, and so paving the way for the instruction of a succeeding generation.

In their Order of the 17th April last, No. 144, the Government instructed the Director "to intimate to the several Inspectors and Deputy Inspectors of Schools that the Government of India attach great importance to the extension and improvement of female education, and look to them to take advantage of any openings which may occur for pressing the subject upon the consideration of enlightened Natives."

In connexion with this subject, it is to be noticed that upon the application of this Government, the Government of India have sanctioned the establishment of a Normal School for training female teachers at Madras, the arrangements for which are now under consideration.

The Acting Inspector of Schools in the 1st Division reports that an impetus has been given to female education in that division during the year, owing to the intelligent and liberal interest taken in the matter by the Maharajah of Vizianagram. The Maharajah has established two schools for girls, one at Vizianagram and another at Rajahmundry.

418. In the year under review the Book Department was re-organized, and a fresh mode of keeping its accounts was introduced. V. Kristnama Chari, an experienced officer of the Educational Department, who had previously done excellent work as a Deputy Inspector of Schools, was appointed Curator of Government Books under the new arrangements. The expenditure on account of the printing, purchase, and distribution of books in 1867-68 was Rupees 33,030-5-4, exclusive of the cost of the establishment of the Central Book Depôt, which amounted to Rupees 4,636-1-0. The number of English and Vernacular books sold was 106,477, and their value Rupees 40,680-6-1; of which particulars are shewn below:—

Book Department.

Languages.	Number of Copies.	Value.		
		RS.	A.	P.
English	29,567	19,313	13	4
Tamil	42,248	9,355	8	6
Telugu	22,769	6,322	8	3
Hindustani	291	172	7	0
Uriya...	1,655	264	4	6
Malayalum	3,167	1,102	1	0
Canarese	6,785	4,149	11	6
Total ...	1,06,477	40,680	6	1

The following statement exhibits the works printed during the year :—

Name of Book.	Language.	Number of Copies.
Selections in English, Prose No. 1	English ...	1,000
Do. Poetry No. 1	Do. ...	3,000
Do. do. No. 2	Do. ...	1,000
1st Book of Lessons	Tamil ...	20,000
2nd do. do.	Do. ...	5,000
Clift's Geography	Do. ...	5,000
Practical Dictionary (Romanized)	Do. ...	2,000
1st Book of Lessons	Telugu ...	5,000
2nd do. do.	Do. ...	4,000
3rd do. do.	Do. ...	3,000
Parsing and analysis	Do. ...	500
Manual of Geography, Part I	Do. ...	5,000
Practical Dictionary (Romanized)	Do. ...	2,000
Baskar's Ramayanam	Do. ...	1,000
Poetical Anthology...	Canarese ...	2,000
1st Book of Lessons	Malayalum..	5,000
Catechism of Grammar	Do. ...	3,000
Do. do.	Do. ...	1,000
Symonds' Map of India with English names	English ...	500
	Total ...	69,000

Uncovenanted Civil Service Examinations.

419. Three Examinations were held by the Commissioner during the year under review, as follows :—

1.—A Modified Special Test Examination in July 1867.

2.—The Special Test Examination in August 1867.

3.—The General Test Examination in February 1868.

Modified Special Test.

420. The Modified Special Test Examination was the fifth and last of those instituted by order of Government in 1865, for the benefit of officials of long standing in the service. It resulted in the success of ten out of nineteen candidates, making in all seventy-five of the candidates declared eligible for the post of Tahsildar and Sub-Magistrate.

Special Tests.

421. The Special Test Examination included, for the first time, a test for Pleaders in District Moonsiffs' Courts. Papers were set in the Law of Evidence and Civil Procedure as for the Lower Grade of the Judicial Test, and others in Hindu and Mahomedan Law as for the Higher Grade of that test. Other Special Tests were made applicable to many appointments which had hitherto been exempt from the operation of the rules ; and candidates for the higher grade of the Translation Test were required to pass in two languages instead of one as formerly.

The number of candidates for the Special Test Examination was 2,866, or 1,330 more than in 1866. Of these 876 were candidates for the new test for Pleaders in District Moonsiffs' Courts. The following table shews the per-centage of successful candidates in the principal subjects for the last three years :—

Tests.	1865.	1866.	1867.
I.—A. Judicial, Civil, Higher Grade	76	48	41
II.—A. Do. Criminal, do. ...	79	42	51
I.—B. Do. Civil, Lower Grade	83	75	61
II.—B. Do. Criminal, do. ...	79	85	29
III.—A. Revenue, Higher Grade ...	45	40	34
III.—B. Do. Lower Grade ...	53	59	21
VII.—B. Translation, do. ...	87	52	18
VIII.—A. Precis Writing, Higher Grade	29	29	37
VIII.—B. Do. Lower Grade	27	66	15
Pleaders in District Moonsiffs' Courts...	...	...	14

The papers set for the Judicial Tests (I. and II.) were rather harder than usual, as also were those set for the Revenue Tests (III.); the per-centage of successful candidates was thus somewhat lowered, but the almost universal failure to pass in Translation (VII. B.) can only be accounted for on the supposition that every one who has a smattering of English thinks he can pass, and that as such superficial knowledge extends, the number of unfit candidates increases. The average of marks assigned in this subject was very low. On the other hand, the improvement in the Higher Grade of the Precis-Writing Test (VIII. A.) is most satisfactory, and shews that a sound knowledge of English, and habits of thought, qualifications which can only be gauged by this part of the examination, are gaining ground.

The subjoined statement shews the number of candidates who having passed in one or more tests, completed their qualifications for the different offices in 1867-68 :—

Offices.	Number who completed their qualifications.
Principal Sudder Ameen and District Moonsiff and Pleader	11
Court Sheristadar	18
Deputy Collector and Magistrate ...	17
Tahsildar and Sub-Magistrate	34

422. Out of 195 candidates who presented themselves for the Police Test, which includes the Lower Grade of the Judicial Test, and a paper on departmental subjects, twenty were declared successful. Police Test.

423. The General Test was held as usual in February. The large number of 3,354 candidates registered their names, and 3,159 were examined. Of these 732 passed, or only twenty-three per cent., against thirty-four per cent. in the previous year. The failures, as might be expected, were chiefly in Grammar and Composition and Arithmetic. The number registered and examined was greater than in any former year, but the per-centage of success was lower than it has ever been except in 1865. The General Test.

Commissioner attributes this partly to the increased severity of the examination in hand-writing, spelling, and dictation, and partly to the increasing eagerness which is shewn to use this examination, not only as a key to the Uncovenanted Service, but as a touch-stone of ordinary education. With the increasing numbers which present themselves every year, there is an increasing proportion of youths whose mere smattering of knowledge gives but little chance of passing, but this is an evil which will be diminished by time and the progress of education, whilst the advantage which the institution presents of offering a standard by which the less ambitious schools may compare themselves and be stimulated to greater efforts will remain.

The following table shews the agency by which the candidates were instructed :—

Instructing Agency.	Anglo-Vernacular Branch.	English Branch.	Vernacular Branch.	Total.
Government Schools...	81	72	161	314
Schools receiving Grants-in-aid	64	56	99	219
Other Schools	24	48	26	98
Private Tuition	6	36	59	101
Total...	175	212	345	732

General result of the system of U. C. S. Examination for 1867-68.

424. Viewed as a Government Institution for supplying candidates qualified by previous mental cultivation for public employment as far as it can be tested by examination, the system of Uncovenanted Civil Service Examination has continued to be successful during the year under review. Viewed as a test of education, it shews neither an advance nor a retrogression.

Receipts and Expenditure.

425. The receipts during the year amounted to Rupees 36,936; the disbursements (excluding the Secretary's salary) to Rupees 35,931, shewing a balance in favor of Government of Rupees 1,005.

Section XI.—ECCLESIASTICAL.

426. The number of Clergy belonging to the Madras diocese at the close of the year was 169, forty of these were Government Chaplains, five were engaged in education, sixty were Missionaries, European or Eurasian, fifty-two were Native clergymen, six were without cure, and six were receiving Government grants. Ten of the clergy (already included as Missionaries) of the Society for the Propagation of the Gospel received Government grants.

Number of Clergy.

427. Thirty-one Chaplains were on duty in the diocese, six were absent on leave, two employed in Calcutta, and one was with the Abyssinian Force as Chaplain.

Chaplains.

428. The salaries of the Senior Chaplains have been raised to an equality with those of the Senior Chaplains in Bengal.

Pay of Senior Chaplains.

429. The Bishop held one Ordination, viz., on the 8th of March 1868, in St. George's Cathedral, at which, one East Indian and two Natives were ordained Priests, and two Europeans were ordained Deacons.

Ordination.

430. The number of persons confirmed in the year was 690, viz., 114 Europeans and East Indians, and 576 Natives.

Confirmations.

431. The Bishop continued his visitation in the early part of 1868. He visited Trichinopoly, Tanjore, Negapatam, Tranquebar, and the principal Mission Stations in that part of the diocese.

Visitation.

432. The Station of Kurnool has been constituted a Chaplaincy. The Joint Chaplaincies of Black Town and of Secunderabad have each been divided into two separate Chaplains' Stations.

New Chaplaincies.

433. The district of Lovedale, in which the Lawrence Asylum is situated, has been separated from the Station of Ootacamund for Ecclesiastical purposes, and placed under the spiritual charge of the Principal of the Asylum for the time being, who is always a Clergyman.

Other new cures.

A Clergyman has been appointed to the charge of the Railway Stations from Salem to Arconum. But hitherto he has not been able to find a residence for himself and family nearer to his work than Bangalore.

A sum of money, amounting to £1,870, has been promised by shareholders in the Madras Railway Company to provide a Chaplain for the Stations on their line. Steps have been taken, in consequence, to procure a Clergyman from

England, who will probably reside at Coimbatore, and have charge of all the western portion of the line.

Church Building.

434. At Chudderghaut the new Church has been completed and opened for divine worship. The work of building new Churches, or of raising subscriptions for the purpose, has been progressing at Ootacamund, Tellicherry, Cuddapah, Coimbatore, and Salem.

Burial Grounds.

435. Mr. Glasson has given a piece of ground at Vythery, in Wynaad, for the purpose of being used as a Church-yard. One Burial ground has been consecrated in the year, viz., at Vellore.

Wants.

436. Owing to the want of Chaplains, Cuddalore was without a resident Clergyman for almost the whole of the year under review; and other Stations have only been imperfectly supplied. A Clergyman is very much required in Wynaad, and at the Station of Cuddapah.

Section XII.—MISCELLANEOUS.

MEDICAL.

437. During the past official year the public health throughout the Madras Presidency has been generally satisfactory, especially as compared with the year preceding.

Public health.

438. There has been no general outbreak of cholera. The disease has appeared, from time to time, in different parts of the country, but has nowhere prevailed to any great extent, or in a very severe form. In April, May, and June, there was an outbreak of a mild type in the Kurnool district; in July, August, and September, the disease appeared in South Arcot; it was epidemic in the neighbourhood of Negapatam in June and July; and in the Salem district an outbreak occurred in January and February, which at first seemed so alarming that extra medical aid was sent from Madras at the Collector's request. The disease, however, proved most unusually amenable to treatment, and the death-rate was remarkably low. In some other districts a few cases are reported, but the disease does not appear to have assumed the epidemic form.

Cholera.

439. Malarious fevers have been frequent in some of the Northern districts, specially Rajahmundry and Nellore; also in the Bellary Collectorate; in the Kurnool district, and throughout the whole of South Canara. In the early months of the present year they prevailed, to some extent, in the neighbourhood of Pulicat, and in the North Arcot District.

Malarious fevers.

440. Small-pox has been unusually prevalent during the year in various parts of the country; most severely in the Malabar district, where it has caused great mortality.

Small-pox.

441. There does not appear to have been any marked scarcity of the necessaries of life in any part of the Presidency; and in most districts food is reported to have been plentiful and cheap.

Cost of necessaries of life.

442. The health of the population of the town of Madras has been satisfactory on the whole, and would have been remarkably so, but for the unfortunate prevalence of small-pox, which has been unusually fatal. Only twenty-five deaths are recorded from cholera during the whole official year.

Health of the population of the town of Madras.

443. These institutions continue to afford most valuable relief to the sick poor of the districts in which they have been established. There has been a marked increase in the number of sick treated, compared with the previous year, as shewn by the annexed figures :—

Working of Civil Dispensaries.

1866-67, total treated	240,314
1867-68, do. do.	278,276
Increase...	37,962

This number is a little in excess of the *decrease* reported last year, and shews that that decrease was due to temporary causes ; probably, in great part, to the widespread distress and sickness prevalent throughout the country having prostrated many of those who would otherwise have resorted to the Dispensaries for relief.

Financial condition of Civil Dispensaries.

444. The financial condition of the dispensaries cannot be considered generally satisfactory, and it is owing to this, no doubt, that the increase in the number of *in*-patients, treated during last year, is not at all in proportion to that of *out*-patients, being only 1,952, which is very far from counterbalancing the large *decrease* of 6,580, in the previous year. Great difficulty is experienced generally in collecting the subscriptions promised by Natives, who have evidently a special dislike to this form of contribution ; and no dispensary can, as a rule, be considered in a thoroughly satisfactory state, as regards income, until all its requirements are adequately provided for by the *interest of funded capital.* Very few of these institutions are as yet in this enviable position ; but the *principle* seems to be more and more recognized, and efforts are being made in several places to carry it into effect.

Funded capital of Civil Dispensaries.

445. The total funded capital, which stood at Rupees 3,42,203-10-6 on the 31st December 1866, was Rupees 5,87,103-15-2 at the close of last year.

New Dispensaries opened.

446. Eight new Dispensaries have been opened during the year, viz., at Adoni, Hospett, Kimedy (Estate Dispensary), Myaveram, Ongole (for out-patients only), Ramnad (Estate Dispensary), Shealy, and Chellumbrum.

The following table shews the number treated and died of In and Out-patients in Civil Hospitals and Dispensaries for the official year 1867-68 :—

	IN-PATIENTS.				OUT-PATIENTS.				TOTAL.			
	Treated.	Died.	Average daily sick.	Per-centage of deaths to treated.	Treated.	Died.	Average daily sick.	Per-centage of deaths to treated.	Treated.	Died.	Average daily sick.	Per-centage of deaths to treated.
Presidency ...	9,420	402	697	4·2	98,916	72	763	0·07	108,336	474	1,460	0·4
Northern ...	1,005	87	81	8·6	24,419	11	252	0·04	25,424	98	333	0·3
Southern ...	5,791	249	188	4·2	77,928	144	511	0·1	83,719	393	699	0·4
Mysore	916	128	64	13·9	15,634	23	116	0·1	16,550	151	180	0·9
Ceded Districts	894	37	41	4·1	31,434	17	405	0·05	32,328	54	446	0·1
Hyderabad Subsidiary Force	247	29	19	11·7	4,400	...	54	...	4,647	29	73	0·6
Nagpore Force	253	41	12	16·2	7,019	3	73	0·04	7,272	44	85	0·6
	18,526	973	1,102	5·2	2,59,750	270	2,174	0·1	278,276	1,243	3,276	0·4
								Total of 1866-67 ...	240,314			
								Increase in 1867-68...	37,962			

447. In the health of prisoners there has been a most striking improvement, the per-centage of deaths to strength having fallen from 11·6 (in 1866-67) to 3·9, and the per-centage of deaths to treated from 9·6 to 3·7.

Health of Prisoners in Jails.

448. A comparison of these death-rates with those of the Native Army, which though also considerably lower than last year, have not fallen in the same proportion, would seem to indicate that while the improvement is no doubt owing in part to the general healthiness of the year, it must also be greatly due to improved sanitary and conservancy arrangements, to a better dietary, and to there having been in most Jails little or no over-crowding.

Compared with that of the Native Army.

Native Army.	Per-centage of	
	Deaths to strength.	Deaths to treated.
1866-67	1·2	1·4
1867-68	0·7	0·9

The appended table shews the extent of sickness and mortality among Prisoners in Jails during the official year 1867-68 :—

		Average annual strength.	Average daily sick.	Treated.	Died.	Per-centage of		
						Treated to strength.	Deaths to strength.	Deaths to treated.
1866-67.	Presidency ...	2,752	107	2,633	202	95·6	17·3	7·6
	Southern ...	3,239	130	3,613	232	111·5	7·1	6·4
	Mysore ...	89	53	1,680	167	181·9	18·6	10·2
	Ceded Districts	1,587[6]	71	1,778	225	112·03	14·1	12·6
	Northern ...	1,553	77	2,395	341	154·2	21·9	14·2
		10,027	438	12,049	1,167	120·1	11·6	9·6
1867-68.	Presidency ...	2,855	82	2,266	64	79·3	2·2	2·8
	Northern ...	1,356	59	1,778	37	131·1	2·7	2·08
	Southern ...	4,660	110	4,204	161	90·2	3·4	3·8
	Mysore ...	1,025	10	1,488	88	145·1	8·5	5·9
	Ceded Districts	991	66	1,600	76	161·4	7·6	4·7
		10,887	327	11,336	426	104·1	3·9	3·7

Vaccination.

449. The total number of operations performed during the official year, from 1st April 1867 to 31st March 1868, was 2,74,582, shewing an increase of 58,198 over the same period of 1866-67.

Total number of Vaccination.

The largest number of operations has been in the North Arcot Vaccine Circle, and the smallest in the Cuddapah Circle.

The ratio per cent. of success for the total number operated on was 89·79.

Small-pox has been very generally prevalent throughout the entire Presidency during the year, but more so in the last quarter of the official (first quarter of present) year. The mortality from the disease throughout the Presidency is not known, but judging from the deaths in the Presidency town, it must have been very great. Small-pox appears to be now declining in the Presidency town.

The whole Vaccine Department has worked steadily and well during the year under review.

In the Appendix will be found a general statement of the work of the department.

EMIGRATION.

450. No emigration to any British Colony has been carried on during the past year, the Colonists not having sufficiently recovered from their financial difficulties, consequent on bad seasons and the numerous failures in England and elsewhere. Natal and the Mauritius, however, keep up their Agents, with the intention of shortly recommencing operations; and the latter Colony in February, despatched orders to resume them, but it transpired that the fever, which prevailed with such fatal effects there last year, had broken out again. It was, therefore, absolutely necessary to suspend emigration to that Colony, till its sanitary condition had improved.

With reference to this fever, which was at one time supposed to be closely allied to the Yellow Fever, a vessel named the "Hindoostan," returning from the Mauritius with time-expired Emigrants for Madras and Calcutta, arrived here in June 1867, and was placed in quarantine at Ennore, where the Madras passengers were landed and kept in camp, under medical inspection, for a few days, when no disease of consequence appearing among them, they were allowed to disperse.

The "Earl Russel," and "Allum Ghur," which arrived from the same Colony, were also placed in quarantine.

The entire number that returned from the Mauritius, during the year under review, was 243 souls in three ships, to which may be added 206 who engaged their passage to Pondicherry in a French ship, hoping probably (as was really the case) to escape thereby the quarantine anticipated at Madras.

Two vessels have brought forty-three invalid and other emigrants from Natal.

No recruiting has taken place under Act V of 1866, the Indian Labor Act. The Officer in charge of the Upper Godavery had the intention of recruiting 2,000 laborers at Madras, with a view to the rapid prosecution of the works: an Agent was sent to Madras to commence operations; but when he found that the Labor Act applied to the case, the project was abandoned.

451. Only three ships have left Pondicherry and Karikal during the year, carrying 884 souls from the first named settlement, and 542 from the last, making in all 1,426. Two vessels were bound to Guadaloupe, and one to Martinique.

French Emigration.

Trading interests were in too depressed a state at Réunion for her Colonists to call for further labor. They indeed at one time refused to receive the emigrants sent to them, and many left that Colony for the Mauritius.

No emigrants have returned from the French Antilles, but Réunion has sent back 482 to Pondicherry. The French ship "Marie," also brought to Pondicherry, from the Mauritius, 206 return emigrants, who, however, came over as private passengers, paying for themselves.

Serious complaints having been made by the British Consul at Réunion of the emigrants having been robbed of their advances before leaving Pondicherry and Karikal, an order was issued by the Madras Government, that no advance shall be made prior to embarkation. The French authorities at Pondicherry remonstrated against this order, as being likely entirely to check emigration to the French Colonies. This order was subsequently withdrawn. The Consular Agents have been instructed to take additional precautions with the assistance of the French emigration Agents for the control of the Emigration Maistries and the protection of the coolies.

Few complaints have been made against the French recruiters, licensed or unlicensed, during the year; but there is no doubt that the law is constantly evaded by persons being surreptitiously induced to leave their homes for the purpose of emigrating, without being registered by a Magistrate. It is very difficult to bring the offence home, and only two men have been convicted during the year, and sentenced to hard labor for three months. They were unlicensed, and had enticed from Madras a young woman, whom they robbed of her jewels on the road, and after leaving her in the depôt at Pondicherry, robbed her of the three months' advance she there received.

MUNICIPAL COMMISSIONS.

Madras.

452. The Municipal Commission has been extensively altered during the year. From the 1st November 1867, Act IX of 1867 of the Madras Government came into operation, by which the Town of Madras was divided into eight Districts, from each of which four persons are appointed Commissioners, the President of the Commission being also appointed by Government, but being a paid officer. The former arrangement was that there were three paid Commissioners, and none unpaid. The two paid Commissioners were provided with employment on the new Commission establishment, the President remaining unchanged. The effects of the change had, of course, been little felt before the close of the year, when the Municipal report is made up.

The receipts of the year were Rupees 5,50,259-10-11 or Rupees 62,708-11-3 in excess of the income of 1866. It was mainly derived from the house and land rate Rupees 2,50,668, tax on professions and callings Rupees 1,02,300, and on vehicles and animals Rupees 88,892-5-8. The other items being the balance from 1866, the Government grant for roads, &c., rents and fees, fines, value of land sold, &c., &c.

The expenditure was Rupees 4,33,192-4-2, and was divided over Police 1,41,704 Rupees, Management, &c., 83,511 Rupees, Scavenging 89,548 Rupees, Roads 61,809 Rupees, Lighting 11,045 Rupees, Constructions, Repairs, &c., 11,062 Rupees, the People's Park 8,035 Rupees, and Miscellaneous charges 26,474 Rupees.

A balance remained at the credit of the Municipality of Rupees 1,19,073 at the end of the year.

Municipalities in the Districts.

453. Of these there are forty-one in the principal towns in the Presidency, whose names are given below :—

Districts.	Towns.	Districts.	Towns.
Bellary ...	... Adoni.	Nellore ...	... Nellore.
	Bellary.	North Arcot	... Vellore.
Coimbatore	... Coimbatore.		Wallajahpett.
	Coonoor.	Salem ...	... Salem.
	Ootacamund.	South Arcot	... Cuddalore.
Cuddapah	... Cuddapah.	South Canara	Mangalore.
Ganjam ...	... Berhampore.	Tanjore ...	... Combaconum.
	Chicacole.		Mayaveram,
Godavery	... Cocanada.		Manargoody.
	Ellore.		Negapatam.
	Rajahmundry.		Tanjore.
Kistna ...	... Guntoor.	Tinnevelly	... Palamcottah.
	Masulipatam.		Tinnevelly.
Kurnool	... Cumbum.		Tuticorin.
	Kurnool.	Trichinopoly	Trichinopoly.
Madras ...	... Conjeveram.	Vizagapatam	Bimlipatam.
Madura	... Dindigul.		Vizagapatam.
	Madura.		Vizianagram.
Malabar	... Calicut.		
	Cannanore.		
	Cochin.		
	Paulghat.		
	Tellicherry.		

These are constituted under Madras Act X of 1865, and provide for the Police, Conservancy, and general improvement of the Towns. The past year is the first in which the Act has been so fully in operation as to afford any accurate idea of its working. As a rule, it has excited little active opposition. In two or three towns, where the exclusive religious element had a strong preponderance great opposition was made, and much angry feeling shewn, but the general tone of feeling was one of indifference. Where, however, the objects of the Act were intelligently explained, and the introduction was made carefully, the interest of the Native Commissioners was aroused, and the Act has been carried out with much heartiness. At present, even in the towns first mentioned, opposition has very much disappeared, and the objects of the Act appear to be more truly appreciated.

The receipts of the several Municipalities from the following sources, amounted to Rupees 9,45,146; the disbursements to Rupees 8,13,924; leaving a balance of Rupees 1,31,222.

Receipts.

Rate on houses, buildings, and lands	Rupees	1,71,623
Tax on Arts, Trades, and Professions	„	1,73,572
Tolls...	„	2,31,535
Tax on Vehicles and Animals	„	52,952
Registration of Carts	„	21,143
Miscellaneous	„	50,503
Government contribution	„	1,58,345
Balance from last year	„	85,473
	„	9,45,146

Disbursements.

New works and improvements	„	1,21,833
Repairs	„	1,21,187
Conservancy	„	1,75,881
Police...	„	2,43,026
Establishment	„	1,17,870
Miscellaneous	„	18,136
For purposes other than those specified in Section 25 of the Act as lighting the town, &c.	„	15,991
	„	8,13,924

A detailed account of the receipts, &c., of each Municipality appears in the Appendix.

The large amount raised by means of tolls has attracted serious notice, and measures are in contemplation for greatly reducing the amount thus raised. In the greater number of towns all the sources for raising money allowed by the Act are employed. The professional tax, as might be expected, seems the most obnoxious.

On the whole, however, the unpleasant feeling has been slight, and it is to be hoped that a few years will quite destroy it.

TELEGRAPH.

Extent of Line, and arrangement of Sub-divisions.

454. The Division extending from Hyderabad (Deccan) to Masulipatam, and from Bezwarah to Thanicar Point (Island of Ramiswaram), comprises 855 miles of line, and ten offices, arranged in Sub-divisions as follows :—

	Miles.
I.—Sub-division Hyderabad, through Secunderabad, to Bezwarah, including Bezwarah Office	166
II.—Sub-division Masulipatam to Ongole, including Masulipatam Office	130
III.—Sub-division Ongole to Madras, including Nellore Office...	181
IV.—Sub-division Madras to Negapatam, including Mount, Pondicherry, Cuddalore, and Karikal Offices	198
V.—Sub-division Negapatam to Thanicar Point, including Negapatam and Paumben Offices (about)	180

There is some difference between these distances and the distances given in the last Administration Report, but these are correct.

First Sub-division.

455. Parties have been employed on the line, Hyderabad to Bezwarah, during nine months of the year, and the line was finished only at the end of last month. The alignment has been greatly improved : iron standards have been erected in place of the wooden posts, a second wire for the Kurnool line has been suspended, on the Bezwarah line posts, for seventeen and a half miles (between Ambareepett and Hyderabad), and a third wire for the Nagpoor line for four and a half miles (between Secunderabad and Hyderabad), and the whole line has been fitted with brackets and insulators, caps, lightning spikes, and earth wires. This line is now in excellent working order, and should not give any trouble for the next five years.

Second and Third Sub-divisions.

456. The second and third Sub-divisions continue in good working order for one wire, but require extensive alterations to fit them for two wires. Estimates for doubling and insulating the lines in these Sub-divisions have been passed by the Director General, and the work will be commenced this month.

Fourth Sub-division.

457. The re-construction and insulation of the line in the fourth Sub-division was commenced in February last, and thirty miles (including the doubling of eleven miles, between Madras and the Mount,) was finished up to the end of last month. Four parties are now occupied on it, and it is hoped the whole will be finished by the end of July next. Some of the tools supplied for this line by the Store department were of a very inferior description. This has caused delay in the progress of the work, and expenses not provided for in the estimate.

458. In the fifth Sub-division nothing has been done beyond making petty repairs, and obtaining a trustworthy report on the state and requirements of the line. Mr. Assistant Superintendent Hervey, who held charge of the Sub-division up to 16th July last, submitted two or three estimates for the re-construction of the line; but they contained so little reliable information, that it was considered advisable to have the line inspected closely by a superior officer before making any arrangement for its re-construction. Mr. Officiating Superintendent T. Blissett (who held charge of the Division for two months, during Mr. Bailey's absence on leave,) made a thorough inspection in September last, and his report led to the consideration whether it would not be advisable to take a new line from Negapatam to Paumben, *viâ* Trichinopoly, Madura, and Ramnad, doing away with the coast line altogether, and orders were received to defer arrangements for the re-construction of the coast line till further orders. The proposed new route was inspected by the Superintendent in January and February last, and his report, dated 12th February, will, it is believed, decide the question. The route proposed is nearly 100 miles longer than the one now followed, but it is better adapted in every respect for a Telegraph line, and has two large stations (Trichinopoly and Madura), in which offices may be opened with profit to the department. The present line is in a weak state, but may be kept up till the beginning of next year with some slight repairs.

Fifth Sub-division.

459. There have been thirty-nine cases of total stoppage, and twelve of imperfect communication, a great improvement on the last year.

Interruptions.

460. No complaint of any consequence has been made, directly or indirectly, in the Division during the year, and the total of fines for errors, &c., in messages is less than for the eleven months ended 31st March 1867, being only 135, amounting to Rupees 127-14-0, against 176, amounting to Rupees 134-5-0.

Complaints.

461. A Telegraph class, under an experienced Telegraph Master, for the instruction of orphan boys from the different charitable institutions in Madras, was opened in the Male Orphan Asylum in December last, but it has not yet been long enough at work to furnish reliable results. The Principal of the Asylum takes great interest in the class, and as far as can be seen at present there is every prospect of its fulfilling the purpose for which it has been established.

Telegraph class in Madras.

OBSERVATORY.

462. For some time the question of the abolition or continuance of this institution has been under the consideration of the Home Government. It has now been settled that the Observatory shall be continued in its present condition long as the Astronomer, Mr. Pogson, retains his connexion with it.

Owing to the smallness of the staff of the institution, which the Astronomer has allowed to diminish as vacancies occurred, in the hope of obtaining European aid, which has not yet been sanctioned by the Secretary of State, the scientific results have accumulated, unpublished, to a considerable extent. Observing is now to be suspended with a view to the publication of the records of observations which extend over a period of six years.

Instruments.

463. The Meridian Circle is in perfect order. The two Equatoreals, the large new one by Troughton and Simms, erected in 1866, and the smaller one by Lerebours and Secretan, in use since 1850, are both in efficient observing condition. There are also six other available Telescopes, viz., a portable five-foot Equatoreal, by Dollond; a handy free Telescope of the same size, with ordinary altitude and azimuth motion, the object glass of which formerly belonged to the old transit instrument; a small but very fine universal Equatoreal, with two thirty-inch Telescopes; and two others, also by Dollond, of forty-two inches focal length, formerly much used for observations of occultations, phenomena of Jupiter's satellites, and similar casual wants.

Labours of the past year.

464. The Meridional observations have been carried on with more than usual activity, their number during the official year being 2,636, or 225 above the average; and realizing a total of 14,465 complete but unpublished observations, made with the new Transit Circle, between June 1st, 1862, and March 31st, 1868. The moon was observed on sixty-two nights; and sixty-five meridian positions of twenty-one of the minor planets were also obtained. The reductions are never long behind, rarely three months in arrears; so that simple arrangement of the Star Catalogues, and examination and rectification of the discrepancies are alone required to prepare for press.

Arranged by calendar years, and remembering that the records of 1862 were for seven months only, the synopsis of meridian circle observations awaiting publication is as follows:—

Year.	Minor Planets.	Mars.	Moon.	Stars.	Total.
1862	81	43	33	832	939
1863	62	...	62	2,077	2,201
1864	97	23	65	2,434	2,619
1865	69	...	58	2,396	2,523
1866	69	...	52	2,455	2,576
1867	69	33	66	2,552	2,720
Total ...	397	99	336	12,746	13,578

The subjects of observation with the Equatoreals have been, as in each successive year, such as were considered best suited to the geographical position of the Observatory, and least likely to be undertaken elsewhere. The variable

Star Atlas has been advanced as much as possible, and the usual search for new celestial objects has been maintained, though this year without success. Thirty-six observations of nine minor planets, and seven of the second comet of 1867, have also been taken, but time has not permitted their reduction. The planet Sylvia, discovered in May 1866, was re-found, and observed at her next opposition in September 1867, by means of the excellent elements and ephemeris calculated by Prof. C. A. F. Peters, Director of the Altona Observatory.

465. The scheme of telegraphic Time Signals, so long under consideration, having at last received definite sanction, and information having been afforded from England that the indent for the requisite machinery would be complied with, it is hoped that the regular discharge of the noon and 8 P. M. guns, at Fort St. George and St. Thomas's Mount, as well as the establishment of three public electrical clocks in Madras, will ere long be carried out.

Time Signals.

466. Improved rain gauges have been constructed, and five hundred glass measures have been had out from England; but these last proved to be so inaccurate, as to require the alteration of every rain gauge rim, to make it correspond to the glass supplied. The consequence has been the delay of the intended fresh issue of rain gauges throughout the Presidency

Revenue Board Rain Returns.

METEOROLOGICAL.

467. The establishment of sixteen Meteorological stations, fairly distributed over the Madras Presidency, including the Observatory as head-quarters, was mentioned in the last Report as having been duly sanctioned by Government, and then under preparation. Many difficulties necessarily attend the starting of any widespread scientific scheme, and as, in this instance, all the instruments required careful selection and comparison with the Madras standards, sheds had to be constructed and despatched, and many appliances, peculiar to tropical meteorology, had to be designed on the spot, much progress was not made in the first year. Eleven of the stations have, however, been provisionally started since November, and the instruments for the remaining seven are ready.

Meteorological Stations.

468. The excellent tables of Hourly Corrections, deduced by Mr. J. Glashier from the Records of the Royal Observatory at Greenwich, afford to English observers a ready means of computing their daily and monthly mean values of atmospheric pressure, temperature, hygrometry, &c., but as such corrections depend, for the most part, upon the sun's rising, setting, and altitude at the different hours of the day, and seasons of the year, they could not, under any circumstances, be employed for tropical regions. The Madras hourly observations taken during the twenty years, 1841 to 1860, had, therefore, to be completely discussed, and Tropical Hourly

Tables of Corrections.

Correction tables to be deduced, and this long and heavy work, in hand for many months past, has at last been completed. The tables are now passing through the press, and immediately that the observers employed have been sufficiently instructed as to their application, past and current results will be available for publication, and will, it is hoped, be found of material value, alike for sanitary, medical, and engineering enquiries.

Instruments used.

469. The main feature of the new Meteorological establishment will be, that all the results obtained at each station will be strictly comparable with each other, and with those of the Kew Observatory. Every barometer, thermometer, and anemometer in use will have been carefully examined and corrected, and nothing taken on trust or with the maker's corrections. A plan of the thermometer shed supplied to each station is appended hereto. The instruments supplied are by first class English makers, either Messrs. Negretti and Zambra, or Mr. Browning. Repairs of the numerous damages incurred on the passage out as well as the construction of a number of anemometers, ozone cages, and of the observing sheds issued, and the general packing arrangements, have been ably executed by Mr. F. Doderet, the Mathematical Instrument-maker of the Public Works Department, without whose valuable aid the scheme must have been greatly delayed.

Superintendence.

470. The observer at each station is under the immediate charge of the local Medical Officer. The general superintendence of the whole scheme rests with the Government Astronomer, to whom the reduced registers are to be transmitted half-monthly, and by whom the publication of the whole has to be effected.

Arrangement of Instruments.

471. The thermometers at the Madras Observatory have hitherto been recorded in a verandah facing the north, but too much shielded on all other sides by surrounding walls and buildings. Since January 1st, however, a fresh set has been employed, placed in an open shed, under precisely similar conditions to those at all the new up-country stations, the verandah readings still being continued, so as to shew any difference due to the change of position. The stations at which observations are now being regularly made are Bangalore, Bellary, Cochin, Coimbatore, Kurnool, Madras, Madura, Salem, Secunderabad, and Trichinopoly. The eight about to be started are Cannanore, Kamptee Masulipatam, Negapatam, Rangoon, Tinnevelly, Vizagapatam, and Wellington.

GOVERNMENT CENTRAL MUSEUM.

472. The total number of specimens added to the collection during the past year was 7,084, of which the following are the most important.

Birds.

473. Forty-six examples of the birds of North America, from the Smithsonian Institution, Washington; 582 specimens of the birds of the Neilgherries, collected by the Head Taxidermist.

These include about sixty species; about the same number of species are still wanting, and it is hoped that most of them will be obtained during the present year. Fifteen examples of the birds of Madras were contributed by Mr. J. M. Mitchell, and thirty-eight birds were purchased.

A set of casts of the bones of the Dodo was received from the Derby Museum, Liverpool.

474. Four snakes were contributed by lady Napier, ten by Major R. H. Beddome, and sixteen were obtained by the Taxidermist on the Neilgherries and on the slopes of the Hills—he also procured eighteen lizards of various kinds.

Reptiles.

475. One hundred and twelve fish were obtained by the Head Taxidermist from the Neilgherry streams, of which four were stuffed, and the remainder preserved in spirit.

Fish.

Two stuffed salmon were received from the Derby Museum, Liverpool, and twenty-four fish were purchased at Madras.

476. 3,193 shells, chiefly marine, were contributed by Mrs. Sherman; Major R. H. Beddome added 835 land and fresh water shells to the collection, and thirty-five were obtained on the Neilgherries by the Taxidermist.

Shells.

477. Mrs. Sherman also contributed 246 insects, and the Taxidermist obtained 652 on the Neilgherries.

Insects.

478. A very fine example of the Hyalonema Japonica was presented by Lieutenant-Colonel R. G. H. Grant of the Horse Artillery.

Sponges.

479. A skeleton of *Aquila fulvescens* has been set up, and skeletons of a Bustard, a Hare, and a Tiger are in hand. The skeleton of an Elephant has been delayed in consequence of the absence of the Head Taxidermist at the Neilgherries.

Skeletons.

480. 437 specimens have been added to the Herbarium, and fifty-four specimens of woods were also received from the Forest department.

Herbarium and specimens of Timber.

481. A cabinet containing 221 specimens was contributed by C. Fisher, Esq., and thirty-five examples of stone implements and rock specimens were contributed by R. B. Foote, Esq., of the Geological Survey.

Mineral and Rock specimens.

482. Thirteen gold coins, received from the Lucknow Treasury, were contributed by Government; and one gold, fourteen silver, four bronze, and one copper coin were received from Major W. Osborne, Political Agent, Sehore, in exchange for coins previously sent to him.

Coins.

483. The following additions have been made to the Library, viz., eighty-four volumes of Standard Works, 146 parts, or numbers, of scientific periodicals, and 128 volumes of Government Reports. 4,096 numbers of the London Patent Office papers have also been received.

Books.

484. Eighty-seven specimens of Madras shells to the Mysore Museum, Bangalore; 237 to the Indian Museum, Calcutta; 138 to F. Layard, Esq.; 155 specimens of birds to A. O. Hume, Esq., C. B., Commissioner of Customs, Agra. The Museum is still deeply indebted to this gentleman.

Specimens contributed to other Museums or exchanged with Naturalists.

485. 403 specimens of the fossils of the Cretaceous Rocks of South India, which had been lent to Dr. Oldham for examination, were returned by him in April last, duly named. The Museum is much indebted to Dr. Oldham and the Madras Members of the Survey for much valuable service most courteously rendered.

Fossils.

486. The number of visitors during the year was 109,340, of whom 27,736 signed their names in the Visitors' book.

Visitors.

487. The balance in hand at the beginning of the year was 1,656 Rupees, and the receipts Rupees 769, or in all Rupees 2,425. The expenditure was 1,170 Rupees.

Local Museum at Rajahmundry.

Some additions have been made by gifts, and the Committee are trying to furnish the Museum with specimens of manufactures.

The number of visitors was 11,237.

APPENDIX I.

A.

Statement of Acts passed by the Legislature of the Madras Presidency in the official year 1867-68, *and sanctioned as required by Law.*

Title of Act.	By whom proposed.	Object and character of Act.	Date on which sanctioned.
An Act to repeal Section 37 of Regulation XIV of 1816, relating to Government Pleaders.	By the Local Government.	To leave the Government to do as they think best in the appointment of their own Pleaders, without being shackled by any legal enactment on the subject.	9th May 1867.
An Act to provide for the examination and settlement of claims against His Highness Prince Azim Jah Bahadur.	Do.	To legalize the official acts of the Commissioner appointed by Her Majesty's Government to investigate the claims of such of the creditors of His Highness Prince Azim Jah Bahadur as elect to submit the same to that Officer, and abide by the award made thereupon, with reference to the allotment made by that Government of a sum of fifty lacs of Rupees towards the payment of such creditors.	1st June 1867.
An Act to repeal Madras Act I of 1863, *(to enable Subordinate Magistrates of the second class to take cognizance of offences under Section* 174 *of the Indian Penal Code.)*	Do.	To remove from the Statute Book a local enactment which has been superseded by Act VIII of 1866, *(an Act further to amend the Schedule annexed to the Code of Criminal Procedure.)*	10th June 1867.
An Act to repeal parts of certain Regulations and Acts relating to the offices of Hindoo and Mahomedan Law Officers.	Do.	To remove from the Statute Book all such enactments affecting the Madras Presidency as relate to the offices of Hindoo and Mahomedan Law Officers; these offices having been abolished by Act XI of 1864.	21st June 1867.

A.—*(Concluded.)*

Statement of Acts passed by the Legislature of the Madras Presidency, &c.

Title of Act.	By whom proposed.	Object and character of Act.	Date on which sanctioned.
An Act to amend Act XII of 1851, *(an Act for securing the Land Revenue of Madras.)*	By the Local Government and the Select Committee of the Council of the Governor of Fort Saint George for making Laws.	To give the Collector of Madras the power of distraining and selling moveable property, *by forcible entry*, for the recovery of arrears of revenue due upon land situated within the Town of Madras, as well as the power of selling the land itself in case of there being no other means of realizing the revenue.	27th June 1867.
An Act to consolidate and amend the Laws relating to the levy of Port dues and fees at Ports within the Presidency of Fort Saint George.	Do.	To embody in one single Act the provisions of the several enactments regulating Port dues and fees in the Madras Presidency, with such amendments as experience has shewn to be absolutely necessary or highly desirable.	12th July 1867.
An Act to incorporate the Police of the Town of Madras with the General Police of the Madras Presidency; to extend the jurisdiction of the Town Police Magistrates, and to amend and consolidate the provisions of Act XIII of 1856, *(for regulating the Police of the Towns of Calcutta, Madras, and Bombay,* and of Act XLVIII of 1860, *to amend Act XIII of* 1856.*)*	By the Honorable J. D. Mayne.	To amalgamate the Police of the Town of Madras with the General Police of the Presidency; to enable the Town Police Magistrates to deal summarily with all offences under the Indian Penal Code which are cognizable by a Magistrate of the District under the Criminal Procedure Code, with certain restrictions; and to consolidate the provisions of the existing law relating to the Town Police, with the necessary amendments.	24th July 1867.

An Act to amend the Law relating to the appointment of Municipal Commissioners for the Town of Madras, and the management of its Municipal affairs, and to make better provision for the Police, Conservancy, and Improvement of the said Town, and to enable the said Commissioners to levy taxes, tolls, and rates therein.	By the Honorable R. S. Ellis, C. B.	To effect changes in the Municipal Law in force at Madras, which the experience derived from the working of Madras Act IX of 1865, has shewn to be very necessary, as regards the constitution of the Municipal Corporation, as well as regards the classification, made in the Schedules annexed to that Act, of persons liable to the tax on trades and callings, and as to the conservancy of the town; and to provide for the levy of lighting and water rates, for the registration of births and deaths, and for the taking of a census; and also for the levy of additional taxes in the form of a Registration fee for every Retail Liquor Shop, and of a sea-toll on boats and rafts conveying goods exported or imported into Madras, to meet the expenditure on account of the works necessary for the supply of pure water to the Town, and for its complete drainage.	5th September 1867.

B.

Statement of Bills proposed or pending in the Legislature of the Madras Presidency in the official year 1867-68.

Title of Bill.	By whom proposed.	Object and character of Bill.	When introduced.	When rejected or withdrawn.	If pending, why, and in what state.
A Bill to declare more precisely the legal efficacy of Wills among Hindoos, and to legalize the alienation of self-acquired property of Hindoos in land.	The late Honorable V. Sadagopah Charlu; at present in charge of the Honorable G. Lutchmenarasu Chettigaru, C. S. I.	The object and character of this Bill are indicated by its title.	28th Feb. 1863.	...	This is a very long standing Bill. It is believed that its consideration was deferred, pending the result of a proposal from the Government of India as to the expediency of introducing a Bill into the imperial Legislature "to extend the testamentary portion of the Indian Succession Act to Hindus, Mahomedans, and Budhists; but nothing seems to have been done in this matter as yet."
A Bill to make provision for improving the sanitary condition of places in the immediate vicinity of Railway stations.	The Honorable H. D. Phillips.	Do.	9th Aug. 1865.	This Bill has been withdrawn since the close of the official year, special legislation on the subject having been considered unnecessary.	......

A Bill to enable the Government to prescribe Rules for regulating the navigation of rivers, canals, and other inland waters, and for the management of ferries, and for the levying of tolls and license fees.	Do.	The main object of this Bill is to regulate the use of the canals in the Godavery and Kistna Districts, which, it is believed, are managed in a very loose way.	16th Dec. 1865.	...	Since the close of the official year, a new Select Committee has been appointed to report on the Bill, the majority of the Members of the Committee originally appointed having resigned their seats in Council.
A Bill to enable land-holders in certain localities to levy tolls upon roads and bridges constructed by them at their own expense, and also on roads constructed at the expense of the State, the repair and maintenance of which may be undertaken by such land-holders.	The Honorable A. J. Arbuthnot.	This Bill is designed to enable the planters in Wynaad (Malabar) and other planting Districts, who may join in constructing and maintaining cross-roads for the purpose of connecting their estates with the main lines of road constructed by the State, to reimburse themselves by levying tolls on such roads.	15th June 1867.	...	The Bill has been passed by the Local Council since the close of the official year.

C.

Statement of Draft Bills submitted by the Madras Government for the consideration of the Legislature of India, during the official year 1867-68.

Title of Bill.	By whom proposed.	Object and character of Act.	Fate, result, or present position of the proposed Bill.
A Bill to repeal Act No. XIX of 1866, in the places to which the Madras Salt Excise Act may be made applicable.	By the Madras Government.	The object of this Bill is sufficiently indicated by its title. The Local Legislature cannot repeal Act XIX of 1866, as it was passed by the Governor General's Council after the coming into operation of the Indian Council's Act of 1861.	Passed as Act No. XXXV of 1867, having received the assent of the Governor General on the 1st August 1867.
A Bill to provide for European Vagrancy.	Do.	To secure immediate relief to European Vagrants, to afford them every facility for obtaining employment in the country, and to provide for their ultimate removal from India, if it is found that no fitting occupation is procurable here.	Under the consideration of the Government of India in the Legislative Department.

APPENDIX II.

A.

Statement shewing the number of Suits instituted and disposed of by the High Court of Judicature at Madras in its Ordinary Original Jurisdiction, during the year 1867.

Suits		Disposed of on merits		Dismissed for default.	Withdrawn		Adjusted.		Otherwise disposed of.	Depending on 31st December 1867.	Cases remaining from the late Supreme Court disposed of.
Remaining from 1866.	Instituted in 1867.	At settlement of issues.	On final disposal.		With leave to bring fresh suit.	Absolutely.	Before hearing.	At hearing.			
84	567	219	150	7	5	103	...	...	9	158	6

B.

GENERAL ABSTRACT STATEMENT.

CIVIL.

No. 1.—*Panchayets.*

	1863.	1864.	1865.	1866.	1867.
Depending 1st January	58	47	71	101	159
Instituted during the year	122	348	582	588	350
Total...	180	395	653	689	509
Decided on merits	59	67	400	407	284
Dismissed on default...	22	15	33	56	32
Adjusted or withdrawn.	33	111	77	60	40
Otherwise disposed of...	19	131	42	7	6
Total...	133	324	552	530	362
Depending 31st December...	47	71	101	159	147

No. 2.—Village Moonsiffs.

	1863.	1864.	1865.	1866.	1867.
Depending 1st Jan.	15,341	14,503	11,885	11,941	11,615
Instituted during the year	42,910	38,181	40,222	39,806	39,168
Total ...	58,251	52,684	52,107	51,747	50,783
Decided on merits ...	16,946	15,359	18,29 0	21,012	21,226
Dismissed on default	8,213	8,153	6,919	7,208	6,900
Adjusted or with-drawn	15,399	15,685	13,671	10,962	10,432
Otherwise disposed of	3,190	1,602	1,286	950	935
Total ...	43,748	40,799	40,166	40,132	39,493
Depending 31st Dec.	14,503	11,885	11,941	11,615	11,290

No. 3.—District Moonsiffs.

	1863.	1864.	1865.	1866.	1867.
Depending 1st Jan.	1,09,345	73,173	47,062	47,199	48,362
Instituted during the year	75,823	99,988	1,11,433	1,12,193	1,09,409
Remanded	447	376	1,908	1,849	1,958
Received by transfer	18,315	6,590	3,185	5,699	2,025
Total ...	2,03,930	1,80,127	1,63,588	1,66,940	1,61,754
Decided on merits ...	61,555	73,336	74,264	76,564	77,014
Dismissed on default	13,620	12,548	6,677	5,701	7,101
Adjusted or with-drawn	33,799	34,107	29,669	28,499	26,223
Otherwise disposed of	21,783	13,074	5,779	7,814	4,902
Total ...	1,30,757	1,33,065	1,16,389	1,18,578	1,15,240
Depending 31st Dec.	73,173	47,062	47,199	48,362	46,514

No. 4.—Cantonment Small Cause Courts.

	1863.	1864.	1865.	1866.	1867.
Depending 1st January	...	...	...	97	65
Instituted during the year ...	...	...	331	1,774	1,805
Remanded	...	...	...	...	...
Receivod by transfer	...	...	...	...	...
Total ...	...	...	331	1,871	1,870
Decided on merits	...	...	183	1,170	1,169
Dismissed on default	...	...	14	128	236
Adjusted or withdrawn	...	...	36	184	410
Otherwise disposed of	...	...	1	324	...
Total ...	...	...	234	1,806	1,815
Depending 31st December ...	...	...	97	65	55

No. 5.—Principal Sudder Ameens.

	1863.		1864.		1865.		1866.		1867.	
	Original.	Appeal.	Original.	Appeal.	Original.	Appeal.	Original.	Appeal.	Original.	Appeal.
Depending 1st January	2,117	1,047	1,203	1,329	1,365	1,841	1,427	1,529	1,246	1,615
Instituted during the year ...	1,125	16	2,439	50	4,034	22	2,793	...	2,757	2
Remanded	17	20	29	21	20	55	39	44	71	48
Received by transfer	79	3,404	162	3,503	59	2,627	124	3,199	561	2,918
Total...	3,338	4,487	3,833	4,903	5,478	4,545	4,383	4,772	4,635	4,583
Decreed for Plaintiff or Appellant	747	982	1,142	1,000	2,130	1,010	1,797	1,114	2,101	1,087
Decreed for Defendant or Respondent	307	1,758	338	1,723	514	1,615	520	1,607	484	1,709
Remanded	...	83	...	80	...	84	...	131	...	165
Dismissed on default	288	151	186	115	197	121	88	97	80	104
Adjusted or withdrawn	457	119	652	86	1,063	81	680	112	570	124
Otherwise disposed of...	336	65	150	58	147	105	52	96	95	71
Total...	2,135	3,158	2,468	3,062	4,051	3,016	3,137	3,157	3,330	3,260
Depending 31st December ...	1,203	1,329	1,365	1,841	1,427	1,529	1,246	1,615	1,305	1,323

No. 6.—Judges of the Court of Small Causes.

	1863.	1864.	1865.	1866.	1867.
	Original.	Original.	Original.	Original.	Original.
Depending 1st January	1,439	706	671	683	367
Instituted during the year	10,033	8,251	10,205	9,934	9,064
Received by transfer	...	...	...	...	...
Total...	11,472	8,957	10,876	10,617	9,431
Decreed for Plaintiff or Appellant ...	6,103	4,967	6,158	5,841	5,559
Decreed for Defendant or Respondent.	894	573	937	850	632
Dismissed on default	1,005	539	512	518	431
Adjusted or withdrawn...	2,764	2,207	2,586	3,041	2,442
Otherwise disposed of	...	...	...	...	...
Total...	10,766	8,286	10,193	10,250	9,064
Depending 31st December	706	671	683	367	367

No. 7.—Assistant Agents.

	1863.		1864.		1865.		1866.		1867.	
	Original.	Appeal.	Original.	Appeal.	Original.	Appeal.	Original.	Appeal.	Original.	Appeal.
Depending 1st January ...	391	115	1	...	5	...	10	...	8	...
Instituted during the year...	286	24	32	...	12	...	36	...	43	...
Remanded	8	...	...	...	...	...	1	...	...	...
Received by transfer	18	19	2	...	19	...	1	...	...	...
Total...	703	158	35	...	36	...	48	...	51	...
Decreed for Plaintiff or Appellant	287	18	19	...	9	...	21	...	26	...
Decreed for Defendant or Respondent	22	72	4	...	2	...	6	...	2	...
Remanded	...	5	...	...	...	...	...	...	...	...
Dismissed on default	34	4	...	...	12	...	5	...	...	...
Adjusted or withdrawn ...	46	1	6	...	2	...	8	...	11	...
Otherwise disposed of	313	58	1	...	1	...	...	...	3	...
Total...	702	158	30	...	26	...	40	...	42	...
Depending 31st December ...	1	...	5	...	10	...	8	...	9	...

No. 8.—Judges of Small Causes with the powers of a Principal Sudder Ameen.

	1863.		1864.		1865.		1866.		1867.	
	Original.	Appeal.	Original.	Appeal.	Original.	Appeal.	Original.	Appeal.	Original.	Appeal.
Depending 1st January ...	...	...	...	...	...	...	146	116	193	114
Instituted during the year ...	...	...	...	...	348	...	312	27	266	27
Remanded	...	...	...	...	5	2	6	3	3	2
Received by transfer	...	...	...	...	1	474	35	276	51	558
Total...	...	...	...	...	354	476	499	422	513	701
Decreed for Plaintiff or Appellant	...	...	...	...	103	86	193	69	182	97
Decreed for Defendant or Respondent	...	...	...	...	47	153	59	180	84	258
Remanded	...	...	...	...	...	17	...	6	...	13
Dismissed on default	...	...	...	...	7	32	4	17	3	77
Adjusted or withdrawn ...	...	...	...	...	46	16	44	13	101	18
Otherwise disposed of	...	...	...	...	5	56	6	23	3	11
Total...	...	...	...	...	208	360	306	308	373	474
Depending 31st December ...	...	...	...	...	146	116	193	114	140	227

No. 9.—Civil Judges.

	1863.		1864.		1865.		1866.		1867.	
	Original.	Appeal.	Original.	Appeal.	Original.	Appeal.	Original.	Appeal.	Original.	Appeal.
Depending 1st January	434	3,989	503	3,755	582	3,782	717	4,918	829	5,377
Instituted during the year ...	455	5,677	532	6,053	962	6,263	1,064	6,217	865	5,123
Remanded	15	16	2	13	15	49	24	35	22	50
Received by transfer	8,127	320	2,469	62	1,777	159	1,604	111	651	73
Total ...	9,031	10,002	3,506	9,883	3,336	10,253	3,409	11,281	2,367	10,623
Decreed for Plaintiff or Appellant	147	812	170	711	446	670	534	839	611	827
Decreed for Defendant or Respondent	88	1,333	120	1,491	135	1,206	154	1,156	157	1,754
Remanded	...	118	...	112	...	80	...	161	...	216
Dismissed on default	30	132	40	128	35	129	20	119	33	101
Adjusted or withdrawn	110	153	143	161	198	122	269	142	247	181
Otherwise disposed of	8,153	3,699	2,451	3,498	1,805	3,128	1,603	3,487	753	3,494
Total ...	8,528	6,247	2,924	6,101	2,619	5,335	2,580	5,904	1,801	6,573
Depending 31st December ...	503	3,755	582	3,782	717	4,918	829	5,377	566	4,050

No. 10.—*High Court.*

	1863.		1864.		1865.		1866.		1867.	
	Regular.	Special.	Regular.	Special.	Regular.	Special.	Regular.	Special.	Regular.	Special.
Depending 1st January	76	552	63	252	48	156	48	273	31	179
Admitted during the year...	76	526	83	487	87	661	94	566	115	611
Total...	152	1,078	146	739	135	817	142	839	146	790
Dismissed on default...	6	57	5	30	...	22	...	23	2	10
Adjusted or withdrawn.	2	4	2	5	...	3	...	5	1	4
Confirmed	55	690	68	498	52	456	68	530	50	458
Amended	6	11	7	9	5	18	7	10	8	15
Reversed	11	49	10	31	19	28	20	48	13	18
Remanded	9	15	4	8	8	13	14	18	4	11
Otherwise disposed of...	...	...	2	2	3	4	2	26	1	...
Total...	89	826	98	583	87	544	111	660	79	516
Depending 31st Dec. ...	63	252	48	156	48	273	31	179	67	274

No. 11.—*Aggregate of Original Jurisdiction.*

	1863.	1864.	1865.	1866.	1867.
Depending 1st January	1,29,125	90,136	61,641	62,321	62,844
Instituted during the year...	1,57,780	1,59,401	1,68,129	1,68,500	1,63,727
Remanded or re-admitted (not including suits received by transfer)	...	...	1,948	1,919	2,054
Total...	2,86,905	2,49,537	2,31,718	2,32,740	2,28,625
Decided on merits ...	87,155	96,095	1,03,618	1,09,128	1,09,531
Dismissed on default...	23,212	21,481	14,406	13,728	14,816
Adjusted or withdrawn.	52,608	52,911	47,348	43,747	40,476
Otherwise disposed of (not including suits merely transferred)	33,794	17,409	4,025	3,293	3,409
Depending 31st Dec...	90,136	61,641	62,321	62,844	60,393
Decided by European Judges...	19,679	11,536	11,740	13,370	12,412
Do. by Native Judges	1,76,957	1,76,036	1,57,105	1,55,996	1,55,458
Do. by Panchayets...	133	324	552	530	362
Total decided...	1,96,769	1,87,896	1,69,397	1,69,896	1,68,232

No. 12.—Aggregate of Appellate Jurisdiction.

	APPEALS FROM																							
	CIVIL JUDGES.										ASSISTANT AGENTS.										PRINCIPAL SUDDER AMEENS.			
	1863.		1864.		1865.		1866.		1867.		1863.		1864.		1865.		1866.		1867.		1863.		1864.	
	Regular.	Special.	Regular.	Special.	Regular.	Special.	Regular.	Special.	Regular.	Special.	Regular.	Special.	Regular.	Special.	Regular.	Special.	Regular.	Special.	Regular.	Special.	Regular.	Special.	Regular.	Special.
Suits appealable	213	2,145	219	2,202	280	1,876	237	1,995	317	2,581	182	62	17	19	...	...	...	...	...	...	755	159	528	250
Appealed	76	289	83	301	87	378	94	248	115	325	101	...	...	...	...	...	...	...	...	...	315	237	244	186
Appeals depending on the 1st January	76	337	63	142	48	80	48	164	31	73	95	31	28	3	...	...	...	...	...	...	159	184	292	107
Total ...	152	626	146	443	135	458	142	412	146	398	196	31	28	3	...	...	...	...	...	...	474	421	536	293
Affirmed	55	409	68	312	52	236	68	276	50	232	43	23	9	2	...	...	...	...	...	...	103	258	167	184
Modified	6	7	7	6	5	8	7	4	8	8	6	...	3	...	...	...	...	...	...	...	18	4	38	3
Reversed	11	28	10	18	19	20	20	34	13	7	13	...	7	1	...	...	...	...	...	...	33	21	45	12
Remanded	9	11	4	5	8	10	14	11	4	8	2	1	7	...	...	...	...	...	...	...	13	3	22	3
Dismissed on default	6	25	5	16	...	13	...	7	2	6	3	4	1	...	...	...	...	...	...	...	2	28	12	14
Adjusted or withdrawn...	2	4	2	4	...	3	...	2	1	3	8	...	...	...	...	...	...	...	...	...	4	...	15	1
Otherwise disposed of	...	...	2	2	3	4	2	5	1	...	93	...	1	...	...	...	...	...	...	...	4	...	3	...
Total ...	89	484	98	363	87	294	111	339	79	264	168	28	28	3	...	...	...	...	...	...	182	314	302	217
Depending 31st December	63	142	48	80	48	164	31	73	67	184	28	3	...	...	...	...	...	...	...	...	292	107	234	76

No. 12.—Aggregate of Appellate Jurisdiction.—(Concluded.)

	APPEALS FROM																									
	PRINCIPAL SUDDER AMEENS.						COLLECTORS.					SUDDER AMEENS.					DISTRICT MOONSIFFS.									
	1865.		1866.		1867.		1863	1864	1865	1866	1867	1863	1864	1865	1866	1867	1863.	1864.	1865.	1866.	1867.
	Regular.	Special.	Regular.	Special.	Regular.	Special.	Regular.	Regular.	Regular.	Regular.	Regular.	Regular.	Regular.	Regular.	Regular.	Regular.	Regular.	Regular.	Regular.	Regular.	Regular.
Suits appealable	713	324	780	2,970	1,106	3,151	214	186	179	171	253	14	2	6	...	...	27,419	24,099	21,249	21,440	23,343
Appealed	231	283	317	318	381	286	141	53	117	65	165	11	1	...	...	...	8,928	9,404	9,303	9,530	8,255
Appeals depending on the 1st January...	234	76	210	109	325	106	59	134	28	79	53	537	127	27	1	...	4,301	4,503	5,334	6,273	6,728
Total ...	465	359	527	427	706	392	200	187	145	144	218	548	128	27	1	...	13,229	13,907	14,637	15,803	14,983
Affirmed	155	220	108	254	233	226	82	106	29	21	47	173	59	10	...	...	2,746	2,793	2,684	2,904	3,346
Modified	42	10	22	6	53	7	4	6	7	1	8	36	7	1	...	...	405	508	572	523	598
Reversed	27	8	31	14	66	11	16	13	25	29	37	63	19	...	...	...	1,279	1,145	1,188	1,326	1,349
Remanded	12	3	17	7	22	3	...	9	...	39	15	15	2	...	...	...	177	152	169	242	357
Dismissed on default	11	9	10	16	5	4	1	11	...	...	2	13	5	13	1	...	272	214	258	222	275
Adjusted or withdrawn...	8	...	12	3	21	1	5	12	2	1	6	6	9	2	...	...	245	208	207	254	296
Otherwise disposed of	...	...	2	21	...	...	8	2	3	...	19	115	...	...	...	...	3,602	3,553	3,286	3,604	3,557
Total ...	255	250	202	321	400	252	66	159	66	91	129	421	101	26	1	...	8,726	8,573	8,364	9,075	9,778
Depending 31st December	210	109	325	106	306	140	134	28	79	53	89	127	27	1	...	...	4,503	5,334	6,273	6,728	5,205

No. 13.—*Description of Original Suits instituted.*

	1863.	1864.	1865.	1866.	1867.
Connected with Land Revenue...	2,852	3,420	5,646	5,775	5,580
Otherwise connected with land.	10,442	12,111	13,395	13,583	10,298
For houses or other fixed property	3,845	4,484	5,192	5,530	4,169
Connected with debts and wages, &c.	1,11,837	1,27,579	1,41,156	1,41,070	1,41,879
Connected with caste, religion, &c.	421	420	458	416	380
Connected with Indigo, Sugar, Silk, &c.	1,357	1,757	2,282	2,126	1,421
Total ...	1,30,754	1,49,771	1,68,129	1,68,500	1,63,727

No. 14.—*Result of Original Suits.*

In favor of Plaintiffs.	In favor of Defendants.
89,811	19,720

No. 15.—*Average duration of Suits.*

	1863.			1864.			1865.			1866.			1867.		
	Years.	Months.	Days.	Years.	Months.	Days.	Years.	Months.	Days.	Years.	Months.	Days.	Years.	Months.	Days.
High Court, Appellate side ...	...	8	1	...	6	10	...	4	......	...	3	1	...	3	23
Civil Judges	1	3	5	1	2	23	1	2	27	1	1	27	1	1	13
Assistant Agents	...	9	13	...	...	23	...	9	18	2	7	20	...	6	7
Judges of the Small Cause Courts	...	...	19	...	...	23	...	...	22	...	...	20	...	...	20
Do. with the powers of a Principal Sudder Ameen ...	...	...	...	...	...	...	...	9	10	...	4	19	...	6	27
Principal Sudder Ameens	...	9	25	...	10	2	1	4	7	1	1	26	...	9	11
Cantonment Small Cause Courts	...	...	...	...	...	...	...	...	$12\frac{1}{4}$	...	...	11	...	...	14
District Moonsiffs	...	10	28	...	10	17	...	9	29	1	...	23	1	1	27

No. 16.—*Total value of Suits depending.*

	1863.	1864.	1865.	1866.	1867.
Before the High Court Appellate side...	24,61,493	15,19,437	14,01,125	18,37,659	24,53,329
Do. other Courts, Original...	1,20,18,282	1,27,77,335	1,50,22,438	1,74,84,076	1,69,96,355
Do. do. Appeal	14,76,546	13,64,234	15,08,287	20,19,733	17,50,868
Total ...	1,59,56,321	1,56,61,006	1,79,31,850	2,13,41,468	2,12,00,552

C.

POLICE ESTABLISHMENT AND COST FOR THE YEAR 1867-68.

Ranges.	DISTRICTS.	Area.	Population.	Sanctioned Strength.	Strength of Force on 31st March 1867.	Police Establishments. Supervising Staff.	Superintendents.	Assistant Superintendents.	Inspectors.	Constables General Duty.	Salt Guard.	Jail Guard.
				No.	No.	No	No	No.	No.	No.	No.	No.
	Inspr. Genl., & Asst. Inspr. Genl. of Police including Establishment	...	...	63	42	2	...	...	38	25	...	...
	Town of Madras including Establishment	27	460,000	1,135	1,200	3	...	...	20	*1,039	...	67
Northern Range.	Dy. Inspector Genl. of Police.	...	...	...	...	1	...	...	...	...	...	...
	Ganjam	7,757	1,136,926	1,577	1,560	...	1	2	23	1,286	220	38
	Vizagapatam ...	9,935	1,415,652	1,479	1,542	...	1	2	29	†1,295	100	60
	Jeypore	9,000	300,000	424	310	...	1	...	6	375	...	..
	Godavery ...	7,534	1,366,831	1,472	1,379	...	1	1	26	1,191	95	65
	Kistua	8,353	1,194,421	1,416	1,465	...	1	1	24	1,222	138	38
	Total...	42,579	5,413,830	6,368	6,256	1	5	6	108	5,369	553	201
Central Range.	Dy. Inspector Genl. of Police.	...	...	...	...	1	...	...	...	...	...	...
	Nellore	8,341	999,254	1,426	1,368	...	1	1	25	1,131	210	36
	Kurnool	7,470	725,768	1,000	1,098	...	1	1	17	793	...	27
	Bellary	11,496	1,234,674	1,384	1,584	...	1	2	31	1,298	...	68
	Cuddapah ...	9,177	1,050,104	1,230	1,243	...	1	2	20	1,053	...	30
	North Arcot ...	7,526	1,654,557	1,372	1,338	...	1	1	27	1,258	...	133
	Madras District.	3,100	675,390	990	962	...	1	...	17	621	299	48
	Total...	47,110	6,339,747	7,402	7,588	1	6	7	137	6,154	509	342
Southern Range.	Dy. Inspector Genl. of Police.	...	...	...	...	1	...	...	...	...	...	...
	South Arcot ...	4,765	1,128,430	1,259	1,211	...	1	1	21	945	145	58
	Tanjore	3,736	1,652,170	1,491	1,483	...	1	1	20	1,210	178	51
	Trichinopoly ...	3,097	939,400	815	774	...	1	...	14	754	...	24
	Madura	8,790	1,856,406	1,366	1,353	...	1	2	25	1,141	67	79
	Tinnevelly ...	5,144	1,670,262	1,078	1,028	...	1	1	21	913	51	30
	Total...	25,532	7,246,668	6,009	5,849	1	5	5	101	4,963	441	242
Western Range.	Dy. Inspector Genl. of Police.	...	...	...	...	1	...	...	...	...	...	...
	Salem	7,617	1,493,221	1,182	1,248	...	1	1	23	1,043	...	58
	Coimbatore ...	8,417	1,215,920	1,321	1,179	...	1	1	25	898	...	312
	South Malabar. } North Malabar. }	6,259	1,709,081	{ 864	895	...	1	1	20	790	...	45
				{ 579	560	...	1	...	12	481	...	23
	South Canara...	4,205	788,042	867	740	...	1	..	14	577	107	25
	Total...	26,498	5,206,264	4,813	4,622	1	5	3	94	3,789	107	463
	Grand Total...	141,746	24,666,509	25,790	25,557	9	21	21	498	21,339	1,610	1,315

* Includes Marine Police 259 strong.

† Includes 50 Constables employed with the Trigonometrical Survey Party.

C.—(*Continued.*)

Ranges.	DISTRICTS.	POLICE ESTABLISHMENT AND COST FOR THE YEAR 1867-68.								
		Land Custom Guard.	Total strength.	Pay and Allowances.	Clothing and Accoutrements.	Rent, Stationery, and other charges.	Total.	Village Police.		Grand Total.
		No.	No.	Rs.	Rs.	Rs.	Rs.	No.	Rs.	Rs.
	Inspr. Genl., & Asst. Inspr. Genl. of Police including Establishment	...	65	63,259	462	3,674	67,395	...	...	67,395
	Town of Madras including Establishment	...	1,129	2,05,919	12,721	13,904	2,32,544	...	...	2,32,544
Northern Range.	Dy. Inspector Genl. of Police.	...	1	15,025	..	533	15,558	..	...	15,558
	Ganjam	...	1,570	1,93,927	17,673	9,582	2,21,182	56	2,758	2,23,940
	Vizagapatam ..	...	1,487	1,85,166	17,123	5,625	2,07,914	48	1,144	2,09,058
	Jeypore ..	...	382	48,198	4,401	1,243	53,842	171	4,106	57,948
	Godavery ...	13	1,392	1,66,396	18,704	4,277	1,89,377	36	858	1,90,235
	Kistna ..	...	1,424	1,67,484	16,089	3,699	1,87,272	20	723	1,87,995
	Total...	13	6,256	7,76,196	73,990	24,959	8,75,145	331	9,589	8,84,734
Central Range.	Dy. Inspector Genl. of Police.	...	1	13,636	...	890	14,026	...	...	14,026
	Nellore	...	1,404	1,64,253	17,209	3,658	1,85,120	96	3,495	1,88,615
	Kurnool ...	...	839	1,33,113	13,638	2,228	1,48,979	12	329	1,49,308
	Bellary ...	...	1,400	1,83,529	20,254	4,442	2,08,225	...	...	2,08,225
	Cuddapah ...	...	1,106	1,57,909	16,008	4,089	1,78,006	...	...	1,78,006
	North Arcot ...	...	1,420	1,65,208	18,553	4,088	1,87,849	...	...	1,87,849
	Madras District.	...	986	1,19,034	13,107	2,496	1,34,637	...	...	1,34,637
	Total...	...	7,156	9,36,682	98,769	21,891	10,56,842	108	3,824	10,60,666
Southern Range.	Dy. Inspector Genl. of Police.	...	1	16,951	...	76	17,027	...	...	17,027
	South Arcot ...	83	1,254	1,52,094	17,713	3,564	1,73,371	2,524	21,795	1,95,166
	Tanjore ...	30	1,491	1,74,132	21,885	4,799	2,00,816	...	...	2,00,816
	Trichinopoly ...	...	793	91,609	9,079	3,147	1,03,835	...	...	1,03,835
	Madura ...	...	1,315	1,65,570	16,348	3,112	1,85,030	...	...	1,85,030
	Tinnevelly ...	...	1,017	1,39,568	14,203	3,898	1,57,669	...	...	1,57,669
	Total...	113	5,871	7,39,924	79,228	18,596	8,37,748	2,524	21,795	8,59,543
Western Range.	Dy. Inspector Genl. of Police.	...	1	19,516	...	468	19,984	...	...	19,984
	Salem ...	...	1,126	1,55,724	13,267	5,476	1,74,467	...	...	1,74,467
	Coimbatore ...	...	1,237	1,61,502	15,052	7,386	1,83,940	14	266	1,84,206
	South Malabar.	...	857	1,20,613	11,707	4,749	1,37,069	...	...	1,37,069
	North Malabar.	28	545	69,444	7,934	1,628	79,006	8	453	79,459
	South Canara...	...	724	87,790	10,550	2,169	1,00,509	...	...	1,00,509
	Total...	28	4,490	6,14,589	58,510	21,876	6,94,975	22	719	6,95,694
	Grand Total...	154	24,967	33,36,569	3,23,680	1,04,400	37,64,649	2,985	35,927	38,00,576

C.—*(Continued.)*

Ranges.	DISTRICTS.	STRENGTH OF FORCE, ESTABLISHMENTS, AND CASUALTIES DURING THE OFFICIAL YEAR 1867-68.								
		Sanctioned strength of Force.	Actual strength of Force on the 31st March 1867.	Actual strength of Force on the 31st March 1868.	CASUALTIES DURING THE YEAR.					
					Dismissed and discharged.	Resigned, deserted, and transferred.	Died.	Total.	Per-centage.	Enlisted during the year.
1	2	3	4	5	6	7	8	9	10	11
	Madras Town...	1,135	1,200	1,090	40	27	6	73	7·0	119
Northern Range.	Ganjam	1,577	1,507	1,567	133	74	15	222	14·1	282
	Vizagapatam...	1,479	1,521	1,484	41	131	24	196	13·2	167
	Jeypore	424	309	381	23	50	4	77	20·2	143
	Godavery ...	1,472	1,370	1,390	53	72	21	146	10·5	168
	Kistna	1,416	1,466	1,422	100	30	35	165	11·6	121
	Total...	6,368	6,173	6,244	350	357	99	806	12·9	881
Central Range.	Nellore	1,426	1,355	1,402	75	85	9	169	12·0	220
	Kurnool... ...	1,000	1,069	837	341	112	9	462	53·4	251
	Bellary	1,384	1,476	1,397	116	84	10	210	15·0	131
	Cuddapah ...	1,230	1,231	1,103	134	76	13	223	20·2	94
	North Arcot ...	1,372	1,325	1,418	72	108	19	199	14·0	279
	Madras	990	957	955	71	65	8	144	16·0	155
	Total...	7,402	7,413	7,112	809	530	68	1,407	19·7	1,130
Southern Range.	South Arcot ...	1,259	1,176	1,224	86	50	9	145	11·8	192
	Tanjore	1,491	1,447	1,459	101	65	15	181	12·4	195
	Trichinopoly ...	815	762	792	57	32	11	100	12·6	130
	Madura	1,366	1,347	1,312	105	79	18	202	14·9	166
	Tinnevelly ...	1,078	1,017	1,009	86	111	15	212	20·7	204
	Total...	6,009	5,749	5,796	435	337	68	840	14·4	887
Western Range.	Salem	1,182	1,222	1,124	75	91	11	177	15·7	79
	Coimbatore ...	1,321	1,165	1,235	90	139	13	242	19·5	312
	South Malabar	864	893	855	37	24	18	79	9·2	46
	North Malabar	579	543	544	33	35	16	84	15·4	85
	South Canara	867	710	706	53	92	10	155	21·9	118
	Total...	4,813	4,533	4,464	288	381	68	737	16·5	640
	Grand Total..	25,727	25,068	24,706	1,922	1,632	309	3,863	15·6	3,657

C.—*(Continued.)*

Ranges.	DISTRICTS.	State of Education on 31st December 1867. Can read and write.	Cannot read and write.	Passed General Test.	Remarks.
1	2	3	4	5	6
	Madras Town	...	...	...	
Northern Range.	Ganjam	766	747	4	
	Vizagapatam	694	740	2	
	Jeypore	196	183	1	
	Godavery	911	458	5	
	Kistna	721	632	6	
	Total...	3,288	2,760	18	
Central Range.	Nellore	507	823	...	
	Kurnool	307	567	3	
	Bellary	679	705	11	
	Cuddapah	404	725	2	Three exempted from General Test by special orders of Government.
	North Arcot	839	385	7	
	Madras	602	847	4	
	Total...	3,338	3,552	27	
Southern Range.	South Aroot	690	496	4	
	Tanjore	1,341	122	6	
	Trichinopoly	689	105	2	
	Madura	1,096	243	15	
	Tinnevelly	824	170	4	
	Total...	4,640	1,136	31	
Western Range.	Salem	818	817	8	
	Coimbatore	776	438	3	
	North Malabar	460	109	1	
	South Malabar	631	203	2	
	South Canara	376	311	7	
		3,061	1,378	21	
	Total...	14,327	8,826	97	

Abstract of the above according to Grades.

Rank.	Can read and write.	Cannot read and write.	Passed General Test.
Inspectors	435	...	70
Head Constables	1,079	34	19
Deputy Constables	1,697	76	7
Constables	11,116	8,716	1
Total...	14,327	8,826	97

C.—(*Continued.*)

Ranges.	DISTRICTS.	Instruction during the Calendar year 1867. Number who have been in District Head Quarter School.	Passed prescribed Test of Rank.	Passed Special Test.*	Remarks.
1	2	3	4	5	6
	Madras Town	...	...	...	
Northern Range.	Ganjam	654	125	...	
	Vizagapatam	398	162	3	
	Jeypore	179	3	...	
	Godavery	325	172	4	
	Kistna	248	122	4	
	Total ..	1,804	584	11	
Central Range.	Nellore	287	145	5	
	Kurnool	365	66	4	
	Bellary	199	54	3	
	Cuddapah	96	90	2	
	North Arcot	322	113	4	
	Madras	43	37	7	
	Total...	1,312	505	25	
Southern Range.	South Arcot	207	25	5	
	Tanjore	143	122	12	
	Trichinopoly	191	137	...	
	Madura	259	147	2	
	Tinnevelly	247	227	2	
	Total..	1,047	658	21	
Western Range.	Salem	192	109	6	
	Coimbatore	295	127	6	
	North Malabar...	258	169	3	
	South Malabar	149	101	8	
	South Canara	136	51	...	
	Total...	1,030	557	23	
	Grand Total...	5,193	2,304	80	

Abstract of the above according to Grades.

Rank.	Number who have been in District Hd. Qr. School.	Passed prescribed Test of Rank.	Passed Special Test.
Inspectors	33	16	39
Head Constables	135	58	26
Deputy do.	339	181	6
Constables	4,686	2,049	9
Total...	5,193	2,304	80

* Inspectors' Test.

C.—*(Continued.)*

Ranges.	DISTRICTS.	POLICE OFFICERS CONVICTED IN 1867. CONVICTED BY MAGISTRATES.															
		Robbery.	House-breaking.	Theft and Receiving.	Extortion and Bribery.	Assault and Criminal Force.	Cheating.	False evidence and causing disappearance of evidence.	Furnishing false information to a Public Servant.	Criminal Breach of Trust and Misappropriation.	Causing Hurt.	Negligent Escape.	Neglect of duty.	False charge.	Wrongful confinement.	Miscellaneous.	Total.
1	2	3	4	5	6	7	8	9	10	11	12	13	14	15	16	17	18
	Madras Town ...	...	...	4	...	1	...	...	...	1	...	...	1	...	...	4	11
Northern Range.	Ganjam ...	...	2	3	4	3	...	...	...	...	10	6	4	...	...	2	34
	Vizagapatam ...	...	...	4	5	1	...	...	...	...	...	4	...	...	3	1	18
	Jeypore ...	...	...	1	2	3	...	...	...	...	...	6	...	...	...	1	13
	Godavery ...	...	...	1	3	1	...	...	...	1	1	2	9	...	...	3	21
	Kistna ...	...	...	...	4	3	...	...	...	1	1	4	4	...	...	9	26
	Total...	...	2	9	18	11	...	...	...	2	12	22	17	...	3	16	112
Central Range.	Nellore ...	...	...	...	1	...	...	...	...	...	3	...	1	1	...	...	6
	Kurnool ...	...	...	...	...	...	...	...	...	...	...	...	15	...	...	...	15
	Bellary ...	...	1	1	3	...	...	...	...	...	...	5	9	...	...	3	22
	Cuddapah ...	...	...	2	4	...	...	...	...	...	...	1	1	...	...	...	8
	North Arcot ...	...	...	7	7	1	...	...	...	...	1	..	10	...	...	3	29
	Madras ...	...	...	8	...	1	1	...	...	...	...	...	6	...	..	1	17
	Total...	...	1	18	15	2	1	...	...	...	4	6	42	1	...	7	97
Southern Range.	South Arcot ...	...	1	2	1	...	...	...		...	...	2	4	...	...	3	14
	Tanjore ...	...	...	4	1	2	...	...	...	1	1	4	6	...	...	3	22
	Trichinopoly ...	..	...	1	...	6	...	...	...	...	2	...	2	..	...	4	15
	Madura ...	...	...	7	...	2	...	1	1	2	...	...	...	1	...	3	17
	Tinnevelly ...	...	...	3	1	...	...	...	1	1	...	...	5	..	...	1	12
	Total...	...	1	17	3	10	...	1	3	4	3	6	17	1	...	14	80
Western Range.	Salem ...	...	..	3	17	...	...	5	...	...	2	...	...	...	...	2	29
	Coimbatore ...	1	..	7	...	5	...	..	...	...	1	2	...	...	...	20	36
	South Malabar ...	...	1	...	...	5	...	...	...	...	1	1	1	...	...	1	10
	North Malabar ...	...	...	...	...	...	...	...	...	...	...	...	1	...	...	2	3
	South Canara ...	...	...	...	1	...	1	..	...	...	...	1	...	...	...	...	3
	Total...	1	1	10	18	10	1	5	...	...	4	4	2	...	...	25	81
	Grand Total...	1	5	58	54	34	2	6	3	7	23	38	79	2	3	66	381

Abstract of the above according to Grades.

RANK.	Number convicted by Magistrates.
Inspectors	5
Head Constables	23
Deputy do.	39
Constables	314
Total...	381

C.—(*Continued.*)

Ranges.	DISTRICTS.	Murder.	Attempt to Murder.	Robbery.	Lurking House Trespass, House-breaking.	Extortion, &c.	Causing grievous hurt.	Kidnapping.	Rape.	False evidence.	Criminal force to a woman.	Negligent escape.	Neglect of duty.	Miscellaneous.	Total.
		POLICE OFFICERS CONVICTED IN 1867.—(*Concluded.*)													
		CONVICTED BY COURTS.													
1	2	3	4	5	6	7	8	9	10	11	12	13	14	15	16
	Madras Town...	...	...	...	...	...	...	...	...	...	...	...	...	...	...
Northern Range.	Ganjam	...	...	...	...	...	...	...	...	...	...	...	...	...	...
	Vizagapatam ...	...	...	...	...	...	...	...	...	...	...	...	...	...	...
	Jeypore ...	...	...	...	...	...	...	...	...	...	...	...	...	1	1
	Godavery ...	...	...	...	...	...	...	...	...	...	...	...	...	...	...
	Kistna ...	...	2	...	...	...	...	...	...	...	...	1	...	...	3
	Total...	...	2	...	...	...	...	...	...	...	...	1	...	1	4
Central Range.	Nellore ...	...	...	...	...	...	2	...	...	...	...	...	...	...	2
	Kurnool ...	...	...	...	...	...	1	...	...	...	...	...	...	...	1
	Bellary ...	...	...	...	...	...	...	...	...	...	...	...	...	...	...
	Cuddapah ...	1	...	...	...	...	...	...	...	...	...	...	...	...	1
	North Arcot ...	...	...	...	...	...	...	...	...	...	...	...	...	...	...
	Madras ..	...	..	...	...	...	...	...	...	...	...	...	...	...	...
	Total...	1	...	...	...	...	3	...	...	...	...	...	...	...	4
Southern Range.	South Arcot ...	...	...	...	...	...	...	...	...	...	1	...	...	...	1
	Tanjore ...	...	...	2	...	...	...	...	...	1	...	...	...	...	3
	Trichinopoly ...	...	...	..	...	...	...	...	...	...	...	...	...	...	...
	Madura ...	...	...	...	...	...	...	...	...	...	...	...	...	1	1
	Tinnevelly ...	...	...	...	...	4	1	...	...	1	...	...	...	1	7
	Total...	...	...	2	...	4	1	...	...	2	1	...	...	2	12
Western Range.	Salem ..	...	...	...	1	...	...	...	...	...	...	...	1	...	2
	Coimbatore ...	...	...	...	...	...	...	1	1	...	...	...	...	...	2
	South Malabar	...	...	...	...	...	1	...	...	...	...	...	...	...	1
	North Malabar	...	...	...	...	...	...	...	...	...	...	...	...	1	1
	South Canara...	...	...	...	...	...	...	...	...	...	...	...	...	...	...
	Total...	...	...	...	1	...	1	1	1	...	...	...	1	1	6
	Grand Total...	1	2	2	1	4	5	1	1	2	1	1	1	4	26

Abstract of the above according to Grades.

RANK.	Number convicted by Courts.
Inspectors	2
Head Constables	1
Deputy do.	1
Constables	22
Total...	26

C.—*(Continued.)*

Ranges.	DISTRICTS.	Europeans.	East Indians.	Foreigners not British subjects.	Brahmins.	Rajaputs and Mahrattas.	Naidoos.	Moodeliars.	Sattanies.	Chetties.	Komatties.	Vunniers.	Weavers.	Yaddiers.	Conicopolies.	Nairs.	Moplas.	Teers.	Oryas.	Christians.	Mahomedans.	Pariahs.	Koravers, &c.	Total.
		CASTES AND RACES ON 31ST MARCH 1867.																						
		INSPECTORS.																						
1	2	3	4	5	6	7	8	9	10	11	12	13	14	15	16	17	18	19	20	21	22	23	24	25
	Madras Town*	10	2	...	...	...	1	...	...	...	...	...	...	...	...	...	...	...	...	...	...	...	...	13
Northern Range.	Ganjam ...	3	3	...	2	2	7	...	...	...	...	...	...	...	...	...	...	...	3	...	3	...	...	23
	Vizagapatam ...	2	3	...	5	...	10	...	1	...	...	...	...	...	...	...	...	...	2	1	3	...	2	29
	Jeypore ...	...	3	...	...	...	2	...	...	...	...	...	...	...	...	...	...	...	...	1	...	...	...	6
	Godavery ...	5	2	...	3	...	11	...	...	...	1	...	...	...	...	...	...	...	...	...	4	...	...	26
	Kistna ...	2	...	...	7	2	12	...	...	...	...	...	...	...	...	...	...	...	...	...	1	...	...	24
	Total...	12	11	...	17	4	42	...	1	...	1	...	...	...	...	...	...	...	5	2	11	...	2	108
Central Range.	Nellore ...	2	2	...	9	1	4	4	...	...	...	...	...	...	...	...	...	...	...	1	...	...	2	25
	Kurnool ...	2	3	...	4	2	4	1	...	...	1	...	...	...	...	...	...	...	...	...	...	...	...	17
	Bellary ...	1	4	...	16	4	3	...	...	...	1	...	...	...	...	...	...	...	...	...	2	...	...	31
	Cuddapah ...	1	4	...	5	2	5	3	...	...	...	...	...	...	...	...	...	...	...	...	...	...	...	20
	North Arcot ...	3	2	...	10	1	5	3	...	...	...	...	...	...	...	...	...	...	...	...	3	...	...	27
	Madras ...	3	2	...	4	...	3	1	...	...	...	...	...	...	...	...	...	...	...	2	2	...	...	17
	Total...	12	17	...	48	10	24	12	...	...	2	...	...	...	...		...	...	...	3	7	...	2	137
Southern Range.	South Arcot ...	3	4	1	7	...	1	2	...	...	...	...	...	...	...	...	...	...	...	...	1	...	2	21
	Tanjore ...	3	2	...	5	...	2	5	...	...	...	1	...	...	...	...	...	...	...	2	...	...	...	20
	Trichinopoly ...	2	2	...	...	...	1	3	...	...	...	...		...	4	...	...	...	...	1	1	...	...	14
	Madura ...	1	3	...	7	1	1	11	...	...	...	...	...	...	...		...	...	...	1	...	...	...	25
	Tinnevelly ...	4	1	...	4	...	3	8	...	...	...	...	...	...	...	...	...	...	...	...	1	...	...	21
	Total...	13	12	1	23	1	8	29	...	...	...	1	...	...	4	...	...		...	4	3	...	2	101
Western Range.	Salem ...	4	4	...	6	...	5	2	...	...	...	...	...	...	...	...	...	...		1	1	...	...	23
	Coimbatore ...	4	5	...	4	2	5	3	...		...	...	...	...	...	...	...	...	...	1	1	...	...	25
	South Malabar ...	2	6	...	1	...	...	...	...	...	...	...	...	...	...	9	1	...	...	...	1	...	...	20
	North Malabar ...	1	2	...	1	...	...	...	...	...	...	...	...	...	...	4	...	4	...	...	...	...	...	12
	South Canara...	1	...	...	9	...	...	...	...	...	...	...	...	...	...	...	...	...	...	1	...	...	3	14
	Total...	12	17	...	21	2	10	5	...	...	...	...	...	...	...	13	1	4	...	3	3	...	3	94
	Grand Total...	59	59	1	109	17	85	46	1	...	3	1	...	...	4	13	1	4	5	12	24	...	9	453

* Including Marine and Mounted Police.

C.—*(Continued.)*

Ranges.	DISTRICTS.	CASTES AND RACES ON 31ST MARCH 1867.—*(Continued.)*										
		CONSTABULARY.										
		Europeans.	East Indians.	Foreigners not British subjects.	Brahmins.	Rajaputs and Mahrattas.	Naidoos.	Moodeliars.	Sattanies.	Chetties.	Komatties.	Vunniers.
		1	2	3	4	5	6	7	8	9	10	11
	Madras Town* ...	32	7	...	30	97	259	191	...	...	...	...
Northern Range.	Ganjam	...	1	...	1	15	828	1	...	...	...	...
	Vizagapatam ...	...	4	...	28	20	988	1	1	...	...	...
	Jeypore	...	1	...	4	5	104	1	...	...	...	...
	Godavery	2	2	...	43	48	687	...	...	...	1	...
	Kistna	1	3	...	36	61	661	1	...	...	...	...
	Total ...	3	11	...	112	149	3,268	4	1	...	1	...
Central Range.	Nellore	1	3	...	50	80	553	19	...	...	...	...
	Kurnool	1	...	...	77	119	128	11	...	...	1	...
	Bellary	4	...	...	86	92	293	82	...	...	...	2
	Cuddapah ...	...	2	...	23	74	402	25	...	...	...	...
	North Arcot ...	1	1	...	31	170	340	161	...	...	...	...
	Madras	2	8	...	17	33	256	155	...	...	...	...
	Total ...	9	14	...	284	568	1,972	403	...	...	1	2
Southern Range.	South Arcot ...	2	11	1	7	37	265	190	...	...	...	...
	Tanjore	4	12	...	25	116	553	289	4	6	...	40
	Trichinopoly ...	8	8	...	12	32	239	7	1	4	...	...
	Madura	3	4	...	20	55	273	367	...	...	...	196
	Tinnevelly ...	3	1	...	10	38	252	332	...	...	...	...
	Total ...	20	36	1	74	278	1,582	1,185	5	10	...	236
Western Range.	Salem	1	4	...	69	83	270	160	...	...	...	...
	Coimbatore	2	12	...	52	78	328	199	...	...	...	...
	South Malabar ...	...	3	...	...	9	19	...	...	2	...	...
	North Malabar ...	...	8	...	5	16	19	...	...	3	...	...
	South Canara ...	...	...	...	47	12	87	210	...	...	...	...
	Total ...	3	27	...	173	198	723	569	...	5	...	...
	Grand Total ...	67	95	1	673	1,290	7,804	2,352	6	15	2	238

* Including Marine Police.

C.—*(Continued.)*

CASTES AND RACES ON 31ST MARCH 1867.—*(Concluded.)*

CONSTABULARY.

Weavers.	Yaddiers.	Conicopolies.	Nairs.	Moplas.	Teers.	Oryas.	Christians.	Mahomedans.	Pariahs.	Koravers, &c.	Total.
12	13	14	15	16	17	18	19	20	21	22	23
...	..	...	...	...	...	...	8	274	10	27	985
...	..	...	...	...	...	573	...	117	8	...	1,544
...	...	...	...	...	...	204	1	159	7	43	1,456
...	...	...	...	...	...	188	1	12	1	58	375
...	...	...	...	...	...	...	1	383	12	185	1,364
...	...	...	...	...	...	...	2	514	2	117	1,398
...	...	...	...	...	...	965	5	1,185	30	403	6,137
...	...	...	...	...	...	...	6	605	11	49	1,377
...	...	...	...	...	...	...	...	462	...	21	820
...	9	...	...	...	...	...	4	733	81	30	1,366
...	...	...	...	...	...	...	...	556	1	...	1,088
...	...	...	...	...	...	...	14	528	44	101	1,391
...	...	...	...	...	...	...	41	406	20	...	938
...	9	...	...	...	..	...	65	3,290	157	201	6,975
...	...	...	...	...	...	...	29	419	23	219	1,203
...	37	...	...	...	...	...	18	147	...	188	1,439
...	214	...	...	...	...	...	4	233	12	4	778
...	...	...	...	—	...	...	38	261	5	65	1,287
25	31	...	...	...	...	...	17	214	8	57	988
25	282	...	...	...	...	...	106	1,274	48	533	5,695
...	...	...	...	...	...	...	15	460	18	21	1,101
...	...	...	...	...	...	...	40	445	13	41	1,210
...	14	...	488	85	44	...	23	132	11	4	834
...	...	...	270	6	82	...	10	82	5	34	540
...	...	...	...	...	...	...	119	142	...	76	693
...	14	...	758	91	126	...	207	1,261	47	176	4,378
25	305	...	758	91	126	965	391	7,284	292	1,340	24,120

C.—*(Continued.)*

Ranges.	DISTRICTS.	POLICE PATIENTS IN HOSPITAL DURING THE CALENDAR YEAR 1867. Number of men treated in Hospital.	Remarks.
1	2	3	4
	Madras Town	246	
Northern Range.	Ganjam	1,839	
	Vizagapatam...	705	
	Jeypore	197	Seven deaths occurred in Hospital.
	Godavery	840	Men detained and treated for a
	Kistna	504	day or two are included in this.
	Total ...	4,085	
Central Range.	Nellore	436	
	Kurnool	913	
	Bellary	294	
	Cuddapah	374	
	North Arcot	436	
	Madras	135	
	Total ...	2,588	
Southern Range.	South Arcot	388	
	Tanjore	721	
	Trichinopoly	184	
	Madura	167	
	Tinnevelly	185	Several of these men have gone
	Total ...	1,645	into Hospital a second, third, fourth, and fifth time.
Western Range.	Salem	582	
	Coimbatore	1,051	
	North Malabar	191	
	South Malabar	298	
	South Canara	249	
	Total ...	2,371	
	Grand Total ...	10,935	

C.—*(Continued.)*

Ranges.	DISTRICTS.	WARRANTS AND SUMMONS ISSUED BY MAGISTRATES, SUB-MAGISTRATES AND COURTS DURING THE YEAR 1867. GRAVE CASES. Warrants originally issued. Number of Processes.	Warrants originally issued. Number of Persons.	Warrants issued on neglect of Summons. Number of Processes.	Warrants issued on neglect of Summons. Number of Persons.	Summons. Number of Processes.	Summons. Number of Persons.	Total. Number of Processes.	Total. Number of Persons.	Proportion to Population.
1	2	3	4	5	6	7	8	9	10	11
										One in
Northern Range.	Madras Town ...	Information not obtainable for the past year.								
	Ganjam	170	170	47	47	1,339	1,339	1,556	1,509	758
	Vizagapatam ...	765	838	262	308	3,702	3,702	4,729	4,540	311
	Jeypore	No Returns.								
	Godavery	260	260	18	18	1,388	1,388	1,666	1,648	829
	Kistna	911	926	20	22	4,035	4,035	4,966	4,961	240
	Total ...	2,106	2,194	347	395	10,464	10,464	12,917	12,658	403
Central Range.	Nellore	328	360	17	17	2,159	2,159	2,504	2,519	396
	Kurnool	150	213	6	12	402	573	558	786	923
	Bellary	263	425	31	31	2,678	2,692	2,972	3,117	396
	Cuddapah ...	343	343	...	...	3,706	3,706	4,049	4,049	259
	North Arcot ...	1,181	1,181	93	93	7,312	7,312	8,586	8,493	194
	Madras	179	179	...	...	846	846	1,025	1,025	658
	Total ...	2,444	2,701	147	153	17,103	17,288	19,694	19,989	317
Southern Range.	South Arcot ...	544	557	14	14	1,686	1,686	2,244	2,243	503
	Tanjore	874	874	16	16	5,212	5,212	6,102	6,086	271
	Trichinopoly ...	450	450	...	...	1,604	1,604	2,054	2,054	457
	Madura	808	808	114	114	7,822	7,322	8,244	8,130	228
	Tinnevelly ...	628	628	47	47	4,627	4,627	5,302	5,255	317
	Total ...	3,304	3,317	191	191	20,451	20,451	23,946	23,768	304
Western Range.	Salem	1,130	1,178	10	10	6,167	6,169	7,307	7,347	203
	Coimbatore	606	606	83	83	4,307	4,307	4,996	4,913	247
	South Malabar ...	991	1,019	94	94	2,265	2,298	3,350	3,317	} 416
	North Malabar ...	205	208	39	39	576	579	820	787	
	South Canara ...	157	157	44	44	1,656	1,656	1,857	1,818	434
	Total ...	3,089	3,168	270	270	14,971	15,009	18,320	18,177	286
	Grand Total ...	10,943	11,380	955	1,009	62,989	63,212	74,887	74,592	320

N. B.—Persons against whom Warrants have been issued on neglect of Summons (Col. 6) are not included in Total number of Persons (Col. 10.)

C.—(Continued.)

Ranges.	DISTRICTS.	WARRANTS AND SUMMONS ISSUED BY MAGISTRATES, SUB-MAGISTRATES AND COURTS DURING THE YEAR 1867.—Continued. PETTY CASES. Warrants originally issued. Number of Processes.	Warrants originally issued. Number of Persons.	Warrants issued on neglect of Summons. Number of Processes.	Warrants issued on neglect of Summons. Number of Persons.
1	2	3	4	5	6
	Madras Town	Information not obtainable for the past year.			
Northern Range.	Ganjam	197	197	106	106
	Vizagapatam	225	333	651	942
	Jeypore	No Returns.			
	Godavery	651	651	652	652
	Kistna	1,261	1,296	435	436
	Total...	2,334	2,477	1,844	2,136
Central Range.	Nellore	466	471	522	567
	Kurnool	589	927	246	324
	Bellary	472	928	315	517
	Cuddapah	262	262	759	759
	North Arcot	272	272	107	107
	Madras	504	504	1,012	1,012
	Total...	2,565	3,364	2,961	3,286
Southern Range.	South Arcot	1,146	1,152	459	467
	Tanjore	319	319	129	129
	Trichinopoly	849	849	188	188
	Madura	287	287	123	123
	Tinnevelly	439	439	86	86
	Total...	3,040	3,046	985	993
Western Range.	Salem	565	572	638	638
	Coimbatore	391	391	313	313
	South Malabar	197	216	385	385
	North Malabar	148	148	121	121
	South Canara	64	64	102	102
	Total...	1,365	1,391	1,559	1,559
	Grand Total...	9,304	10,278	7,349	7,974

C.—*(Continued.)*

WARRANTS AND SUMMONS ISSUED BY MAGISTRATES, SUB-MAGISTRATES AND COURTS DURING THE YEAR 1867.—*Concluded.*

PETTY CASES.				
SUMMONS.		TOTAL.		
Number of Processes.	Number of Persons.	Number of Processes.	Number of Persons.	Proportion to Population.
7	8	9	10	11
Information not obtainable for the past year.				One in
5,028	5,028	5,331	5,225	217
13,436	13,436	14,312	13,709	102
		No Returns.		
14,039	14,039	15,342	14,690	93
18,306	18,306	20,002	19,602	60
50,809	50,809	54,987	53,286	95
16,789	16,789	17,777	17,260	57
5,305	7,789	6,140	8,666	83
8,878	8,970	9,665	9,898	124
8,342	8,342	9,363	8,604	122
5,744	5,744	6,123	6,016	275
11,297	11,297	12,813	11,801	57
56,355	58,881	61,881	62,245	101
20,330	20,330	21,935	21,482	52
16,697	16,697	17,145	17,016	97
8,620	8,620	9,657	9,469	99
13,964	13,964	14,374	14,251	130
8,951	8,951	9,476	9,390	177
68,562	68,562	72,587	71,608	101
13,351	13,386	14,554	13,958	106
14,419	14,419	15,123	14,810	82
7,345	7,444	7,927	7,660	} 143
4,080	4,092	4,349	4,240	
3,398	3,398	3,564	3,462	227
42,598	42,739	45,517	44,130	117
218,319	220,991	234,972	231,269	103

N. B.—Persons against whom Warrants have been issued on neglect of Summons (Col. 6) are not included in Total number of Persons (Col. 10.)

C.—(Continued.)

Ranges.	DISTRICTS.	MISCELLANEOUS PROCESSES ISSUED IN 1867. Number of Miscellaneous Processes including Remand Warrants, Levy of Distress, Committals, &c. — Number of Processes.	Number of Persons.	Number of Search Warrants.	Number of houses searched.
1	2	3	4	5	6
	Madras Town	Information not obtainable for the past year.			
Northern Range.	Ganjam	2,192	2,526	47	51
	Vizagapatam	2,066	3,414	99	223
	Jeypore		No Returns.		
	Godavery	2,574	3,585	68	128
	Kistna	2,301	3,971	76	81
	Total ...	9,133	13,496	290	483
Central Range.	Nellore	1,255	2,010	18	25
	Kurnool...	301	536	45	86
	Bellary	2,592	3,938	37	51
	Cuddapah	1,291	1543	205	207
	North Arcot	1,958	2,907	292	292
	Madras	453	558	43	49
	Total ...	7,850	11,492	640	710
Southern Range.	South Arcot	2,535	3,656	145	154
	Tanjore	1,028	1,040	144	144
	Trichinopoly	1,335	1,452	102	117
	Madura	1,607	1,766	76	76
	Tinnevelly	852	1,422	89	114
	Total ...	7,357	9,336	556	605
Western Range.	Salem	3,429	4,660	49	51
	Coimbatore	1,941	2,602	38	43
	South Malabar	2,006	2,125	29	29
	North Malabar	1,070	1,377	33	69
	South Canara	1,308	1,618	52	57
	Total ...	9,754	12,382	201	249
	Grand Total ...	34,094	46,706	1,687	2,047

C.—*(Continued.)*

Ranges.	DISTRICTS.	Average number of Prisoners.	CONVICTS GUARDED IN JAILS IN 1867-68. POLICE GUARDS. No.	Cost.			REMARKS.
1	2	3	4	5	6	7	8
	Madras Town	490	57	6,228	0	0	
Northern Range.	Ganjam	379	54	6,006	0	0	
	Vizagapatam	304	42	4,650	0	0	
	Jeypore*	...	...	...	...	...	
	Godavery	845	120	13,716	0	0	
	Kistna	298	42	4,650	0	0	
	Total ...	1,826	258	29,022	0	0	
Central Range.	Nellore	252	36	4,266	0	0	
	Kurnool	226	32	3,690	0	0	
	Bellary	485	69	8,388	0	0	
	Cuddapah	265	38	4,470	0	0	
	North Arcot	798	114	12,858	0	0	
	Madras	269	38	4,470	0	0	
	Total ...	2,295	327	38,142	0	0	
Southern Range.	South Arcot	500	71	7,986	0	0	
	Tanjore	439	62	7,044	0	0	
	Trichinopoly	464	66	8,088	0	0	
	Madura	577	82	9,246	0	0	
	Tinnevelly	244	35	3,900	0	0	
	Total ...	2,224	316	36,264	0	0	
Western Range.	Salem...	561	80	9,006	0	0	
	Coimbatore	1,786	299	29,292	0	0	
	South Malabar	286	46	5,226	0	0	
	North Malabar	444	74	8,466	0	0	
	South Canara	203	29	3,720	0	0	
	Total ...	3,280	528	55,710	0	0	
	Grand Total ...	10,115	1,486	1,65,366	0	0	

* No Jails in this District.

C.—*(Continued.)*

Ranges.	DISTRICTS.	Short-sentenced Prisoners in Subsidiary Jails during the year 1867.			
		Number of Jails.	Total number of Convicts during the year.	Total number of days.	Average duration of confinement.
1	2	3	4	5	6
	Madras Town	...	...	...	...
Northern Range.	Ganjam	5	338	3,285	9·71
	Vizagapatam	15	863	4,777	5·53
	Jeypore	4	101	1,919	19
	Godavery	6	534	7,330	13·72
	Kistna	21	410	2,183	5·32
	Total ...	51	2,246	19,494	8·67
Central Range.	Nellore	18	394	2,700	6·85
	Kurnool	13	892	8,623	9·66
	Bellary	11	1,224	11,924	9·74
	Cuddapah	11	820	16,005	19·51
	North Arcot	16	644	3,665	5·69
	Madras	10	1,129	10,060	8·91
	Total ...	79	5,103	52,977	10·38
Southern Range.	South Arcot	17	1,317	14,054	10·67
	Tanjore	9	911	12,336	13·54
	Trichinopoly	6	548	6,931	12·64
	Madura	17	672	5,689	8·46
	Tinnevelly	16	920	9,648	10·48
	Total ...	65	4,368	48,658	11·13
Western Range.	Salem	11	1,231	13,732	11·15
	Coimbatore	10	1,503	14,668	9·75
	South Malabar	13	1,339	9,073	6·77
	North Malabar	10	526	4,423	8·40
	South Canara	9	517	7,818	15·12
	Total ...	53	5,116	49,714	9·71
	Grand Total ...	248	16,833	170,843	10·14

C.—*(Continued.)*

Ranges.	DISTRICTS.	PRISONERS ESCAPED DURING THE YEAR 1867							
		FROM JAILS.		FROM SUBSIDIARY JAILS.		FROM OTHER CUSTODY.		TOTAL.	
		Escaped.	Re-captured.	Escaped.	Re-captured.	Escaped.	Re-captured.	Escaped.	Re-captured.
1	2	3	4	5	6	7	8	9	10
	Madras Town	...	...	...	...	6	4	6	4
Northern Range.	Ganjam	...	...	4	4	11	6	15	10
	Vizagapatam	...	...	...	...	8	4	8	4
	Jeypore			No Returns.					
	Godavery	1	1	...	...	8	8	9	9
	Kistna	...	...	...	...	10	9	10	9
	Total ...	1	1	4	4	37	27	42	32
Central Range.	Nellore	...	...	...	...	...	...	...	...
	Kurnool	...	...	2	2	2	1	4	3
	Bellary	...	1	8	3	14	8	22	12
	Cuddapah	...	...	1	1	9	8	10	9
	North Arcot	6	1	12	6	10	7	28	14
	Madras	...	...	5	5	2	2	7	7
	Total ...	6	2	28	17	37	26	71	45
Southern Range.	South Arcot	3	3	4	1	19	15	26	19
	Tanjore	5	3	...	...	14	9	19	12
	Trichinopoly	5	2	...	...	6	4	11	6
	Madura	11	5	2	2	13	11	26	18
	Tinnevelly	2	1	..	...	5	5	7	6
	Total ...	26	14	6	3	57	44	89	61
Western Range.	Salem	1	1	10	9	13	11	24	21
	Coimbatore...	11	9	...	...	25	20	36	29
	South Malabar	2	...	7	4	15	4	24	8
	North Malabar	1	1	...	...	4	3	5	4
	South Canara	...	...	...	..	2	2	2	2
	Total ...	15	11	17	13	59	40	91	64
	Grand Total ...	48	28	55	37	196	141	299	206

C.—*(Continued.)*

Ranges.	DISTRICTS.	Fall of Rain and Price of Food during the Calendar year 1867, as compared with the last five years.				Remarks.
		Average fall of rain during the past five years.	Fall of rain during present year 1867.	Staple articles of food and average price during past five years.	Price during present year 1867.	
1	2	3	4	5	6	7
	Madras Town ...	...	...	...	...	
Northern Range.	Ganjam ...	58·59	49·33	190	162	
	Vizagapatam ... Jeypore ...	37·85	51·68	179	126	
	Godavery ...	32·90	32·80	166	142	
	Kistna ...	26·62	29·68	176	202	
	Total...	38·99	40·87	178	158	
Central Range.	Nellore ...	27·77	21·62	204	239	
	Kurnool ...	28·18	22·05	285	233	
	Bellary ...	19·45	14·27	321	200	
	Cuddapah ...	19·63	17·11	274	272	
	North Arcot ...	26·50	15·34	227	229	
	Madras ...	30·01	12·49	245	273	
	Total...	25·26	17·15	259	241	
Southern Range.	South Arcot ...	41·26	21·30	198	215	
	Tanjore ...	39·54	19·34	211	223	
	Trichinopoly ...	46·70	26·18	216	219	
	Madura ...	28·18	22·32	250	260	
	Tinnevelly ...	29·60	24·82	279	255	
	Total...	37·06	22·79	231	234	
Western Range.	Salem ...	18·06	23·12	212	242	
	Coimbatore ...	30·83	20·99	268	258	
	North Malabar... South Malabar...	155·36	97·17	227	263	
	South Canara ...	153·19	127·19	253	255	
	Total...	89·36	67·12	240	255	
	Grand Total...	47·67	36·98	227	222	

C.—(*Continued.*)

Ranges.	DISTRICTS.	DEPREDATORS, OFFENDERS, AND SUSPECTED PERSONS. Number of Depredators, Offenders, and Suspected Persons at large on 31st December 1867. Known Thieves and Depredators. Males.	Known Thieves and Depredators. Females.	Receivers of stolen goods. Males.	Receivers of stolen goods. Females.	Prostitutes.	Suspected persons. Males.	Suspected persons. Females.
1	2	3	4	5	6	7	8	9
	Madras Town	204	18	64	18	419	55	8
Northern Range.	Ganjam	411	41	68	6	677	388	41
	Vizagapatam	1,413	112	97	48	665	1,292	130
	Jeypore	No Returns.						
	Godavery	169	20	27	9	15	377	17
	Kistna	531	8	102	12	...	1,142	82
	Total ...	2,524	181	289	75	1,357	3,199	270
Central Range.	Nellore	980	24	212	18	35	1,023	22
	Kurnool	324	4	37	6	29	576	17
	Bellary	1,344	18	137	18	246	1,936	53
	Cuddapah	1,009	100	63	20	...	916	37
	North Arcot	739	23	81	12	35	900	25
	Madras	154	14	15	1	113	461	11
	Total ...	4,550	183	545	75	458	5,812	165
Southern Range.	South Arcot	773	9	145	35	77	1,124	93
	Tanjore	976	27	131	13	498	1,634	41
	Trichinopoly	203	...	24	1	213	730	13
	Madura	554	10	130	19	322	892	53
	Tinnevelly	425	20	111	28	...	647	18
	Total ...	2,931	66	541	96	1,110	5,027	218
Western Range.	Salem	421	3	29	5	20	633	20
	Coimbatore	410	20	49	20	204	441	27
	South Malabar ...	228	...	36	1	130	364	...
	North Malabar ...	659	18	35	4	119	460	23
	South Canara	115	...	1	...	...	74	...
	Total ...	1,833	41	150	30	473	1,972	70
	Grand Total ...	12,042	489	1,589	294	3,817	16,065	731

C.—*(Continued.)*

Ranges.	DISTRICTS.	DEPREDATORS, OFFENDERS, AND SUSPECTED PERSONS.—*(Concluded.)* Number of Depredators, Offenders, and Suspected Persons at large on 31st December 1867. Vagrants and Wandering Gangs. Males.	Vagrants and Wandering Gangs. Females.	Total. Males.	Total. Females.	Number of Houses of Bad Repute. Toddy shops resorted to by thieves, &c.	Brothels in Cantonments.	Receivers of Stolen Goods.	Notorious Gambling Houses.
		10	11	12	13	14	15	16	17
	Madras Town ...	41	20	364	483	1	...	3	6
Northern Range.	Ganjam	44	7	906	772	52	5	46	100
	Vizagapatam... ...	417	49	3,219	1,004	219	159	101	151
	Jeypore	No Returns.							
	Godavery	171	71	744	132	122	5	25	248
	Kistna	1,300	1,176	3,075	1,278	145	...	68	34
	Total ...	1,932	1,303	7,944	3,186	538	169	240	533
Central Range.	Nellore	938	697	3,153	796	20	...	9	3
	Kurnool...	87	48	1,024	104	13	...	15	7
	Bellary	2,048	1,790	5,465	2,125	94	94	98	84
	Cuddapah	24	7	2,012	164	29	...	74	14
	North Arcot	595	216	2,315	311	60	10	44	63
	Madras	92	33	722	172	7	30	8	11
	Total ...	3,784	2,791	14,691	3,672	223	134	248	182
Southern Range.	South Arcot	336	83	2,378	297	60	...	102	16
	Tanjore	333	28	3,074	607	246	...	92	73
	Trichinopoly	57	...	1,[illegible]4	227	23	33	10	22
	Madura	111	...	1,687	404	93	...	60	65
	Tinnevelly	210	44	1,393	110	53	...	82	88
	Total ...	1,047	155	9,546	1,645	475	33	346	264
Western Range.	Salem	65	26	1,148	74	5	...	18	33
	Coimbatore	388	26	1,288	297	34	11	42	54
	South Malabar ...	4	...	632	131	...	2	25	8
	North Malabar ...	19	...	1,173	164	...	2	7	16
	South Canara ...	...	...	190	...	...	...	...	4
	Total ...	476	52	4,431	666	39	15	92	115
	Grand Total ..	7,280	4,321	36,976	9,652	1,276	351	929	1,100

C.—*(Continued.)*

Ranges.	DISTRICTS.	ACCIDENTAL DEATHS AND SUICIDES IN 1867.									
		ACCIDENTAL DEATHS						SUICIDES			
		By drowning.		By other causes.		Total.		By drowning		By hanging.	
		Males.	Females.	Males.	Females.	Males.	Females.	Males.	Females.	Males.	Females.
1	2	3	4	5	6	7	8	9	10	11	12
	Madras Town ...	28	8	20	1	48	9	5	12	2	...
Northern Range.	Ganjam	68	83	135	81	203	164	3	6	15	27
	Vizagapatam ...	177	115	147	40	324	155	15	44	8	8
	Jeypore ...			No Returns.							
	Godavery ...	117	77	88	30	205	107	18	59	5	5
	Kistna ...	87	79	54	15	141	94	23	62	3	4
	Total...	449	354	424	166	878	520	59	171	31	44
Central Range.	Nellore	151	159	99	37	250	196	16	55	5	...
	Kurnool ...	48	66	56	19	104	85	7	36	1	1
	Bellary ...	135	187	109	56	244	243	27	61	6	6
	Cuddapah ...	135	262	71	33	206	295	21	72	6	3
	North Arcot ...	236	400	73	15	309	415	24	41	6	4
	Madras	104	96	51	24	155	120	8	17	2	...
	Total......	809	1,170	459	184	1,268	1,354	103	282	26	14
Southern Range.	South Arcot ...	185	184	62	23	247	207	13	19	12	6
	Tanjore ...	133	104	59	8	192	107	...	6	6	3
	Trichinopoly ...	69	73	36	7	105	80	2	11	4	4
	Madura ...	137	113	36	10	173	123	12	23	10	7
	Tinnevelly ...	143	108	88	9	231	117	8	34	11	18
	Total...	667	582	281	52	948	634	35	93	43	38
Western Range.	Salem ...	269	262	28	3	297	265	2	9	8	8
	Coimbatore ...	239	277	61	19	300	296	29	55	11	3
	South Malabar...	131	92	116	16	247	108	4	1	30	7
	North Malabar...	60	33	35	5	95	38	3	5	16	...
	South Canara ...	75	75	118	40	193	115	6	15	19	13
	Total...	774	739	358	83	1,132	822	44	85	84	31
	Grand Total...	2,727	2,853	1,542	486	4,269	3,339	246	643	186	127

C.—*(Continued.)*

Ranges.	DISTRICTS.	ACCIDENTAL DEATHS AND SUICIDES IN 1867.—*(Concluded.)*							
		SUICIDES							
		By poison.		By lethal weapons.		By other causes.		Total.	
		Males.	Females.	Males.	Females.	Males.	Females.	Males.	Females.
		13	14	15	16	17	18	19	20
	Madras Town ...	...	...	1	...	...	...	8	12
Northern Range.	Ganjam	...	...	3	...	...	...	21	33
	Vizagapatam	...	2	3	...	1	2	27	56
	Jeypore	No Returns.							
	Godavery	2	...	1	1	...	...	26	65
	Kistna	...	...	4	...	...	1	30	67
	Total...	2	2	11	1	1	3	104	221
Central Range.	Nellore	...	...	...	...	...	...	21	55
	Kurnool	...	...	...	...	...	...	8	87
	Bellary	1	...	4	...	...	1	38	68
	Cuddapah	1	2	4	1	...	1	32	79
	North Arcot	1	...	1	...	1	...	83	45
	Madras	...	1	2	...	...	...	12	18
	Total...	3	3	11	1	1	2	144	302
Southern Range.	South Arcot	5	1	...	...	1	...	31	26
	Tanjore	...	2	...	...	1	...	7	11
	Trichinopoly	1	...	2	...	...	1	9	16
	Madura	...	1	...	...	...	...	22	31
	Tinnevelly	3	5	1	...	1	1	24	58
	Total...	9	9	3	..	3	2	93	142
Western Range.	Salem	...	...	...	...	...	...	10	17
	Coimbatore	...	1	1	1	...	...	41	60
	South Malabar ...	2	...	2	...	6	...	44	8
	North Malabar ...	...	...	1	...	...	...	20	5
	South Canara... ...	2	3	1	...	...	...	28	31
	Total...	4	4	5	1	6	...	143	121
	Grand Total...	18	18	31	3	11	7	492	798

C.—(*Concluded.*)

Ranges.	DISTRICTS.	Statement of Fires and Property lost during the Calendar year 1867. Number of Fires.	Number of Houses, &c., burnt.	Value of property destroyed.	Number of lives lost.	REMARKS.
1	2	3	4	5	6	7
	Madras Town ...	7	7	90	...	
Northern Range.	Ganjam	313	3,307	44,892	4	
	Vizagapatam ...	268	3,403	24,990	9	
	Jeypore	No Returns		received.		
	Godavery	672	6,963	63,348	11	
	Kistna	394	2,611	1,13,213	1	
	Total...	1,647	16,284	2,46,443	25	
Central Range.	Nellore	333	*1,592	55,337	...	* 464 grass heaps are included in this.
	Kurnool	108	921	32,039	4	
	Bellary	434	806	11,312	3	
	Cuddapah	448	638	19,962	3	
	North Arcot	650	752	22,602	7	
	Madras	249	288	10,644	4	
	Total...	2,222	4,997	1,51,896	21	
Southern Range.	South Arcot	400	982	40,392	21	
	Tanjore	116	922	11,543	11	
	Trichinopoly ...	311	1,255	24,600	16	
	Madura	411	3,255	60,083	37	
	Tinnevelly	475	2,387	48,374	4	
	Total...	1,713	8,801	1,84,992	89	
Western Range.	Salem	344	441	19,876	3	
	Coimbatore	205	1,189	13,587	5	
	North Malabar ...	70	72	13,916	...	
	South Malabar ...	238	316	33,344	3	
	South Canara ...	234	309	53,887	10	
	Total...	1,091	2,327	1,34,610	21	
	Grand Total...	6,680	32,416	7,18,031	156	

D.

No. I.—Number of Offences against the Indian Penal Code, and for the year 1867 *; and the*

DESCRIPTION OF OFFENCES.	OPERATIONS			
	Number of offences committed and charges preferred in 1867.	Persons concerned.	Property	
			Lost.	Recovered.
No. 1.—Offences against the person.				
Murder	222	534	2,622	278
Attempt to murder	45	64	606	...
Culpable homicide	80	242	...	...
Attempt at do.	2	8	...	...
Abetment of suicide	2	2	...	...
Attempt to commit suicide	245	247	...	...
Causing miscarriage	93	178	...	...
Exposure or abandonment of children	20	22	...	...
Concealment of birth	49	66	...	...
Causing grievous hurt	368	1 043	57	...
Causing hurt	246	496	1,664	100
Causing hurt, (Petty cases)	5,110	14,464	89	26
Causing hurt or grievous hurt to extort confession.	38	135	...	...
Wrongful restraint	1,234	2,893	54	54
Do. to extort confession	4	7	...	...
Assault	159	396	...	...
Petty assault	13,822	33,603	77	28
Assault in attempting theft	59	208	34	16
Kidnapping or abducting	87	185	1,069	843
Kidnapping with intent to take property	6	8	104	4
Slave dealing	1	1	...	...
Prostitution of minors	9	16	...	...
Compulsory labor	2	2	...	...
Rape	84	99	11	...
Unnatural Offences	6	6	...	...
Total of No. 1...	21,493	54,920	6,387	849
No. 2.—Offences against property with violence.				
Robbery	595	1,523	25,997	3,033
Robbery on the highway	101	292	4,829	768
Robbery (aggravated)	75	222	3,701	376
Attempt at robbery	41	116	...	...
Dacoity	504	5,525	94,504	16,309
Dacoity (aggravated)	29	394	5,399	839
Being a dacoit, &c.	4	20	19	14
Preparing or assembling for dacoity	6	64	...	...
House-trespass with intent to commit an offence...	127	247	236	103
Lurking house-trespass, house-breaking...	715	987	27,673	4,155
House-breaking by night	6,162	9,278	4,17,181	51,198
Do. with aggravating circumstances	6	26	1,484	13
Breaking open closed receptacle of property ...	267	530	4,779	814
Total of No. 2...	8,632	19,224	5,85,802	77,622

D.—(*Continued.*)

of persons concerned in the Districts of the Madras Presidency, result of the proceedings.

OF THE POLICE.						JUDICIAL OPERATIONS OF MAGISTRATES' COURTS, JUSTICES OF THE PEACE AND OTHER COURTS. SUMMARILY DISPOSED OF BY MAGISTRATES.					
				Bailed by Police.		By Sub-Magistrates of 2nd Class.			By Sub-Magistrates of 1st Class.		
Number of cases detected in which convictions followed.	Persons arrested with and without Warrant.	Persons summoned.	Total persons compelled to appear.	Cases.	Persons.	Number of cases tried.	Persons tried.	Persons convicted.	Number of cases tried.	Persons tried.	Persons convicted.
109	463	9	472	1	1	...	...	...	...	...	...
18	54	...	54	...	...	...	...	...	...	...	...
49	209	...	209	...	1	...	...	...	...	...	...
1	3	...	3	..	...	...	...	...	...	...	...
...	2	...	2	...	...	...	...	...	...	...	...
116	217	6	223	3	3	...	...	...	...	...	...
10	121	16	137	...	...	...	...	...	...	...	...
9	16	...	16	...	...	...	...	...	...	...	...
28	52	...	52	1	1	...	...	...	...	...	...
229	587	290	877	2	2	158	469	283	62	150	74
124	254	138	392	3	4	29	65	38	77	136	85
2,366	1,050	12,043	13,093	3	6	3,168	8,434	3,968	529	1,442	600
8	85	17	102	...	...	...	...	...	..	...	..
356	515	2,008	2,523	1	3	433	980	469	98	250	91
...	3	2	5	...	...	...	...	...	...	...	...
70	190	110	300	...	...	24	60	4	41	98	52
3,739	1,139	27,943	29,082	6	9	4,164	10,356	4,784	877	2,420	1,080
21	80	98	178	...	...	42	129	26	9	16	8
22	126	17	143	2	12	...	...	...	...	...	...
1	5	...	5	...	...	...	...	...	...	...	...
...	...	1	1	...	...	...	...	...	...	...	...
1	9	5	14	...	...	...	...	...	...	...	...
...	1	1	2	...	...	2	2	...	...	...	...
14	65	25	90	3	3	...	...	...	...	...	...
1	8	2	5	...	...	...	...	...	...	...	...
7,292	5,249	42,731	47,980	25	45	8,015	20,495	9,572	1,693	4,512	1,990
141	502	15	517	8	16	...	...	...	...	...	...
22	105	...	105	...	...	...	...	...	...	...	...
26	104	...	104	2	4	...	...	...	...	...	...
7	14	...	14	...	...	...	...	...	...	...	...
124	1,584	...	1,584	12	57	...	...	...	...	...	...
6	115	...	115	1	2	...	...	...	...	...	...
4	20	...	20	...	...	...	...	...	...	...	...
1	14	...	14	...	...	...	...	...	...	...	...
72	136	66	202	...	...	51	90	53	27	68	31
358	622	11	633	...	...	...	...	...	180	243	189
1,081	2,855	34	2,889	46	91	...	...	...	511	871	600
1	7	...	7	...	...	...	...	...	...	...	..
51	205	15	220	1	5	...	...	...	87	93	81
1,894	6,283	141	6,424	70	175	51	90	53	755	1,275	901

D.—(Continued.)

No. I.—Number of Offences against the Indian Penal Code, and for the year 1867; and the

DESCRIPTION OF OFFENCES.	JUDICIAL OPERATIONS — SUMMARILY DISPOSED OF — By Justices and Magistrates with full powers. Number of cases tried.	Persons tried.	Persons convicted.
No. 1.—Offences against the person.			
Murder ...	...	...	...
Attempt to murder	...	...	...
Culpable homicide	...	...	...
Attempt at do.	...	...	...
Abetment of suicide	...	...	...
Attempt to commit suicide	198	200	111
Causing miscarriage	...	...	...
Exposure or abandonment of children	...	...	...
Concealment of birth	...	...	...
Causing grievous hurt	50	133	75
Causing hurt	66	141	55
Causing hurt, (Petty cases)	69	154	89
Causing hurt or grievous hurt to extort confession	5	9	1
Wrongful restraint	82	207	85
Do. to extort confession	1	3	...
Assault ...	63	120	49
Petty assault	733	1,254	476
Assault in attempting theft	2	26	22
Kidnapping or abducting...	...	...	...
Kidnapping with intent to take property	...	...	...
Slave dealing	...	...	...
Prostitution of minors	...	...	...
Compulsory labor	...	...	...
Rape	...	...	...
Unnatural offences	...	...	...
Total of No. 1...	1,269	2,247	963
No. 2.—Offences against property with violence.			
Robbery...	188	387	200
Robbery on the highway	23	54	24
Robbery (aggravated)...	...	...	...
Attempt at robbery	8	10	8
Dacoity ...	...	...	...
Dacoity (aggravated)	...	...	...
Being a dacoit, &c.	...	...	...
Preparing or assembling for dacoity	...	...	...
House-trespass with intent to commit an offence...	25	40	17
Lurking house-trespass, house-breaking	236	332	232
House-breaking by night	752	1,347	810
Do. with aggravating circumstances	1	2	...
Breaking open closed receptacle of property	32	104	32
Total of No. 2...	1,265	2,276	1,323

D.—*(Continued.)*

of persons concerned in the Districts of the Madras Presidency, result of the proceedings.—(Continued.)

OF MAGISTRATES' COURTS, JUSTICES OF THE PEACE AND OTHER COURTS.											
by Magistrates.			Operations in Committable Cases.								
Total.			By Sub-Magistrates of 2nd Class.				By Sub-Magistrates of 1st Class.				
					Committed to Higher Court.				Committed to Higher Court.		
Number of cases tired.	Persons tried.	Persons convicted.	Number of cases inquired into.	Persons charged.	Cases.	Persons.	Number of cases inquired into.	Persons charged.	Cases.	Persons.	
...	...	...	127	306	109	217	42	109	38	78	
...	...	...	26	38	19	28	6	6	4	4	
...	...	...	45	112	41	88	22	45	20	41	
...	...	...	2	8	1	2	...	...	...	...	
...	...	...	1	1	...	...	...	...	...	...	
198	200	111	11	11	6	6	2	2	...	...	
...	...	...	45	92	18	34	14	34	3	18	
...	...	...	10	10	7	7	3	5	3	5	
...	...	...	30	42	25	28	3	5	3	5	
265	752	432	41	90	40	89	11	13	11	13	
172	342	178	13	18	10	14	2	2	2	2	
3,766	10,030	4,657	5	11	5	11	...	...	...	...	
5	9	1	13	48	6	21	6	21	4	15	
613	1,437	645	4	10	4	8	...	...	...	...	
1	3	...	...	...	...	...	1	2	...	...	
128	278	105	...	...	...	...	...	...	...	...	
5,774	14,030	6,340	2	4	2	4	1	1	1	1	
53	171	56	1	1	1	1	...	...	...	...	
...	...	...	89	84	18	33	10	22	5	9	
...	...	...	3	4	3	4	1	1	...	...	
...	...	...	...	...	...	...	...	...	...	...	
...	...	...	5	10	2	2	1	2	6	2	
2	2	...	...	...	...	...	...	...	...	...	
...	...	...	40	48	14	14	17	21	...	6	
...	...	...	3	3	1	1	...	...	...	...	
10,977	27,254	12,525	466	946	332	607	142	291	101	199	
188	387	200	40	82	29	53	18	28	3	5	
23	54	24	12	31	9	21	1	2	1	2	
...	...	...	32	71	28	57	7	14	4	8	
8	10	8	2	4	2	4	...	...	...	...	
...	...	...	196	1,126	142	684	49	285	31	149	
...	...	...	13	73	6	25	3	20	3	20	
...	...	...	1	7	1	7	...	...	...	...	
...	...	...	3	9	2	8	1	2	1	2	
103	198	101	3	3	...	...	...	...	...	...	
416	575	421	19	45	14	31	1	2	1	2	
1,263	2,218	1,410	159	454	112	246	27	45	27	45	
1	2	...	2	4	2	4	...	...	...	...	
69	197	113	5	18	3	10	...	...	...	...	
2,071	3,641	2,277	487	1,927	350	1,150	102	398	71	233	

D.—*(Continued.)*

No. 1.—*Number of Offences against the Indian Penal Code, and for the year* 1867 *; and the*

DESCRIPTION OF OFFENCES.	JUDICIAL OPERATIONS OF — OPERATIONS — By Justices and Magistrates with full powers.			
	Number of cases inquired into.	Persons charged.	Committed to Higher Court. — Cases.	Committed to Higher Court. — Persons.
No. 1.—Offences against the person.				
Murder	17	51	12	33
Attempt to murder	5	10	4	6
Culpable homicide	7	50	6	49
Attempt at do.	...	...	...	...
Abetment of suicide	1	1	...	...
Attempt to commit suicide	8	8	8	8
Causing miscarriage	5	7	3	4
Exposure or abandonment of children	...	...	...	...
Concealment of birth	3	4	2	2
Causing grievous hurt	3	6	3	6
Causing hurt	7	11	7	11
Causing hurt (Petty cases)	...	...	...	...
Causing hurt or grievous hurt to extort confession	7	25	2	5
Wrongful restraint	2	2	2	2
Do. to extort confession	...	...	...	...
Assault	2	2	2	2
Petty Assault	...	...	...	...
Assault in attempting theft	...	...	...	...
Kidnapping or abducting	14	24	7	10
Kidnapping with intent to take property	...	...	...	...
Slave dealing	...	...	...	...
Prostitution of minors	1	1	...	...
Compulsory labor	...	...	...	...
Rape	13	16	2	3
Unnatural offences	2	2	1	1
Total of No. 1	92	215	56	137
No. 2.—Offences against property with violence.				
Robbery	1	2	1	2
Robbery on the highway	6	18	5	14
Robbery (aggravated)	5	15	5	14
Attempt at robbery	...	...	...	...
Dacoity	13	113	10	50
Dacoity (aggravated)	1	15	1	14
Being a dacoit, &c.	3	13	3	13
Preparing or assembling for dacoity	...	...	...	...
House-trespass with intent to commit an offence	...	...	...	...
Lurking house-trespass, house-breaking	5	8	5	8
House-breaking by night	28	62	28	61
Do. with aggravating circumstances	...	...	...	...
Breaking open closed receptacle of property	...	...	...	...
Total of No. 2	62	246	58	176

D.—(*Continued.*)

of persons concerned in the Districts of the Madras Presidency, result of the proceedings.—(Continued.)

MAGISTRATES' COURTS, JUSTICES OF THE PEACE AND OTHER COURTS.

IN COMMITTABLE CASES.

By Principal Sudder Ameens.					By Session Judges.		
Number of cases tried.	Persons tried.	Persons convicted.	Committed to Higher Court. Cases.	Committed to Higher Court. Persons.	Number of cases tried.	Persons tried.	Persons convicted.
...	...	...	...	...	150	816	172
...	...	...	...	...	26	32	20
...	...	...	...	...	66	177	112
...	...	...	...	...	1	2	1
...	...	...	...	...	...	...	...
4	4	3	...	...	2	2	1
...	...	...	...	...	23	5	16
...	...	...	...	...	10	1	10
...	...	...	...	...	29	32	32
4	10	2	...	...	48	94	67
2	2	1	...	...	14	23	10
...	...	...	...	...	5	12	4
...	...	...	...	...	13	41	18
2	3	3	...	...	2	5	1
...	...	...	...	...	...	...	...
...	...	...	...	...	...	...	...
...	...	...	...	...	3	5	3
...	...	...	...	...	1	1	1
...	...	...	...	...	25	47	28
...	...	...	...	...	2	3	1
...	...	...	...	...	...	...	...
...	...	...	...	...	3	4	1
...	...	...	...	...	...	...	...
...	...	...	...	...	22	23	15
...	...	...	...	...	2	2	1
12	19	9	...	...	446	887	514
5	7	4	...	...	28	53	37
...	...	...	...	...	13	32	19
...	...	...	...	...	37	79	51
...	...	...	...	...	2	4	1
...	...	...	...	...	182	873	484
...	...	...	...	...	10	59	46
...	...	...	...	...	4	20	20
...	...	...	...	...	3	10	7
...	...	...	...	...	...	...	...
8	17	13	...	...	9	19	8
33	47	35	...	...	117	274	141
...	...	...	...	...	2	4	2
1	5	1	...	...	2	5	2
47	76	53	...	...	409	1,432	818

D.—*(Continued.)*

No. 1.—Number of Offences against the Indian Penal Code, and for the year 1867 *; and the*

DESCRIPTION OF OFFENCES.	JUDICIAL OPERATIONS — OPERATIONS IN COMMITTABLE — By High Court. Number of cases tried.	Persons tried.	Persons convicted.
No. 1.—Offences against the person.			
Murder	8	11	8
Attempt to murder	1	1	...
Culpable homicide	1	1	1
Attempt at do.	...	...	...
Abetment of suicide	...	...	...
Attempt to commit suicide	3	3	2
Causing miscarriage	1	1	...
Exposure or abandonment of children	...	...	...
Concealment of birth	1	1	1
Causing grievous hurt	2	5	4
Causing hurt	3	3	3
Causing hurt (Petty cases)	...	...	...
Causing hurt or grievous hurt to extort confession	...	...	...
Wrongful restraint	2	2	...
Do. to extort confession	...	...	...
Assault	2	2	2
Petty assault	...	...	...
Assault in attempting theft	...	...	...
Kidnapping or abducting	5	5	4
Kidnapping with intent to take property	...	...	...
Slave dealing	...	...	...
Prostitution of minors	...	...	...
Compulsory labor	...	...	...
Rape	...	...	...
Unnatural Offences	...	...	...
Total of No. 1	29	35	25
No. 2.—Offences against property with violence.			
Robbery	...	...	...
Robbery on the highway	2	5	2
Robbery (aggravated)	...	...	...
Attempt at robbery	...	...	...
Dacoity	1	8	4
Dacoity (aggravated)	...	...	...
Being a dacoit, &c.	...	...	...
Preparing or assembling for dacoity	...	...	...
House-trespass with intent to commit an offence	...	...	...
Lurking house-trespass, house-breaking	3	5	3
House-breaking by night	17	31	24
Do. with aggravating circumstances	...	...	...
Breaking open closed receptacle of property	...	...	...
Total of No. 2	23	49	33

D.—(*Continued.*)

of persons concerned in the Districts of the Madras Presidency, result of the proceedings.—(Continued.)

OF MAGISTRATES' COURTS, JUSTICES OF THE PEACE AND OTHER COURTS.

CASES.			Total Number of cases summarily disposed of by Magistrates and tried by Courts.	TOTAL NUMBER OF PERSONS CONVICTED BY MAGISTRATES AND COURTS.				
TOTAL.				Adults.		Juveniles.		
Cases tried.	Persons tried.	Persons convicted.		Males.	Females.	Males.	Females.	Total.
158	327	180	158	168	10	2	...	180
27	83	20	27	18	2	...	...	20
67	178	113	67	111	1	1	...	113
1	2	1	1	1	...	...	...	1
...	...	...	...	...	...	...	...	...
9	9	6	207	87	80	...	...	117
24	56	16	24	5	11	...	...	16
10	12	10	10	1	9	...	...	10
30	85	33	30	...	33	...	...	33
54	108	78	819	488	14	3	...	505
19	27	14	191	190	1	1	...	192
5	11	4	3,771	4,410	233	17	1	4,661
12	41	18	17	19	...	...	...	19
6	10	4	619	634	14	1	...	649
...	...	...	1	...	...	...	...	...
2	2	2	130	104	3	...	...	107
3	5	3	5,777	5,946	387	8	2	6,343
1	1	1	54	56	1	...	...	57
30	52	32	30	19	13	...	...	32
2	3	1	2	1	...	...	...	1
...	...	...	...	...	...	...	...	...
3	4	1	3	...	1	...	...	1
...	...	...	2	...	...	...	...	...
22	23	15	22	15	...	...	...	15
2	2	1	2	1	...	...	...	1
487	941	548	11,464	12,274	763	33	3	13,073
33	60	41	221	240	...	1	...	241
15	37	21	38	45	...	...	...	45
37	79	51	37	50	1	...	...	51
2	4	1	10	9	...	...	...	9
183	881	488	183	480	...	8	...	488
10	59	46	10	46	...	...	...	46
4	20	20	4	18	...	2	...	20
3	10	7	3	7	...	...	...	7
...	...	...	103	89	12	...	...	101
20	41	24	436	382	37	25	1	445
167	352	200	1,430	1,550	26	34	...	1,610
2	4	2	3	2	...	...	...	2
3	10	3	72	113	1	2	...	116
479	1,557	904	2,550	3,031	77	72	1	3,181

D.—*(Continued.)*

No. 1.—*Number of Offences against the Indian Penal Code, and for the year* 1867 ; *and the*

DESCRIPTION OF OFFENCES.	PUNISHMENTS.				
		TRANSPORTATION.			
	Death.	Life.	Fourteen years.	Ten years.	Seven years.
No. 1.—*Offences against the person.*					
Murder ...	94	84	...	...	...
Attempt to murder ...	...	1	...	4	...
Culpable homicide ...	...	14	...	2	2
Attempt at do. ...	...	...	...	...	...
Abetment of suicide ...	...	...	...	...	...
Attempt to commit suicide ...	...	...	...	...	...
Causing miscarriage ...	...	...	...	...	...
Exposure or abandonment of children ...	...	...	...	...	...
Concealment of birth ...	...	...	...	...	...
Causing grievous hurt ...	...	...	...	...	...
Causing hurt ...	...	...	...	...	2
Causing hurt, (Petty cases) ...	...	...	...	...	...
Causing hurt or grievous hurt to extort confession	...	...	...	...	...
Wrongful restraint ...	...	...	...	...	...
Do. to extort confession ...	...	...	...	...	...
Assault ...	...	...	...	...	...
Petty assault ...	...	...	...	...	...
Assault in attempting theft ...	...	...	...	...	...
Kidnapping or abducting ...	...	...	...	...	...
Kidnapping with intent to take property ...	...	...	...	...	...
Slave dealing ...	...	...	...	...	...
Prostitution of minors ...	...	...	...	...	...
Compulsory labor ...	...	...	...	...	...
Rape ...	...	1	...	1	2
Unnatural offences ...	...	...	...	...	...
Total of No. 1...	94	100	...	7	6
No. 2.—*Offences against property with violence.*					
Robbery ...	...	1	...	...	1
Robbery on the highway ...	...	...	...	3	...
Robbery (aggravated) ...	...	...	...	...	...
Attempt at robbery ...	...	...	...	...	...
Dacoity ...	...	20	3	5	10
Dacoity (aggravated) ...	1	2	...	2	6
Being a dacoit, &c. ...	...	...	...	...	...
Preparing or assembling for dacoity ...	...	...	...	...	...
House-trespass with intent to commit an offence	...	...	...	...	...
Lurking house-trespass, house-breaking... ...	...	...	...	...	...
House-breaking by night ...	...	...	...	2	5
Do. with aggravating circumstances ...	...	...	...	...	...
Breaking open closed receptacle of property ...	...	...	...	...	...
Total of No. 2...	1	23	3	12	22

D.—(*Continued.*)

of persons concerned in the Districts of the Madras Presidency, result of the proceedings.—(Continued.)

PUNISHMENTS.											
IMPRISONMENT.										Flogged.	Flogged in addition to other punishment.
Life.	Not exceeding fourteen years.	Do. ten years.	Do. seven years.	Do. five years.	Do. three years.	Do. two years.	Do. one year.	Do. six months.	Do. one month.		
...	...	...	...	...	...	...	...	...	...	...	...
...	...	3	1	5	2	2	...	1	...	...	...
...	...	27	13	19	2	11	11	7	3	1	...
...	...	...	...	...	...	...	...	1	...	...	...
...	...	...	...	...	...	...	...	...	..	...	...
...	...	...	...	...	...	1	...	51	62	...	...
...	...	...	1	3	3	1	3	5	...	...	...
...	...	...	1	2	2	1	2	1	2	...	...
...	...	...	...	...	...	8	8	15	1	...	...
...	...	1	1	4	10	32	17	78	176	2	2
...	...	...	1	...	2	4	3	62	42	2	...
...	...	...	...	..	...	...	1	55	1,000	3	...
...	...	1	4	2	...	5	3	2	1	1	...
...	...	...	...	...	1	2	5	27	88	1	...
...	...	...	...	...	...	...	...	...	...	...	...
...	...	...	...	...	...	1	5	21	14	...	...
...	...	...	...	...	...	...	...	22	661	...	...
...	...	...	...	...	...	...	1	5	13	...	...
...	...	...	1	10	5	9	1	5	1	...	...
...	...	...	...	1	...	...	...	...	...	...	...
...	...	...	...	...	...	...	...	...	...	...	...
...	...	...	...	1	...	...	...	...	...	..	...
...	...	..	...	...	...	...	...	...	...	...	...
...	...	1	1	7	...	1	1	...	...	...	...
...	...	...	...	1	...	...	...	...	...	...	...
...	...	33	24	55	27	78	61	358	2,064	10	2
...	...	1	2	...	23	66	52	78	14	5	2
...	...	...	6	2	3	18	5	7	...	1	...
...	...	2	5	36	6	2	...	...	...	...	...
...	...	...	...	...	..	2	3	4	...	...	...
...	5	29	125	176	59	25	10	6	...	15	4
...	...	10	21	3	...	...	1	...	...	...	..
...	...	...	3	17	...	...	...	...	...	...	1
...	...	...	...	...	5	...	2	...	...	...	...
...	...	...	...	...	...	...	3	18	63	2	...
...	...	...	...	4	2	21	45	198	61	107	20
...	...	5	14	36	51	182	199	6[illegible]5	122	388	74
...	...	...	...	2	...	...	...	...	...	...	...
...	...	...	...	...	...	3	13	42	36	21	2
...	5	47	176	276	149	319	333	958	296	539	103

D.—(*Continued.*)

No. I.—Number of Offences against the Indian Penal Code, and for the year 1867 ; *and the*

DESCRIPTION OF OFFENCES.	PUNISHMENTS.				
	Fined.		Fined in addition to other punishment.		
	Persons.	Amount.	Persons.	Amount.	Insane.
No. 1.—Offences against the person.					
Murder	...	...	...	...	2
Attempt to murder...	...	...	...	...	1
Culpable homicide	1	50	1	500	...
Attempt at do.	...	...	...	...	...
Abetment of suicide	...	...	...	...	...
Attempt to commit suicide	3	31	6	44	...
Causing miscarriage	...	...	...	...	...
Exposure or abandonment of children...	...	...	...	...	...
Concealment of birth	...	...	...	...	...
Causing grievous hurt	186	1,579	124	2,753	1
Causing hurt	75	966	19	598	...
Causing hurt, (Petty cases)...	3,630	18,373	351	3,796	...
Causing hurt or grievous hurt to extort confession.	...	...	2	400	...
Wrongful restraint	526	3,921	44	667	...
Do. to extort confession	...	...	..	...	...
Assault	66	1,180	9	692	...
Petty assault	5,681	24,215	147	1,236	...
Assault in attempting theft	38	330	2	20	...
Kidnapping or abducting	...	...	1	250	...
Kidnapping with intent to take property	...	...	...	...	1
Slave dealing	...	...	...	...	...
Prostitution of minors	...	...	...	...	...
Compulsory labor	...	...	...	...	...
Rape	...	...	...	...	...
Unnatural Offences	...	...	...	...	...
Total of No. 1...	10,206	50,645	706	10,956	5
No. 2.—Offences against property with violence.					
Robbery	...	...	9	655	...
Robbery on the highway	...	...	4	97	...
Robbery (aggravated)	...	...	5	138	...
Attempt at robbery...	...	...	...	...	...
Dacoity	...	...	8	930	...
Dacoity (aggravated)	...	...	...	...	...
Being a dacoit, &c.	...	...	...	...	...
Preparing or assembling for dacoity	...	...	...	...	...
House-trespass with intent to commit an offence	15	150	19	394	...
Lurking house-trespass, house-breaking	7	155	12	593	...
House-breaking by night	7	94	69	22,816	1
Do. with aggravating circumstances	...	...	...	...	...
Breaking open closed receptacle of property ...	1	5	...	...	...
Total of No. 2...	30	404	126	25,618	1

D.—*(Continued.)*

of persons concerned in the Districts of the Madras Presidency, result of the proceedings.—(Continued.)

CASES OTHERWISE DISPOSED OF.							
Dismissed for default and neglect to prosecute.		Withdrawn by parties.		Transferred to Military Authorities; Juveniles handed over to Parents; Cautioned; Escaped from custody; Died before conclusion of trial.		TOTAL.	
Cases.	Persons.	Cases.	Persons.	Cases.	Persons.	Cases.	Persons.
...	...	...	...	3	3	3	3
...	...	...	...	...	...	...	...
...	...	...	...	...	1	...	1
...	...	...	...	...	...	...	...
...	...	...	...	...	...	...	...
...	...	...	...	3	3	3	3
1	1	...	...	2	4	3	5
...	...	...	...	1	1	1	1
...	...	...	...	...	...	...	...
4	11	3	3	1	1	8	15
4	13	2	2	...	...	6	15
258	588	866	2,516	1	1	1,125	3,105
...	...	...	...	...	...	...	...
93	226	386	845	2	2	481	1,073
...	...	...	...	...	...	...	...
1	1	5	12	1	7	7	20
2,650	5,819	4,108	10,428	1	1	6,759	15,748
...	...	2	6	...	...	2	6
1	1	...	...	...	...	1	1
...	...	...	...	...	...	...	...
1	1	...	...	...	...	1	1
1	1	...	...	...	...	1	1
...	...	...	...	...	...	...	...
2	2	...	...	...	...	2	2
...	...	...	...	...	...	...	...
3,016	6,164	5,372	13,812	15	24	8,403	20,000
...	...	...	...	...	2	...	2
...	...	...	...	...	...	...	...
...	...	...	...	...	...	...	...
...	...	...	...	...	...	...	...
...	...	...	...	...	4	...	4
...	...	...	...	1	5	1	5
...	...	...	...	...	...	...	...
...	...	...	...	...	3	...	3
...	...	...	...	...	1	...	1
...	...	...	...	...	1	...	1
...	...	...	...	7	14	7	14
...	...	...	...	1	1	1	1
...	...	...	...	...	...	...	...
...	...	...	...	9	31	9	31

D.—*(Continued.)*

No. 1.—Number of Offences against the Indian Penal Code, and for the year 1867; and the

DESCRIPTION OF OFFENCES.	OPERATIONS OF			
	Number of offences committed and charges preferred in 1867.	Persons concerned.	Property	
			Lost.	Recovered.
No. 3.—Offences against property without violence.				
Frauds relating to weights and measures	83	152	...	...
Theft	19,602	32,552	3,58,316	99,772
Extortion	294	685	1,204	141
Misappropriation	1,091	2,123	25,236	6,426
Criminal Breach of Trust	586	896	71,781	33,126
Receiving or possessing stolen property	502	756	2,955	6,342
Cheating	436	670	4,951	1,104
Total of No. 3 ...	22,594	37,834	4,64,448	1,46,911
No. 4.—Malicious Offences against property.				
Mischief	4,140	11,446	3,506	280
Mischief to animals	309	567	2,958	311
Mischief with aggravating circumstances	193	806	782	...
Mischief by fire	186	269	12,367	61
Mischief by causing inundation to a public drainage	20	148	...	...
Total of No. 4 ...	4,848	13,236	19,613	652
No. 5.—Forgery and Offences against the Currency.				
Counterfeiting or altering coin	11	14	...	...
Uttering or possessing counterfeit or altered coin.	129	156	8	8
Other offences relating to coin	1	2	..	...
Frauds relating to stamps	5	7	...	...
Forgery	186	405	114	11
Offences relating to trade and property marks ...	3	7	...	...
Total of No. 5 ...	335	591	122	19
No. 6.—Contempt and Offences against Public Justice.				
Contempt of legal process or orders	2,204	5,079	...	...
Withholding information	61	78	...	...
Giving false information	93	119	...	...
False statement to a public servant on oath ...	11	12	...	...
Obstructing or omitting to aid public servant ...	150	389	19	19
Illegal bidding at authorised sale	...	...	...	...
False evidence	270	380	...	...
Causing disappearance of evidence	28	63	...	...
False personation in Judicial proceeding	10	14	...	...
Fraudulent disposal of property and false claims.	34	93	86	1
False charge	107	184	...	...
Harbouring offenders	15	24	...	...
Compounding offences	41	72	...	..

D—*(Continued.)*

of persons concerned in the Districts of the Madras Presidency, result of the proceedings.—(Continued,)

THE POLICE.						JUDICIAL OPERATIONS OF MAGISTRATES' COURTS, JUSTICES OF THE PEACE AND OTHER COURTS.					
						SUMMARILY DISPOSED OF BY MAGISTRATES.					
				Bailed by Police.		By Sub-Magistrates of 2nd Class.			By Sub-Magistrates of 1st Class.		
Number of cases detected in which convictions followed.	Persons arrested with and without Warrant.	Persons summoned.	Total persons compelled to appear.	Cases.	Persons.	Number of cases tried.	Persons tried.	Persons convicted.	Number of cases tried.	Persons tried	Persons convicted.
48	47	57	104	...	...	...	...	...	80	53	37
7,931	17,549	1,761	19,810	148	270	5,457	11,101	7,528	1,978	3,766	2,647
56	313	215	528	...	...	...	...	...	22	65	8
491	888	960	1,848	2	2	598	1,197	499	155	284	150
191	480	205	685	1	1	...	...	...	133	201	84
288	708	11	719	2	2	...	...	...	148	210	111
126	311	238	549	1	1	...	...	...	120	173	72
9,131	20,296	3,447	23,743	154	276	6,055	12,298	8,027	2,586	4,752	3,109
1,359	1,048	9,107	10,155	2	9	1,647	4,287	2,069	842	1,048	508
83	256	123	379	2	3	...	...	...	75	179	79
72	242	384	626	...	...	...	...	...	57	164	75
12	79	17	96	2	3	...	...	...	...	...	...
5	88	54	142	...	...	...	...	...	7	12	7
1,531	1,718	9,685	11,398	6	15	1,647	4,287	2,069	481	1,408	669
1	10	2	12	2	2	...	...	...	...	...	...
60	133	3	136	4	6	...	...	...	20	23	16
1	2	...	2	...	...	...	...	...	...	...	...
2	7	...	7	1	1	...	...	...	...	...	...
51	245	117	362	...	1	...	...	...	...	...	...
1	7	...	7	...	...	...	...	...	1	1	1
116	404	122	526	7	10	...	...	...	21	24	17
1,860	3,369	1,482	4,851	...	...	1,666	3,702	3,160	324	876	678
24	42	24	66	...	...	...	...	...	...	...	...
57	61	45	106	...	...	...	...	...	33	42	32
8	7	5	12	...	...	...	...	...	...	...	...
88	123	215	338	...	...	...	...	...	69	139	81
...	...	...	...	...	...	...	...	...	...	...	...
110	293	66	359	...	...	...	...	...	...	...	...
8	48	6	54	...	...	3	3	3	3	11	11
4	11	...	11	...	...	...	...	...	...	...	...
6	32	37	69	1	2	...	...	...	7	29	3
44	119	49	168	...	...	...	...	...	...	...	...
6	22	...	22	...	...	1	1	1	1	1	...
20	84	25	59	1	3	11	22	13	6	11	5

D.—*(Continued.)*

No. 1.—*Number of Offences against the Indian Penal Code, and for the year* 1867; *and the*

DESCRIPTION OF OFFENCES.	JUDICIAL OPERATIONS — SUMMARILY DISPOSED — By Justices and Magistrates with full power. Number of cases tried.	Persons tried.	Persons convicted.
No. 3.—Offences against property without violence.			
Frauds relating to weights and measures	39	48	28
Theft	2,323	3,848	2,584
Extortion	149	341	83
Misappropriation	90	145	73
Criminal breach of trust	221	312	123
Receiving or possessing stolen property	265	409	228
Cheating	119	160	58
Total of No. 3...	3,206	5,263	3,177
No. 4.—Malicious Offences against property.			
Mischief	115	256	154
Mischief to animals	79	153	42
Mischief with aggravating circumstances	69	306	102
Mischief by fire...	...	...	...
Mischief by causing inundation to a public drainage ...	5	84	...
Total of No. 4...	268	799	298
No. 5.—Forgery and Offences against the Currency.			
Counterfeiting or altering coin	...	...	...
Uttering or possessing counterfeit or altered coin.	19	20	13
Other offences relating to coin	...	...	...
Frauds relating to stamps	3	4	2
Forgery	...	...	...
Offences relating to trade and property marks	2	6	...
Total of No. 5...	24	30	15
No. 6.—Contempt and Offences against Public Justice.			
Contempt of legal process or orders	166	291	217
Withholding information...	39	56	26
Giving false information	44	52	32
False statement to a public servant on oath	9	9	7
Obstructing or omitting to aid public servant	54	166	79
Illegal bidding at authorised sale	...	...	...
False evidence	...	...	...
Causing disappearance of evidence...	6	10	...
False personation in Judicial proceeding	...	...	..
Frandulent disposal of property and false claims	20	37	6
False charge	53	82	32
Harbouring offenders	6	10	3
Compounding offences	6	7	5

D.—*(Continued.)*

of persons concerned in the Districts of the Madras Presidency, result of the proceedings.—(Continued.)

OF MAGISTRATES' COURTS, JUSTICES OF THE PEACE AND OTHER COURTS.

OF BY MAGISTRATES. TOTAL.			OPERATIONS IN COMMITTABLE CASES. By Sub-Magistrates of 2nd Class.				By Sub-Magistrates of 1st Class.			
					Committed to Higher Court.				Committed to Higher Court.	
Number of cases tried.	Persons tried.	Persons convicted.	Number of cases inquired into.	Persons charged.	Cases.	Persons.	Number of cases inquired into.	Persons charged.	Cases.	Persons
69	101	65	3	3	1	1	...	...	...	...
9,758	18,715	12,759	90	186	90	186	8	23	8	23
171	406	91	38	90	9	15	5	12	2	5
843	1,626	722	3	10	3	10	1	1	1	1
354	513	207	53	92	19	36	2	3	2	3
413	619	339	40	65	30	44	5	8	5	8
239	333	130	64	121	11	16	5	6	5	6
11,847	22,313	14,313	291	567	163	308	26	53	23	46
2,104	5,591	2,731	8	13	3	13	...	...	...	...
154	332	121	17	34	3	3	...	...	...	...
126	470	177	12	63	2	10	11	55	...	...
...	...	...	39	59	17	22	15	31	5	7
12	96	7	2	40	...	...	...	...	...	...
2,396	6,489	3,036	73	209	25	48	26	86	5	7
...	...	...	5	7	2	2	1	1	...	...
39	43	29	56	67	36	43	12	13	9	9
...	...	...	1	2	1	2	...	...	...	...
3	4	2	1	2	1	2	...	...	...	...
...	...	...	122	273	49	79	27	61	10	15
3	7	1	...	...	...	...	...	...	...	...
45	54	32	185	351	89	128	40	75	19	24
2,156	4,869	4,055	1	1	1	1	...	...	...	...
89	56	26	4	6	...	...	2	3	1	2
77	94	64	4	10	3	5	...	...	...	...
9	9	7	1	2	1	2	...	...	...	...
123	305	160	9	20	2	2	...	...	...	...
...	...	...	...	...	...	...	...	...	...	...
...	...	...	126	188	95	117	45	62	28	40
12	24	14	3	7	...	...	5	20	5	18
...	...	...	6	9	4	6	1	1	1	1
27	66	9	1	1	...	...	...	...	...	...
53	82	32	32	58	19	25	8	22	4	5
8	12	4	6	10	2	3	...	...	...	...
23	40	23	6	10	4	6	1	1	...	...

D.—*(Continued.)*

No. 1.—Number of Offences against the Indian Penal Code, and for the year 1867 *; and the*

DESCRIPTION OF OFFENCES.	JUDICIAL OPERATIONS — OPERATIONS IN — By Justices and Magistrates with full powers.			
	Number of cases inquired into.	Persons charged.	Committed to Higher Court.	
			Cases.	Persons.
No. 3.—Offences against property without violence.				
Frauds relating to weights and measures	...	...	...	...
Theft	35	38	35	38
Extortion	4	11	3	10
Misappropriation	4	4	4	4
Criminal breach of trust	15	15	15	15
Receiving or possessing stolen property	17	22	17	22
Cheating	9	17	9	17
Total of No. 3...	84	107	83	106
No. 4.—Malicious Offences against property.				
Mischief	...	...	...	...
Mischief to animals	4	6	4	5
Mischief with aggravating circumstances	...	...	...	...
Mischief by fire...	3	3	1	1
Mischief by causing inundation to a public drainage	...	...	...	...
Total of No. 4...	7	9	5	6
No. 5.—Forgery and Offences against the Currency.				
Counterfeiting or altering coin	1	2	...	...
Uttering or possessing counterfeit or altered coin	5	7	5	7
Other offences relating to coin...	...	...	...	...
Frauds relating to stamps	...	...	...	...
Forgery	19	24	17	22
Offences relating to trade and property marks	...	...	...	...
Total of No. 5...	25	33	22	29
No. 6.—Contempt and Offences against Public Justice.				
Contempt of legal process or orders	...	...	...	...
Withholding information...	...	...	...	...
Giving false information	...	...	...	...
False statement to a public servant on oath...	...	...	...	...
Obstructing or omitting to aid public servant	...	...	...	...
Illegal bidding at authorised sale	...	...	...	...
False evidence	59	69	45	48
Causing disappearance of evidence	3	3	1	1
False personation in Judicial proceeding	...	...	...	...
Fraudulent disposal of property and false claims	...	...	...	...
False charge	4	7	4	7
Harbouring offenders	...	...	...	...
Compounding offences.	1	5	1	5

D.—*(Continued.)*

of persons concerned in the Districts of the Madras Presidency, result of the proceedings.—(Continued.)

OF MAGISTRATES' COURTS, JUSTICES OF THE PEACE AND OTHER COURTS.

COMMITTABLE CASES.

By Principal Sudder Ameens.					By Session Judges.		
Number of cases tried.	Persons tried.	Persons convicted.	Committed to Higher Court.		Number of cases tried.	Persons tried.	Persons convicted.
			Cases.	Persons.			
1	1	...	...	...	...	...	...
54	77	56	...	...	45	133	82
6	12	4	...	...	8	18	7
2	2	2	...	...	2	9	...
8	19	11	...	...	19	26	13
8	17	5	...	...	30	40	29
4	4	...	...	...	12	18	7
83	132	78	...	...	116	244	138
2	12	9	...	...	1	1	...
2	2	1	...	...	3	4	4
1	9	3	...	...	1	1	...
...	...	...	...	...	23	30	13
...	...	...	...	...	...	...	...
5	23	13	...	...	28	36	17
...	...	...	...	...	2	2	1
...	...	...	...	...	46	52	36
...	...	...	...	...	1	2	1
...	...	...	...	...	1	2	...
...	...	...	...	...	70	106	61
...	...	...	...	...	...	...	...
...	...	...	...	...	120	164	99
1	1	...	...	...	...	...	...
...	...	...	...	...	1	1	1
1	2	2	...	...	2	3	2
...	...	...	...	...	2	3	2
2	2	1	...	...	...	...	...
...	...	...	...	...	...	...	...
...	...	...	4	4	187	224	130
...	...	...	...	...	6	19	2
...	...	...	...	...	6	8	6
...	...	...	...	...	...	...	...
1	1	1	...	...	25	34	22
...	...	...	...	...	2	3	3
...	...	...	...	...	5	10	8

D.—(*Continued.*)

No. 1.—*Number of Offences against the Indian Penal Code, and for the year* 1867; *and the*

DESCRIPTION OF OFFENCES.	JUDICIAL OPERATIONS		
	OPERATIONS IN		
	By High Court.		
	Number of cases tried.	Persons tried.	Persons convicted.
No. 3.—Offences against property without violence.			
Frauds relating to weights and measures	...	...	...
Theft	34	37	33
Extortion	...	...	...
Misappropriation	4	4	4
Criminal breach of trust	9	9	9
Receiving or possessing stolen property	14	17	13
Cheating...	9	17	13
Total of No. 3..	70	84	72
No. 4.—Malicious Offences against property.			
Mischief	...	...	...
Mischief to animals	2	2	1
Mischief with aggravating circumstances	...	...	...
Mischief by fire	...	...	...
Mischief by causing inundation to a public drainage...	...	...	...
Total of No. 4...	2	2	1
No. 5.—Forgery and Offences against the Currency.			
Counterfeiting or altering coin	...	...	...
Uttering or possessing counterfeit or altered coin ...	4	6	3
Other offences relating to coin	...	...	...
Frauds relating to stamps	...	...	...
Forgery	6	6	6
Offences relating to trade and property marks ...	...	...	...
Total of No. 5...	10	12	9
No. 6.—Contempt and Offences against Public Justice.			
Contempt of legal process or orders	...	...	...
Withholding information	...	...	...
Giving false information	...	...	...
False statement to a public servant on oath	...	...	...
Obstructing or omitting to aid public servant	...	...	...
Illegal bidding at authorised sale	...	...	...
False evidence	2	2	1
Causing disappearance of evidence	...	...	...
False personation in Judicial proceeding	...	...	...
Fraudulent disposal of property and false claims ...	...	...	...
False charge	1	1	1
Harbouring offenders	...	...	...
Compounding offences	...	...	...

D.—*(Continued.)*

of persons concerned in the Districts of the Madras Presidency, result of the proceedings.—(Continued.)

OF MAGISTRATES' COURTS, JUSTICES OF THE PEACE AND OTHER COURTS.								
COMMITTABLE CASES.			Total Number of cases summarily disposed of by Magistrates and tried by Courts.	TOTAL NUMBER OF PERSONS CONVICTED BY MAGISTRATES AND COURTS.				
TOTAL.				Adults.		Juveniles.		
Cases tried.	Persons tried.	Persons convicted.		Males.	Females.	Males.	Females.	Total.
1	1	...	70	52	13	...	...	65
138	247	171	9,891	12,110	496	288	36	12,930
14	30	11	185	102	...	...	...	102
8	15	6	851	693	32	3	...	728
36	54	33	390	233	3	4	...	240
52	74	47	465	347	35	4	...	386
25	39	20	264	145	4	1	...	150
269	460	288	12,116	13,682	583	300	36	14,601
3	13	9	2,107	2,695	42	2	1	2,740
7	8	6	161	125	2	...	...	127
2	10	3	128	180	...	...	...	180
23	30	13	23	11	2	...	...	13
...	...	...	12	7	...	...	...	7
35	61	31	2,431	3,018	46	2	1	3,067
2	2	1	2	1	...	...	...	1
50	58	39	89	66	1	1	...	68
1	2	1	1	1	...	...	...	1
1	2	...	4	2	...	...	...	2
76	112	67	76	67	...	...	...	67
...	...	...	3	1	...	...	...	1
130	176	108	175	138	1	1	...	140
1	1	...	2,157	3,945	102	7	1	4,055
1	1	1	40	27	...	...	...	27
3	5	4	80	67	...	1	...	68
2	3	2	11	9	...	...	...	9
2	2	1	125	157	4	...	...	161
...	...	...	...	...	...	...	...	...
189	226	131	189	122	8	1	...	131
6	19	2	18	16	...	...	...	16
6	8	6	6	6	...	...	...	6
...	...	...	27	9	...	...	...	9
27	36	24	80	53	3	...	...	56
2	3	3	10	7	...	...	...	7
5	10	8	28	31	...	...	...	31

D.—(*Continued.*)

No. 1.—Number of Offences against the Indian Penal Code, and for the year 1867; *and the*

DESCRIPTION OF OFFENCES.	PUNISHMENTS.				
		TRANSPORTATION.			
	Death.	Life.	Fourteen years.	Ten years.	Seven years.
No. 3.—Offences against property without violence.					
Frauds relating to weights and measures	...	...	...	...	...
Theft	...	...	...	...	6
Extortion	...	...	...	...	...
Misappropriation	...	...	...	...	...
Criminal breach of trust	...	...	...	...	...
Receiving or possessing stolen property	...	...	...	...	...
Cheating	...	...	...	...	1
Total of No. 3...	...	...	...	...	7
No. 4.—Malicious Offences against property.					
Mischief	...	...	...	...	...
Mischief to animals	...	...	...	...	...
Mischief with aggravating circumstances	...	...	...	...	...
Mischief by fire	...	...	...	...	...
Mischief by causing inundation to a public drainage	...	...	...	...	...
Total of No. 4.	...	...	...	...	...
No. 5.—Forgery and Offences against the Currency.					
Counterfeiting or altering coin	...	...	...	...	...
Uttering or possessing counterfeit or altered coin.	...	...	...	...	...
Other offences relating to coin	...	...	...	...	...
Frauds relating to stamps	...	...	...	...	...
Forgery	...	...	...	...	2
Offences relating to trade and property marks ...	...	...	...	...	...
Total of No. 5...	...	...	...	...	2
No. 6.—Contempt and Offences against Public Justice.					
Contempt of legal process or orders	...	...	...	...	...
Withholding information	...	...	...	...	...
Giving false information	...	...	...	...	...
False statement to a public servant on oath ...	...	...	...	...	...
Obstructing or omitting to aid public servant ...	...	...	...	...	...
Illegal bidding at authorised sale...	...	...	...	...	...
False evidence	...	...	...	...	1
Causing disappearance of evidence	...	...	...	...	...
False personation in Judicial proceeding	...	...	...	...	...
Fraudulent disposal of property and false claims...	...	...	...	...	...
False charge	...	...	...	...	...
Harbouring offenders	...	...	...	...	...
Compounding offences	...	...	...	...	...

D.—(*Continued.*)

of persons concerned in the Districts of the Madras Presidency, result of the proceedings.—(Continued.)

PUNISHMENTS.											
IMPRISONMENT.										Flogged.	Flogged in addition to other punishment.
Life.	Not exceeding fourteen years.	Do. ten years.	Do. seven years.	Do. five years.	Do. three years.	Do. two years.	Do. one year.	Do. six months.	Do. one month.		
...	...	...	...	...	...	...	...	1	2	...	...
...	...	...	3	6	19	221	356	1,562	6,730	1,829	262
...	...	...	...	2	...	9	9	30	12	3	...
...	...	...	...	...	...	...	9	61	305	1	...
...	...	...	2	4	4	21	21	115	42	3	...
...	...	1	1	2	6	44	35	155	68	40	5
...	...	..	...	...	1	12	11	65	26	1	...
...	...	1	6	14	30	307	441	1,989	7,185	1,877	267
...	..	...	...	...	...	2	1	27	486	2	...
...	...	...	...	...	...	9	11	67	12	1	...
...	...	...	...	...	...	...	3	12	24	...	...
...	...	...	1	2	6	2	...	2	...	...	...
...	...	...	...	...	...	...	...	...	...	...	...
...	...	...	1	2	6	13	15	108	522	3	...
...	...	...	...	...	1	...	...	...	...	...	...
...	...	...	1	1	4	18	7	24	2	1	...
...	...	...	...	...	...	1	...	...	...	...	...
...	...	...	...	...	...	...	...	...	...	...	...
...	...	1	3	21	9	20	5	5	1	...	...
...	...	...	...	...	...	...	...	...	...	...	...
...	...	1	4	22	14	39	12	29	3	1	...
...	...	...	...	...	...	...	1	7	301	...	...
...	...	...	...	...	...	...	...	4	4	...	...
...	...	...	...	...	...	1	1	21	22	...	...
...	...	...	...	...	...	...	...	5	4	...	...
...	...	...	...	...	1	4	...	10	36	...	...
...	...	...	...	...	...	...	...	...	...	...	...
...	...	1	5	8	16	19	30	40	9	2	...
...	...	...	...	1	...	1	...	...	18	...	...
...	...	...	...	...	1	...	...	1	...	...	...
...	...	...	...	...	...	...	...	2	...	...	...
...	...	...	1	3	4	7	10	10	13	1	...
...	...	...	...	1	...	2	...	1	1	...	...
...	...	...	1	...	...	4	...	5	11	...	...

D.—(Continued.)

No. 1.—Number of Offences against the Indian Penal Code, and for the year 1867; and the

DESCRIPTION OF OFFENCES.	PUNISHMENTS.				
	Fined.		Fined in addition to other punishment.		
	Persons.	Amount.	Persons.	Amount.	Insane.
No. 3.—Offences against property without violence.					
Frauds relating to weights and measures	62	866	...	...	...
Theft	2,222	11,872	888	10,561	5
Extortion	87	1,393	22	1,566	...
Misappropriation	352	2,763	63	1,567	...
Criminal breach of trust...	27	1,019	45	4,318	1
Receiving or possessing stolen property	34	1,508	16	997	...
Cheating	38	1,225	15	1,609	...
Total of No. 3...	2,767	20,646	1,049	20,613	6
No. 4.—Malicious Offences against property.					
Mischief	2,229	11,970	179	1,171	...
Mischief to animals	27	382	16	359	...
Mischief with aggravating circumstances	141	1,587	11	660	...
Mischief by fire	...	...	...	...	...
Mischief by causing inundation to a public drainage	7	215	...	...	...
Total of No. 4...	2,404	14,154	206	2,190	...
No. 5.—Forgery and Offences against the Currency.					
Counterfeiting or altering coin	...	...	...	...	...
Uttering or possessing counterfeit or altered coin.	10	208	2	60	...
Other offences relating to coin	...	...	...	...	...
Frauds relating to stamps	2	60	...	...	...
Forgery	...	...	10	3,050	...
Offences relating to trade and property marks ...	1	50	...	...	...
Total of No. 5...	13	318	12	3,110	...
No. 6.—Contempt and Offences against Public Justice.					
Contempt of legal process or orders	3,761	10,938	13	90	...
Withholding information	19	289	2	15	...
Giving false information	23	687	13	590	...
False statement to a public servant on oath ...	...	...	3	210	...
Obstructing or omitting to aid public servant ...	110	1,234	1	50	...
Illegal bidding at authorised sale	...	...	...	...	...
False evidence	...	...	18	1,800	...
Causing disappearance of evidence	1	10	3	6	...
False personation in Judicial proceeding	4	115	...	...	...
Fraudulent disposal of property and false claims.	7	180	...	...	...
False charge	7	240	2	35	...
Harbouring offenders	2	20	...	...	...
Compounding offences	10	151	4	350	...

D.—*(Continued.)*

of persons concerned in the Districts of the Madras Presidency, result of the proceedings.—(Continued.)

CASES OTHERWISE DISPOSED OF.							
Dismissed for default and neglect to prosecute.		Withdrawn by parties.		Transferred to Military Authorities; Juveniles handed over to Parents; Cautioned; Escaped from custody; Died before conclusion of trial.		Total.	
Cases.	Persons.	Cases.	Persons.	Cases.	Persons.	Cases.	Persons.
...	...	...	...	...	...	...	...
16	31	3	7	18	26	37	64
4	6	1	1	...	...	5	7
47	120	41	98	3	3	91	221
14	23	21	48	1	1	36	72
...	...	...	...	1	1	1	1
21	30	29	41	...	...	50	71
102	210	95	195	23	31	220	436
471	1,231	1,283	3,443	6	6	1,760	4,680
1	1	4	9	...	...	5	10
6	28	4	10	...	...	10	38
...	...	...	...	...	...	...	...
...	...	2	6	...	...	2	6
478	1,260	1,293	3,468	6	6	1,777	4,734
...	...	...	...	...	...	...	...
...	...	...	...	...	1	...	1
...	...	...	...	...	...	...	...
...	...	...	...	...	...	...	...
1	2	...	...	1	1	2	3
...	...	...	...	...	...	...	...
1	2	...	...	1	2	2	4
9	15	6	12	...	...	15	27
...	...	1	1	...	...	1	1
...	...	1	2	...	1	1	3
...	...	...	...	...	...	...	...
3	10	3	3	1	1	7	14
...	...	...	...	...	...	...	...
8	15	3	4	1	4	12	23
...	...	...	...	...	...	...	...
...	...	...	...	...	...	...	...
...	...	...	...	...	...	...	...
...	...	...	...	...	...	...	...
...	...	...	...	...	...	...	...
...	...	...	...	...	1	...	1

D.—(Continued.)

No. 1.—Number of Offences against the Indian Penal Code, and for the year 1867 *; and the*

DESCRIPTION OF OFFENCES.	OPERATIONS OF			
	Number of offences committed and charges preferred in 1867.	Persons concerned.	Property	
			Lost.	Recovered.
No. 6.—Contempt and Offences, &c.—Contd.				
Taking gift to recover stolen property	30	61	434	182
Omission to apprehend by public servant	12	30	...	...
Negligent escape	56	68	...	...
Escape	232	330	65	...
Rescue	29	129	5	...
Return from transportation	...	...	...	...
Contempt of Court	139	178	...	...
Total of No. 6 ...	3,522	7,298	609	202
No. 7.—Offences not included in the above Classes.				
Abetment	39	130	...	...
Concealment of criminal designs	1	1	...	...
Offences against the State	...	...	...	...
Spreading false and alarming rumours	...	...	...	...
Abetment of Military and Naval offences	...	...	...	...
Unlawful assembly	78	979	...	...
Rioting	257	2,522	165	133
Landholders, &c., failing to prevent a riot	1	1	...	...
Affray	258	1,174	...	...
Giving or receiving illegal gratification	184	295	475	125
Breaches of duty by public servant	30	40	...	...
Personating public servant	28	45	...	...
Spreading dangerous diseases, &c.	8	14	...	...
Adulteration and selling noxious food, &c.	22	32	...	...
Nuisance	970	4,072	...	...
Acts against public safety	204	358	...	...
Acts against decency	31	59	...	...
Offences against religion	50	190	...	...
Criminal trespass	8,333	24,334	27	7
House-trespass	491	1,266	79	42
Criminal breach of contract	25	51	...	...
Bigamy...	4	9	...	...
Adultery	133	169	91	10
Other offences relating to marriage	109	189	553	87
Defamation	120	257	...	...
Insult	887	1,831	...	...
Criminal intimidation	59	125	...	...
Misconduct in public by a drunken person	141	208	...	...
Attempts not otherwise provided for	1,424	2,191	...	...
Total of No. 7 ...	13,887	40,542	1,390	404
Grand Total ...	75,311	1,73,645	10,78,366	2,26,659

D.—*(Continued.)*

of persons concerned in the Districts of the Madras Presidency, result of the proceedings.—(Continued.)

THE POLICE.						JUDICIAL OPERATIONS OF MAGISTRATES' COURTS, JUSTICES OF THE PEACE AND OTHER COURTS.					
				Bailed by Police.		SUMMARILY DISPOSED OF BY MAGISTRATES.					
						By Sub-Magistrates of 2nd Class.			By Sub-Magistrates of 1st Class.		
Number of cases detected in which convictions followed.	Persons arrested with and without Warrant.	Persons summoned.	Total persons compelled to appear.	Cases.	Persons.	Number of cases tried.	Persons tried.	Persons convicted.	Number of cases tried.	Persons tried.	Persons convicted.
22	46	4	50	...	...	...	...	...	...	...	...
4	17	1	18	...	...	...	...	...	1	1	1
37	55	11	66	...	...	...	...	...	18	24	19
164	206	13	219	...	...	...	...	...	62	73	66
14	66	7	73	1	1	...	...	...	10	44	36
...	...	...	...	...	...	...	...	...	...	...	...
134	97	57	154	...	...	97	118	116	17	18	17
2,610	4,648	2,047	6,695	3	6	1,778	3,846	3,293	551	1,269	949
14	83	40	123	...	...	5	35	82	1	2	...
...	1	...	1	...	...	...	...	...	...	...	...
...	...	...	...	...	...	...	...	...	...	...	...
...	...	...	...	...	...	...	...	...	...	...	...
...	...	...	...	...	...	...	...	...	...	...	...
45	399	296	695	1	4	52	541	351	9	69	46
166	1,135	965	2,100	...	...	185	1,562	948	30	253	156
...	1	...	1	...	...	...	...	...	1	1	...
280	542	541	1,083	...	...	187	808	665	36	155	118
56	96	162	258	1	1	9	16	11	21	30	20
16	29	9	38	...	...	...	...	...	9	10	5
16	30	2	32	...	...	10	10	10	6	13	9
5	5	9	14	...	...	...	...	...	2	2	1
18	14	17	31	...	...	...	...	...	9	12	8
773	1,664	2,063	3,727	2	7	715	3,075	2,601	105	357	252
143	191	134	325	3	4	109	207	156	54	81	64
18	24	22	46	...	...	...	...	...	6	18	7
23	79	67	146	...	...	...	...	...	...	...	...
2,041	1,838	17,842	19,680	2	6	3,158	8,331	3,656	611	1,643	757
226	497	497	994	4	5	234	698	299	69	151	57
13	5	33	48	...	...	...	...	...	10	24	20
...	5	4	9	...	...	...	...	...	...	...	...
14	86	73	159	3	3	...	...	...	...	...	...
21	79	52	131	...	...	...	...	...	...	...	...
36	69	167	236	...	...	...	...	...	...	...	...
430	278	1,456	1,734	...	...	524	1,057	496	77	175	78
14	51	67	118	2	2	...	...	...	15	24	8
126	16	35	204	...	...	94	117	108	37	70	68
117	24	34	275	3	5	90	125	61	33	36	27
4,561	7,611	24,592	32,203	21	37	5,422	16,582	9,394	1,141	3,126	1,701
27,135	46,204	82,765	1,28,969	286	564	22,968	57,598	32,408	7,228	16,361	9,336

D.—(Continued.)

No. 1.—Number of Offences against the Indian Penal Code, and for the year 1867; and the

DESCRIPTION OF OFFENCES.	JUDICIAL OPERATIONS — SUMMARILY DISPOSED OF — By Justices and Magistrates with full powers.		
	Number of cases tried.	Persons tried.	Persons convicted.
No. 6.—Contempt and Offences against Public Justice.—Contd.			
Taking gift to recover stolen property ...	27	46	29
Omission to apprehend by public servant	4	7	2
Negligent escape...	33	39	25
Escape ...	103	119	105
Rescue..	13	20	9
Return from transportation	...	...	...
Contempt of Court ...	24	31	29
Total of No. 6...	607	982	606
No. 7.—Offences not included in the above Classes.			
Abetment ...	17	23	9
Concealment of criminal designs ...	...	...	...
Offences against the State...	...	...	...
Spreading false and alarming rumours...	...	...	...
Abetment of Military and Naval offences	...	...	...
Unlawful assembly ...	4	15	13
Rioting ...	20	207	107
Landholders, &c., failing to prevent a riot ...	...	...	...
Affray ...	23	143	80
Giving or receiving illegal gratification...	100	160	46
Breaches of duty by public servant	14	21	11
Personating public servant... ...	5	8	2
Spreading dangerous diseases, &c.	6	12	7
Adulteration and selling noxious food, &c.	11	18	10
Nuisances ...	65	153	108
Acts against public safety	17	24	15
Acts against decency ...	19	25	17
Offences against religion ...	44	125	50
Criminal trespass	68	165	69
House-trespass ...	40	72	42
Criminal breach of contract	6	15	5
Bigamy ...	...	...	...
Adultery ...	9	10	2
Other offences relating to marriage	56	91	17
Defamation ...	79	149	46
Insult ...	43	64	42
Criminal intimidation	16	41	8
Misconduct in public by a drunken person ...	6	12	4
Attempts not otherwise provided for ...	55	83	47
Total of No. 7...	723	1,636	757
Grand Total...	7,862	13,233	7,139

D.—*(Continued.)*

of persons concerned in the Districts of the Madras Presidency, result of the proceedings.—(Continued.)

OF MAGISTRATES' COURTS, JUSTICES OF THE PEACE AND OTHER COURTS.

BY MAGISTRATES.			OPERATIONS IN COMMITTABLE CASES.							
TOTAL.			By Sub-Magistrates of 2nd Class.				By Sub-Magistrates of 1st Class.			
					Committed to Higher Court.				Committed to Higher Court.	
Number of cases tried.	Persons tried.	Persons convicted.	Number of cases inquired into.	Persons charged.	Cases.	Persons.	Number of cases inquired into.	Persons charged.	Cases.	Persons.
27	46	29	1	2	...	...	...	...	...	...
5	8	3	2	5	1	1	2	5	1	4
51	63	44	2	2	2	2	...	...	...	...
165	192	171	16	19	16	19	4	5	4	5
23	64	45	2	6	1	4	1	2	1	1
...	...	...	...	...	...	...	...	...	...	...
138	167	162	...	...	...	...	...	...	...	...
2,936	6,097	4,848	222	356	151	193	69	121	45	76
23	60	41	8	10	8	10	2	6	2	6
...	...	...	...	...	...	...	...	...	...	...
...	...	...	...	...	...	...	...	...	...	...
...	...	...	...	...	...	...	...	...	...	...
...	...	...	...	...	...	...	...	...	...	...
65	625	410	...	...	...	...	...	...	...	...
235	2,022	1,211	3	37	3	37	...	...	...	...
1	1	...	...	...	...	...	...	...	...	...
246	1,106	863	...	...	...	...	...	...	...	...
130	206	77	26	37	7	10	2	2	1	1
23	31	16	4	5	4	5	...	...	...	...
21	81	21	...	...	...	...	...	...	...	...
8	14	8	...	...	...	...	...	...	...	...
20	30	18	...	...	...	...	...	...	...	...
885	3,585	2,961	...	...	...	...	...	...	...	...
180	812	235	...	...	...	...	...	...	...	...
25	43	24	2	2	2	2	...	...	...	...
44	125	50	1	21	1	21	...	...	...	...
3,837	10,139	4,482	...	...	...	...	...	...	...	...
393	921	398	...	...	...	...	...	...	...	...
16	89	25	...	...	...	...	...	...	...	...
...	...	...	2	4	1	1	...	...	...	...
9	10	2	43	62	19	23	17	24	5	5
56	91	17	11	22	4	7	1	1	...	...
79	149	46	7	16	1	1	5	16	2	13
144	1,296	616	...	...	...	...	...	...	...	...
31	65	16	13	28	3	5	1	1	1	1
137	199	180	...	...	...	...	1	2	1	2
178	244	135	13	17	12	16	1	1	1	1
7,286	21,344	11,852	183	261	65	138	30	53	13	29
87,558	87,192	48,883	1,857	4,617	1,175	2,572	435	1,077	277	614

D.—*(Continued.)*

No. 1.—*Number of Offences against the Indian Penal Code, and for the year* 1867 ; *and the*

DESCRIPTION OF OFFENCES.	JUDICIAL OPERATIONS — OPERATIONS IN — By Justices and Magistrates with full powers. Number of cases inquired into.	Persons charged.	Committed to Higher Court. Cases.	Committed to Higher Court. Persons.
No. 6.—Contempt and Offences against Public Justice.—Contd.				
Taking gift to recover stolen property ...	2	2	2	2
Omission to apprehend by public servant ...	...	...	...	...
Negligent escape ...	...	...	...	...
Escape...	...	...	...	...
Rescue...	...	...	...	...
Return from transportation ...	...	...	..	...
Contempt of Court ...	...	...	...	...
Total of No. 6...	69	86	53	63
No. 7.—Offences not included in the above Classes.				
Abetment ...	3	46	3	40
Concealment of criminal designs ...	1	1	1	1
Offences against the State ...	...	...	...	...
Spreading false and alarming rumours ...	...	...	...	...
Abetment of Military and Naval offences ...	...	...	...	...
Unlawful assembly ...	...	...	...	...
Rioting...	1	1	1	1
Land-holders, &c., failing to prevent a riot ...	...	...	...	...
Affray ...	...	...	...	...
Giving or receiving illegal gratification ...	2	5	2	5
Breaches of duty by public servant ...	1	1	1	1
Personating public servant ...	...	...	...	...
Spreading dangerous diseases, &c....	...	...	...	...
Adulteration and selling noxious food, &c....	...	...	...	...
Nuisance ...	1	1	1	1
Acts against public safety ...	...	...	...	...
Acts against decency...	...	...	...	...
Offences against religion ...	...	...	...	...
Criminal trespass ...	...	...	...	...
House-trespass ...	...	...	...	...
Criminal breach of contract ...	...	...	...	...
Bigamy...	...	...	...	...
Adultery ...	23	29	11	14
Other offences relating to marriage ...	4	4	3	3
Defamation ...	1	1	1	1
Insult ...	...	...	...	...
Criminal intimidation ...	...	...	...	...
Misconduct in public by a drunken person ...	...	...	...	...
Attempts not otherwise provided for ...	2	5	2	5
Total of No. 7...	39	94	26	72
Grand Total...	378	790	303	589

D.—*(Continued.)*

of persons concerned in the Districts of the Madras Presidency, result of the proceedings.—(Continued.)

OF MAGISTRATES' COURTS, JUSTICES OF THE PEACE AND OTHER COURTS.

COMMITTABLE CASES.

By Principal Sudder Ameens.					By Session Judges.		
			Committed to Higher Court.				
Number of cases tried.	Persons tried.	Persons convicted.	Cases.	Persons.	Number of cases tried.	Persons tried.	Persons convicted.
...	...	...	...	...	2	2	2
...	...	...	...	...	2	5	4
2	2	1	...	...	...	...	...
8	9	9	...	...	12	15	14
1	4	8	...	...	1	1	1
...	...	...	...	...	...	...	...
...	...	...	...	...	...	...	...
16	21	17	4	4	253	328	197
1	1	...	...	...	10	53	5
...	...	...	...	...	1	1	...
...	...	...	...	...	...	...	...
...	...	...	...	...	...	...	...
...	...	...	...	...	...	...	...
...	...	...	...	...	...	...	...
...	...	...	...	...	3	37	22
...	...	...	...	...	...	...	...
...	...	...	...	...	...	...	...
5	7	...	...	...	5	9	...
1	1	1	...	...	4	5	1
...	...	...	...	...	...	...	...
...	...	...	...	...	...	...	...
..	...	...	...	...	...	...	...
...	...	...	...	...	...	...	...
...	...	...	...	...	...	...	...
2	2	1	...	...	...	...	...
1	21	3	...	...	...	...	...
...	...	...	...	...	...	...	...
...	...	...	...	...	...	...	...
...	...	...	...	...	...	...	...
...	...	...	...	...	1	1	...
1	1	...	...	...	30	35	11
1	1	1	...	...	4	7	3
3	14	6	...	...	...	...	...
...	...	...	...	...	...	...	...
...	...	...	...	...	4	6	...
...	...	...	...	...	1	2	...
1	3	...	...	...	13	18	10
16	51	12	...	...	76	174	52
179	322	182	4	4	1,448	3,265	1,835

D.—(Continued.)

No. 1.—Number of Offences against the Indian Penal Code, and for the year 1867; and the

DESCRIPTION OF OFFENCES.	JUDICIAL OPERATIONS		
	OPERATIONS IN		
	By High Court.		
	Number of cases tried.	Persons tried.	Persons convicted.
No. 6.—Contempt and Offences against Public Justice.—Contd.			
Taking gift to recover stolen property	...	...	...
Omission to apprehend by public servant	...	...	...
Negligent escape	...	...	...
Escape	...	...	...
Rescue	...	...	...
Return from transportation	...	...	...
Contempt of Court	...	...	...
Total of No. 6...	8	8	2
No. 7.—Offences not included in the above Classes.			
Abetment	2	2	1
Concealment of criminal designs	...	...	...
Offences against the State...	...	...	...
Spreading false and alarming rumours	...	...	...
Abetment of Military and Naval offences	...	...	...
Unlawful assembly	...	...	...
Rioting	1	1	...
Landholders, &c., failing to prevent a riot	...	...	...
Affray	...	...	...
Giving or receiving illegal gratification...	...	...	...
Breaches of duty by public servant...	...	...	...
Personating public servant	...	...	...
Spreading dangerous diseases, &c.	...	...	...
Adulteration and selling noxious food, &c.	...	...	...
Nuisance	1	1	1
Acts against public safety	...	...	...
Acts against decency...	...	...	...
Offences against religion	...	...	...
Criminal trespass	...	...	...
House-trespass	...	...	...
Criminal breach of contract	...	...	...
Bigamy	...	...	...
Adultery...	3	3	1
Other offences relating to marriage...	1	1	1
Defamation	1	1	...
Insult	...	...	...
Criminal intimidation	...	...	...
Misconduct in public by a drunken person	...	...	...
Attempts not otherwise provided for	1	1	1
Total of No. 7...	10	10	5
Grand Total...	147	195	147

D.—(*Continued.*)

of persons concerned in the Districts of the Madras Presidency, result of the proceedings.—(Continued.)

OF MAGISTRATES' COURTS, JUSTICES OF THE PEACE AND OTHER COURTS.									
COMMITTABLE CASES.			Total Number of cases summarily disposed of by Magistrates and tried by Courts.	TOTAL NUMBER OF PERSONS CONVICTED BY MAGISTRATES AND COURTS.					
TOTAL.				Adults.		Juveniles.		Total.
Cases tried.	Persons tried.	Persons convicted.		Males.	Females.	Males.	Females.	
2	2	2	29	31	...	...	...	31
2	5	4	7	7	...	...	...	7
2	2	1	58	45	...	...	...	45
20	24	23	185	191	3	...	...	194
2	5	4	25	49	...	...	...	49
...	...	...	...	...	...	...	...	...
...	...	...	138	162	...	...	...	162
272	352	216	3,208	4,934	120	9	1	5,064
13	56	6	36	47	...	...	...	47
1	1	...	1	...	...	...	...	...
...	...	...	...	...	...	...	...	...
...	...	...	...	...	...	...	...	...
...	...	...	...	...	...	...	...	...
...	...	...	65	406	3	1	...	410
4	38	22	239	1,208	23	2	...	1,233
...	...	...	1	...	...	...	...	...
...	...	...	246	762	97	4	...	863
10	16	...	140	77	...	...	...	77
5	6	2	28	18	...	...	...	18
...	...	...	21	21	...	...	...	21
...	...	...	8	5	3	...	...	8
...	...	...	20	18	...	...	...	18
1	1	1	886	2,886	76	...	...	2,962
...	...	...	180	224	10	1	...	235
2	2	1	27	19	5	1	...	25
1	21	8	45	52	1	...	...	53
...	...	...	3,837	4,361	109	12	...	4,482
...	...	...	398	360	38	...	...	398
...	...	...	16	26	...	...	...	25
1	1	...	1	...	...	...	...	...
34	39	12	43	14	...	...	...	14
6	9	5	62	21	1	...	...	22
4	15	6	88	49	3	...	...	52
...	...	...	644	564	52	...	...	616
4	6	...	35	16	...	...	...	16
1	2	...	138	179	1	...	...	180
15	22	11	198	141	2	3	...	146
102	235	69	7,388	11,473	424	24	...	11,921
1,774	3,782	2,164	39,332	48,550	2,014	441	42	51,047

D.—*(Continued.)*

No. 1.—Number of Offences against the Indian Penal Code, and for the year 1867; and the

DESCRIPTION OF OFFENCES.	PUNISHMENTS.				
		TRANSPORTATION.			
	Death.	Life.	Fourteen years.	Ten years.	Seven years.
No. 6.—Contempt and Offences, &c.—Continued.					
Taking gift to recover stolen property	...	...	1	...	...
Omission to apprehend by public servant	...	...	...	...	...
Negligent escape	...	...	...	...	...
Escape	...	...	...	...	...
Rescue	...	...	...	...	...
Return from transportation	...	...	...	...	...
Contempt of Court	...	...	...	...	...
Total of No. 6....	...	...	1	...	1
No. 7.—Offences not included in the above Classes.					
Abetment	1	...	...	...	...
Concealment of criminal designs	...	...	...	...	...
Offences against the State	...	...	...	...	...
Spreading false and alarming rumours	...	...	...	...	...
Abetment of Military and Naval offences	...	...	...	...	...
Unlawful assembly	...	...	...	...	...
Rioting	...	...	...	...	...
Landholders, &c., failing to prevent a riot	...	...	...	...	...
Affray	...	...	...	...	...
Giving or receiving illegal gratification	...	...	...	...	...
Breaches of duty by public servant	...	...	...	...	...
Personating public servant	...	...	...	...	...
Spreading dangerous diseases, &c.	...	...	...	...	...
Adulteration and selling noxious food, &c.	...	...	...	...	...
Nuisance	...	...	...	...	...
Acts against public safety	...	...	...	...	...
Acts against decency	...	...	...	...	...
Offences against religion	...	...	...	...	...
Criminal trespass	...	...	...	...	...
House-trespass	...	...	...	...	...
Criminal breach of contract	...	...	...	...	...
Bigamy	...	...	...	...	...
Adultery	...	...	...	...	...
Other offences relating to marriage	...	...	...	...	...
Defamation	...	...	...	...	...
Insult	...	...	...	...	...
Criminal intimidation	...	...	...	...	...
Misconduct in public by a drunken person	...	...	...	...	...
Attempts not otherwise provided for	...	...	...	1	1
Total of No. 7....	1	...	...	1	1
Grand Total...	96	123	4	20	39

D.—(*Continued.*)

of persons concerned in the Districts of the Madras Presidency, result of the proceedings.—(Continued.)

PUNISHMENTS.											
IMPRISONMENT.										Flogged.	Flogged in addition to other punishment.
Life.	Not exceeding fourteen years.	Do. ten years.	Do. seven years.	Do. five years.	Do. three years.	Do. two years.	Do. one year.	Do. six months.	Do. one month.		
...	...	...	1	1	...	5	5	10	4	2	...
...	...	...	...	...	...	5	...	2	...	...	...
...	...	...	...	...	...	...	2	19	11	...	...
...	...	...	...	...	...	10	17	95	59	5	...
...	...	...	...	...	...	4	2	4	7	...	...
...	...	...	...	...	...	...	...	...	...	...	...
...	...	...	...	...	...	...	...	...	11	...	...
...	...	1	7	14	22	62	68	236	506	10	...
...	...	1	...	1	2	1	2	3	4	...	...
...	...	...	...	...	...	...	...	...	...	...	...
...	...	...	...	...	...	...	...	...	...	...	...
...	...	...	...	...	...	...	...	...	...	...	...
...	...	...	...	...	...	...	...	...	...	...	...
...	...	...	...	...	...	...	...	...	85	...	...
...	...	...	...	...	...	6	11	41	302	1	...
...	...	...	...	...	...	...	...	...	...	...	...
...	...	...	...	...	...	...	...	...	180	...	...
...	...	...	...	...	...	2	10	6	6	...	...
...	...	...	...	...	...	...	5	2	4	...	...
...	...	...	...	...	...	...	...	2	8	...	...
...	...	...	...	...	...	...	...	5	...	...	...
...	...	...	...	...	...	...	...	...	...	...	...
...	...	...	...	...	...	...	...	2	137	...	...
...	...	...	...	...	...	...	1	8	22	1	2
...	...	...	...	...	...	...	...	2	7	1	...
...	...	...	...	...	...	...	...	12	4	...	...
...	...	...	...	...	...	...	1	10	506	...	...
...	...	...	...	...	...	...	1	24	109	...	...
...	...	...	...	...	...	...	...	...	16	...	...
...	...	...	...	...	...	...	...	...	...	...	...
...	...	...	...	1	...	3	2	4	3	...	...
...	...	...	...	...	...	4	3	14	...	...	...
...	...	...	...	...	...	...	...	6	7	...	...
...	...	...	...	...	...	...	...	9	76	...	...
...	...	...	...	...	...	...	...	5	2	...	...
...	...	...	...	...	...	...	...	...	88	...	...
...	...	...	1	...	4	2	8	40	72	4	1
...	...	1	1	2	6	18	44	195	1,628	7	3
...	5	84	219	385	254	836	974	3,873	12,204	2,447	375

D.—(*Continued.*)

No. 1.—*Number of Offences against the Indian Penal Code, and for the year* 1867 ; *and the*

DESCRIPTION OF OFFENCES.	PUNISHMENTS.				
	Fined.		Fined in addition to other punishment.		
	Persons.	Amount.	Persons.	Amount.	Insane.
No. 6.—*Contempt and Offences, &c.*—(*Contd.*)					
Taking gift to recover stolen property ...	3	95	6	330	...
Omission to apprehend by public servant...	...	...	1	10	...
Negligent escape	13	152	2	35	...
Escape	8	91	4	101	...
Rescue	32	360	1	15	...
Return from transportation	...	...	...	...	...
Contempt of Court...	151	1,226	...	...	...
Total of No. 6...	4,151	15,788	73	3,697	...
No. 7.—*Offences not included in the above Classes.*					
Abetment...	32	95	1	10	...
Concealment of criminal designs...	...	...	...	...	...
Offences against the State	...	...	...	...	...
Spreading false and alarming rumours ...	...	...	...	...	...
Abetment of Military and Naval offences ...	...	...	...	...	...
Unlawful assembly...	325	1,720	26	390	...
Rioting	898	9,252	108	1,684	...
Landholders, &c., failing to prevent a riot...	...	...	...	...	...
Affray	690	2,628	50	394	...
Giving or receiving illegal gratification ...	53	1,545	3	1,100	...
Breaches of duty by public servant	7	1,205	...	...	...
Personating public servant	16	74	1	50	...
Spreading dangerous diseases, &c.	3	16	...	...	...
Adulteration and selling noxious food, &c...	18	271	...	...	...
Nuisance	2,835	6,917	1	15	...
Acts against public safety	202	2,085	3	70	...
Acts against decency	15	82	...	...	...
Offences against religion	33	489	...	...	...
Criminal trespass	3,966	21,733	178	2,864	1
House-trespass	267	3,785	14	162	...
Criminal breach of contract...	7	71	...	...	...
Bigamy	...	...	...	...	...
Adultery	1	100	2	80	...
Other offences relating to marriage	1	40	5	505	...
Defamation	39	946	2	50	...
Insult	533	2,336	11	122	...
Criminal intimidation	9	187	...	...	...
Misconduct in public by a drunken person..	98	259	8	48	...
Attempts not otherwise provided for... ...	15	70	10	172	...
Total of No. 7...	10,063	55,901	423	7,716	1
Grand Total...	29,634	1,57,856	2,595	73,900	13

D.—*(Continued.)*

of persons concerned in the Districts of the Madras Presidency, result of the proceedings.—(Concluded.)

CASES OTHERWISE DISPOSED OF.							
Dismissed for default and neglect to prosecute.		Withdrawn by parties.		Transferred to Military Authorities; Juveniles handed over to Parents; Cautioned; Escaped from custody; Died before conclusion of trial.		TOTAL.	
Cases.	Persons.	Cases.	Persons.	Cases.	Persons.	Cases.	Persons.
...	...	...	...	...	...	...	...
...	...	...	...	...	...	...	...
...	...	...	...	...	...	...	...
...	...	...	...	2	2	2	2
...	...	...	...	...	...	...	...
...	...	...	...	...	...	...	...
...	...	...	...	...	...	...	...
20	40	14	22	4	9	38	71
1	1	...	...	...	...	1	1
...	...	...	...	...	...	...	...
...	...	...	...	...	...	...	...
...	...	...	...	...	...	...	...
...	...	...	...	...	...	...	...
2	2	5	68	...	...	7	70
3	8	9	33	...	...	12	41
...	...	...	...	...	...	...	...
2	7	3	11	...	...	5	18
...	...	2	7	...	...	2	7
1	1	...	...	...	...	1	1
...	...	1	1	...	...	1	1
...	...	...	...	...	...	...	...
1	1	...	...	...	...	1	1
14	59	31	86	...	...	45	145
2	8	6	6	...	...	8	9
...	...	1	1	...	...	1	1
...	...	...	...	...	...	...	...
1,268	3,155	2,865	7,005	1	1	4,134	10,161
16	35	17	47	...	...	33	82
1	1	2	3	...	...	3	4
...	...	2	5	...	...	2	5
10	10	18	22	2	2	30	34
4	4	6	9	1	1	11	14
7	9	8	45	...	...	15	54
72	150	132	314	...	...	204	464
5	18	4	4	...	...	9	22
...	...	2	4	...	...	2	4
2	2	...	...	1	1	3	3
1,411	3,466	3,114	7,671	5	5	4,530	11,142
5,028	11,142	9,888	25,168	63	108	14,979	36,418

E.

Extracts from the Administration Report of the Acting Inspector General of Police, for 1867-68.

PARA. 27. *Offences.*—* * * By far the largest number of offences are reported in the Central and Southern Ranges, the former greatly predominating. The Western Range shews the highest averages of detective results at all points, and Madras Town the lowest, save in the item of recovery of property. In the results of particular crimes of the gravest kind there are very great differences as will afterwards be shewn.

28. *Murder.*—222 Murders were reported during the year, of which 109, or forty-nine per cent., were prosecuted to conviction. In five cases, returned as undetected, the murderers committed suicide, and in four cases in Coimbatore mothers jumped into wells with their children in their arms. Including these cases the ratio of detection would be 53·1 per cent. The Western Range shews the best average of detection in murder cases, viz., 62·9 per cent. Local causes facilitate detection on the Western Coast. The Southern Range shews the next best average in this class of crime, 56·2 per cent. On the whole, detection of murder has improved during 1867. Only 38·1 of persons arrested have been convicted, which is a poor average. In rural parts, evidence is frequently withheld by persons well cognizant of the facts, so that persons arrested on the strongest suspicion sometimes escape. The proportion of convictions to every 100 offences, however, is eighty-one, which is better than the English average, and a considerable improvement on former years. Taking results by districts, it will be found that North Malabar has an entirely clean sheet of murder in 1867—a very rare occurrence. South Malabar has sixteen murders, the whole of which were detected. In no single case did the murderers escape punishment. Twenty-three persons were arrested, of whom twenty-two were brought to trial and twenty-one were convicted. The open manner in which murders are frequently committed in Malabar of course contributes greatly to these results, but still they are highly creditable. If certainty of detection could prevent murder, then it should now cease in Malabar. Coimbatore has sixteen cases, of which nine were detected. In four cases women threw themselves into wells with their children. Deducting these four from the total of sixteen, Coimbatore has detected seventy-five per cent. of cases in which conviction was possible. This district distinguishes itself by detective results in almost all descriptions of grave crime, and it is perhaps worthy of remark, that in no district is there so small a proportion of Natives of the District serving in the Police force. A large number of men are drawn from other parts of the country. Godavery and Trichinopoly Districts also shew a high per-centage of detection in murder cases. One case in Trichinopoly was that of Serjeant Dalton, a man of previously irreproachable character, who openly mur-

dered his wife one Sunday, under circumstances of great brutality. He was convicted before the High Court at Madras, and sentenced to penal servitude for life, instead of hanging, owing to some doubt as to the exact state of his mind when he battered his wife's brains out in his children's presence. Tinnevelly, too, shews well in murder cases. Detection in Kurnool is poor, only twenty-nine per cent. The only Districts which shew really *bad* results are Bellary and Kistna. In the former only one case out of twelve has been detected, and in the latter only two cases out of thirteen. Even the Southern Range, so poor in general detection, retrieves its character in Murder, Culpable Homicide, and Drugging cases. Five murders were committed in Madras City, of which only two are shewn as detected, but in a third case the murderer being found to be insane was merely produced before the High Court, and transferred without trial to the Lunatic Asylum. Fifty per cent. of cases may, therefore, be said to have been detected by the Madras City Police. In one of these cases, a high caste youth of nineteen, from Northern India, named Baladeen, was decoyed at the dead of night into a deserted choultry, in an unfrequented cocoanut grove, and there drugged, strangled, and buried, for the sake of his gold bangles. For sometime nothing was known save that the youth had suddenly disappeared. Finally, the Police traced out the case under circumstances of great difficulty. Five persons were brought to trial before the High Court for this offence. Three (including a Brahmin devotee) were convicted and hanged; one was made Queen's Evidence, though he confessed but little; the fifth, a woman, Ram Bhoye, wife of one of the convicted prisoners, the paramour of the youthful victim, and herself the arch contriver of this diabolical murder, escaped through a missing link of evidence. Throughout she maintained a demeanour of calm and conscious innocence, but after witnessing the execution of her husband and friends, she quietly told the Police that the five persons brought to trial were the real murderers, but that the worst of the lot had been allowed to escape. Equal in genius and daring to Mrs. Manning, Ram Bhoye was more fortunate in her fate. Chief Constable Roop Ram distinguished himself by great detective ability in this case. All the persons concerned, save one, were Natives of Northern India, though long settled in Madras.

29. *Culpable Homicide.*—Under the head of Culpable Homicide, 61·2 per cent. of cases were detected, and 56·5 per cent. of persons arrested, were convicted. The Southern Range was most successful in detecting this class of cases, reaching the high average of 76·1 per cent. The Western Range comes next. In a large number of Culpable Homicide cases, the dying person's statement is available. Taking Murder and Culpable Homicide combined, 52·3 per cent. of cases were detected, forty-three per cent. of persons arrested were convicted, and ninety-seven per cent. of convictions were obtained to every 100 offences. These rates shew considerable improvement on results in former years.

30. *Offences against property with violence.*—Under the head of offences against property with violence, there has been the highly satisfactory decrease of 25·4 per cent. Excluding Madras Town, (not previously entered in the Returns) there were only 8,277 of these grave descriptions of offence against 11,102 in 1866. And there has been a decrease of 19·4 per cent. as compared with the average of three years antecedent to the year of scarcity. The per-centage of detection has, however, fallen from 27·8 in 1866 to 21·3 in the present year. Only 49·3 per cent. of persons arrested have been convicted, against 50·9 per cent. in the previous year, and 13·2 per cent. of property has been recovered against 15·5 per cent. in 1866. Thus, notwithstanding decrease of crime, there has been a slight falling off in detection, as compared with the year preceding, though the average of four years past has been exceeded. Rupees 5,85,546 of property were lost, against Rupees 6,40,313 in 1866. The decrease of crime has been common to all Ranges save the Southern, where there has been a slight increase. At the same time the per-centage of detection in the Southern Range has fallen from nineteen in 1866, to the very low ratio of 15·4, which is much to be lamented. The per-centage of property recovered is also far lower than in any other range. The Western Range has again the highest average of detection, and Madras Town the highest averages of conviction and of recovery of property. Thirty-one per cent. of property lost has been recovered by the Madras Town Police, which is a very creditable ratio.

31. *Dacoities.*—The number of dacoities has fallen from 1,025 to 533, a decrease of forty-eight per cent., or very nearly one-half. In 1865, the year before the famine, the number was 558. Analysis shews that, out of a total of 533, 145 were committed in houses, 212 in fields or jungles, and 176 on highways and thoroughfares. The per-centages of detection are 31·7, 25·4, and 17 respectively, so that highway dacoity would seem the most difficult of detection. Four persons on an average were convicted in each case of dacoity successfully prosecuted. The average of property lost in each dacoity was 187 Rupees. Exclusive of torchlight gang robbery, the average loss was Rupees 119. In the great majority of dacoities the amount lost is trifling, but a few heavy cases swell the average. In forty-four cases only did the amount of property lost exceed Rupees 500. In 55·9 per cent. of the cases, the amount lost was under Rupees 50. The number of dacoities in Bellary has fallen from 355 in 1866, to seventy in 1867, a result which strikingly illustrates the effect of prices upon crime. The numerous convictions in 1866 would also have a great effect. In the year before the famine, there were 104 dacoities in Bellary. Even Madras City shews one dacoity, due to the wide embracing definition of the Penal Code, and not to the actual presence of dacoits in Madras. It was a drunken row in a highway, committed by more than four persons, in which some property changed hands. Two persons were convicted and sentenced to two years' imprisonment. No single district shews a clean

sheet of this offence, but the Northern Circars and the Districts of the Western Coast have the lightest score. Nellore, too, shews only eight, Madras District nine, and Tinnevelly nine. Even Kurnool, with its wild mountain passes, shews but fifteen dacoities, while South Arcot, ever fruitful in crime, heads the list with seventy-two. Madura is the only district in which there has been an actual increase this year, the number being sixty-one against thirty-four in 1866, an increase of 44·2 per cent. The district has been subject to the disadvantage of frequent change of officers, but is now being thoroughly worked up. The detection of dacoity has slightly improved from 23·5 in 1866, to 24·3 in 1867. Here Bellary fails most utterly and lamentably, having detected only three cases out of seventy (4·2 per cent.) This is a sad falling off, even from the sufficiently miserable per-centage of 13·8 last year. In Cuddapah, the detection of dacoity is almost equally miserable. Only three have been detected out of forty-seven, or 6·4 per cent. These figures are a disgrace to the criminal statistics. Canara has detected three out of four cases, or seventy-five per cent. In Ganjam and Vizagapatam, fifty per cent. of the small number of cases have been detected. In Coimbatore, out of forty-six cases, twenty-one, (or 45·7, have been detected. This district therefore, on the whole, stands at the head of detection in dacoity.

32. *Robberies.*—There have been 812 robberies against 1,124 in 1866. The Analysis shews that 134 occurred in towns, 419 in fields and jungles, and 259 on highways. Here again the per-centage of detection is least in highway robbery; though there is but little difference between the classes. 24·1 per cent. of all robberies were detected, and an average of about two persons were sentenced in each convicted case of robbery. The average of property lost in each case was 42½ Rupees. The amount exceeded Rupees 500 in six cases only, and in 83·5 per cent. of the whole cases, the amount of property lost was below 50 Rupees. Bellary still heads the list with 132 robberies, but the decrease from last year is 41·3 per cent. In detection of robbery Bellary has struggled nearly up to the general average, shewing 20·5 per cent. of cases detected. South Arcot comes next in the number of robberies, shewing ninety-nine, of which twenty-two, or 22·2 per cent. were detected. This is a great improvement on the miserable detection in this district last year (12·7 per cent.), though still below the general average. Madras City shews six robberies on highways, of which only one was detected. Madras District shews only seven, of which four (fifty-seven per cent.) were detected. Salem has detected twenty-three robberies out of fifty-nine, or thirty-nine per cent. of its cases.

33. *Torchlight Gang Robbery.*—There have been only sixty-five torchlight robberies in 1867, against an annual average of 165 for four years past. The present year shews the lowest record of this hideous crime ever yet

exhibited in the Police annals of the Madras Presidency. Rupees 44,090 have been plundered against an annual average of Rupees 63,227, a striking decrease of 30·2 per cent., while the recovery of property has risen to 25·3 per cent. from the previous very poor annual average of 6·4 per cent. These improved results are very satisfactory. In Kistna District the high average of sixty-seven per cent. was recovered, and in North Arcot 41·8 per cent. The average of property plundered was 678 Rupees per case. Here again a few heavy cases swell the average. The majority of gang robberies now-a-days are but paltry attempts at plunder, compared with the bold and successful midnight raids of bygone years. One case, resembling the old type, occurred at Greenspett, a suburb of Chittoor, the Zillah station of North Arcot. A large gang attacked the house of a goldsmith, but being disturbed by a Beat Constable, fled with 8,000 Rupees worth of property. The crime was subsequently brought home to a gang of professional thieves, residing and cultivating land in the Madras District, who were successfully prosecuted to conviction. 6,000 Rupees worth of property was recovered by the Police in this case. The credit of detection belongs mainly to Inspector Ali Dost, of the Madras District, a first class Police officer. The per-centage of detection in gang robbery was 27·7, which shews no improvement on former years. In 1866, 29·9 per cent. of cases were detected. 28·4 per cent. of persons arrested were convicted, a slight advance on the average of the four previous years. From the nature of the crime, a large number of persons are frequently arrested on reasonable grounds of suspicion, against many of whom it is difficult to bring home individual proof. Nearly seven persons on an average were convicted in each case successfully prosecuted in a Sessions Court. Bellary shews only eight cases of torchlight robbery, against sixty-six in 1866, but not one single case could the Bellary Police force succeed in detecting. Cuddapah, formerly the favorite home of gang robbers, shews only three cases, not one of which, however, was detected. The educated force in Madras District has not succeeded in detecting a single case out of six scored against them. Madura also has three cases, and no detection. In North Arcot there were seven cases, of which six were detected in 1867, and the seventh, (the Greenspett case,) has been successfully prosecuted to conviction in the current year. Thus North Arcot has detected the whole of its cases, a result which is highly creditable to the Police force in that District. Gang robbery proved a crime very difficult to grapple with in North Arcot, where the local robbers are cunning and clever, and drawn from various classes of society. But during the last few years there has been a marked and progressive decrease of torchlight robbery.

North Arcot.	Cases.
1864	39
1865	23
1866	15
1867	7

This speaks well for the persistent efforts of the Police in the face of great difficulties. There has been a slight increase of gang robbery in Kistna, Madras, South Arcot, Trichinopoly, and Madura Districts. The following districts are quite free from this crime :—

Madras Town.	Godavery.	Canara.
Ganjam.	Kurnool.	Nellore.
Vizagapatam.	Malabar.	

Nellore is infested with wandering gangs of Yerkulas, and torchlight robberies were once rife in this district. The close vigilance of the Police, under the superintendence of able officers, has succeeded in effectually controlling these gangs, and in eradicating this phase of crime. In the Ceded Districts also, once so notorious for organized bands of robbers, comparative peace has fallen on the land. The more civilized provinces of South Arcot and Trichinopoly now head the list of gang robbery. Here the crime is still probably fostered by persons of higher class, and more subtle device. It has sometimes been asserted that the dacoits and criminal tribes of the Upper and Central Provinces make their way even into the far South, and there commit their favourite crime of dacoity with an impunity from detection, which requires the interference of a special agency. If so, then these bold and far-reaching marauders confine their exploits now-a-days to very insignificant enterprises. But it is not true. The records of conviction, and all the circumstances of this crime in the Madras Presidency, prove that it is purely home-made. And it is gradually but surely being trampled out by the District Police, each on their own ground, without the aid of any special agency.

34. *House-breaking cases.*—There has been a large decrease of 21·2 per cent. in the total number of house-breaking cases during the year, as compared with 1866. In the Southern Range, however, a slight increase appears, 20·9 per cent. of cases were detected, 58·3 of persons arrested were convicted, and 12·4 per cent. of property lost has been recovered. On all these points there is a slight falling off from last year, which is much to be regretted, although the results far exceed the average of three years previous to 1866. The Southern Range, as usual, shews worst at all points. Although the number of cases reported is less than in the Central Range, yet only the miserable per-centage of 13·3 has been detected, while only 6·6 per cent. of property has been recovered. These results are very melancholy, and materially affect the general average for the whole Presidency. Last in the rank comes South Arcot District, shewing 10·7 per cent. only of cases detected. Tanjore and Trichinopoly (also of the Southern Range) struggle barely ahead with 11·9 per cent. of detection, and neck-and-neck with them comes Kistna District, of the Northern Range, shewing also only 11·9 per cent. of detection. Why Kistna District should shew this low per-centage of detection, when Nellore, immediately south, shews 22·8 per cent., and Godavery, immediately north, shews 18·6

per cent., it is hard to say, except that the efforts of the Police must be more slack. In the Southern Range, Tinnevelly makes the nearest approach to a respectable average, with 17·3 per cent. of cases detected. Madura shews 16· per cent. So that, with the exception of Kistna in the Northern Range, and Kurnool in the Central Range (17·1 per cent.), which just equals Tinnevelly, the districts of the Southern Range are separately and collectively the worst in the Presidency for detection of house-breaking. This crime is of comparatively rare occurrence in the Western Range, probably because the buildings are stronger, and the inmates, if roused, rather troublesome customers. The per-centage of detection is also best in this Range, standing at 35·3 per cent. Canara District comes in first of the whole Presidency, with 44·4 per cent. detected, out of thirty-six cases only reported. Ganjam comes next, with 41·5 per cent. detected out of 416 cases. The remaining four Districts of the Western Range come next in order. Then follow Vizagapatam, Nellore, Madras, and Bellary. Madras Town, which with its strongly organised city Police, might have been expected to be the winner, cuts but a poor figure, with 21·3 per cent. only of detection. The Western and Northern Ranges have convicted 64·5 per cent., and 60·9 per cent. respectively of persons arrested. The Central and Southern Ranges are equal with fifty-four per cent. each. In the Western Range 17·1 per cent. of property lost has been recovered. The per-centages of recovery in the other Ranges are too poor to be quoted. On examining the number of cases reported, the effects of the famine of 1866 upon Ganjam District will again be obvious, the figures having fallen from 1,161 in 1866, to 416 only in 1867, while in Bellary there have been but 418 cases, against 732 in the previous year. The total number of cases has decreased in all districts save South Arcot, Tanjore, Madura, and Tinnevelly, of the Southern Range, which shew an increase not to be surprised at when detection is so poor. Madras Town has 211 cases, against 117 only in the previous year of exceptional scarcity and crime, but this apparent increase has been caused by the operation of Act VIII of 1867, under which all house-breaking cases are tried according to the Penal Code, whereas, formerly, all petty house-breakings were conveniently merged into the English definition of larceny.

35. *House-breaking in Towns.*—Looking to the operations of the Police in *towns* only, as compared with rural parts, it will be found that 29·3 per cent. of cases have been detected, against 19·4 per cent. in villages. The Northern Range stands highest, with fifty-four per cent. of detection, and the Western Range comes next. Even in towns the Southern Range can only detect 19·7 per cent. of its cases. Among Districts, South Malabar stands highest, with 83·3 per cent. of cases detected. Ganjam and Vizagapatam come next, with seventy and 63·6 per cent. The Town Police in Nellore and North Arcot shew good detective results. Kistna District, too, so poor in general detection under this head, has detected 47·8 per cent. of its town cases.

The detection in Madras City is below that of the towns in any rural district, save South Arcot, Tanjore, and Trichinopoly (the last most wretched). This may partly be accounted for by local peculiarities, such as the large assemblage of loose characters bent upon prey, and the practice of leaving the numerous small bazaars totally unprotected at night, save by the flimsiest tatty doors and the most ridiculous padlocks. The padlock is picked, a handful of curry-stuff is stolen, and a fresh house-breaking is added to the list. In the per-centage of persons convicted, the Northern Range stands highest, with 91·3 per cent., (a highly creditable average,) and the Central Range lowest, with 59·8 per cent. Here again the working of the Towns Police in many districts contrasts favorably with that of the Madras City Police. In the recovery of property, North Malabar comes first, with sixty seven per cent. Vizagapatam comes next, with 44·8 per cent., and Kistna takes a forward place, with 38·2 per cent. of property recovered. Madras City has recovered thirty-one per cent. Bellary shews very creditably. The per-centages of recovery in the Southern Range are not fit to be looked at.

36. *Amount of property lost in House-breaking cases.*—The average amount of property lost in each case of house-breaking was 67 Rupees. In 134 cases only, out of 6,650, did the amount lost exceed Rupees 500, in 75·3 per cent. of the whole the amount was less than 50 Rupees, and in no less than 1,392 cases the amount lost was under one rupee.

37. *General remarks on House-breaking.*—The results under this head of crime have been analysed at some length, because as the more violent and, so to say, *interesting* crimes of dacoity and robbery are repressed, the crime of house-breaking becomes of great importance, as being the chief field for the depredations of the criminal classes, and consequently demanding the keenest energies of the Police. As yet they cannot be said to have shewn satisfactory results in dealing with this phase of crime. Accustomed to the higher zest of gang and highway robbery, their palate is dull as yet to the flavour of house-breaking. Great effort is, therefore, needed to stimulate them to the necessary pitch of activity, and in the Southern Range, and in the Kistna District particularly, it would seem from this analysis that a sad condition of apathy has prevailed. The small proportion of detection cannot be accounted for by supposing that crime is there more accurately reported, because (with the exception of Tanjore) the actual number of cases reported in each district of the Southern Range is not greater than in many other districts, where the per-centage of detection is far higher. The present district officers are able, earnest, and energetic, and whatever the local difficulties may be, they will doubtless be conquered by persistent effort.

38. *Thuggee and Robbery by drugging.*—No conviction for Thuggee under Section 311 of the Penal Code was recorded during the year. Twenty-three cases of robbery by drugging have come to light, in six of which death ensued.

In most cases datura is the deleterious substance used. Seven persons fell victims. Nine cases (39 per cent.) were detected, and twelve persons were convicted. These results are good, considering the circumstances under which this crime is usually committed. The perpetrators are strangers to their victims, whom they leave insensible on decamping. Little can be got from the sufferers on recovery, save a confused description of the robbers. Either this crime passed unnoticed before, or it has from some unknown cause increased of late. It is remarkable that the Northern Range of Districts should be entirely free from it. The Southern Range, so backward in general detective ability, comes well to the front in this class of cases, having detected fifty per cent. The case convicted in Tanjore furnished a remarkable instance of keen detective genius. Three cases in Bellary District passed entirely undetected. In the Western Range, four out of ten cases were detected, and seven out of ten persons were convicted. In Coimbatore, a gang of four prisoners robbed four cattle merchants, two of whom died, and the other two recovered. Two of the prisoners were convicted, one being sentenced to death, and the other to transportation for life. Two of the members of this gang had before been tried in Salem for a similar offence but were acquitted. There is no doubt they were professional Thugs.

39. *Detective Results in Grave cases.*—There has been a marked decrease in the number of cases as compared with 1866, save in the Southern Range, where a larger number of grave crimes has been reported than in any of the four previous years. The ratio of detection has fallen off from that of 1866, but is much better than the average of three previous years. The Western Range shews the best detection under these heads of crime, and the Southern Range the worst. Tanjore, North Arcot, Bellary, South Arcot, and Cuddapah shew by far the largest number of cases reported. Grave crime is very heavy in these districts.

40. The following is the order of districts according to the ratio of detection in these grave crimes, which chiefly test the ability of the Police :—

	Districts.	Per-centage of detected cases.
1.	South Canara	43·5
2.	Ganjam	40·8
3.	South Malabar	39·9
4.	Salem	38·4
5.	North Malabar	35·2
6.	Coimbatore	34·
7.	Vizagapatam	26·9
8.	Nellore	24·5
9.	Madras District	23·9
10.	Madras Town	21·9

	Districts.	Per-centage of detected cases.
11.	Godavery... ... ... Madura	20·1
12.	North Arcot ... ... Tinnevelly... ... .,.	19·8
13.	Bellary	19·7
14.	Cuddapah	19·
15.	Kurnool	15·9
16.	Trichinopoly	15·1
17.	South Arcot	14·7
18.	Kistna	13·7
19.	Tanjore	12·9

South Canara comes in first of all. This is not an absolute test of efficiency and must not be taken to shew that the South Canara Police are the best in the Presidency. In South Canara there is very little crime. Only sixty-two cases under these heads have been reported in all, so that the Police must have been able to devote the most careful and protracted attention to each case. Local circumstances may facilitate detection, and all crime may not be reported. But in districts which present no striking differences in area, population, strength of Police, and the character and the condition of the people with regard to crime, undoubtedly the test here laid down (viz., per-centage of detection of cases) is the best that can be obtained. Ganjam, of the Northern Range, comes next to Canara, having been very successful in house-breaking. Then follow the remaining districts of the Western Range. In North and South Malabar there has been comparatively little crime to deal with, but Salem and Coimbatore, which come fourth and sixth on the list, are heavy districts. Salem has taken the lead by success in house-breaking, and, in robbery, is very slightly in advance of Coimbatore. In murder and dacoity Coimbatore is superior. The detective results in these two difficult districts are most satisfactory. Vizagapatam stands seventh on the list, and then the Central Range makes its appearance with Nellore and Madras Districts. Madras Town stands only tenth on the list. Madura, the first of the Southern Range, is bracketed with Godavery, as No. 11 and Tinnevelly, with North Arcot, as No. 12. Then follow the remaining districts of the Central Range. Detection in Kurnool has fallen from 25·6 in 1866, to 15·9 in the year under review. This is a great falling off, but the district has been in trouble, and improved results may now be confidently expected. The remaining three districts of the Southern Range bring up the rear, accompanied, however, by Kistna of the Northern Range, which is last but one on the list. Tanjore, the strongest manned district of the whole Presidency, bears the wooden spoon. Detection has fallen in this district from 25·2 in 1866, to the miserable ratio of 12·9 in

1867. The Police force is superabundant in number, but in quality must be sadly defective.

41. *Offences against Revenue Laws.*—There has been a decrease of offences under the Revenue Laws, only 1,895 cases having been reported against 2,256 in 1866, while 3,398 persons were convicted against 4,541 in the previous year. The decrease is entirely under the head of Breaches of Salt Laws. The number of cases fell from 1,126 cases in 1866, to 468 cases in 1867, possibly, the result of closer guarding. Abkarry cases increased from 1,130 cases in 1866, to 1,427 cases in 1867. The Police are beginning to scent rewards.

42. *Petty Thefts tried by Heads of Villages.*—There were 10,337 cases of Petty Thefts triable by heads of villages under Regulation IV of 1821, against 14,657 in the famine year of 1866. The average of three years has been 10,026 cases. 12,974 persons were convicted under this head in 1867.

43. *Cases reported to be false by the Police.*—Under Section 137 C. C. P., groundless complaints are reported by the Police to the Magistrates for orders, and, under Section 153, if an accused person has been groundlessly arrested, he is released on bail, and the case is similarly reported for orders. Should the Magistrate concur with the Police in considering a complaint false, the alleged offence is struck out of the Register of offences reported. Obviously, therefore, this is a point of Police working which demands great watchfulness, for besides other temptations to give a wrong colouring to a case, there is always a direct advantage to be gained by lessening the number of undetected cases on the Station House List ; and if true cases should with any frequency be struck out as false, the statistics of prevention and detection of crime would be rendered unreliable. To ensure close check, every case reported as false is required to be submitted to the Magistrate, through the Divisional Inspector, and no case can be struck out without the Magistrate's order. In 96·3 per cent. of cases the Magistrates have concurred with the Police, and have ordered the cases referred to them to be struck off as false. In several districts every case has been accepted as false. Either, therefore, the Police are really scrupulously exact in this matter, or they succeed in representing the facts so plausibly, according to the view they wish to be taken, as to convince the Magistracy that this view is correct. But it is difficult to account satisfactorily for the great differences that exist in different districts with regard to the number of cases reported as false, unless, indeed, the inhabitants of certain districts are really more prone than others to make false accusations. The following table shews the number of cases of *grave* crime referred (as false) in different districts, and may be compared with the detective results under the same heads of offence exhibited in paragraphs 39 and 40.

Statement of Grave Cases referred by Police, to Magistrates, for orders under Sections 137 *and* 153 *C. C. P.*

DISTRICTS.	Murder.		Dacoity.		Robbery.		Lurkinghouse trespass and House-breaking.		Total.			Per-centage of Referred to Total Cases.
	Reported.	Referred.	Reported.	Referred.	Reported.	Referred.	Reported.	Referred.	Reported.	Referred.	Struck off as false.	
Madras Town.	Information for the past year not obtainable.											
Ganjam	13	6	8	1	31	11	416	51	468	69	54	12·8
Vizagapatam...	28	...	2	3	18	13	383	26	431	42	42	8·8
Jeypore	No Returns.											
Godavery ...	7	4	3	5	6	40	242	97	258	146	137	36·1
Kistna	13	...	7	6	24	36	403	44	447	86	85	16·1
Total...	61	10	20	15	79	100	1,444	218	1,604	343	318	17·6
Nellore	5	2	8	4	38	48	330	73	381	127	127	25
Bellary	No Returns.											
Kurnool... ...	7	3	15	6	39	21	303	56	364	86	85	19·1
Cuddapah ...	15	...	47	7	98	40	471	84	631	131	124	17·1
North Arcot...	16	2	54	11	90	26	570	94	730	133	118	15·4
Madras	7	...	9	3	7	22	238	31	261	56	52	17·6
Total...	50	7	133	31	272	157	1,912	338	2,367	533	506	18·3
South Arcot ...	2	4	72	20	99	39	457	95	630	158	149	20
Tanjore	6	3	22	83	28	88	688	163	744	337	323	31·1
Trichinopoly...	4	1	28	16	38	36	254	31	324	84	73	20·5
Madura	9	2	61	30	37	48	362	74	469	154	154	24·7
Tinnevelly ...	11	7	9	20	15	43	358	134	393	204	204	34·1
Total...	32	17	192	169	217	254	2,119	497	2,560	937	903	26·8
Salem	14	2	48	40	59	79	268	100	389	221	217	36·1
Coimbatore ...	16	9	46	22	28	100	309	118	399	249	247	38·4
South Malabar.	16	1	16	17	7	20	104	67	143	105	105	42·3
North Malabar	...	...	3	2	6	11	62	30	71	43	43	37·7
South Canara..	16	6	4	3	6	9	36	26	62	44	44	41·5
Total...	62	18	117	84	106	219	779	341	1,064	662	656	38·3
Grand Total...	205	52	462	299	674	730	6,254	1,394	7,595	2,475	2,383	24·5

Of all cases (true and false) reported, twenty per cent. of Murder cases, 39·3 per cent. of Dacoities, 52 per cent. of Robberies, and 18·2 per cent. of House-breaking cases have been referred as false. By far the largest per-centage of cases reported to be false (38·3 per cent. under all heads of grave crime) is in the Western Range, where also by far the best detective results are exhibited. On the other hand, the Southern Range, where detection is worst, exhibits the next largest per-centage of referred cases (26·8 per cent.) In the Northern and Central Ranges the proportion of Referred cases is much smaller. Godavery, however, shews a large number (36·1 per cent.), and Nellore of the Central Range shews 25 per cent. Ganjam, which shews so well in detection, has struck off only the small proportion of 12·8 per cent. as false. The largest proportion of false charges are under the heads of dacoity and robbery. In Tanjore, no less than 79· per cent. of charges of dacoity, and 76· per cent. of charges of robbery were pronounced to be false. Tinnevelly shews 69· per cent., and 74· per cent. respectively, of false cases under these heads. All the districts of the Western Range shew very high averages. It would seem, therefore, that the inhabitants of districts in the Western and Southern Ranges are specially addicted to the concoction of false charges, or else that the Police in those parts are keener to detect flaws. But why 36· per cent. of all cases reported in Salem should be false, and only 15·4 per cent. in North Arcot, immediately adjoining, it is difficult to determine. This much only can be said, that the propensity to prefer false complaints is undoubtedly strong amongst Natives of India, while at the same time the action of the Police in this matter must continue to be (as it is now) most closely and jealously watched. The Magistracy would seem to be satisfied.

44. *Cases disposed of by Sessions Court.*—Conviction was obtained in 66·3 per cent. of cases tried by the High and Sessions Courts, and 54·1 per cent. of persons brought to trial were convicted. This last proportion is unsatisfactory. The Northern and Western Ranges have been most successful in their averages. The Southern Range stands lowest in the conviction of cases, and the Central Range in the conviction of persons. In Madras Town, eighty-four per cent. of cases tried by the High Court have been successfully prosecuted, and 73·6 per cent. of persons brought to trial have been convicted. In South Malabar the averages are equally high, 85·4 per cent. of cases and 73·2 per cent. of persons. North Malabar, Coimbatore, and Madras Districts also shew very good results. The averages are comparatively poor in Kistna, Bellary, Cuddapah, North Arcot, Tanjore, Tinnevelly, Salem, and South Canara. Tanjore stands lowest of the whole Presidency in the conviction of cases (53·7 per cent.), and Kistna in the conviction of persons (36·5 per cent.)

F.

Statement shewing Sickness and Mortality in the Jails of the Madras Presidency, during the year ending 31*st March* 1868.

JAILS.	Average daily number of Prisoners during the year.		Remaining in Hospital 31st March 1867.		Cholera.			
					Admissions.		Deaths.	
	Males.	Females.	Males.	Females.	Males.	Females.	Males.	Females.
Russelcondah	109·06	2·12	4	...	...	...	...	...
Berhampore	214·	18·	27	3	...	...	...	...
Chicacole	23·	1·	...	...	...	...	...	...
Vizagapatam...	298·	20·06	14	...	...	...	...	...
Rajahmundry, Central ...	710·50	...	23	...	...	...	...	...
Do. District...	78·50	19·25	4	1	...	...	...	...
Masulipatam	109·60	·92	3	...	...	...	...	...
Guntoor	174·88	15·10	7	...	...	...	...	...
Nellore	228·80	24·80	4	...	...	...	...	...
Kurnool	223·50	7·70	19	...	2	...	2	...
Bellary	451·	27·	39	...	...	...	...	...
Cuddapah	252·	20·	24	3	...	...	...	...
Chittoor	300·	33·	17	2	...	...	...	...
Vellore, Central	294·26	...	...	...	...	...	...	...
Do. Fort	197·98	...	8	...	...	...	...	...
Salem	532·89	35·53	27	1	...	...	...	...
Guindy	71·20	...	1	...	...	...	...	...
Chingleput	190·91	12·26	14	...	...	...	...	...
Cuddalore	495·	13·	8	...	2	...	1	...
Tranquebar	167·27	11·39	17	...	...	...	...	...
Tanjore	152·74	17·02	...	...	2	...	2	...
Trichinopoly, Central ...	297·71	...	...	...	...	...	...	...
Do. District ...	189·54	8·62	5	...	...	...	...	...
Madura	482·25	8·75	17	...	7	...	1	...
Tinnevelly	225·	28·	10	...	...	...	...	...
Paumben	113·94	·01	6	1	1	...	...	...
Cochin	19·	·10	...	...	...	...	...	...
Calicut	220·26	5·51	12	1	1	...	...	...
Tellicherry	129·18	3·19	13	...	...	...	...	...
Cannanore, Central ...	256·09	...	...	...	...	...	...	...
Do. Fort	64·61	...	2	...	...	...	...	...
Mangalore	200·	10·	18	...	...	...	...	...
Paulghat	53·20	...	3	...	...	...	...	...
Coimbatore, Central ...	893·09	15·29	11	...	...	...	...	...
Do. District ...	165·64	12·50	12	...	...	...	...	...
Ootacamund, Native ...	84·22	3·82	4	...	...	...	...	...
Lawrence Asylum Works	362·46	...	11	...	...	...	...	...
Dodabett	71·16	...	1	...	...	...	...	...
Neddivuttum	177·14	...	1	...	...	...	...	...
European Prison	14·91	...	1	...	...	...	...	...
Total ...	9294·49	373·94	387	12	15	...	6	...
Penitentiary	445·75	45·	23	...	...	...	...	...
Grand Total ...	9740·24	418·94	410	12	15	...	6	...

F.—*(Continued.)*

Statement shewing Sickness and Mortality in the Jails of the Madras

JAILS.	Small-Pox.				Fevers.			
	Admissions.		Deaths.		Admissions.		Deaths.	
	Males.	Females.	Males.	Females.	Males.	Females.	Males.	Females.
Russelcondah	...	...	...	...	150	2	1	...
Berhampore	...	...	...	...	67	5	2	...
Chicacole	...	...	...	...	6	...	...	...
Vizagapatam	...	...	...	...	86	4	2	...
Rajahmundry, Central ...	...	...	...	...	244	...	3	...
Do. District...	...	...	...	...	56	6	...	...
Masulipatam	...	...	...	...	29	...	...	...
Guntoor	...	...	...	...	36	3	...	..
Nellore	...	...	...	...	28	...	...	...
Kurnool	...	...	...	...	161	1	1	...
Bellary	...	...	...	...	60	...	...	...
Cuddapah	...	...	...	...	180	21	...	...
Chittoor	...	...	...	...	58	36	3	...
Vellore, Central	...	...	...	...	53	...	...	...
Do. Fort	...	...	...	...	45	...	1	...
Salem	...	...	...	...	56	4	4	...
Guindy	...	...	...	...	44	...	...	...
Chingleput	...	...	...	...	48	7	...	...
Cuddalore	...	...	...	...	39	3	...	...
Tranquebar	1	...	...	...	56	6	1	...
Tanjore	5	...	2	...	5	...	...	...
Trichinopoly, Central ...	...	...	...	...	26	...	...	...
Do. District ...	1	...	...	...	25	...	2	...
Madura	...	...	...	...	46	...	...	...
Tinnevelly	...	...	...	...	10	...	...	...
Paumben	...	...	...	...	18	...	...	...
Cochin	...	...	...	...	9	...	...	...
Calicut	7	...	2	...	30	2	...	...
Tellicherry	5	...	4	...	56	...	1	...
Cannanore, Central ...	...	...	...	...	202	...	...	...
Do. Fort	4	...	1	...	2	...	...	...
Mangalore	...	...	...	...	75	...	...	...
Paulghat	...	...	...	...	25	...	...	...
Coimbatore, Central ...	...	...	...	...	63	1	1	...
Do. District ..	2	...	...	...	27	...	...	...
Ootacamund, Native ...	...	...	...	...	9	...	...	...
Lawrence Asylum Works	...	...	...	...	111	...	1	...
Dodabett	...	...	...	...	36	...	...	...
Neddivuttum	3	...	...	...	43	...	...	...
European Prison	...	...	...	...	1	...	...	...
Total ...	28	...	9	...	2,321	101	23	...
Penitentiary...	2	...	...	...	96	10	...	...
Grand Total ...	30	...	9	...	2,417	111	23	...

F.—*(Continued.)*

Presidency, during the year ending 31st March 1868.—*(Continued.)*

Dysentery.				Diarrhœa.				Diseases of the Brain.			
Admissions.		Deaths.		Admissions.		Deaths.		Admissions.		Deaths.	
Males.	Females.	Males.	Females.	Males.	Females.	Males.	Females.	Males.	Females.	Males.	Females.
29	...	1	...	32	2	1	...	10	1	...	...
34	6	5	...	19	2	1	...	1	...	...	...
3	...	...	...	...	...	...	...	...	...	...	...
20	...	2	...	4	...	...	...	1	...	...	...
25	...	...	...	48	...	...	...	21	...	1	...
6	...	...	...	13	1	...	...	1	...	...	...
1	...	...	...	4	...	...	...	1	...	...	...
2	...	1	...	...	...	...	...	3	...	...	...
5	1	1	...	5	...	...	...	...	...	...	...
30	...	7	...	34	...	7	...	2	...	1	...
1	...	...	...	4	...	...	...	1	...	...	...
20	1	3	...	14	1	1	...	7	...	...	...
5	1	2	...	26	8	...	...	5	1	...	...
5	...	1	...	21	...	1	...	2	...	...	...
4	...	1	...	10	...	1	...	1	...	...	...
29	1	3	...	9	...	1	...	4	...	...	...
4	...	...	...	3	...	...	...	...	...	...	...
8	1	...	...	29	3	...	...	1	...	...	...
53	1	4	...	14	3	3	3	1	...	...	...
13	...	1	...	15	...	2	...	...	...	...	...
22	...	4	...	19	...	10	...	...	...	...	...
18	...	...	...	22	...	6	...	1	...	...	...
29	1	1	...	39	1	4	1	6	...	2	...
16	...	3	...	20	...	4	...	1	...	...	...
2	...	1	...	41	3	15	...	1	...	...	...
5	...	2	...	2	...	...	...	...	...	...	...
...	...	...	...	7	1	...	...	...	...	...	...
6	...	...	...	13	...	...	...	1	...	...	...
37	1	3	...	23	...	2	...	2	...	...	...
14	...	3	...	63	...	4	...	...	...	...	...
2	...	...	...	3	...	1	...	1	...	...	...
24	...	2	...	47	1	7	1	6	...	1	...
8	...	...	...	16	...	...	...	...	...	...	...
13	...	3	...	12	...	...	...	1	...	...	...
6	...	3	...	4	...	...	...	...	...	...	...
9	...	1	...	4	1	1	...	2	...	...	...
50	...	3	...	21	...	4	...	4	...	...	...
12	...	...	...	17	...	...	...	36	...	...	...
22	...	4	...	31	...	1	...	...	...	...	...
1	...	...	...	1	...	...	...	...	...	...	...
593	14	65	...	709	27	77	5	126	2	5	...
21	2	1	...	73	...	4	...	4	...	1	...
614	16	66	...	782	27	81	5	130	2	6	...

(F.—*Continued.*)

Statement shewing Sickness and Mortality in the Jails of the Madras

JAILS.	Diseases of the Liver.				Diseases of the Lungs.			
	Admissions.		Deaths.		Admissions.		Deaths.	
	Males.	Females.	Males.	Females.	Males.	Females.	Males.	Females.
Russelcondah	1	...	...	...	10	...	...	...
Berhampore...	...	...	...	...	3	2	...	...
Chicacole	...	...	...	...	1	...	...	...
Vizagapatam...	...	...	...	...	6	...	...	...
Rajahmundry, Central ...	2	...	...	...	26	...	...	...
Do. District...	...	...	...	...	2	...	...	...
Masulipatam	...	...	...	...	2	...	1	...
Guntoor	...	...	...	...	...	...	...	...
Nellore...	...	...	...	...	1	...	1	...
Kurnool	1	...	...	...	4	...	1	...
Bellary	4	...	...	...	13	...	4	...
Cuddapah	15	...	...	...	6	...	1	...
Chittoor	...	...	...	...	13	1	...	...
Vellore, Central	1	...	...	...	5	...	...	...
Do. Fort...	...	...	...	...	2	...	...	...
Salem	...	...	...	...	21	...	1	...
Guindy	3	...	...	...	...	...	...	...
Chingleput	...	...	1	...	11	2	...	...
Cuddalore	...	...	...	...	5	...	3	...
Tranquebar	...	...	...	...	4	...	...	...
Tanjore...	...	...	...	...	2	...	1	...
Trichinopoly, Central ...	...	...	...	...	5	...	...	...
Do. District ...	...	...	...	...	17	...	2	...
Madura...	...	...	...	...	3	...	1	...
Tinnevelly	...	...	...	...	...	1	...	...
Paumben	...	...	...	...	3	...	2	...
Cochin	...	...	...	...	3	...	...	...
Calicut	3	...	...	...	19	...	2	...
Tellicherry	...	...	...	...	5	...	1	...
Cannanore, Central ...	...	...	...	...	6	...	2	...
Do. Fort	...	...	...	...	...	...	...	...
Mangalore	...	...	...	...	6	...	...	...
Paulghat	...	...	...	...	6	...	...	...
Coimbatore, Central ...	...	...	...	...	22	...	5	...
Do. District ...	...	...	...	...	5	...	...	...
Ootacamund, Native ...	2	...	...	...	...	...	...	...
Lawrence Asylum Works	1	...	...	...	42	...	1	...
Dodabett	...	...	...	...	7	...	...	...
Neddivuttum	...	...	...	...	9	...	1	...
European Prison	...	...	...	...	...	...	...	...
Total ..	33	...	1	...	295	6	30	...
Penitentiary...	1	...	...	...	27	1	2	...
Grand Total ...	34	...	1	...	322	7	32	...

F.—*(Continued.)*

Presidency, during the year ending 31st March 1868.—*(Continued.)*

Dropsy.				Anasarca.				Atrophy.			
Admissions.		Deaths.		Admissions.		Deaths.		Admissions.		Deaths.	
Males.	Females.	Males.	Females.	Males.	Females.	Males.	Females.	Males.	Females.	Males.	Females.
...	...	...	...	...	...	...	...	1	...	...	...
...	...	...	...	15	1	4	1	3	1	...	...
...	...	...	...	...	...	...	...	...	...	...	...
...	...	...	...	3	...	...	...	5	...	2	...
...	...	...	...	4	...	3	...	8	...	...	...
...	...	...	...	1	1	1	...	1	...	...	...
...	...	...	...	...	...	...	...	2	...	...	...
...	...	...	...	1	...	...	...	1	...	1	...
...	...	...	...	...	...	...	...	3	...	...	...
...	...	...	...	8	...	5	...	6	...	2	...
...	...	...	...	6	...	6	...	33	...	23	...
...	...	...	...	3	1	1	...	...	...	...	...
...	...	...	...	2	...	...	...	1	...	1	...
...	...	...	...	1	...	...	...	17	...	...	...
...	...	...	...	3	...	2	...	6	...	2	...
...	...	...	...	2	...	...	...	2	...	2	...
...	...	...	...	...	...	...	...	...	...	...	...
...	...	...	...	...	...	...	...	5	1	2	1
...	...	...	...	1	...	2	...	27	2	8	...
...	...	...	...	...	...	...	...	1	...	2	...
...	...	...	...	...	...	...	...	2	...	1	...
...	...	...	...	...	...	...	...	...	...	...	...
...	...	...	...	3	...	3	...	4	...	1	...
...	...	...	...	3	...	...	...	4	...	...	...
1	...	1	...	2	1	1	1	4	...	2	...
...	...	...	...	...	...	...	...	9	...	2	...
...	...	...	...	...	...	...	...	...	...	...	...
...	...	...	...	3	...	1	...	...	...	...	...
...	...	...	...	1	...	2	...	...	...	...	...
2	...	2	...	3	...	2	...	5	...	1	...
...	...	...	...	...	...	...	...	...	...	...	...
...	...	...	...	1	...	...	...	33	...	7	...
...	...	...	...	...	...	...	...	...	...	...	...
...	...	...	...	...	...	...	...	20	...	8	...
...	...	...	...	...	...	...	...	7	...	1	...
...	...	...	...	...	...	...	...	1	...	...	...
...	...	...	...	...	...	...	...	31	...	4	...
...	...	...	...	...	...	...	...	4	...	...	...
...	...	...	...	3	...	2	...	1	...	...	...
...	...	...	...	...	...	...	...	...	...	...	...
3	...	3	...	69	4	35	2	247	4	72	1
...	...	...	...	...	...	...	...	5	...	1	...
3	...	3	...	69	4	35	2	252	4	73	1

F.—*(Continued.)*

Statement shewing Sickness and Mortality in the Jails of the Madras

JAILS.	Scurvy.				Rheumatism.			
	Admissions.		Deaths.		Admissions.		Deaths.	
	Males.	Females.	Males.	Females.	Males.	Females.	Males.	Females.
Russelcondah	1	...	...	...	33	1	...	...
Berhampore	...	...	...	...	7	1	...	...
Chicacole	...	...	...	...	2	...	...	...
Vizagapatam	...	...	...	...	12	3	...	...
Rajahmundry, Central...	1	...	...	...	30	...	1	...
Do. District	...	...	...	...	6	2	...	...
Masulipatam	...	...	...	...	10	...	...	...
Guntoor	...	...	...	...	1	...	...	...
Nellore	...	...	...	...	8	...	...	...
Kurnool	...	..	...	...	10	...	...	...
Bellary	27	...	...	...	20	...	...	...
Cuddapah	...	...	...	...	6	1	...	...
Chittoor	...	...	...	...	5	1	...	...
Vellore, Central	...	...	...	...	10	...	...	...
Do. Fort	...	...	...	...	2	...	...	...
Salem	6	...	...	...	13	1	...	...
Guindy	...	...	...	...	13	...	...	...
Chingleput	...	...	...	...	2	2	...	...
Cuddalore	...	...	...	..	15	...	...	...
Tranquebar	...	...	...	...	9	...	1	...
Tanjore	...	...	...	...	...	...	...	...
Trichinopoly, Central ...	...	...	...	...	8	...	...	...
Do. District ...	...	...	...	...	8	...	1	...
Madura	1	...	...	...	9	...	1	...
Tinnevelly	...	...	...	...	4	3	...	...
Paumben	...	...	...	...	10	...	1	...
Cochin	1	...	...	...	1	...	...	...
Calicut	6	...	1	...	10	...	2	...
Tellicherry	4	...	1	...	5	...	...	...
Cannanore, Central ...	60	...	...	...	24	...	9	...
Do. Fort	...	...	...	...	...	...	...	...
Mangalore	...	...	...	...	5	...	...	...
Paulghat	...	...	...	...	7	...	...	...
Coimbatore, Central ...	4	...	1	...	12	...	1	...
Do. District ...	...	...	...	...	8	...	...	...
Ootacamund, Native ...	...	...	...	...	3	...	...	...
Lawrence Asylum Works	...	...	...	...	24	...	...	...
Dodabett	...	...	...	...	24	...	...	...
Neddivuttum	...	...	...	...	6	...	...	...
European Prison	...	...	...	...	...	...	...	...
Total ...	111	...	3	...	382	15	17	...
Penitentiary	1	...	...	...	9	...	...	...
Grand Total ...	112	...	3	..	391	15	17	...

F.—*(Continued.)*

Presidency, during the year ending 31*st March* 1868.—*(Continued.)*

Venereal.				Abscess and Ulcers.				Wounds and Injuries.			
Admissions.		Deaths.		Admissions.		Deaths.		Admissions.		Deaths.	
Males.	Females.	Males.	Females.	Males.	Females.	Males.	Females.	Males.	Females.	Males.	Females.
1	2	...	...	111	...	...	...	40	...	...	...
8	1	...	...	8	...	...	...	10	...	...	...
9	...	...	...	8	...	...	...	4	...	...	...
3	...	...	...	26	1	...	...	14	...	...	...
6	...	...	...	171	...	...	...	93	...	2	...
10	1	...	...	51	...	...	...	10	...	...	...
2	...	...	...	9	...	...	...	5	...	...	...
6	1	...	...	7	...	...	...	4	...	...	...
7	2	...	...	13	...	...	...	7	...	1	...
9	1	...	...	32	1	...	...	20	...	...	...
9	...	...	...	113	...	2	...	46	...	...	...
19	...	...	...	96	1	5	...	64	...	2	...
21	4	...	...	47	...	...	...	36	1	...	...
3	...	...	...	41	...	...	...	13	...	...	...
3	...	...	...	22	...	...	...	25	...	...	...
13	3	...	...	63	...	...	...	35	...	...	...
...	...	...	...	14	...	...	...	15	...	...	...
17	...	...	...	46	...	...	...	44	...	...	...
8	2	...	...	15	...	...	...	11	...	...	...
2	1	...	...	59	...	...	...	37	...	...	...
...	...	...	...	2	...	...	...	1	...	...	...
2	...	...	...	7	...	...	...	10	...	...	...
9	...	1	...	6	...	...	...	6	...	...	...
13	...	...	...	27	...	...	...	19	...	...	...
5	...	...	...	45	3	...	...	25	...	...	...
3	...	...	...	15	...	...	...	12	...	...	...
...	...	...	...	4	...	...	...	4	...	...	...
7	...	...	...	29	...	1	...	10	...	...	...
5	...	...	...	14	...	...	...	3	...	...	...
1	...	...	...	27	...	2	...	34	...	1	...
...	...	...	...	3	...	...	...	1	...	...	...
5	...	...	...	62	...	...	...	50	...	...	...
...	...	...	...	16	...	...	...	3	...	...	...
16	2	...	...	63	1	1	...	29	1	...	...
13	2	...	...	47	...	...	...	18	...	...	...
3	...	...	...	4	...	...	...	1	...	...	...
...	...	...	...	35	...	...	...	49	...	...	...
...	...	...	...	8	...	...	...	10	...	...	...
1	...	...	...	34	...	...	...	11	...	...	...
...	...	...	...	...	...	...	...	...	...	...	...
239	22	1	...	1,400	7	11	...	829	2	6	...
28	4	...	...	12	...	...	...	14	...	...	...
267	26	1	...	1,412	7	11	...	843	2	6	...

F.—(Continued.)

Statement shewing Sickness and Mortality in the Jails of the Madras

JAILS.	Diseases of the Eye.				Diseases of the Skin.			
	Admissions.		Deaths.		Admissions.		Deaths.	
	Males.	Females.	Males.	Females.	Males.	Females.	Males.	Females.
Russelcondah	8	...	...	...	13	...	...	...
Berhampore	2	1	...	...	2	...	...	...
Chicacole	...	...	...	...	1	...	...	...
Vizagapatam	4	1	...	...	17	2	...	1
Rajahmundry, Central ...	9	...	...	...	24	...	...	...
Do. District ...	1	3	...	...	2	...	...	...
Masulipatam	...	...	...	...	1	...	...	...
Guntoor	...	...	...	...	...	...	...	...
Nellore	5	...	...	...	...	...	...	...
Kurnool	4	...	...	...	7	...	...	...
Bellary	1	...	...	...	6	...	...	...
Cuddapah	2	1	...	...	46	...	...	...
Chittoor	3	...	...	...	22	1	...	...
Vellore, Central	1	...	...	...	1	...	...	...
Do. Fort	...	...	...	...	...	...	...	...
Salem	3	...	...	...	1	...	...	...
Guindy	3	...	...	...	3	...	...	...
Chingleput	2	...	...	...	11	...	...	...
Cuddalore	9	...	...	...	25	...	...	...
Tranquebar	2	...	...	...	22	...	...	...
Tanjore	...	...	...	...	...	...	...	...
Trichinopoly, Central ...	1	...	...	...	3	...	...	...
Do. District ...	1	...	...	...	3	...	...	...
Madura	5	...	...	...	14	...	...	...
Tinnevelly	3	...	...	...	7	1	...	...
Paumben	5	...	...	...	1	...	...	...
Cochin	1	...	...	...	1	...	...	...
Calicut	5	...	...	...	6	...	...	...
Tellicherry	6	...	...	...	3	...	...	...
Cannanore, Central ...	10	...	...	...	1	...	...	...
Do. Fort	...	...	...	...	...	...	...	...
Mangalore	5	...	...	...	5	...	...	...
Paulghat	...	...	...	...	1	...	...	...
Coimbatore, Central ...	6	...	...	...	11	...	...	...
Do. District ...	...	...	...	...	15	...	...	...
Ootacamund, Native ...	...	...	...	...	1	...	...	...
Lawrence Asylum Works	1	...	...	...	10	...	...	...
Dodabett	1	...	...	...	...	...	...	...
Neddivuttum	8	...	...	...	...	...	...	...
European Prison	...	...	...	...	...	...	...	...
Total ...	117	6	...	...	286	4	...	1
Penitentiary	8	4	...	...	39	2	...	...
Grand Total ...	125	10	...	...	325	6	...	1

F.—*(Continued.)*

Presidency, during the year ending 31st March* 1868.—*(Continued.)

Other Cases.				Total Admissions.		Total Deaths.	
Admissions.		Deaths.					
Males.	Females.	Males.	Females.	Males.	Females.	Males.	Females.
56	2	...	...	496	10	3	...
16	5	...	...	195	25	12	1
2	...	...	...	36	...	...	...
19	1	2	...	220	12	8	1
69	...	...	...	781	...	10	...
14	3	...	3	174	17	1	3
15	...	...	...	81	...	1	...
24	1	...	...	85	5	2	...
23	2	2	...	105	5	5	...
79	...	...	...	409	3	26	...
118	1	4	...	462	1	39	...
1	1	...	...	479	28	13	...
27	4	2	...	271	58	8	...
33	...	...	...	207	...	2	...
15	...	1	...	138	...	8	...
86	1	2	...	343	10	13	...
12	...	1	...	114	...	1	...
23	5	...	...	247	21	3	1
57	...	1	...	282	11	22	3
47	3	2	...	268	10	9	...
1	...	...	...	61	...	20	...
6	...	...	...	109	...	6	...
16	...	1	...	173	2	18	1
27	...	1	...	215	...	11	...
9	3	...	...	159	15	20	1
14	...	1	...	98	...	8	...
16	1	...	...	47	2	...	...
33	...	9	...	189	2	18	...
9	...	...	...	178	1	14	...
21	...	1	...	473	...	27	...
5	...	1	...	21	...	3	...
27	...	...	...	351	1	17	1
...	...	...	...	82	...	...	...
153	5	3	...	425	10	23	...
54	...	...	...	206	2	4	...
1	...	...	...	40	1	2	...
62	...	...	...	441	...	13	...
27	...	...	...	182	...	...	...
23	...	...	...	195	...	8	...
...	...	...	...	5	...	...	...
1,240	38	34	3	9,043	252	398	12
71	5	3	...	411	28	12	...
1,311	43	37	3	9,454	280	410	12
						13	

F.—*(Continued.)*

Statement shewing Sickness and Mortality in the Jails of the Madras

JAILS.	Remaining in Hospital, 31st March 1868.		Average daily Sick during the year.	
	Males.	Females.	Males.	Females.
Russelcondah	13	...	9·24	·04
Berhampore	3	...	8·50	·50
Chicacole...	2	...	2·	...
Vizagapatam	10	...	8·46	·25
Rajahmundry, Central	18	...	24·50	...
Do. District	4	...	3·84	1·43
Masulipatam	5	...	1·53	...
Guntoor	3	...	4·60	·59
Nellore	2	...	3·68	·06
Kurnool	13	1	16·60	·80
Bellary	20	...	26·90	·05
Cuddapah	12	...	20·72	·85
Chittoor	15	2	22·25	4·50
Vellore, Central	12	...	9·11	...
Do. Fort	5	...	3·70	...
Salem	10	1	20·34	1·13
Guindy	4	...	3·03	...
Chingleput	8	...	10·01	·52
Cuddalore	22	...	16·	1·
Tranquebar	4	...	11·27	·32
Tanjore	3	...	2·23	...
Trichinopoly, Central	2	...	4·05	...
Do. District	8	...	8·10	·09
Madura	11	...	10·25	...
Tinnevelly	4	...	5·95	·59
Paumben...	3	...	6·	...
Cochin	1	...	·10	...
Calicut	4	...	6·58	·11
Tellicherry	3	...	6·66	...
Cannanore, Central...	13	...	16·50	...
Do. Fort	3	...	1·10	...
Mangalore	18	...	16·	...
Paulghat	2	...	·22	...
Coimbatore, Central	24	...	14·16	·61
Do. District	11	...	9·08	·06
Ootacamund, Native	2	...	3·84	·14
Lawrence Asylum Works	10	...	10·37	...
Dodabett	...	...	1·09	...
Neddivuttum	10	...	6·41	...
European Prison	...	...	1·79	...
Total...	317	4	356·76	13·64
Penitentiary	10	3	15·	·50
Grand Total...	327	7	371·76	14·14

F.—*(Concluded.)*

Presidency, during the year ending 31*st March* 1868.—*(Concluded.)*

Per-centage of Sick to daily strength.	Per-centage of Deaths to daily strength.	Deaths out of Hospital. Suicide. Males.	Deaths out of Hospital. Suicide. Females.	Deaths out of Hospital. Sudden or Accidental Deaths. Males.	Deaths out of Hospital. Sudden or Accidental Deaths. Females.	REMARKS.
8·34	2·69	...	...	...	...	
3·87	5·60	1	...	...	...	
8·33	...	...	...	...	...	
2·73	2·82	...	...	...	...	
3·44	1·40	...	...	...	...	
5·39	4·09	...	...	...	...	
1·38	·90	...	...	...	...	
2·73	1·05	...	...	...	...	
1·47	1·97	...	...	...	1	Heart Disease.
7·52	11·24	...	...	...	...	
5·63	8·15	...	...	...	...	
7·93	4·77	...	...	*1	...	* Lung Disease, Hæmoptysis.
8·03	2·40	1	...	...	...	
3·09	·67	...	...	...	...	
1·86	4·04	...	...	...	...	
3·77	2·28	...	...	...	...	
4·25	1·40	...	...	...	...	
5·18	1·96	...	...	...	...	
3·34	4·92	...	...	...	...	
6·48	5·03	...	...	...	...	
1·31	11·78	...	...	...	...	
1·36	2·01	...	...	...	...	
4·13	9·58	...	...	...	...	
2·08	2·24	...	...	...	...	
2·58	8·30	...	...	...	...	
5·26	7·02	...	...	...	...	
·52	...	...	...	...	...	
2·96	7·97	...	...	...	...	
5·03	10·57	...	...	...	...	
6·44	10·54	...	...	...	...	
1·70	4·64	...	...	...	...	
7·61	8·57	...	...	...	...	
·41	...	...	...	...	...	
1·62	2·53	...	...	...	...	
5·13	2·24	...	...	...	...	
4·52	2·27	...	...	...	...	
2·86	3·58	...	...	...	...	
1·53	...	...	...	...	...	
3·61	4·51	...	...	...	...	
12·	...	...	...	...	...	
3·83	4·24	2	...	1	1	
3·15	2·44	...	...	...	...	
3·79	4·15	2	...	1	1	

G.

Statement of Expenses incurred in the several Jails of the

JAILS.	Average daily number of Prisoners dieted.	Fixed Establishment.			Extra Establishment.		
		RS.	A.	P.	RS.	A.	P.
Russelcondah	112	539	10	10	...	...	...
Berhampore	228	3,299	4	9	35	12	11
Chicacole	23	470	0	0	...	...	...
Vizagapatam...	302	3,399	10	4	...	...	...
Rajahmundry, Central...	710	11,245	5	2	...	...	...
Do. District ...	90	1,710	6	5	...	...	...
Masulipatam...	109	2,197	8	3	...	...	...
Guntoor	177	2,879	6	1	...	...	...
Nellore	249	3,134	8	0	...	...	...
Kurnool.	220	3,417	3	5	...	...	...
Bellary	468	3,242	2	5	95	0	7
Cuddapah	255	3,640	6	9	...	...	...
Chittoor	305	4,330	4	6	...	...	...
Vellore, Central	269	2,802	12	0	...	...	...
Do. Fort	198	2,063	14	9	...	...	...
Salem	547	11,420	15	5	...	...	...
Guindy	71	1,294	0	0	...	...	...
Chingleput	197	5,557	10	3	...	...	...
Cuddalore	488	4,290	10	7	...	...	...
Tranquebar	167	2,758	7	5	...	...	...
Tanjore	157	2,781	12	0	...	...	...
Trichinopoly, Central ...	304	2,386	11	7	...	...	...
Do. District ...	183	3,056	9	3	...	...	...
Madura	459	3,352	15	4	112	0	0
Tinnevelly	236	3,057	8	7	...	...	...
Paumben	113	1,724	4	10	...	...	...
Cochin	18	880	15	4	...	...	...
Calicut	213	4,597	12	5	...	...	...
Tellicherry	92	2,709	3	1	...	...	...
Cannanore, Central ...	249	2,817	11	10	...	...	...
Do. Fort ...	64	696	0	0	...	...	...
Mangalore	202	3,635	11	10	...	...	...
Paulghat	53	653	8	0	...	...	...
Coimbatore, Central ...	904	16,303	6	3	...	...	...
Do. District ...	155	2,887	2	8	...	...	...
Ootacamund, Native ...	86	2,405	15	11	...	...	...
Lawrence Asylum Works	371	...	...	...	...	...	...
Dodabett	71	...	...	...	...	...	...
Neddivuttum	177	...	...	...	...	...	...
Pykarrah	40	...	...	...	...	...	...
Total...	9,332	1,27,641	8	3	242	13	6
European Prison... ...	15	5,746	5	4	...	...	...
Grand Total...	9,347	1,33,387	13	7	242	13	6

G.—*(Continued.)*

Madras Presidency, during the year ending 31*st March* 1868.—(Continued.)

Batta paid to discharged Prisoners.			Diet to Prisoners.			Extra allowance granted to sick.			Cost per head.		
RS.	A.	P.	RS.	A.	P.	RS.	A.	P.	RS.	A.	P.
24	8	0	3,346	5	7	2	2	2	29	14	4
84	0	6	7,245	7	10	347	6	5	33	4	10
27	6	8	422	14	2	...	...	...	18	6	2
162	11	3	9,012	14	0	27	3	5	29	14	11
499	11	0	27,687	14	9	234	10	11	39	5	3
90	8	6	3,561	11	10	31	12	2	39	14	10
18	5	0	4,802	11	10	221	6	2	46	1	6
153	9	5	8,133	13	1	35	5	11	46	2	6
179	7	0	11,530	13	11	60	11	11	46	8	10
151	5	0	6,918	1	6	111	12	9	31	15	3
144	10	6	19,690	14	1	1,509	3	3	45	4	9
204	5	0	9,910	11	2	153	14	11	39	7	6
114	4	0	12,170	3	11	139	6	8	40	5	9
257	13	9	13,987	14	3	263	0	5	52	15	8
110	3	3	9,668	6	3	212	0	9	49	14	5
280	3	9	26,657	13	5	104	14	3	48	14	10
14	8	0	3,226	9	7	10	4	0	45	9	8
99	0	0	11,116	0	3	164	10	6	57	4	2
75	8	0	24,972	3	7	...	...	...	51	2	9
83	6	0	9,545	8	4	81	5	4	57	10	4
14	3	8	10,004	13	9	152	9	6	64	11	2
40	7	6	14,330	7	0	...	...	...	47	2	3
31	1	0	5,923	2	6	323	13	0	34	2	2
104	9	0	38,336	0	9	134	13	6	83	13	0
...	...	...	11,635	5	7	38	7	0	49	7	5
49	8	0	5,734	4	3	180	3	3	52	5	5
22	8	0	704	5	2	0	13	6	39	2	10
35	7	10	15,750	14	6	1,456	8	9	80	12	7
4	6	0	6,299	4	0	191	13	2	70	8	10
44	2	0	17,650	14	11	219	3	4	72	0	11
57	2	0	2,653	3	6	16	1	10	41	11	4
64	2	0	10,622	12	11	1,045	7	3	57	12	3
8	6	6	1,840	12	11	53	13	1	35	11	11
709	2	9	51,328	4	7	...	...	...	56	12	6
168	4	3	8,612	15	5	...	...	...	55	9	1
110	7	4	5,532	7	0	451	5	6	69	9	3
205	3	11	25,559	15	5	343	9	6	69	13	2
24	10	0	4,295	7	3	0	12	3	60	8	2
12	4	0	12,175	11	0	1	8	0	63	2	4
...	...	...	465	14	4	...	...	...	11	10	4
4,481	6	4	4,73,066	2	1	8,322	2	4	49	2	7
58	7	0	2,362	4	2	218	12	1	171	1	1
4,539	13	4	4,75,428	6	3	8,540	14	5	...	...	...

G.—*(Continued.)*

Statement of Expenses incurred in the several Jails of the

JAILS.	Clothing and Bedding.			Cost per head.			Lighting.		
	RS.	A.	P.	RS.	A.	P.	RS.	A.	P.
Russelcondah	238	7	2	2	2	1	117	0	2
Berhampore	385	7	9	1	11	1	252	15	7
Chicacole	19	5	4	0	13	5	31	4	0
Vizagapatam...	567	5	4	1	14	1	625	5	0
Rajahmundry, Central...	3,006	14	1	4	3	9	1,128	12	5
Do. District...	316	1	0	3	8	2	241	3	11
Masulipatam...	245	6	0	2	4	0	168	1	2
Guntoor	1,041	4	9	5	14	2	304	0	8
Nellore...	1,125	7	10	4	8	4	254	1	0
Kurnool	574	15	0	2	9	9	307	1	2
Bellary...	1,168	8	0	2	11	4	298	6	2
Cuddapah	847	0	10	3	5	2	320	2	0
Chittoor	1,098	9	1	3	9	7	292	4	0
Vellore, Central	1,671	5	2	6	3	5	274	14	4
Do. Fort	852	15	0	4	4.	11	241	6	6
Salem	1,687	2	0	3	1	4	99	9	8
Guindy...	397	4	0	5	9	6	316	4	3
Chingleput	656	12	8	3	5	4	571	7	8
Cuddalore	1,594	13	3	3	4	3	252	4	3
Tranquebar	1,014	11	4	6	1	2	234	4	5
Tanjore...	522	10	0	3	5	11	196	7	0
Trichinopoly, Central ...	1,582	12	10	5	3	3	83	11	7
Do. District ...	655	9	0	3	9	4	71	10	9
Madura...	1,797	12	3	3	14	8	480	8	10
Tinnevelly	386	15	4	1	10	3	351	13	3
Paumben	477	8	0	4	3	7	241	15	10
Cochin	31	1	2	1	11	8	113	10	10
Calicut	1,376	4	0	6	7	4	953	1	0
Tellicherry	116	2	7	1	4	2	318	13	9
Cannanore, Central ...	884	6	6	3	8	0	683	7	5
Do. Fort	240	4	6	3	12	1	330	11	3
Mangalore	581	10	6	2	14	1	543	5	6
Paulghat	120	8	8	2	4	6	143	4	7
Coimbatore, Central ...	3,097	7	0	3	6	9	19	0	2
Do. District ...	520	1	8	3	5	8	13	15	3
Ootacamund, Native ...	992	9	8	11	8	8	245	8	3
Lawrence Asylum Works	2,908	8	9	7	13	5	929	2	10
Dodabett...	762	13	0	10	11	11	169	4	11
Neddivuttum	1,334	5	0	7	8	7	209	2	8
Pykarrah	5	0	0	0	2	0	23	0	8
Total...	36,904	2	0	3	15	9	12,452	8	8
European Prison	406	8	2	27	9	9	140	0	4
Grand Total...	37,310	10	2	...	...	...	12,592	9	0

G.—*(Continued.)*

***Madras Presidency, during the year ending* 31*st March* 1868.**—(Continued.)

Rent and Repairs of Buildings.			Purchase and Repair of Chains, Fetters, Tools, and Implements.			Furniture purchased or repaired.			Stationery.		
RS.	A.	P.	RS.	A.	P.	RS.	A.	P.	RS.	A.	P.
19	15	0	81	0	3	4	2	0	...	...	...
21	13	6	51	7	0	...	...	...	0	2	6
114	12	3	14	14	10	21	1	8	0	6	0
72	11	7	116	4	0	...	...	...	10	4	0
2	0	0	1,099	8	3	...	...	...	43	4	3
9	6	0	216	9	10	25	12	0	3	4	6
12	9	7	170	15	6	4	0	0	...	...	...
247	4	9	302	5	3	129	10	8	8	5	10
300	11	9	231	14	9	102	15	6	4	9	9
164	11	8	50	13	1	24	15	0	0	6	0
86	12	0	74	8	0	281	11	0	22	10	0
44	4	0	195	4	0	42	2	6	...	...	...
275	9	8	365	0	11	...	...	...	12	4	6
0	12	0	19	15	6	142	14	6	7	4	0
25	5	0	36	14	6	86	8	6	2	1	0
132	6	3	134	5	9	3	0	0	1	2	8
34	12	0	290	12	10	32	0	0	...	...	...
80	8	7	296	6	4	20	0	0	0	11	6
135	14	4	12	12	5	24	0	0	11	9	8
91	15	3	183	14	10	18	12	10	4	6	0
646	6	6	237	9	2	...	...	...	1	5	0
...	...	...	156	6	6	166	6	0	32	1	9
26	12	0	143	11	7	3	1	4	18	12	0
12	0	0	204	1	4	1	0	0	4	0	0
12	1	4	218	14	0	...	...	...	...	...	...
1	2	6	8	0	0	15	11	3	3	0	6
42	8	3	17	8	4	...	...	...	...	...	...
187	5	2	204	2	11	...	...	...	...	...	...
13	13	7	79	6	1	0	12	0	0	2	0
...	...	...	1	12	8	957	9	4	8	4	0
28	5	8	75	1	1	9	12	0	...	...	...
161	14	8	37	5	11	5	0	0	4	9	0
38	12	8	16	15	0	...	...	...	0	1	0
800	3	0	129	5	7	3	12	0	0	3	0
129	2	2	1	4	0	38	0	0	3	0	0
466	0	0	47	12	0	256	7	6	4	5	0
...	...	...	...	...	...	...	...	...	10	5	3
...	...	...	7	2	0	37	0	0	...	...	...
...	...	...	1	6	0	71	8	0	4	4	0
...	...	...	...	...	...	...	...	...	0	4	0
4,440	10	8	5,533	8	0	2,529	9	7	227	4	8
462	5	0	10	8	0	24	0	0	6	8	0
4,902	15	8	5,544	0	0	2,553	9	7	233	12	8

G.—*(Continued.)*

Statement of Expenses incurred in the several Jails of the

JAILS.	Executions.			Transportation and transfer of Prisoners.			Sundries.			Batta to Prisoners' children.		
	RS.	A.	P.	RS.	A.	P.	RS.	A.	P.	RS.	A.	P.
Russelcondah	14	12	0	...	...	...	70	14	5	...	...	...
Berhampore...	36	10	0	1,038	6	11	219	4	6	5	10	3
Chicacole	...	...	...	...	...	...	32	7	5	...	...	...
Vizagapatam	26	1	10	318	13	11	87	2	8	...	...	...
Rajahmundry, Central...	...	...	...	211	6	10	764	8	2	...	...	...
Do. District...	33	11	4	42	10	0	230	11	2	...	...	...
Masulipatam...	...	...	...	...	...	...	313	5	3	...	...	...
Guntoor	...	...	...	158	0	1	272	13	5	3	11	0
Nellore	5	0	0	12	6	4	158	6	10	...	...	...
Kurnool	7	0	0	349	3	5	254	14	9	18	11	3
Bellary	0	5	0	1,680	15	0	330	15	11	...	...	...
Cuddapah	26	11	0	426	3	0	312	1	0	...	...	...
Chittoor	2	12	8	29	11	0	256	4	3	...	...	...
Vellore, Central	...	...	...	...	...	...	263	10	3	...	...	...
Do. Fort	...	...	...	80	14	6	139	0	9	...	...	...
Salem	5	1	0	604	13	9	171	1	10	...	...	...
Guindy	...	...	...	...	...	...	70	12	4	...	...	...
Chingleput	29	0	4	...	...	...	410	1	1	...	...	...
Cuddalore	28	0	0	656	5	6	862	10	3	...	...	...
Tranquebar	58	4	3	274	7	0	382	6	1	...	...	...
Tanjore...	16	14	9	94	5	6	496	12	5	47	9	0
Trichinopoly, Central ...	...	...	...	...	...	...	670	2	4	...	...	...
Do. District ...	36	4	9	38	1	8	635	10	9	...	...	...
Madura	83	12	6	508	7	11	869	7	8	...	...	...
Tinnevelly	14	0	0	364	15	2	113	8	4	...	...	...
Paumben	...	...	...	34	11	3	116	4	0	...	...	...
Cochin	...	...	...	...	...	...	28	11	0	...	...	...
Calicut	58	0	0	338	6	8	456	6	4	...	...	...
Tellicherry	...	...	...	4	4	0	23	8	10	...	...	...
Cannanore, Central ...	...	...	...	...	...	...	840	9	10	...	...	...
Do. Fort	...	...	...	...	...	...	...	...	...	...	...	...
Mangalore	14	0	0	507	15	9	80	3	6	...	...	...
Paulghat	...	...	...	122	4	10	23	10	4	...	...	...
Coimbatore, Central ...	13	12	0	378	6	4	1,058	11	1	...	...	...
Do. District ...	14	0	0	...	...	...	187	15	6	...	...	...
Ootacamund, Native ...	...	...	...	1	8	0	760	9	0	...	...	...
Lawrence Asylum Works	...	...	...	54	9	11	1,323	12	8	...	...	...
Dodabett	...	...	...	...	...	...	267	9	11	...	...	...
Neddivuttum	...	...	...	136	6	9	649	13	7	...	...	...
Pykarrah	...	...	...	...	...	...	55	2	8	...	...	...
Total...	524	1	5	8,468	13	0	14,262	2	1	75	9	6
European Prison	...	...	...	59	12	9	1,107	4	8	...	...	...
Grand Total...	524	1	5	8,528	9	9	15,369	6	9	75	9	6

G.—*(Concluded.)*

Madras Presidency, during the year ending 31st *March* 1868.—(Concluded.)

Rewards paid for the re-apprehension of escaped Convicts.			Supplied Hospital on Medical requisition (exclusive of diet.)			Manufacture.			Total.			Remarks.
RS.	A.	P.	RS.	A.	P.	RS.	A.	P.	RS.	A.	P.	
...	...	...	2	1	6	...	...	...	4,460	15	1	
...	...	...	74	3	6	...	...	...	13,098	1	11	
...	...	...	3	9	0	...	...	...	1,158	1	4	
...	...	...	52	0	11	...	...	...	14,478	8	3	
...	...	...	502	3	9	13,002	10	11	59,428	14	6	
15	0	0	99	7	3	...	...	...	6,628	3	11	
...	...	...	127	15	8	125	3	6	8,407	7	11	
...	...	...	144	12	11	...	...	...	13,814	7	10	
...	...	...	64	12	5	298	8	11	17,464	7	11	
...	...	...	...	...	...	...	...	...	12,351	2	0	
25	0	0	...	...	...	807	0	6	29,458	10	5	
...	...	...	165	2	6	254	1	4	16,542	6	0	
...	...	...	113	12	11	123	5	10	19,323	13	11	
...	...	...	119	9	11	...	...	...	19,811	14	1	
20	0	0	160	3	11	...	...	...	13,699	14	8	
...	...	...	86	15	1	3,758	13	11	45,148	6	9	
...	...	...	52	0	0	...	...	...	5,739	3	0	
...	...	...	70	8	11	2,775	5	3	21,848	3	4	
...	...	...	...	...	...	2,122	12	8	35,039	8	6	
30	0	0	212	4	11	...	...	...	14,974	2	0	
20	0	0	38	13	10	939	9	5	16,211	13	6	
...	...	...	249	15	8	...	...	...	19,699	2	9	
...	...	...	126	3	7	...	...	...	11,090	7	2	
100	0	0	...	...	...	...	...	...	46,101	9	1	
...	...	...	92	14	6	...	...	...	16,286	7	1	
...	...	...	...	...	...	32	15	4	8,619	9	0	
...	...	...	...	...	...	...	...	...	1,842	1	7	
...	...	...	429	11	1	...	...	...	25,844	0	8	
40	0	0	65	9	8	...	...	...	9,867	2	9	
25	0	0	92	9	3	...	...	...	24,225	11	1	
...	...	...	6	0	0	...	...	...	4,112	9	10	
...	...	...	61	9	2	799	11	9	18,165	7	9	
...	...	...	29	15	4	...	...	...	3,052	0	11	
...	...	...	...	...	...	9,153	9	1	82,995	2	10	
...	...	...	...	...	...	162	15	0	12,738	11	11	
50	0	0	239	5	5	...	...	...	11,564	4	7	
295	0	0	168	0	7	...	...	...	31,798	4	10	Rs. 14,847-8-0 credited on account of convict labor.
...	...	...	15	2	9	...	...	...	5,579	14	1	
...	...	...	73	5	11	...	...	...	14,669	10	11	
...	...	...	...	...	...	...	...	...	549	5	8	Rs. 269-14-8 credited on account of convict labor for April and May 1867.
620	0	0	3,741	1	10	34,356	11	5	7,37,890	3	4	
...	...	...	85	4	10	1,399	3	5	12,087	3	9	
620	0	0	3,826	6	8	35,755	14	10	7,49,977	7	1	

APPENDIX III.

A.

Prices of Grains, &c., for six years.

Items.	1862-63.	1863-64.	1864-65.	1865-66.	1866-67.	1867-68.
	RS.	RS.	RS.	RS.	RS.	RS.
Rice, 2nd sort, per garce ...	346	352	411	431	522	383
Paddy, do. do ...	157	158	189	198	242	179
Cholum, per garce	201	214	227	260	334	214
Cumboo, do. ...	173	186	209	237	296	179
Raggy, do. ...	175	185	210	231	313	212
Veragoo, do. ...	139	132	161	164	208	158
Wheat, do. ...	445	553	668	700	800	616
Salt, do. ...	265	272	276	272	330	291
Cotton, per candy.	159	270	227	151	166	124

B.

General Receipts.

Items.	1863-64.		1864-65.		1865-66.		1866-67. (for eleven months.)		1867-68.		Results of 1867-68 compared with 1866-67.	
	Receipts.	Per-centage.	Receipts.	Per-centage.	Receipts.	Per-centage.	Receipts.	Per-centage.	Receipts.	Per-centage.	Increase.	Decrease
	RS.		RS.		RS.		RS.		RS.		RS.	RS.
Land Revenue	429,65,352 (Land and Forest Revenue)	68·9 (Land and Forest Revenue)	418,11,620	66·7	429,02,557	67·6	363,55,087	64·5	423,97,052	64·3	60,41,965	......
Forest Revenue			2,92,527	0·5	3,21,581	0·5	3,39,155	0·6	4,24,184	0·6	85,029	......
Abkarry	40,51,918	6·5	39,60,490	6·3	41,42,805	6·5	42,74,529	7·6	50,67,411	7·8	7,92,882	......
Income Tax	16,45,522	2·6	14,65,652	2·3	6,70,548	1·1	18,911	0·2	215	......	....	13,696
License ax	....	......	....	......	....	......	....	......	8,07,135	1·3	8,07,135	......
Moturpha Tax on Profession	2,456	0·1	2,518	0·1	....	......	....	......	....	......	....	......
Sea Customs	20,37,378	3·2	18,10,046	2·9	19,51,019	3·2	18,26,743	3·2	23,71,941	3·7	5,45,198	......
Land Customs	2,61,146	·5	2,28,733	·3	1,34,465	·2	1,06,745	0·1	1,47,080	0·2	40,335	......
Salt	89,79,243	14·4	103,45,973	16·6	101,27,596	16·1	104,72,038	18·7	109,38,017	16·7	4,65,979	......
Stamps	23,81,746	3·8	26,83,918	4·3	30,66,558	4·8	28,25,533	5·1	35,37,234	5·4	7,11,701	......
Total...	623,24,756	100	626,01,477	100	633,17,129	100	562,13,741	100	656,90,269	100	94,90,224	13,696
£ ...	6,232,475	......	6,260,147	......	6,331,712	......	5,621,374	......	6,569,026	Net. ...	9,476,528	......

C.

General Charges.

Items.	1863-64.	1864-65.	1865-66.	1866-67 (for eleven months.)	1867-68.
	RS.	RS.	RS.	RS.	RS.
Land Revenue, including Board of Revenue, Settlement Offices and Revenue Survey ...	39,24,787	38,12,095	39,84,523	37,08,331	39,35,888
Forests		1,58,616	2,59,802	2,17,149	2,72,240
Abkarry	1,89,817	1,56,331	2,70,416	1,95,670	2,16,121
Income Tax...	37,900	32,506	17,433	....	....
License Tax...	....	....	....	....	27,230
Sea Customs	1,48,901	1,58,680	1,57,201	1,42,672	1,58,935
Land Customs	14,292	10,406	8,489	7,999	7,825
Salt	9,15,864	14,25,062	14,87,686	14,48,193	13,48,996
Stamps	1,43,305	1,49,131	1,24,113	1,20,408	1,55,759
Total...	58,24,866	59,03,279	63,09,668	58,30,422	61,73,594
Allowance to District and Village Officers	3,30,472	3,60,015	3,58,901	3,41,845	3,58,518
Miscellaneous payments	1,39,122	66,311	....	....	....
Grand Total...	57,94,460	63,29,605	66,68,564	61,72,267	65,32,112
£...	579,446	632,960	666,856	617,226	653,211

D.

Abstract of Receipts and Charges.

Items.	1863-64.	1864-65.	1865-66.	1866-67.	1867-68.
1	2	3	4	5	6
	RS.	RS.	RS.	RS.	RS.
Receipts ...	623,24,756	626,01,477	633,17,129	562,13,741	656,90,269
Charges ...	57,94,460	63,29,605	66,68,564	61,72,267	65,32,112
Per-centage of charges ...	9·3	10·1	10·5	10·9	9·9

E.

Import and Export Duties.

Districts.	Import duty.	Export duty.	Re-export duty.	Miscellaneous items.	Total.
	RS.	RS.	RS.	RS.	RS.
1. Ganjam	992	84,969	...	86	86,047
2. Vizagapatam...	4,180	69,997	...	114	74,291
3. Godavery ...	10,070	68,082	...	181	78,333
4. Kistna	1,249	5,336	...	137	6,722
5. Nellore	4	208	...	22	234
6. Madras, SeaCustoms	11,78,287	1,75,447	26	27,134	13,80,894
7. South Arcot ...	11,925	56,383	...	173	68,481
8. Tanjore	1,43,910	2,87,364	...	2,743	4,34,017
9. Madura	21,078	6,118	...	5	27,201
10. Tinnevelly ...	60,328	18,983	...	341	79,652
11. South Canara...	10,913	39,532	...	766	51,211
12. Malabar... ...	35,413	47,534	...	1,911	84,858
Total...	14,78,349	8,59,953	26	33,613	23,71,941

F.

Value of Imports and Exports from 1856-57 *to* 1867-68.

Years.	Value of Imports.				Value of Exports.				Value of Re-Exports.		Gross duty.
	Merchandize.	Treasure.	Total.	Duty.	Merchandize.	Treasure.	Total.	Duty.	Merchandize.	Duty.	
	RS.	RS.	RS.	RS.	RS.	RS.	RS.	RS.	RS.	RS.	RS.
1856-57	235,25,244	170,38,582	405,63,826	7,18,443	367,26,978	33,33,678	400,60,656	5,34,044	7,78,134	......	12,52,487
1857-58	246,85,453	186,23,162	433,08,615	6,34,817	403,65,161	117,00,866	520,66,027	5,97,599	9,10,155	......	12,32,416
1858-59	293,08,408	142,96,207	436,04,615	8,82,161	337,99,807	57,28,536	395,28,343	4,29,528	17,16,376	......	13,11,689
1859-60	299,07,033	174,39,684	473,46,717	16,01,718	387,82,800	45,47,547	433,30,347	7,13,038	12,56,494	......	23,14,750
1860-61	316,55,812	207,25,887	523,81,699	17,22,731	445,98,338	62,88,632	508,86,970	8,56,058	15,07,146	675	25,79,464
1861-62	344,94,138	222,85,900	567,80,038	13,58,719	542,92,250	39,58,486	582,50,736	7,12,211	11,60,099	260	20,71,390
1862-63	303,30,148	303,86,890	607,17,038	10,91,820	635,58,990	61,90,551	697,49,541	6,79,052	11,96,496	306	17,70,178
1863-64	402,65,473	360,75,985	763,41,458	12,75,208	877,78,126	223,39,284	11,01,17,410	7,19,579	17,35,648	126	19,94,913
1864-65	418,02,487	303,13,958	721,16,445	11,17,875	836,71,790	181,50,942	10,18,22,732	6,67,464	10,04,383	88	17,85,427
1865-66	479,87,412	366,42,492	846,29,904	12,19,300	900,15,155	126,10,223	10,26,25,378	7,00,548	14,61,719	660	19,20,508
1866-67	416,74,201	136,86,606	553,60,807	12,77,505	445,86,571	175,29,881	621,16,452	5,23,008	4,86,237	79	18,00,592
1867-68	508,27,573	112,93,529	621,21,102	14,78,349	580,09,230	101,55,634	681,64,864	8,59,953	4,39,318	26	23,38,328

G.

IMPORTS.

Principal Staples of Trade.

ARTICLES.	1866-67 (eleven months.)	1867-68. For April 1867.	1867-68. From May 1867 to March 1868, (eleven months.)	1867-68. Total.
	RS.	RS.	RS.	RS.
Military and wearing apparel.	9,86,402	66,518	10,85,271	11,51,789
Books	1,45,646	6,679	1,40,266	1,46,945
Twist	80,81,785	5,48,081	78,02,107	83,50,188
Cotton Piece Goods, plain ...	78,94,570	6,69,695	87,03,602	93,73,297
Do. dyed and printed ...	26,08,441	1,20,457	22,75,410	23,95,867
Coral, unwrought	1,84,749	9,900	1,65,471	1,75,371
Drugs and medicines	3,88,645	52,536	4,17,518	4,70,054
Dyeing and colouring materials.	63,011	15,020	79,978	94,998
Earthen and Porcelain ware ...	80,782	3,771	1,09,962	1,13,733
Glass, manufactures of ...	1,91,027	11,800	1,92,202	2,04,002
Paddy	13,88,560	3,17,222	30,74,478	33,91,700
Rice...	14,52,911	4,17,712	10,58,652	14,76,364
Wheat	5,04,226	44,932	2,21,332	2,66,264
Grain of sorts	6,33,534	54,942	3,64,308	4,19,250
Jewelry	63,302	4,822	84,401	89,223
Jute, manufactures of	3,61,105	23,934	2,45,667	2,69,601
Machines and machinery ...	1,54,197	7,210	4,42,290	4,49,500
Malt liquors	8,28,988	43,437	7,00,514	7,43,951
Metals	30,32,582	3,12,698	36,99,879	40,12,577
Paper	2,01,830	52,857	4,65,737	5,18,594
Provisions and Oilman's stores.	4,78,853	36,206	5,78,054	6,14,260
Railway stores	14,80,860	3,53,325	27,73,341	31,26,666
Seeds	10,89,873	74,294	3,24,546	3,98,840
Silk, raw...	3,07,995	500	1,92,455	1,92,955
Silk, manufactures of	1,98,940	21,042	2,31,205	2,52,247
Spices, including betel-nut ...	11,43,925	70,827	15,52,099	16,22,926
Spirits	5,67,972	45,216	6,23,930	6,69,146
Stationery, except paper ...	90,813	7,510	91,910	99,420
Tea	28,381	11,434	2,75,987	2,87,421
Timber and planks	10,52,598	89,035	11,37,699	12,26,734
Wines	8,60,789	34,846	8,99,574	9,34,420
Wool, manufactures of... ...	3,68,295	19,344	4,72,609	4,91,953
Other articles*	48,13,664	4,82,184	63,15,133	67,97,317
Total...	416,74,201	40,29,986	467,97,587	508,27,573
£..	4,167,420	402,998	4,679,758	5,082,757
* Government Stores	8,50,079	75,665	9,18,116	9,93,781
Do. Salt on the West Coast ..	35,712	19,874	2,89,501	3,09,375

G.—*(Concluded.)*

EXPORTS.

ARTICLES.	1866-67, (eleven months.)	1867-68. For April 1867.	1867-68. From May 1867 to March 1868, (eleven months.)	1867-68. Total.
	RS.	RS.	RS.	RS.
Cocoanuts	25,04,079	1,23,277	30,47,592	31,70,869
Coffee	41,91,785	11,31,068	69,23,269	80,54,337
Cotton Wool	94,37,789	21,14,486	102,71,894	123,86,380
Cotton Goods	29,75,738	2,73,591	31,06,683	33,80,274
Coir and Coir rope	10,56,216	63,247	11,14,670	11,77,917
Dregs of Gingelly-oil	2,82,451	41,789	2,52,859	2,94,648
Drugs	1,32,104	16,408	1,45,014	1,61,422
Indigo	14,20,215	3,93,973	39,21,031	43,15,004
Dyes of sorts	4,70,705	28,006	3,09,723	3,37,729
Feathers...	14,681	2,733	30,957	33,690
Fruits and vegetables... ...	1,39,416	10,571	1,40,996	1,51,567
Paddy	7,19,520	34,215	6,13,854	6,48,069
Rice	84,51,383	8,31,861	62,12,628	70,44,489
Wheat	40,420	23,470	47,576	71,046
Grain of sorts	3,79,898	31,872	1,60,052	1,91,924
Hemp, manufactures of ...	9,228	871	22,537	23,408
Hides and Skins	28,53,898	2,56,629	26,41,648	28,98,277
Horns	1,41,898	28,346	1,80,902	2,09,248
Ivory and Ivory ware	17,708	82	13,512	13,594
Jewelry	61,106	...	47,000	47,000
Mats	21,954	1,924	21,894	23,818
Oils	11,97,479	3,76,825	20,66,878	24,43,703
Precious stones	57,255	800	40,300	41,100
Provisions and Oilman's stores.	4,05,828	10,539	4,02,053	4,12,592
Salt	88,319	2,787	31,856	34,643
Saltpetre	22,761	...	65,900	65,900
Seeds	4,89,748	1,19,477	33,07,253	34,26,730
Silk, manufactures of	74,917	4,878	64,481	69,359
Spices	21,96,828	2,32,905	23,92,928	26,25,833
Spirits	7,024	807	9,434	10,241
Sugar and other Saccharine matter...	18,58,020	8,389	8,94,457	9,02,846
Timber and wood	8,75,442	50,351	10,12,421	10,62,772
Tobacco	3,43,965	18,478	3,48,238	3,66,716
Wax	40,938	270	28,022	28,292
All other articles	21,06,430	5,64,727	13,19,066	18,83,793
Total...	445,86,571	67,99,652	512,09,578	580,09,230
£...	4,458,657	679,965	5,120,958	5,800,923
Government Stores	21,668	...	...	...

H.

Export trade in Coffee, Cotton, Indigo, &c.

Articles.	1865-66.		1866-67.		1867-68.	
	Quantity.	Value.	Quantity.	Value.	Quantity.	Value.
		RS.		RS.		RS.
Coffee ... ... lbs...	3,45,27,695	78,13,813	1,73,49,508	41,91,785	3,76,06,333	80,54,337
Cotton Wool ... ... „ ...	12,00,34,216	484,16,348	2,43,67,331	94,37,789	4,70,26,932	123,86,380
Cotton Piece Goods	......	20,43,953	......	29,75,738	......	33,80,274
Indigo ... ... lbs...	16,00,925	34,57,070	6,58,224	14,20,215	22,61,616	43,15,004
Rice... ... ... Cwt...	14,43,419	65,88,482	15,28,596	84,51,333	16,99,299	70,44,489
Hides and Skins ... ... No...	44,43,327	19,81,107	1,11,29,993	23,53,398	51,65,385	28,98,277
Oils ... ... Gallons...	15,92,962	15,43,435	11,04,160	11,97,479	17,27,867	24,43,703
Coir and Coir Rope ... ... Cwt...	2,17,907	12,27,560	1,81,427	10,56,216	2,02,571	11,77,917
Oil, &c., Seeds ... ... „ ...	5,96,469	22,69,161	1,12,655	4,89,748	6,36,435	34,26,730
Spices ... ... { Cwt...	1,65,438	23,59,650	2,22,471	21,96,823	1,99,583	} 26,25,833
{ No...	......	......	......	......	1,01,57,316	
Sugar and other saccharine matter ... Cwt...	4,19,559	27,45,800	2,84,631	18,58,020	1,05,554	9,02,846

I.

Area of Cotton cultivation and Exports of Cotton for ten years.

Years.	Quantity.	Value.	Area.
1858-59	3,86,52,542	61,17,902	10,41,848
1859-60	8,25,12,521	95,97,135	9,96,658
1860-61	7,88,22,027	112,91,211	10,60,558
1861-62	8,65,44,471	170,40,215	9,77,728
1862-63	6,23,74,133	238,12,882	13,62,438
1863-64	7,24,90,886	447,18,112	18,24,763
1864-65	7,31,01,578	404,18,937	17,42,078
1865-66	12,00,34,216	484,16,348	15,16,076
1866-67 (eleven months) ...	2,43,67,331	94,37,789	13,75,425
1867-68	4,70,26,932	123,86,380	14,62,432

K.

Bullion.

Years.	IMPORTS			EXPORTS		
	By Government.	By Individuals.	Total.	By Government.	By Individuals.	Total.
	RS.	RS.	RS.	RS.	RS.	RS.
1862-63 ...	51,02,833	252,84,057	303,86,890	35,40,000	26,50,551	61,90,551
1863-64 ...	44,30,000	316,45,985	360,75,985	160,03,000	63,36,284	223,39,284
1864-65 ...	......	303,13,958	303,13,958	89,52,000	91,98,942	181,50,942
1865-66 ...	......	366,42,492	366,42,492	62,00,600	64,09,623	126,10,223
1866-67 for 11 months.	......	186,86,606	186,86,606	67,28,685	108,01,196	175,29,881
1867-68 ...	......	112,93,529	112,93,529	79,00,000	22,55,634	101,55,634

L.

Salt.

Items.	1863-64.	1864-65.	1865-66.	1866-67 11 months.	1867-68.
	In. Mds.	In. Mds.	In. Mds.	In. Mds.	In. Mds.
Home consumption	29,74,214	32,36,772	33,30,837	30,99,750	33,67,710
Inland do.	31,25,278	37,09,269	33,50,364	32,11,132	32,86,245
Total ...	60,99,492	69,46,041	66,81,201	63,10,882	66,53,955
Exportation	3,03,127	5,32,018	12,86,965	5,04,733	1,95,176
Grand Total...	64,02,619	74,78,059	79,68,166	68,15,615	68,49,131
	RS. A. P.	RS. A. P.	RS. A. P.	RS. A. P.	RS. A. P.
Government price for Salt per Indian Maund ...	1 8 0	1 8 0	{ 1 8 0 / 1 11 0 }	1 11 0	1 11 0

M.

Local Funds.

Districts.	Receipts.					Charges.				
	1863-64.	1864-65	1865-66.	1866-67.	1867-68.	1863-64.	1864-65.	1865-66.	1866-67.	1867-68.
	RS.	RS.	RS.	RS.	RS.	RS.	RS.	RS.	RS.	RS.
Ganjam	2,965	3,370	3,446	5,349	31,676	200	5,747	2,587	942	18,339
Vizagapatam	3,167	211	3,655	10,310	1,18,595	1,095	1,232	762	5,182	15,824
Godavery	30,389	51,802	46,107	53,069	1,90,901	30,790	27,849	61,628	65,435	1,05,403
Kistna	42,007	30,792	29,307	43,335	93,030	36,477	16,122	13,338	15,173	84,068
Nellore	16,565	23,575	31,153	29,553	47,017	31,140	28,700	22,647	16,599	49,045
Cuddapah	6,357	5,977	9,575	11,245	60,035	4,580	2,564	9,039	8,985	16,194
Bellary	8,464	15,672	21,576	20,523	32,932	9,879	9,161	19,812	23,612	15,320
Kurnool	5,672	8,801	12,440	30,416	64,668	7,635	9,314	12,928	15,073	18,501
Madras	9,128	9,704	10,581	8,884	34,753	20,858	8,006	12,393	8,175	45,890
North Arcot	51,674	38,540	42,489	63,076	65,554	26,651	38,857	42,623	49,143	76,962
South Arcot	56,377	65,942	65,880	55,410	1,02,993	55,922	72,362	70,145	65,023	45,890
Tanjore	37,083	40,344	47,614	99,294	2,12,397	27,829	26,249	37,473	74,144	59,474
Trichinopoly	4,184	11,287	45,854	63,332	68,564	4,583	2,855	14,109	22,698	27,927
Madura	22,588	26,669	43,445	41,033	82,866	21,885	17,618	31,676	65,404	83,620
Tinnevelly	13,350	26,373	21,827	92,119	71,105	11,654	16,618	26,480	37,125	85,260
Coimbatore	16,147	29,505	38,501	55,341	1,10,270	14,420	23,489	30,800	27,490	1,20,050
Salem	22,252	43,849	65,393	34,339	78,409	27,784	37,071	27,885	63,178	72,861
South Canara	11,924	13,687	13,494	38,541	47,716	14,298	19,153	14,484	7,698	49,455
Malabar	67,823	98,075	1,01,017	99,759	1,44,150	83,229	82,643	1,15,711	98,722	1,53,849
Total...	4,28,116	5,44,175	6,53,354	8,54,928	16,57,631	4,30,909	4,45,610	5,66,520	6,69,801	11,43,932

N.

No. 1.

Statement shewing the Cultivations in the several Districts, for the official year 1867-68.

Districts.	DRY.		WET.		TOTAL.		1866-67.		COMPARISON.			
									INCREASE.		DECREASE.	
	Extent.	Assessment.	Extent.	Assessment.	Extent.	Assessment.	Extent.	Assessment.	Extent.	Assessment.	Extent.	Assessment.
1	2	3	4	5	6	7	8	9	10	11	12	13
	Acres.	Rupees.	Acres.	Rupees.	Acres.	Rupees.	Acres.	Rupees.	Acres.	Rupees.	Acres.	Rupees.
1. Ganjam... ...	99,174	1,27,578	1,71,735	4,97,156	2,70,909	6,24,734	2,62,479	6,06,319	8,430	18,415	...	...
2. Vizagapatam.	51,052	53,056	23,971	1,25,128	75,023	1,78,184	70,628	1,74,846	4,395	3,338	...	...
3. Godavery ...	2,66,876	5,80,394	2,04,991	5,85,250	4,71,867	11,65,644	4,33,003	10,82,987	38,864	82,657	...	...
4. Kistna	14,76,278	22,63,833	1,45,458	8,27,621	16,21,736	30,91,454	16,12,437	30,81,931	9,299	9,523	...	...
5. Nellore ...	5,37,541	7,33,364	1,55,450	7,15,622	6,92,991	14,48,986	6,70,648	15,01,959	22,343	...	...	52,973
6. Cuddapah ...	10,89,379	8,47,270	1,11,822	8,29,703	12,01,201	16,76,973	11,93,648	17,94,862	7,553	...	...	1,17,889
7. Bellary... ...	20,95,192	14,13,715	1,33,421	5,90,478	22,28,613	20,04,193	21,20,874	20,53,912	1,07,739	...	...	49,719
8. Kurnool.. ...	11,57,569	11,27,915	25,437	1,95,871	11,83,006	13,23,786	11,75,225	13,45,561	7,781	...	...	21,775
9. Madras... ...	1,53,209	2,65,300	2,13,215	8,88,431	3,66,424	11,53,731	3,64,827	12,21,038	1,597	...	...	67,307
10. North Arcot..	3,87,900	5,65,171	1,60,267	9,85,776	5,48,167	15,50,947	5,51,309	16,97,595	...	...	3,142	1,46,648
11. South Arcot.	8,11,840	15,30,712	2,51,541	13,75,655	10,63,381	29,06,367	10,36,322	29,21,651	27,059	...	...	15,284
12. Tanjore... ...	1,80,774	2,49,164	7,12,055	35,45,583	8,92,829	37,94,747	8,86,666	37,60,425	6,163	34,322	...	...
13. Trichinopoly.	8,02,180	7,48,038	1,26,685	5,83,979	9,28,865	13,32,017	8,86,764	13,03,705	42,101	28,312	...	...
14. Madura. ...	5,98,734	8,05,837	1,25,526	5,85,837	7,24,260	13,91,674	6,83,476	13,25,316	40,784	66,358	...	...
15. Tinnevelly ...	8,52,538	7,01,413	2,25,233	16,38,220	10,77,771	23,39,633	10,50,101	23,13,973	27,670	25,660	...	...
16. Coimbatore....	18,11,707	17,10,217	74,200	5,92,956	18,85,907	23,03,173	19,07,063	23,01,598	...	1,575	21,156	...
17. Salem	10,04,914	12,92,617	70,241	4,47,441	10,75,155	17,40,058	10,49,349	17,51,014	25,806	...	...	10,956
18. South Canara.	...	...	...	...	...	...	...	...	...	...	...	...
19. Malabar... ...	...	...	The Collector has not forwarded the Cultivation Return.									
Total...	1,33,76,857	150,15,594	29,31,248	150,10,707	1,63,08,105	3,00,26,301	159,54,819	302,38,692	3,77,584	2,70,160	24,298	4,82,551
								Net ...	3,53,286		Net...	2,12,391

O.

No. 2.

Statement shewing the prices of Grain and other chief articles of produce in the several Districts, for the official year 1867-68, *compared with* 1866-67.

DISTRICTS.	RICE, 1st sort, per garce.		RICE, 2nd sort.		PADDY, 1st sort.		PADDY, 2nd sort.	
	1866-67.	1867-68.	1866-67.	1867-68.	1866-67.	1867-68.	1866-67.	1867-68.
1	2	3	4	5	6	7	8	9
	RS.	RS.	RS.	RS.	RS.	RS.	RS.	RS.
Ganjam	541	256	478	232	209	121	192	112
Vizagapatam...	436	222	396	203	188	93	171	85
Godavery ...	373	237	345	222	167	107	157	101
Kistna	461	384	425	351	211	173	196	160
Nellore	451	415	428	380	214	197	203	180
Cuddapah ...	672	561	589	492	319	261	277	231
Bellary	852	526	762	469	367	224	346	204
Kurnool... ...	673	525	607	455	306	231	274	205
Madras	568	450	523	417	252	203	231	183
North Arcot....	569	431	517	391	245	185	229	172
South Arcot....	542	398	503	358	240	176	220	155
Tanjore... ...	533	385	479	359	244	179	224	165
Trichinopoly....	620	468	577	436	292	218	265	198
Madura	681	512	625	477	328	255	297	232
Tinnevelly ...	698	522	569	433	319	247	273	203
Coimbatore.....	762	537	653	474	363	252	316	223
Salem	631	469	577	426	292	210	263	191
South Canara...	479	333	439	308	...	...	210	149
Malabar	599	435	535	389	271	194	255	188
Average...	586	425	522	383	268	196	242	179

O.—*(Continued.)*

No. 2.—(Continued.)

Statement shewing the prices of Grain and other chief articles of produce in the

Districts.	CHOLUM.		CUMBOO.		RAGGY.		VERAGU.	
	1866-67.	1867-68.	1866-67.	1867-68.	1866-67.	1867-68.	1866-67.	1867-68.
	10	11	12	13	14	15	16	17
	RS.	RS.	RS.	RS.	RS.	RS.	RS.	RS.
Ganjam... ...	326	140	228	111	292	151	...	133
Vizagapatam...	234	121	192	86	233	108	158	72
Godavery ...	202	127	167	105	192	118	164	108
Kistna	226	210	213	189	211	167	189	163
Nellore	271	239	246	218	239	200	150	145
Cuddapah ...	367	273	335	264	346	255	240	217
Bellary	502	229	480	233	448	217	...	161
Kurnool... ...	377	208	356	210	339	197	209	144
Madras	357	256	337	246	351	282	281	207
North Arcot...	372	281	331	256	331	263	346	246
South Arcot ...	287	207	277	213	301	221	203	142
Tanjore... ...	326	222	292	187	270	191	160	124
Trichinopoly...	294	187	295	210	295	209	157	135
Madura... ...	349	236	317	228	329	228	162	189
Tinnevelly ...	339	188	332	225	313	204	...	...
Coimbatore ...	475	268	324	204	392	241	304	183
Salem	371	253	311	219	351	247	195	151
South Canara.	...	...	...	...	349	271	...	...
Malabar... ...	...	...	...	...	366	262	...	...
Average...	334	214	296	179	313	212	208	158

O.—*(Continued.)*

No. 2.—(Continued.)

several Districts, for the official year 1867-68, *compared with* 1866-67.

HORSE-GRAM.		ULUNDOO.		WHEAT.		GINGELLY-OIL SEED.		LAMP-OIL SEED.	
1866-67.	1867-68.	1866-67.	1867-68.	1866-67.	1867-68.	1866-67.	1867-68.	1866-67.	1867-68.
18	19	20	21	22	23	24	25	26	27
RS. 352	RS. 154	RS. 429	RS. 289	RS. 774	RS. 302	RS. 462	RS. 360	RS. 497	RS. 370
250	143	387	253	559	292	484	345	424	338
286	141	389	321	686	356	521	352	342	269
304	184	440	400	806	545	511	431	348	335
362	264	547	491	731	702	463	535	298	294
468	262	775	600	890	622	755	636	467	346
593	258	909	619	1,095	555	812	490	573	328
463	233	557	459	970	540	578	267	440	168
470	311	610	506	885	739	...	...	...	...
439	259	626	505	796	629	748	563	481	332
403	243	643	508	923	800	669	521	571	338
416	257	610	565	806	740	834	610	582	429
413	262	659	628	794	739	1,088	636	593	427
508	276	657	644	903	874	902	577	622	449
414	300	713	659	818	750	1,011	667	734	422
522	261	705	583	849	711	838	726	595	350
415	241	610	473	769	659	...	...	...	...
441	297	471	393	601	580	...	...	...	...
460	290	587	490	615	563	...	...	...	...
420	244	590	494	800	616	725	514	504	346

O.—*(Concluded.)*

No. 2.—(Concluded.)

Statement shewing the prices of Grain and other chief articles of produce in the several Districts, for the official year 1867-68 *compared with* 1866-67.

Districts.	SALT.		COTTON, per Candy.		INDIGO, per Candy.		SUGAR, per Candy.	
	1866-67.	1867-68.	1866-67.	1867-68.	1866-67.	1867-68.	1866-67.	1867-68.
	28	29	30	31	32	33	34	35
	RS.	RS.	RS.	RS.	RS.	RS.	RS.	RS.
Ganjam	270	291	148	140	937	957	119	107
Vizagapatam ...	292	281	160	142	740	720	104	100
Godavery... ...	256	244	165	110	900	865	80	99
Kistna	281	266	145	91	1,089	940	47	42
Nellore	260	259	163	114	933	877	93	99
Cuddapah ...	354	328	189	141	1,203	1,104	100	97
Bellary	489	449	181	105	1,216	1,151	96	110
Kurnool	390	330	163	97	1,173	1,075	102	90
Madras	264	269	141	120	986	917	...	...
North Arcot ...	248	250	197	149	1,020	980	80	82
South Arcot ...	263	271	133	120	695	680	42	40
Tanjore	241	247	173	148	249	282	50	45
Trichinopoly ...	294	298	176	118	369	512	49	39
Madura	286	276	125	109	720	716	45	39
Tinnevelly ...	291	278	156	109	620	620	100	...
Coimbatore ...	376	343	137	101	520	500	46	45
Salem	307	304	218	175	757	780	...	...
South Canara ...	245	254	215	141	...	...	...	...
Malabar	305	291	...	...	...	...	...	...
Average...	330	291	166	124	831	809	77	74

P.

Statement shewing the collections of all sources of Revenue in the several Districts, for the official year 1867-68, *compared with* 1866-67.

Districts.	Land Revenue.				Abkarry.				Income Tax.			
	1866-67.	1867-68. (for 11 months.)	Increase.	Decrease	1866-67.	1867-68.	Increase.	Decrease.	1866-67.	1867-68.	Increase.	Decrease.
1	2	3	4	5	6	7	8	9	10	11	12	13
	RS.	RS.	RS.	RS.	RS.	RS.	RS.	RS.	RS.	RS.	RS.	RS.
1. Ganjam... ...	9,01,126	11,65,192	2,64,066	......	60,856	64,784	3,928	...	13	...	...	13
2. Vizagapatam ...	11,09,018	14,39,221	3,30,208	......	81,233	1,02,846	21,613	...	45	...	...	45
3. Godavery ...	35,12,825	38,67,333	3,54,508	......	1,66,105	1,93,194	27,089	...	55	5	...	50
4. Kistna	28,91,821	34,14,438	5,22,617	......	1,19,191	1,44,293	25,102	...	58	...	...	58
5. Nellore... ...	19,02,142	23,33,281	4,31,139	......	62,151	77,866	15,715	...	412	...	...	412
6. Cuddapah ...	17,58,697	18,94,691	1,35,994	......	1,94,946	1,74,594	...	20,352	--	...	...	...
7. Bellary	16,56,575	23,42,500	6,85,925	......	4,88,570	6,90,828	2,02,258	...	92	...	...	92
8. Kurnool ...	13,45,276	14,55,379	1,10,103	......	2,83,785	3,23,388	39,603	...	10	...	...	10
9. Madras... ...	13,70,861	11,94,897	...	1,75,964	10,05,659	10,83,497	77,838	...	4,504	...	...	4,504
10. North Arcot ...	19,84,279	21,37,395	1,53,116	......	2,32,030	3,14,325	82,295	...	11	...	...	11
11. South Arcot ...	25,13,458	26,35,977	1,22,519	......	1,98,284	2,39,291	41,007	...	58	...	...	58
12. Tanjore... ...	33,83,034	41,82,030	7,98,996	......	4,16,082	4,74,637	58,555	...	1,569	210	...	1,359
13. Trichinopoly ...	12,75,134	13,91,946	1,16,812	......	1,04,697	1,21,032	16,335	...	48	...	...	48
14. Madura... ...	17,02,156	20,07,732	3,05,576	......	1,21,468	1,42,577	21,109	...	...	...	...	...
15. Tinnevelly ...	25,86,966	31,24,737	5,37,771	......	61,571	81,459	19,888	...	399	...	...	399
16. Coimbatore ...	20,24,336	25,52,554	5,28,218	......	2,61,849	3,20,556	58,707	...	47	...	...	47
17. Salem	17,70,991	21,42,303	3,71,312	......	1,59,932	2,30,503	70,571	...	...	...	...	...
18. South Canara ..	10,69,612	18,82,214	8,12,602	......	94,749	1,05,774	11,025	...	...	...	...	...
19. Malabar ..	15,96,785	17,33,232	1,36,447	......	1,61,371	1,81,967	20,596	...	1,945	...	...	1,945
Madras Town ...	...	......	...	......	......	...	...	...	...	...	...	...
Total ...	363,55,087	423,97,052	62,17,929	1,75,964	42,74,529	50,67,411	8,13,234	20,352	9,266	215	...	9,051
		Net...	60,41,965			Net...	7,92,882					
					Stoppages made from the salary of the Public Servants at the Presidency.				4,645	...	...	4,645
									18,911	215	...	13,696

P.—(Continued.)

Statement shewing the collections of all sources of Revenue in the several Districts, &c.—(Continued.)

Districts.	License Tax.				Salt.				Sea Customs.			
	1866-67.	1867-68.	Increase	Decrease	1866-67.	1867-68.	Increase.	Decrease.	1866-67.	1867-68.	Increase.	Decrease
	14	15	16	17	18	19	20	21	22	23	24	25
	RS.	RS.	RS.	RS.	RS.	RS.	RS.	RS.	RS.	RS.	RS.	RS.
1. Ganjam	......	16,957	16,957	......	14,26,617	13,17,190	......	1,09,427	5,931	86,047	80,116	......
2. Vizagapatam ...	......	24,010	24,010	......	3,20,607	2,69,507	......	51,100	8,576	74,291	65,715	......
3. Godavery... ...	......	40,427	40,427	......	4,09,473	4,21,328	11,855	......	47,799	78,333	30,534	......
4. Kistna	......	60,011	60,011	......	10,87,864	8,93,425	......	1,94,459	7,885	6,722	......	1,163
5. Nellore	......	38,276	38,276	......	9,84,124	10,88,914	1,04,790	......	124	234	110	......
6. Cuddapah... ...	......	48,289	48,289	......	...	...	......	......	......	......	......	......
7. Bellary	......	1,06,324	1,06,324	......	6,132	10,857	4,725	......	......	......	......	......
8. Kurnool	......	46,831	46,831	......	1,788	1,970	182	......	......	......	......	......
9. Madras	......	13,983	13,983	......	21,52,583	23,63,653	2,11,070	......	......	......	......	......
10. North Arcot ...	......	29,685	29,685	......	...	...	......	......	......	......	......	......
11. South Arcot ...	......	22,599	22,599	......	5,72,718	6,03,438	30,720	......	33,199	68,481	35,282	......
12. Tanjore...... ...	......	60,734	60,734	......	10,41,620	11,19,874	78,254	......	3,08,503	4,34,017	1,25,514	......
13. Trichinopoly ...	......	12,246	12,246	......	...	...	......	......	......	......	......	......
14. Madura	......	40,399	40,399	......	5,52,179	6,24,833	72,654	......	24,728	27,201	2,473	......
15. Tinnevelly ...	......	32,507	32,507	......	6,61,733	7,06,826	45,093	......	64,445	79,652	15,207	......
16. Coimbatore ...	......	36,442	36,442	......	...	...	......	......	......	......	......	......
17. Salem	......	29,428	29,406	......	...	...	......	......	......	......	......	......
18. South Canara ...	......	14,685	14,628	......	4,80,462	5,95,890	1,15,428	......	51,600	51,211	......	389
19. Malabar	......	28,006	28,085	......	7,74,118	9,20,312	1,46,194	......	87,068	84,858	......	2,210
Madras Town ...	......	83,307	83,307	......	...	...	......	......	11,86,885	13,80,894	1,94,009	......
Total ...	......	7,85,146	7,85,146	......	104,72,088	109,88,017	8,20,965	3,54,986	18,26,743	23,71,941	5,48,960	3,762
						Net...	4,65,979			Net...	5,45,198	......
Stoppages made from the salary of the Public Servants at the Presidency	......	21,989	21,989									
	......	8,07,135	8,07,135	......								

P.—*(Concluded.)*

Statement shewing the collections of all sources of Revenue in the several Districts, &c.—(Concluded.)

Districts.	Land Customs.				Stamps.				Total.			
	1866-67.	1867-68.	Increase.	Decrease	1866-67.	1867-68.	Increase.	Decrease	1866-67.	1867-68.	Increase.	Decrease
	26	27	28	29	30	31	32	33	34	35	36	37
	RS.	RS.	RS.	RS.	RS.	RS.	RS.	RS.	RS.	RS.	RS.	RS.
1. Ganjam	......	......	...	......	69,828	80,416	10,588	......	24,64,371	27,30,586	2,66,215	......
2. Vizagapatam ...	......	......	...	......	1,03,538	1,29,898	26,360	......	16,23,012	20,39,773	4,16,761	......
3. Godavery ...	401	986	585	......	1,39,798	1,67,947	28,149	......	42,76,456	47,69,553	4,93,097	......
4. Kistna	......	......	...	......	90,717	1,17,962	27,245	......	41,97,556	46,86,851	4,89,295	......
5. Nellore	4	......	...	4	63,993	92,784	28,791	......	30,12,950	36,31,855	6,18,405	......
6. Cuddapah ..	......	......	...	......	1,16,675	1,45,959	29,284	......	20,70,318	22,63,538	1,93,215	......
7. Bellary	......	......	...	......	1,40,608	1,89,252	48,644	......	22,91,977	33,39,761	10,47,784	......
8 Kurnool	......	......	...	......	94,736	1,15,733	20,997	......	17,25,595	19,48,301	2,17,706	......
9. Madras	......	......	...	......	1,64,747	2,34,042	69,295	......	46,98,354	48,90,072	1,91,718	......
10. North Arcot ...	......	......	...	......	98,236	1,35,102	36,866	......	23,14,556	26,16,507	3,01,951	......
11. South Arcot ...	45,995	55,566	9,571	......	91,869	1,20,671	28,802	......	34,55,581	37,46,023	2,90,442	......
12. Tanjore	55,759	81,634	25,875	......	3,33,908	4,06,598	72,690	......	55,40,475	67,59,734	12,19,259	......
13. Trichinopoly ...	......	......	...	......	75,057	93,544	18,487	......	14,54,936	16,18,768	1,63,832	......
14. Madura	......	......	...	......	2,00,569	2,48,139	47,570	......	26,01,100	30,90,881	4,89,781	......
15. Tinnevelly ...	......	......	...	......	2,00,164	2,49,159	48,995	......	35,75,278	42,74,340	6,99,062	......
16. Coimbatore ...	......	......	...	......	1,26,832	1,50,396	23,564	......	24,13,064	30,59,948	6,46,884	......
17. Salem	......	......	...	......	1,13,976	1,46,139	32,163	......	20,44,899	25,48,351	5,03,452	......
18. South Canara..	......	......	...	......	1,34,841	1,45,195	10,354	......	18,31,264	22,94,912	4,63,648	......
19. Malabar	4,586	8,894	4,308	......	3,79,539	4,66,866	87,327	......	30,05,412	34,24,214	4,18,802	......
Madras Town...	......	......	...	......	85,902	1,01,432	15,530	......	12,72,787	15,65,633	2,92,846	......
Total ...	1,06,745	1,47,080	40,339	4	28,25,533	35,37,234	7,11,701	......	558,69,941	652,44,096	93,74,155	......
		Net...	40,335		Stoppages made from the pay of Public Servants in the Presidency Towns on account of Income-tax				4,645	...	...	4,645
					Do. do. do. on account of License-tax...				...	21,989	21,989	....•
								Total ...	558,74,586	652,66,085	93,96,144	4,645
										Net ...	93,91,499	

APPENDIX IV.

A.

Statement shewing the expenditure on Public Works in 1867-68 *from Imperial Funds, as compared with the allotment for that year, and with the outlay in* 1866-67.

Districts.	Allotment for 1867-68, including Private contributions.	Expenditure in 1867-68.	Expenditure in 1866-67.
	RS.	RS.	RS.
Ganjam	2,09,645	1,86,406	1,32,367
Vizagapatam	1,55,792	1,27,918	1,07,448
Godavery	4,88,937	3,87,193	3,39,664
Kistna	3,75,402	3,57,971	2,57,853
Nellore	2,23,554	2,17,032	1,47,395
Cuddapah...	1,49,602	1,42,896	1,14,166
Kurnool	59,717	55,375	70,786
Bellary	3,36,378	3,07,392	2,54,878
Presidency	4,70,077	4,74,048	3,49,376
Madras	7,28,389	7,08,416	3,48,502
North Arcot	3,60,158	3,61,004	1,85,665
South Arcot	2,73,935	1,98,157	1,58,635
Salem	1,49,307	52,720	92,775
Bangalore...	4,43,819	4,60,199	3,15,375
Tanjore	3,46,699	2,87,924	2,37,713
Trichinopoly	3,44,293	3,39,837	2,04,353
Coimbatore	5,62,259	5,29,238	5,10,940
Malabar	5,88,523	5,86,343	4,05,525
South Canara	65,541	68,245	65,864
Madura	2,39,690	2,40,785	1,80,892
Tinnevelly	1,78,525	1,78,934	1,48,261
Total...	67,50,242	62,68,033	46,28,433

B.

Statement shewing the expenditure on New Works in each District from Imperial Funds under the Budget heads.

Districts.	Military.	Civil Buildings	Agricultural.	Communications.	Miscellaneous Public Improvement.	Total.
	RS.	RS.	RS.	RS.	RS.	RS.
Ganjam	...	14,339	4,230	1,02,265	...	1,20,834
Vizagapatam ...	3,127	32,049	3,602	32,016	858	71,652
Godavery ...	446	64,008	1,48,599	157	1,513	2,14,723
Kistna	...	7,852	2,39,164	3,680	13,854	2,64,550
Nellore	...	3,990	88,691	35,944	...	1,28,625
Cuddapah ...	...	1,625	21,924	12,489	...	36,038
Kurnool... ...	217	869	289	...	...	1,375
Bellary	1,03,534	10,542	31,750	1,354	...	1,47,180
Presidency ...	1,93,868	1,59,025	...	36,310	3,488	3,92,691
Madras	80,417	50,672	3,56,591	8,475	312	4,96,467
North Arcot ...	2,377	82,431	99,796	36,869	...	2,21,473
South Arcot ...	...	10,391	43,117	15,980	...	69,488
Salem	...	12,899	2,180	3,502	...	18,581
Bangalore ...	4,12,728	11,212	...	...	...	4,23,940
Tanjore	...	6,630	92,779	30,563	...	1,29,972
Trichinopoly ...	11,436	1,15,220	42,316	18,319	...	1,87,291
Coimbatore ...	1,36,648	1,26,961	44,923	1,00,272	...	4,08,804
Malabar	97,346	1,37,041	...	2,57,334	...	4,91,721
South Canara...	175	740	...	32,145	...	33,060
Madura	...	84,845	5,907	23,809	5,650	1,20,211
Tinnevelly ...	6,594	4,135	6,786	44,981	...	62,496
Total ...	10,48,913	9,37,476	12,32,644	7,96,464	25,675	40,41,172

C.

Statement shewing the expenditure on Repairs in each District from Imperial Funds under the Budget heads.

Districts.	Military.	Civil Buildings.	Agricultural.	Communications.	Miscellaneous Public Improvement.	Total.
	RS.	RS.	RS.	RS.	RS.	RS.
Ganjam ...	255	2,108	16,964	46,237	13	65,572
Vizagapatam.	4,516	2,474	13,056	36,220	...	56,266
Godavery ...	1,070	2,975	1,34,311	29,141	4,973	1,72,470
Kistna ...	457	4,708	60,878	27,132	246	93,421
Nellore ...	...	1,214	42,883	44,310	...	88,407
Cuddapah ...	1,007	2,884	32,940	70,027	...	1,06,858
Kurnool ...	674	434	16,942	35,950	...	54,000
Bellary ...	17,493	2,818	54,135	85,766	...	1,60,212
Presidency ...	40,743	18,639	1,650	19,732	593	81,357
Madras ...	16,610	5,846	91,943	97,492	58	2,11,949
North Arcot..	5,532	3,217	70,814	59,978	...	1,39,531
South Arcot..	...	1,771	67,854	59,044	...	1,28,669
Salem... ...	...	650	13,747	19,742	...	34,139
Bangalore ...	35,364	895	...	...	...	36,259
Tanjore ...	...	2,721	98,616	56,147	468	1,57,952
Trichinopoly.	6,393	812	86,708	58,633	...	1,52,546
Coimbatore...	6,142	5,176	35,870	72,846	400	1,20,434
Malabar ...	15,889	3,198	400	74,535	600	94,622
South Canara	557	451	...	34,177	...	35,185
Madura ...	...	3,458	52,496	64,620	...	1,20,574
Tinnevelly ...	2,061	2,650	62,959	48,631	137	1,16,438
Total...	1,54,753	69,094	9,55,166	10,40,360	7,488	22,26,861

D.

Statement shewing the expenditure in each District from Local Funds.

Districts.	Income Tax Funds.	District Road, Port, and other Funds.	Educational Funds.	Total.
	RS.	RS.	RS.	RS.
Ganjam	...	39,105	2,549	41,654
Vizagapatam	...	31,241	2,936	34,177
Godavery	...	83,657	...	83,657
Kistna	421	1,12,670	...	1,13,091
Nellore	...	47,540	...	47,540
Cuddapah	...	25,706	...	25,706
Kurnool	...	13,157	662	13,819
Bellary	3,117	46,122	...	49,239
Presidency	68,161	2,780	42,408	1,13,349
Madras	...	58,947	170	59,117
North Arcot	...	63,807	...	63,807
South Arcot	2,241	67,320	8,405	77,966
Salem	...	15,642	3,313	18,955
Bangalore	...	...	...	...
Tanjore	3,989	32,081	...	36,070
Trichinopoly	1,011	48,599	...	49,610
Coimbatore	...	1,09,002	...	1,09,002
Malabar	4,927	1,32,637	6,812	1,44,376
South Canara	1,158	49,705	2,926	53,789
Madura	488	90,800	...	91,288
Tinnevelly	5,807	88,803	...	94,610
Total...	91,320	11,59,321	70,181	13,20,822

E.

Statement shewing the Estimate, Allotment, and Expenditure in 1867-68, *on important Public Works in the Madras Presidency.*

District.	Work.	Estimate.	Expenditure up to 31st March 1867.	Allotment for 1867-68.	Expenditure during 1867-68.
	Military.	RS.	RS.	RS.	RS.
Bellary... ...	New Wash-house for the European Regiment at Bellary.	34,800	21,294	17,000 reduced to 13,505	13,192
Do.	Blacksmith's Forge at do.	3,770	2,305	1,465	1,507
Do.	Collar makers' and Carpenters' Workshop at do.	8,490	4,526	3,964	4,358
Do.	Armourers' shop for the 60th Rifles at do.	5,560	4,326	1,234	1,096
Do.	Drainage of the European Infantry Barracks at do.	17,000	2,707	3,000 increased to 7,248	6,364
Do.	Improvements to six Staff Serjeants' quarters at do.	8,702	...	7,590	7,535
Do.	Canteen with cellar at do.	6,455	...	6,000	5,953
Do.	Improving the supply of water to the Cantonment at do.	69,300	...	12,200	11,806
Do.	Constructing Camel-sheds at Sultanpoor and do ...	23,398	...	16,598	20,299
Do.	Roman Catholic place of worship at do.	20,525	18,613	1,912	1,912
Do.	Building for the performance of Divine worship at Ramandroog.	9,715	9,583	132	357
Do.	Protestant place of worship at do.	20,975	14,432	6,092	7,266
Presidency ...	Constructing a Fives and Racket Court in Fort St. George.	13,900	2,872	6,694	6,694
Do.	Building a Swimming-bath in do. do.	5,340	811	4,510	4,510
Do.	Alterations and additions to the Office of the Controller of Military Accounts in do. do.	39,100	...	39,100 reduced to 36,500	36,499
Do.	Improving the hollows and draining the Perambore Lines.	16,000	5,613	10,387 increased to 16,887	16,951
Madras ...	New Female Hospital at St. Thomas' Mount.	28,000	...	10,000 increased to 17,000	16,993
Do.	Constructing Family quarters near the Horse Artillery Lines at St. Thomas' Mount.	40,800	...	40,000 reduced to 32,243	32,238
Bangalore ...	New Barracks on the Race Course.	12,00,000	7,84,400	Imperial 2,64,788 increased to 2,67,163 Income Tax. 26	2,62,829
Do.	Three Blocks of new Infantry Barracks.	1,05,200	95,326	20,900 reduced to 11,900	10,340

E.—*(Continued.)*

Statement shewing the Estimate, Allotment, and Expenditure in 1867-68, *on important Public Works in the Madras Presidency.*—(Continued.)

District.	Work.	Estimate.	Expenditure up to 31st March 1867.	Allotment for 1867-68.	Expenditure during 1867-68.
	Military.—(Continued.)	RS.	RS.	RS.	RS.
Bangalore ...	Additional Cells to Provost at the new Infantry Barracks.	9,100	...	9,000	9,100
Do.	Ulsoor Water Project ...	72,000	63,687	20,000	73,572
Coimbatore ...	Lawrence Asylum at Ootacamund.	5,36,202	3,55,573	1,40,000 reduced to 1,06,601 (both works)	1,02,280
	Police Constables' huts at the Lawrence Asylum.	21,614	21,730		607
Malabar ...	Married quarters at Cannanore.	1,27,723	1,21,817 (both works)	7,441 incd. to 20,558 (both works)	20,585
	Out-houses to do.	11,810			
Do.	Artillery Barracks at do.	1,05,300	46,697	31,889 increased to 41,000	41,597
Bellary ...	Commissariat Serjeants' quarters at Ramandroog.	5,010	4,014	1,059	1,059
Presidency ...	Making certain alterations in the Criminal side of the Grand Jail, &c., to adapt it for the use of the Commissariat Department.	19,840	16,150	10,840 reduced to 568	462
Do.	Making certain alterations and additions in the Commissariat Arrack and Porter Depôt at the Commissary General's Office.	35,400	15,506	26,000 reduced to 15,894	15,894
Bangalore ...	Bakery and Soojee Mill.	84,100	39,537	30,278 reduced to 28,791	16,020
Malabar ...	Commissariat Godown at Cannanore.	28,780	5,080	8,780 increased to 10,980	10,519
Bellary... ...	Shed for sick carts attached to the Arsenal at Bellary.	4,455	4,334	121	121
Presidency ...	Constructing eighteen Blocks of Family quarters for the Warrant and Non-Commissioned Officers of the Ordnance Department	76,590	5,000	50,000 increased to 60,767	60,767
Do.	Do. a range of quarters for the Overseers attached to the Gun Powder Manufactory.	28,200	12,500	16,200 reduced to 15,700	15,743
Madras ...	Reserve Powder Magazine at St. Thomas' Mount.	46,293	41,099	6,000 reduced to 5,193	5,197
Malabar ...	Grand Powder Magazine at Cannanore.	20,700	11,284	7,200 reduced to 6,500	7,023

E.—*(Continued.)*

***Statement shewing the Estimate, Allotment, and Expenditure in* 1867-68, *on important Public Works in the Madras Presidency.*—(Continued.)**

District.	Work.	Estimate.	Expenditure up to 31st March 1867.	Allotment for 1867-68.	Expenditure during 1867-68.
	Civil Buildings.	RS.	RS.	RS.	RS.
Godavery ...	Constructing Central Jail at Rajahmundry.	3,02,093	1,98,887	40,000	49,065
North Arcot.	Construction of a Central Jail at Vellore.	Approximate 1,38,000	19,249	75,000 reduced to 65,220	64,267
Salem	Additions and alterations to the Salem Central Jail.	35,500	5,037	10,000	10,346
Trichinopoly.	Constructing Central Jail at Trichinopoly.	...	15,048	75,000 increased to 1,13,850	1,13,767
Coimbatore ...	Central Jail at Coimbatore	3,50,000 }	3,28,683	{ 50,000 reduced to 47,317	45,022
	Improvements to do. ...	8,000 }			2,633
Malabar ...	Central Jail at Cannanore.	3,00,305	20,236	75,000 reduced to 72,500	72,460
Vizagapatam.	Constructing Zillah Jail at Vizagapatam.	62,096	43,177	16,644	16,144
Ganjam ...	Improvements to the Zillah Jail at Berhampore.	14,318	4,974	8,606 reduced to 6,386	9,406
Kistna	Guntoor Jail	14,340	6,288	4,150 increased to 5,150	5,150
Bellary... ...	Improvements to the Jail at Bellary.	...	5,046	10,394	10,393
Presidency ...	Compound wall to enclose the Penitentiary on the west side, and adding new buildings.	16,860	15,950	910	900
South Arcot...	Additions and improvements to the Jail at Cuddalore.	Approximate 16,800	8,000	6,562	6,562
Coimbatore...	Central Jail at Ootacamund, and additions to the Zillah Jail.	52,890	...	10,000 increased to 24,570	24,638
Malabar ...	District Jail at Calicut ...	80,000	19,638	40,000 reduced to 36,400	36,409
Madura ...	New Jail at Madura ...	96,794	34,999	30,000 increased to 61,794	61,750
Madras... ...	Constructing a Talook Cutcherry with Subsidiary Jail, &c., at Trivellore.	24,500	...	6,000 increased to 7,000	6,000
Do.	Alterations and additions to the Tahsildar's Cutcherry at Ponnery	4,560	...	4,560	3,597
Madura ...	Small Cause and Principal Sudder Ameen's Court House at Madura.	27,500	9,799	10,000 increased to 17,700	17,700
Presidency ...	Constructing a Lunatic Asylum at Kilpauk.	Approximate 2,20,000	20,028	30,000 increased to 35,522	35,617

E.—*(Continued.)*

***Statement shewing the Estimate, Allotment, and Expenditure in* 1867-68, *on important Public Works in the Madras Presidency.*—(Continued.)**

District.	Work.	Estimate.	Expenditure up to 31st March 1867.	Allotment for 1867-68.	Expenditure during 1867-68.
	Civil Buildings.—(Conld.)	RS.	RS.	RS.	RS.
Presidency ...	Constructing new Wards for the Leper Hospital.	Approximate 32,000	...	2,600	2,896
Do.	Drainage to the General Hospital.	11,160	3,730	6,713	6,713
Do.	Building an additional shed on the north side of the quadrangle of the Public Works Stores.	15,940	2,712	11,728	11,711
Do.	Making certain alterations and additions to the Medical College at Madras.	51,650	43,200	8,390	8,390
Coimbatore ...	Church at Ootacamund.	53,830	15,000	Imperial 10,000 incd. to 13,465 Private contributions 15,481	Imperial 13,480 Private contributions 15,481
	Agricultural.				
Godavery ...	Strengthening the apron of the Godavery anicut.	22,000	...	9,851 increased to 15,000	15,468
South Arcot.	Anicut across the Manimuttanaddy for the supply of the Kullakurchi tank.	4,000	1,600	700 increased to 2,400	2,078
Do.	Do. across do. near Kumaramangalam.	34,750	...	34,750	27,022
Tanjore ...	Constructing a sluice and seven arches, and completing an additional laterite and rough stone apron at the north extremity of the south branch of the Lower Coleroon anicut.	97,880	68,676	31,469 reduced to 28,056	24,219
Do.	Completing a front and rear retaining wall and apron along the south branch of the Lower Coleroon anicut.	70,400	10,996	31,750 increased to 41,896	22,951
Bellary... ...	Improving the supply channel of the Narraindavakerra tank.	12,720	...	8,720	6,615
Do.	Restoration of the Gootloor tank.	39,400	...	39,400 reduced to 21,400	18,549
Do.	Restoration of the Pautha Cottacheroo tank.	5,830	...	5,830 reduced to 2,710	1,952
Do.	Restoration of the Yerrabommanahully tank.	6900	...	6,800	3,452
Cuddapah ...	Restoration of the Somereddypully tank.	6,540	...	6,540	6,230
Do.	Restoration of the Gunganapully Mallapah tank.	11,080	...	7,710	7,355

E.—*(Continued.)*

Statement shewing the Estimate, Allotment, and Expenditure in 1867-68, *on important Public Works in the Madras Presidency.*—(Continued.)

District.	Work.	Estimate.	Expenditure up to 31st March 1867.	Allotment for 1867-68.	Expenditure during 1867-68.
	Agricultural—(Continued.)	RS.	RS.	RS.	RS.
Nellore... ...	Channel from the Vencatagherry river to Chennur tank.	22,400	4,647	4,000 increased to 8,000	8,000
Do.	Nellore tank improvement.	18,130	13,971	3,918 increased to 4,158	4,119
North Arcot	New calingulah to Cauverypauk tank.	6,000	...	6,000	6,000
Godavery ...	Improvements to the Akeed canal.	80,120	22,070	20,000	17,045
Do.	Widening and improving the Samulcottah canal.	1,31,200	...	30,000	25,715
Do.	Works for the cross drainage of the Ellore High Level Canal.	1,05,486	56,611	42,799 reduced to 34,676	25,451
Kistna ...	Enlarging channels in the Masulipatam section of the Kistna Delta.	1,77,000	...	40,000 increased to 43,770	43,014
Do. ...	Widening the head of the Masulipatam canal.	20,080	...	20,080 reduced to 8,000	7,741
Do. ...	East side irrigation channel of the Masulipatam canal	15,610	...	15,610	12,845
Do. ...	West side irrigation channel of the Masulipatam canal.	49,860	...	30,000 reduced to 14,230	14,502
Do. ...	Side channels from Duggeralla to Nizampatam.	48,757	...	25,000 reduced to 18,500	19,097
Do. ...	Constructing 1st Class Lock at Duggeralla.	30,570	19,013	11,225 reduced to 9,395	7,357
Do. ...	Constructing a 2nd Class Lock at Jagarlamoody.	7,760	...	5,000 increased to 9,260	9,570
Do. ...	Extending the Commamore channel and subsidiary works.	1,95,770	75,484	40,000 increased to 52,450	51,293
Do. ...	Widening the lower portion of the Pullairu channel.	1,04,050	95,475	8,569 reduced to 7,069	6,561
Do. ...	Western bank channel ...	1,46,479	1,09,543	19,000 reduced to 15,970	15,844
Do. ...	Sloping down the banks of the main canal from the southern flank of the anicut, and enlarging the head of the main channel from Seetanagram to Duggeralla.	2,76,404	1,72,370	19,000 reduced to 16,000	14,346
Nellore ...	Improvements to the Survapally channel.	4,12,100	...	25,000 increased to 56,483	57,16

E.—*(Continued.)*

Statement shewing the Estimate, Allotment, and Expenditure in 1867-68, *on important Public Works in the Madras Presidency.*—(Continued.)

District.	Work.	Estimate.	Expenditure up to 31st March 1867.	Allotment for 1867-68.	Expenditure during 1867-68.
	Agricultural—(Continued.)	RS.	RS.	RS.	RS.
Cuddapah ...	Excavating a new head, and building a new head sluice and dyke to the Venkish Calwah channel.	6,130	...	6,130	6,1 00
Madras ...	Madras Water Supply Project.	6,11,759	61,683	2,00,000 increased to 3,07,129	2,83,902
Do. ...	Strengthening portions of the Bungaroo channel banks.	7,370	...	7,370	7,523
Do. ...	Cutting a new head to the Nagalapooram Black tank river supply channel, and constructing a head sluice to do.	3,380	...	3,380	3,380
North Arcot..	Widening the Cheyaur channel from Mookoor to Pooroosay.	28,000	Famine Fund. 10,089	28,000 reduced to 17,911	17,911
Do. ...	Alhabad head sluice and channel.	31,700	...	31,700	30,437
Do. ...	Cutting channel from the north end of Cauveripauk tank to the Mahindravady channel, and constructing head sluice and aqueduct.	8,240	...	8,300	8,240
Do. ...	Improving the Mahindravady channel, and constructing flood calingulah in continuation of the Palar anicut project.	7,500	...	7,500	7,500
South Arcot..	Pombay channel from the north end of the Pooniar anicut.	45,400	...	39,524 reduced to 27,524	26,977
Do. ...	Improving the Ragavien channel, &c.	8,830	...	6,000 increased to 8,830	8,830
Tanjore ...	Regulating works for the improvement of the river Cauvery.	1,10,090	...	50,000 reduced to 39,055	28,309
Trichinopoly.	Completion of the Wyacondan extension project	24,800	...	10,000 increased to 15,000	14,999
Do. ...	Constructing ten surplus sluices on the north bank of the Coleroon.	12,380	8,904	3,470 reduced to 2,500	2,500
Do. ...	Constructing ten surplus sluices for the Wyacondan channel.	16,500	5,045	16,500 reduced to 10,414	9,622
Do. ...	Nunthyaur anicut extension project.	30,500	...	20,000 reduced to 15,045	13,950

E.—*(Continued.)*

Statement shewing the Estimate, Allotment, and Expenditure in 1867-68, *on important Public Works in the Madras Presidency.*—(Continued.)

District.	Work.	Estimate.	Expenditure up to 31st March 1867.	Allotment for 1867-68.	Expenditure during 1867-68.
	Agricultural.—(Conld.)	RS.	RS.	RS.	RS.
Coimbatore...	Aqueduct over the Vanipootoor stream.	24,700	...	24,700	7,087
	Communications.				
Ganjam ...	Road from Aska to Pippulponka.	47,690	24,275	7,000 increased to 9,000	9,000
Do. ...	Road from Aska to Russelcondah, *viâ* Bullepudra, Vishnuchuckrum and Belloogoonta, on the northern bank of the Mahanuddy river.	44,640	16,604	8,000 increased to 12,000	12,000
Do. ...	Branch road from Bullepudra to Kurcholly.	27,950	25,582	2,367	2,367
Do. ...	Road from Aska to the Ganjam port and salt pans.	62,700	51,622	5,078	5,241
Do. ...	Excavating a canal from the Chilka lake to the Ganjam river.	1,61,110	15,209	30,000 increased to 40,161	42,176
Vizagapatam..	Road from Vizagapatam to Casseepur.	1,15,000	66,397	7,000 increased to 8,000	8,000
Do. ...	Road from Vizianagram to Bowdara.	63,820	51,370	1,710 increased to 3,210	3,210
Do. ...	Trunk Road No. 6 from Chittavalsa to Chicacole.	1,32,785	48,675	7,000	7,000
Nellore ...	Embanked road and masonry work across the Moosanoor valley on Trunk Road No. 6.	68,630	41,455	8,000 increased to 9,500	11,002
Do.	Constructing Pydauru bridge on Trunk Road No. 6.	23,600	20,028	500 increased to 4,172	4,176
Bellary and Cuddapah.	Road from Bellary to the Cuddapah frontier.	{1,06,431 1,02,200	96,991 1,03,452	{ 5,000 Income Tax 3,121	5,000 Income Tax 3,117
Cuddapah ...	Road from Cuddapah to the Kurnool frontier.	76,008	68,518	5,000 increased to 7,490	7,489
Presidency ...	Cooum river bridge ...	Approximate 1,71,000	31,772	Imperial 35,613 Income Tax 80,051	Imperial 35,613 Inc. Tax 68,161
North Arcot..	Improving the road from the town of Tirupathy to the Railway Station, and thence to Calastry.	28,750	10,600	7,000	7,000
Do.	Road from Calastry to Naidoopett on Trunk Road No. 6.	34,500	10,000	7,000	7,000

E.—*(Continued.)*

***Statement shewing the Estimate, Allotment, and Expenditure in* 1867-68, *on important Public Works in the Madras Presidency.*—(Continued.)**

District.	Work.	Estimate.	Expenditure up to 31st March 1867.	Allotment for 1867-68.	Expenditure during 1867-68.
	Communications.—(Contd.)	RS.	RS.	RS.	RS.
North Arcot..	Constructing a line of road from Bangarpett to Yareepett.	21,400	10,000	7,000	7,000
South Arcot...	Four bridges on the road between Kallakurchi and the Salem frontier.	17,310	1,980	4,000 increased to 5,820	4,592
Do.	Bridge across the Thumbiahpettah Oday on the road from Cuddalore to the Salem frontier.	5,900	2,883	778 increased to 2,778	2,633
Tanjore ...	Opening a canal between Negapatam and Vadarniem.	70,410	15,719	Imperial 30,000 Income Tax 1,211	Imperial 30,000 Inc. Tax 1,211
Trichinopoly..	Road from Trichinopoly to Arealoor and Woodiarpoliem to its junction with Trunk Road No. 9.	43,600	31,848	Imperial 7,000 Income Tax 1,763	Imperial 7,000 Inc. Tax 1,011
Do. ...	Road from Trichinopoly to the Salem frontier, *viâ* Toriore.	50,000	38,712	6,890 increased to 11,289	10,188
Coimbatore ...	Coonoor Ghaut, new trace.	2,40,000	1,56,782	23,667 increased to 50,021	50,021
Do. ...	New Goodaloor Ghaut ...	81,400	31,114	10,000	10,000
Do. ...	New road connecting Kotagherry and Wellington with the Coonoor Ghaut.	33,427	9,427	5,000 increased to 7,000	7,000
Do. ...	New line of road from Ootacamund to the head of the Goodaloor Ghaut at Neddivuttum.	66,762	14,469	8,000 increased to 11,000	11,000
Do. ...	Burghoor Ghaut, new trace	72,100	34,620	5,000 increased to 8,000	8,027
Malabar, Wynaad.	Karkoor Ghaut	1,07,400	51,045	17,960 increased to 22,960	22,960
Do. ...	Karkoor Ghaut to Goodaloor.	64,086	27,305	10,000 increased to 16,000	16,273
Do. ...	Road from Goodaloor to Tippacaudu.	58,388	38,382	10,000 reduced to 6,000	4,960
Do. ...	Periah Ghaut, new trace..	78,000	46,427	25,000 increased to 34,000	45,746
Do. ...	Improvements to the Bowally road towards the Mysore frontier.	Approximate 10,000	1,509	5,500 reduced to 4,500	1,640
Do. ...	Tambracherry Ghaut ...	1,46,413	80,839	25,000 increased to 50,000	55,147

E.—*(Concluded.)*

Statement shewing the Estimate, Allotment, and Expenditure in 1867-68, *on important Public Works in the Madras Presidency.*—(Concluded.)

District.	Work.	Estimate.	Expenditure up to 31st March 1867.	Allotment for 1867-68.	Expenditure during 1867-68.
	Communications.—(Conld.)	RS.	RS.	RS.	RS.
Malabar, Wynaad.	Earth-work and bridges between Luckady and Vythery.	25,150	17,841	7,445 reduced to 1,945	908
Do. ...	Road between Vythery and Culputty.	41,400	15,524	19,403 reduced to 7,703	4,835
Do. ...	Bridge over the Coonooth river.	16,000	10,274	8,000	8,000
Do. ...	Culputty bridge ...	14,500	3,589	8,100 reduced to 3,589	3,579
Do. ...	Road from Culputty to Sultan's Battery.	Approximate 20,000	2,087	12,194 increased to 17,194	18,088
Do. ...	Road from Sultan's Battery to the Mysore frontier.	30,000	11,730	13,000 reduced to 7,500	9,706
Do. ...	Road from Manantoddy to the Coorg frontier.	Approximate 37,500	...	17,500 reduced to 10,500	10,327
Malabar ...	Karkoor Ghaut, road and bridges below.	{ 32,550 54,600 90,230	20,881 18,914 17,408	Imperial 28,802 increased to 32,549 Income Tax 2,736	Imperial 32,549 Inc. Tax 2,736
South Canara.	Bridges on the road to connect Mangalore and Cannanore by Vitla and Hossdroog.	71,134	30,465	5,000 increased to 13,440	14,322
Madura ...	Road from Tirumangalam to the Coimbatore boundary.	1,65,000	36,875	Imperial 15,000 increased to 22,500 Income Tax 488	Imperial 22,662 Inc. Tax 488
Tinnevelly ...	Road No. 4, from Madura to the Travancore country.	30,000 4,000 5,860 }	} 18,844	{ Imperial 12,904 increased to 18,784 Inc. Tax 2,556 increased to 3,114	Imperial 18,784 Inc. Tax 3,114
Do. ...	Road No. 8, from Palamcottah to Tuticorin.	1,30,000	59,072	15,000 increased to 21,197	21,197
	Miscellaneous Public Improvement.				
Madura ...	Cutting the inner angle of the Reef channel at Paumben.	48,340	27,635	7,350 reduced to 5,450	5,450

F.

Statement shewing the principal works which were undertaken from the District Road, Educational, and Port Funds by Officers of the Public Works Department, during the year 1867-68.

District.	Work.	Expenditure in 1867-68.	Remarks.
		RS.	
Ganjam ...	Road from Jagganadpur to Pooroośhotapoor.	1,670	Completed.
Do. ...	Branch road to the Port of Barwah.	6,571	Earth-work thrown up to the full length of road. Three miles of road metalled and 1¾ miles gravelled.
Do. ...	Road between Aska and Soorada to the Soorla Salt platform.	19,974	Earth-work thrown up to 25 miles. Jungle cleared along the whole line 20 yards wide, and a large quantity of materials being collected.
Do. ...	Do. from Cunchilly to the Barwah ferries at Vamsadara.	4,999	Earth-work thrown up to the full length of road and materials being collected.
Do. ...	Zillah School at Berhampore.	2,124	Completed.
Vizagapatam...	Branch road from Nursipatam to Thallapolem.	10,280	Eight miles of road completed, forty-six masonry works built, and two in progress.
Do. ...	Road from Gazpatinagram to Parvatipoor.	18,725	In progress.
Do. ...	Normal School at Vizagapatam.	242	Completed.
Do. ...	Anglo-Vernacular School at Bimlipatam.	1,839	Roofing nearly completed.
Godavery ...	Widening canal road between Samulcottah and Cocanada.	4,478	Completed for half the distance.
Do. ...	Road from Tanuku *viâ* Duva to Prattipaud.	2,284	Road completed as far as the Alumparroo Bapanah tank.
Do. ...	Do. from Sidantam to Martair.	872	Completed.
Do. ...	Do. from Palcole to Doddiputla.	10,162	Road nearly completed.
Do. ...	Do. from Narsapoor to Veeravasaram.	14,447	Do.
Do. ...	Do. from Ellore to Hyderabad *viâ* Chintalapoody.	10,031	Road completed from Ellore to Durneajugudem, a distance of 17 miles.
Do. ...	Do. from Razole to Mooktaswaram.	6,356	Road completed for 19 miles.
Kistna ...	Coast road from Villatoor to Sandole.	3,061	Metalling in progress.
Do. ...	Road from Ponnoor to Baputla.	8,174	Earth-work in progress. Two tunnels built, materials being collected for others.
Do. ...	Improvements to the road from Guntoor to Sattanapally.	17,493	Stones required for metalling between the 3rd and 12th miles are being collected. Stone for gravelling being dug. Embanking road in progress.
Do. ...	Road from Datchapally to Gurazala.	4,625	The first 1½ miles have been opened for traffic.

F.—*(Continued.)*

***Statement shewing the principal works which were undertaken from the District Road, Educational, and Port Funds by Officers of the Public Works Department during the year* 1867-68.—(Continued.)**

District.	Work.	Expenditure in 1867-68.	Remarks.
		RS.	
Kistna ...	Road from Narsarowpett to Chinnapallakaloor.	14,080	Embankment laid throughout, except for 1½ miles. Metalling in progress between the 10th and 18th miles.
Do. ...	Do. from the Hyderabad road opposite Ibrampatam to Mylaveram.	3,360	Eight road dams completed, and three in progress. Two tunnels nearly completed, and three in progress.
Do. ...	Do. from Masulipatam to Cowtaram.	10,104	About 10 miles of road made, two masonry tunnels and two bridges completed, and one bridge in progress.
Do. ...	Roadway across the swamp between Masulipatam and Sallapally.	8,657	Completed.
Do. ...	Embanked road from Masulipatam across the swamp towards Sallapally.	5,001	About 2 miles of road raised.
Nellore ...	Allur and Iskapally road to the beach.	3,349	Fully completed up to the sea.
Do. ...	Road from Sangam to Kaligherry.	7,997	The first 13 miles completed with masonry works.
Do. ...	Do. from the Dornal road to Oodeagherry.	7,537	The first 13 miles completed, as also the masonry works between the 14th and 17th miles.
Do. ...	Road from Nellore to Somaisweram.	6,525	Materials collected on the first 18 miles for road and masonry works.
Do. ...	Constructing the Kaligherry, Kondakur, and Oollapollum road to the beach.	2,287	Completed with the exception of a few masonry works, which will be finished shortly; 18 miles of road gravelled.
Cuddapah ...	Road from Poddatoor to Nundialumpett.	3,122	11,563 cubic yards of earth-work executed, and 8,892 cubic feet of masonry built.
Do. ...	Do. from Gundloor to Condapoor station.	3,916	Earth-work almost completed. All minor masonry works nearly finished, and double 20 feet arch bridge built up to springing.
Kurnool ...	Construction of village roads below the main canal of Madras Irrigation and Canal Company.	6,239	About half completed.
Bellary ...	Road from Anantapoor to Taudpatry.	21,178	Metal to 2,000 yards laid down; metal collected for 2 miles, and gravel for about 5 miles, 850 yards.
Do. ...	Do. from Raidroog to Coodair.	1,859	Road made throughout, and is in fair order.

F.—*(Continued.)*

Statement shewing the principal works which were undertaken from the District Road, Educational, and Port Funds by Officers of the Public Works Department during the year 1867-68.—(Continued.)

District.	Work.	Expenditure in 1867-68.	Remarks.
		RS.	
Presidency ...	Erecting a new Presidency College.	41,473	Completed throughout to the level of the stringing course dividing the lower from the upper story. The interior walls are up to their full height, and the exterior or face walls partly raised. All the girders are raised and fixed, the lower floor is arched in, and the roof arching has been commenced upon. The tower is now 50 feet above the ground, and the false dome partially executed.
Madras ...	Road from Trivellore to Nagalapooram.	4,000	Sixteen miles gravelled and bridged, viz., from Trivellore to Coranee.
Do. ...	Road from Sattivadu to Kowrapet.	3,000	Six tunnels and two road dams completed, and six miles of road metalled.
Do. ...	Road from Oothucottah to Trunk Road No. 6.	3,000	Earth-work completed for 4 miles, and three dams built.
Do. ...	Road from Trivellore to Ponnary.	2,500	Road formed with earth for 2 miles. One tunnel completed, and materials under collection.
North Arcot ...	Road from the Poody Railway Station to the Sirthanoor village.	3,168	Completed.
Do. ...	Bridges on the Chittoor and Goodiattum road.	3,461	One bridge of three arches of 24 feet span completed.
Do. ...	Two large bridges on the Poiney road.	3,499	Finished, except the plastering and approaches.
Do. ...	Road from Coopum to the Coopum Railway Station.	3,833	Finished with the exception of the portion through the Railway compound to the goods shed, which has been left to the Railway Department.
Do. ...	Road from Old Arcot to Trivettur.	2,787	Road gravelled from Arcot to Papantangul, and one tunnel built.
Do. ...	Road from Kannamungalam to South Arcot frontier.	3,573	Completed.
Do. ...	Road from Arnee to Chetput.	3,500	Do.
South Arcot ...	Road from Paloor to Trivady.	3,040	Do. except turfing.
Do. ...	Completing the branch road to Coomaramungalam.	4,692	Do.
Do. ...	Constructing a Government Zillah School at Munjacoopum.	8,405	Do. with the exception of the plastering.
Salem ...	Road from Ahtur to Lathivady.	1,836	Four miles formed.
Do. ...	Extending the Salem Zillah School.	3,313	About two-thirds finished.

F.—(*Continued.*)

Statement shewing the principal works which were undertaken from the District Road, Educational, and Port Funds by Officers of the Public Works Department, during the year 1867-68.—(Continued.)

District.	Work.	Expenditure in 1867-68.	Remarks.
		RS.	
Trichinopoly...	Road from Coolitallay to Manaparah.	12,714	The first 6 miles of this road completed, with the exception of a small portion of metalling; eight more miles are in an advanced stage of progress.
Do. ...	Road from Perambaloor to Kistnapoorem.	4,967	One-eighth of the earth-work, one culvert, and seven road dams finished.
Do. ...	Road along the Coleroon bank from the Lower Anicut to the road between Woodiarpolliem and Combaconum.	7,600	This work provides for converting the Coleroon north bank into a road from the Lower Anicut to Madavacoorchi, a distance of 10 miles, seven and a half of which have been completed.
Do. ...	Road from Mooseri to Cannanore and Toriore.	10,113	The earth-work of this road is almost entirely completed. Petty masonry works are being pushed on, and materials are under collection for three large bridges.
Coimbatore ...	Road from Coonoor Ghaut to Kartairy.	6,426	Completed.
Do. ...	Road from Tirpoor Railway Station to Palladam and Periaputty. Do. from Periaputty to Oodamalpettah.	11 435	A timber bridge and a culvert completed, and road work in progress.
Do. ...	Erecting Chuttrum at Erode.	3,600	58¼ cubic yards brick in chunam, 20 cubic yards rough stone in chunam, 118 cubic yards rough stone in mud, and 41 square yards roofing completed, and 51 cubic feet jungle wood wrought and put up.
Malabar ...	Road from Cherikal to the Coorg boundary.	11,500	Earth-work finished, with the exception of about quarter of a mile near Irrity. Fifteen tunnels and bridges completed, and 3 miles of road made passable for carts.
Do. ...	Road from Quilandy, *viâ* Ullari to Tambercherry.	1,959	Completed.
Do. ...	Road from Tambercherry to Areacode.	10,490	Seven tunnels, 650 cubic feet of masonry work for wooden bridge, and 124¼ cubic yards of gravelling completed, and a large quantity of materials collected.
Do. ...	Road from Manjeri, *viâ* Paudicad and Malatoor, to 2 miles west of Manarow, the Moondoor road.	2,658	Four tunnels built, and 3,227 cubic yards of embankment raised.
Do. ...	Road from Angadipooram to Wundoor as far as Warampooram Angady.	10,806	Road as far as Warampooram Angady completed and open for traffic. Twenty-seven tunnels and nine bridges built.

F.—*(Continued.)*

***Statement shewing the principal works which were undertaken from the District Road, Educational, and Port Funds by Officers of the Public Works Department, during the year* 1867-68.—(Continued.)**

District.	Work.	Expenditure in 1867-68.	Remarks.
		RS.	
Malabar ...	Road from Palghaut, *viâ* Poodoonagaram to Kollengode.	9,000	Road between Poodoonagaram and Kollengode completed, and sixteen tunnels built.
Do. ...	Road from Poodiangady to Kokaloor Amshom.	12,953	Completed.
Do. ...	Road from Taliparamba to the road from Madey to Kavoy near Kunjumungalam.	6,336	Earth-work completed and seven bridges.
Do. ...	Tuta bridge on the road from Angadipooram to Puttamby.	968	Completed and in use by the public.
Do. ...	Chittakadavoo bridge ...	2,532	Completed.
Do. ...	Bridge on the road from Palghaut to Kollengode.	571	Do.
Do. ...	Constructing a Light-house at Cochin.	3,696	Do.
Do. ...	Checking the advances of the Sea at Cochin.	2,119	Work almost completed.
Do. ...	Protecting the Light-house at Cochin from the encroachment of the Sea.	1,100	Completed.
Do. ...	Constructing Normal School at Cannanore.	6,672	Do.
South Canara...	Bridges on the road between Moodbiddry and Beltangady.	15,091	One bridge half completed, and two others in progress.
Do. ...	Widening to 12 feet the road from Vittel to Munjeshwar.	7,304	19¼ miles opened to four yards width.
Do. ...	Completion of the road from Moodbiddry to Beltangady.	394	The whole length opened to four yards width.
Do. ...	Bridging the road from Pootoor, by Vitla to Munjeshwar.	7,198	Four bridges completed, and three others in progress.
Do. ...	Provincial School at Mangalore.	2,926	Materials collected.
Do. ...	Extension of the Quay at Mangalore.	292	Allotment worked out.
Madura ...	Bridge over the Venkatathricottah river.	3,279	Foundations to the west abutments and wings laid, superstructure built to the height of the springing line of the arches; the arches turned, and wing walls and abutments completed to a level with the extrados of the arches.
Do. ...	Do. over the Munjalaur river.	4,122	Completed, with the exception of retaining wall and flooring to arches.
Do. ...	Road between Tondy and Teroopatoor.	14,869	Eleven miles of road, four platforms, and five arched tunnels completed.

F.—*(Concluded.)*

Statement shewing the principal works which were undertaken from the District Road, Educational, and Port Funds by Officers of the Public Works Department, during the year 1867-68.—(Concluded.)

District.	Work.	Expenditure in 1867-68.	Remarks.
		RS.	
Madura ...	Road between Teroopatoor and Cottamputty.	10,000	8½ miles completed, and 3½ miles in progress.
Do. ...	Road between Cottamputty and Nuttum.	10,000	Eight miles completed.
Do. ...	Do. between Nuttum and Dindigul.	9,331	Three tunnels constructed, and 3½ miles of road made.
Do. ...	Do. between Teroomungalam and Ooslumputty.	13,000	Four miles completed, and two in progress.
Do. ...	Do. between Mangalore and Shevagungah.	18,608	Nineteen miles of road and six tunnels completed.
Tinnevelly ...	Do. No. 1 from Madura to Quilon.	5,000	Earth-raising completed, broken stone laid to a length of 2,049 yards, and materials for all masonry works completed.
Do. ...	Completion of road No. 10 between Calladacoorchy and Punnagoody.	14,610	Six miles and 7 furlongs completed, 10 miles and 228 yards embanked and gravelled. Thirty masonry works completed, and 608 yards of earth-work done.
Do. ...	Road from Velathicolum to Tuticorin.	5,000	The whole line has been traced with the exception of 1,340 yards. 2,660 yards of road raised and metalled, and 236½ cubic yards of gravel heaped at the sides.
Do. ...	Do. from Palamcottah to Shermadavy.	8,634	Six miles and 1,016 yards embanked and gravelled. 966 yards of earth-work done. Twenty masonry works completed, and three repaired.
Do. ...	Do. from Palamcottah to Streevelliputtur.	19,907	One bridge of seven arches of 30 feet span and two Chuttrums completed, 5 miles of road almost finished, and three bridges in progress.

APPENDIX V.

A.

Statement shewing the Receipts, Disbursements, and Balances, connected with Port Charges and Dues in the various Ports of the Presidency of Fort Saint George, under the operation of Act XXII. of 1855, *from* 1*st April* 1867 *to* 31*st March* 1868.

Names of the Ports.	Receipts.			Disbursements.			Excess for this year.			Deficit for this year.			Total balance to credit of the Port.			Total deficit against the Port.		
	RS.	A.	P.	RS.	A.	P.	RS.	A.	P.	RS.	A.	P.	RS.	A.	P.	RS.	A.	P.
Eastern Group.																		
Ganjam	277	10	0	579	13	0	...	...	...	302	3	0	...	...	...	275	5	8
Munsoorcottah or Gopaulpore	1,883	9	10	651	12	8	1,231	13	2	...	...	...	5,941	14	8	...	...	...
Calingapatam	2,423	0	4	654	7	0	1,768	9	4	...	...	...	3,823	3	6	...	...	...
Bimlipatam	3,947	11	7	2,198	13	0	1,748	14	7	...	...	...	8,464	15	4	...	...	...
Vizagapatam...	3,442	4	5	2,098	12	0	1,343	8	5	...	...	...	1,470	9	11	...	...	...
Cocanada...	12,739	10	2	13,822	5	4	...	...	...	1,082	11	2	19,877	3	2	...	...	...
Masulipatam...	2,045	12	4	1,534	10	6	511	1	10	...	...	...	6,980	6	5	...	...	...
Madras...	77,403	2	1	1,37,976	6	2	...	...	...	60,573	4	1	66,398	14	1	...	...	...
Cuddalore	758	8	3	424	12	0	333	12	3	...	...	...	3,121	15	1	...	...	...
Tranquebar	1,900	4	7	368	12	0	1,531	8	7	...	...	...	5,260	7	7	...	...	...
Negapatam and Nagore	7,975	7	5	10,368	3	5	...	...	...	2,392	12	0	6,195	10	1	...	...	...
Tuticorin	5,929	15	5	3,409	12	7	2,520	2	10	...	...	...	21,735	4	1	...	...	...
Western Group.																		
Cochin...	9,411	14	1	21,764	0	11	...	...	...	12,852	2	10	...	...	...	2,515	3	5
Calicut and Beypore...	6,884	11	0	4,515	1	8	2,369	9	4	...	...	...	9,788	8	2	...	...	...
Tellicherry	1,487	4	11	1,872	1	8	...	...	...	384	12	9	3,370	3	10	...	...	...
Cannanore	2,869	6	5	1,143	15	2	1,725	7	3	...	...	...	16,748	15	11	...	...	...
Mangalore	8,978	14	3	7,410	12	6	1,568	1	9	...	...	...	4,544	10	9	...	...	...
Total...	1,50,359	3	1	2,10,794	7	7	17,542	3	1	77,087	13	10	1,83,712	14	7	2,790	9	1

B.

Statement shewing the Wrecks which occurred at various Ports within this Presidency during the official year 1867-68.

Dates.	Names of Ships.	Tons.	Particulars.
10th April 1867.	Ship "Abel Tasman."	624	Was wrecked on the Byramgore Reef, on which she was drifted by the current while on the voyage to Bombay from Liverpool. Her cargo was entirely lost, but the crew taking to the ship's boats proceeded to Cannanore and from that port to Bombay.
13th May ,,	Barque "Tar." ...	244	Was stranded on the beach at Vizagapatam, having parted from her last anchor. The rudder being adrift, her crew abandoned her through fear. There was no cargo on board.
19th June ,,	U. S. Steam Frigate "Sacramento."	1,367	Was wrecked at 7-30 P. M. on a shoal at the mouth of the Kottapaulem river, near Cocanada.
4th Sept. ,,	Barque "Douglas"...	303	Was wrecked about 20 miles south of Cocanada, through the Commander's neglect of the lead. Four children among the passengers were washed overboard by the surf and drowned. The cargo was partly saved in a damaged condition.
29th do. ,,	Brig "Stree Vencataswerloo."	159	Was stranded at the port of Calingapatam, having parted her cables in a cyclone. Her entire cargo was lost, but the crew were saved.
29th do. ,,	Ship "Eliza Bencke."	988	Was loading at Calingapatam for London, and was wrecked at that port during a cyclone. Twelve of the crew were saved, but the Captain and thirteen men perished. The greater portion of the cargo, valued at Rupees 1,35,240, was lost.
29th do. ,,	Ship Mercia"	596	Was lost at Calingapatam in the same cyclone as the above. The crew were saved, but most of the cargo, valued at Rupees 15,000, was lost.
29th do. ,,	Brig "Dyrakee Dowlah Cawder Bux."	112	Was wrecked at Calingapatam on the same occasion. The greater part of her cargo was saved. The crew suffered no injury.
30th do. ,,	Barque "Gallant Neill."	244	Parted from her anchors in a cyclone at the port of Vizagapatam, thrown on her beam end, and was wrecked off Waltair. She had a cargo of gram, valued at 6,000 Rupees, which was totally lost.
30th do. ,,	Brig "Maha Letchmy"	130	Do. do. No cargo on board.
31st Oct. ,,	Brig "Streenevasaloo"	76	This vessel was driven ashore at Calingapatam in the cyclone of the 29th September, but sustained no injury. She, however, became a total wreck on the 31st October following, during a gale.
7th Feb. 1868.	Brig "Luke Belas"...	170	Having sprung a leak while proceeding from Chittagong to the Maldive Islands, put into Paumben, and was run on the reef to save her from foundering. The crew were safe, but only part of the cargo, which was valued at 16,000 Rs., was recovered.

C.

Statement of the number of Troops moved by Sea during the year 1867-68.

(Small Detachments not included.)

Dates. Arrived.	Dates. Sailed.	From and to what Ports.	Vessels' Names.	Corps.	Officers.	Men.	Women.	Children.	Convicts.	Horses.	Bullocks.
June 1867.		From Penang to Rangoon	H. M.'s Steamer "Prince Arthur" ...	No. 1 Battery, 5th Brigade, R. A. ...	4	109	12	12	...	...	...
	1868. 25th Jan.	From Madras to Rangoon ...	Steamer "Dacca" and Transport "Alnwick Castle"...	H. M.'s 76th Regiment	18	634	85	96	...	4	...
	6th Feb.	Do.	Steamer "Cashmere"	A. Battery, 23rd Brigade, R. A.... ...	5	200	18	10	...	7	...
				Detachment of 76th Regiment	3	152	2	1	...	...	...
				Other details	1	32	1	3	...	...	...
1868. 19th Feb.	......	From Rangoon to Madras	Do.	C. Battery, 20th Brigade, R. A.... ...	3	198	15	29	...	...	...
				Detachment of 2-19th Foot	2	131	9	18	...	...	...
24th do.	......	Do.	Steamer "Dacca" and Transport "Alnwick Castle"	H. M.'s 2-19th Foot...	20	687	47	78	...	5	...
	2nd March	From Madras to Vizagapatam and Munsoorcottah	Do.	2nd Regiment N. I	14	599	488	107	...	5	...
				Other details	1	14	4	7	...	...	...
	6th do.	From Vizagapatam to Munsoorcottah...	Do.	31st Regiment N. I	13	468	153	142	...	...	4
	7th do.	From Beypore to Bombay	Steamer "Busheer"	European details	2	87	7	18	...	...	...
	9th do.	From Munsoorcottah to Penang ...	Steamer "Dacca" and Transport "Alnwick Castle"	7th Regiment N. I	23	853	12	8	...	8	...
1st April.	......	From Penang to Madras	Do.	35th Regiment N. I...	9	717	10	20	...	6	...
				Other details	1	31	...	...	...	...	...
	3rd April	From Madras to Rangoon	Steamer "Mahratta"	Detachment of 2-24th	3	125	6	5	...	...	...
				Do. of 76th Regiment	1	49	...	...	...	...	...
				Other details	2	30	7	13	...	...	...
	9th do.	Do.	Steamer "Dacca" and Transport "Alnwick Castle"	38th Regiment N. I...	23	831	12	13	...	7	...
	19th do.	From Madras to Hong-Kong	Transport "Theresa"	Detachment of 29th Regiment N. I. ...	9	311	1	3	...	...	...
	19th do.	Do.	Per P. and O. Steamer	Do. ...	3	152	...	...	...	...	...
	27th do.	From Madras to Port Blair	Transport "Chandernagore" ...	I. Company, Sappers and Miners ...	3	143	...	...	...	...	...
				Judicial Department	...	...	...	...	33	...	...
27th do.	......	From Rangoon to Negapatam ...	Steamer "Dacca" and Transport "Alnwick Castle"	26th Regiment N. I...	23	716	14	26	7	...	...
				2-24th Foot	1	58	4	3	...	...	...
				Other details...	1	10	1	2	...	...	...
	4th May.	From Madras to Hong-Kong	Per P. and O. Steamer	Detachment of 29th N. I.	3	152	...	...	...	...	...
	5th do.	From Madras to Vizagapatam ...	Steamer "Dacca" and Transport "Alnwick Castle"	Right Wing of the 2nd N. I.	10	504	516	173	...	3	...

NOTE.—This Statement has been continued beyond the close of the official year, to shew the whole reliefs of the season at once.

D.

Statement of Troops, &c., arrived from England during the year 1867-68.

Names of Vessels.	Date of Arrival.	Rate.	Number of				Remarks.
			Officers.	Men.	Women.	Children.	
	1868.	£ s. d.					
Ship "Himalaya"	March 14th	12 7 10	11	359	20	26	Passage money to be adjusted in England.

Statement of Troops, Invalids, &c., embarked for England during the year 1867-68.

Names of Vessels.	Date of Departure.	Rate for																		Number of				In-sanes.		Con-victs.	
		Invalids.									Effectives.																
		Men.			Women.			Children			Men.			Women.			Children			Officers.	Men.	Women.	Children.	Number.	Rate.	Number.	Rate.
		Rs.	A.	P.	Rs.	A.	P.	Rs.	A.	P.	Rs.	A.	P.	Rs.	A.	P.	Rs.	A.	P.								
	1867.																										
Ship "Gosforth," Effectives	April 18th ...	...	...	...	...	...	...	...	...	...	199	14	8	225	0	0	135	0	0	8	147	17	41	...	...	...	...
,, "Clara"	May 22nd ...	...	...	...	...	...	...	...	...	...	250	0	0	...	...	...	...	...	...	...	3	...	...	...	...	...	...
,, "Clive"	July 3rd ...	...	...	...	...	...	...	...	...	...	...	...	...	500	0	0	...	...	...	...	...	1	...	...	...	...	...
	1868.																										
,, "Renown," Invalids	February 29th...	396	0	0	380	0	0	193	0	0	...	...	...	...	...	...	...	...	...	8	123	13	15	...	...	...	...
,, "Akbar," Invalids and Effectives	March 10th ...	396	0	0	386	0	0	193	0	0	...	...	...	...	...	...	...	...	...	8	90	12	21	3	500	5	450
		...	...	...	...	...	...	...	...	...	386	0	0	386	0	0	193	0	0	...	2	1	4	...	...	...	...
,, "Gosforth," Invalids...	Do. 13th ...	359	14	0	339	14	0	235	0	0	...	...	...	...	...	...	...	...	...	8	132	17	32	1	500	...	...
																				...	1	1	...	...	...	...	...
,, "Derwentwater"...	Do. 31st ...	...	...	...	...	...	...	...	...	...	1,200 lump sum.									...	1	1	2	...	...	...	...
																			Total...	17	499	63	115	4		5	

E.

Statement of Tolls levied on the Madras Pier, from 1st April 1867 to 31st March 1868.

Months.	On Passengers.			On Goods.			On Tarpaulins.			Total.		
	RS.	A.	P.	RS.	A.	P.	RS.	A.	P.	RS.	A.	P.
1867.												
April	365	0	0	461	15	11	3	4	0	830	3	11
May	414	9	0	590	6	3	15	12	0	1,020	11	3
June	404	9	0	641	8	2	28	8	0	1,074	9	2
July	430	5	0	620	10	6	28	4	0	1,079	3	6
August ...	319	14	0	547	5	9	28	12	0	895	15	9
September ...	379	3	0	465	0	9	50	8	0	894	11	9
October ...	329	15	0	353	15	5	32	12	0	716	10	5
November ...	194	15	0	217	4	11	18	4	0	430	7	11
December ...	143	10	0	410	6	3	23	4	0	577	4	3
1868.												
January ...	751	12	0	520	6	5	21	12	0	1,293	14	5
February ...	742	13	0	543	4	11	10	12	0	1,296	13	11
March ...	640	8	0	620	10	4	2	12	0	1,263	14	4
Total...	5,117	1	0	5,992	15	7	264	8	0	11,374	8	7

F.

Table shewing the number of Boats and Rafts using the Pier each month, from April 1867 to March 1868.

Months.	Number of Boats.		Total.	No. of Rafts.
	Export.	Import.		
1867.				
April...	1,414¼	1,033	2,447¼	9
May...	1,521	1,619	3,140	...
June...	1,916½	1,505	3,421½	...
July...	2,186	1,375	3,561	7
August	1,441	1,398	2,839	10
September	1,363	1,019	2,382	15
October	769½	1,272	2,041½	3
November	655½	355	1,010½	7
December	1,069	959	2,028	3
1868.				
January	993½	1,526	2,519½	21
February...	1,189½	1,644	2,833½	8
March	1,895¾	1,405	3,300¾	36
Total...	16,414¼	15,110	31,524¼	119

G.

Statement of Vessels passing through the Paumben Channel, from 1849 *to* 1867 *inclusive.*

Calendar years.	Square rigged vessels.	Tonnage.	Dhonies.	Tonnage.	Total Vessels.	Total Tonnage.	Average Size. Vessels.	Average Size. Dhonies.
							Tons	Tons
1849... ...	1,003	79,234	1,114	58,700	2,117	1,37,934	79	53
1850... ...	1,142	90,656	1,004	60,807	2,146	1,51,457	79½	60½
1851... ...	1,092	82,697	939	57,084	2,031	1,39,781	75¾	60¾
1852... ...	1,178	94,109	924	59,565	2,112	1,53,674	80	64½
1853... ...	1,192	98,189	920	54,264	2,122	1,52,453	82½	59
1854... ...	1,035	78,746	879	59,140	1,914	1,39,886	76	67½
1855... ...	1,220	1,09,326	947	60,771	2,169	1,70,097	89½	64⅛
1856... ...	1,353	1,21,810	990	54,867	2,343	1,76,677	90	55½
1857... ...	1,506	1,38,090	1,025	57,214	2,531	1,95,304	91¾	55¾
1858... ...	1,108	1,13,814	803	43,720	1,911	1,57,534	102¾	54½
1859... ...	974	88,574	742	38,414	1,716	1,26,988	91	51¾
1860... ...	1,366	1,43,082	950	48,763	2,316	1,91,845	104¾	51⅓
1861... ...	1,335	1,33,897	905	45,916	2,240	1,79,813	100¼	50⅔
1862... ...	1,050	1,00,907	894	38,994	1,944	1,39,901	96	43⅔
1863... ...	1,226	1,18,816	789	38,960	2,015	1,57,776	96¾	49⅓
1864... ...	1,265	1,26,471	672	34,313	1,937	1,60,784	100	51
1865... ...	1,359	1,31,165	774	42,298	2,133	1,73,463	96½	54½
1866... ...	1,511	1,55,187	661	34,659	2,172	1,89,846	102⅔	52⅓
1867... ...	1,532	1,63,720	709	52,152	2,241	2,15,872	106¾	73½

H.

Statement of Pilotage levied at Paumben, from 1849 *to* 1867 *inclusive.*

Calendar years.	Pilotage levied.			Pilot's share.			Credited to Government.		
	RS.	A.	P.	RS.	A.	P.	RS.	A.	P.
1849	7,247	2	0	1,811	12	6	5,435	5	6
1850	4,684	8	0	1,171	2	0	3,513	6	0
1851	10,525	5	0	2,628	8	6	7,896	12	6
1852	11,456	12	3	2,861	14	9	8,594	13	6
1853	11,569	5	9	2,890	1	0	8,679	4	9
1854	11,153	1	9	2,786	7	5	8,366	10	4
1855	12,486	8	3	3,120	9	8	9,365	14	7
1856	13,168	5	0	3,292	1	3	9,876	3	9
1857	15,575	5	6	3,891	13	9	11,683	7	9
1858	12,820	8	0	3,203	2	0	9,617	6	0
1859	10,647	1	0	2,661	0	3	7,986	0	9
1860	17,144	5	0	4,286	1	3	12,858	3	9
1861	16,193	9	0	4,048	6	3	12,145	2	9
1862	14,598	4	0	3,177	0	7	11,421	3	5
1863	17,312	10	0	3,461	8	9	13,851	1	3
1864	17,055	6	0	3,410	2	8	13,645	3	4
1865	19,419	2	0	3,883	13	1	15,535	4	11
1866	20,070	13	0	4,012	3	7	16,058	9	5
1867	21,343	11	0	4,266	12	7	17,076	14	5

I.

Statement of the Pilotage levied between Paumben and Keelacarry for the year 1867.

Months and Year.	FROM PAUMBEN TO KEELACARRY.									FROM KEELACARRY TO PAUMBEN.									TOTAL.								
	Pilotage levied.			Pilot's share.			Credited to Govt.			Pilotage levied.			Pilot's share.			Credited to Govt.			Pilotage levied.			Pilot's share.			Credited to Govt.		
1867.	RS.	A.	P.	RS.	A.	P.	RS.	A.	P.	RS.	A.	P.	RS.	A.	P.	RS.	A.	P.	RS.	A.	P.	RS.	A.	P.	RS.	A.	P.
January	130	2	6	104	2	0	26	0	6	43	9	6	34	14	0	8	11	6	173	12	0	139	0	0	34	12	0
February	121	11	6	97	6	0	24	5	6	52	8	0	42	0	0	10	8	0	174	3	6	139	6	0	34	13	6
March	135	15	0	108	12	0	27	3	0	56	6	6	45	2	0	11	4	6	192	5	6	153	14	0	38	7	6
April	254	13	6	203	14	0	50	15	6	123	7	0	98	12	0	24	11	0	378	4	6	302	10	0	75	10	6
May	185	2	6	148	2	0	37	0	6	66	4	0	53	0	0	13	4	0	251	6	6	201	2	0	50	4	6
June	306	4	0	245	0	0	61	4	0	59	11	0	47	12	0	11	15	0	365	15	0	292	12	0	73	3	0
July	444	6	0	355	8	0	88	14	0	74	3	6	59	6	0	14	13	6	518	9	6	414	14	0	103	11	6
August	495	10	0	396	8	0	99	2	0	58	12	0	47	0	0	11	12	0	554	6	0	443	8	0	110	14	0
September	357	15	0	284	2	0	73	13	0	61	11	6	49	6	0	12	5	6	419	10	6	333	8	0	86	2	6
October	285	10	0	228	8	0	57	2	0	59	1	0	47	4	0	11	13	0	344	11	0	275	12	0	68	15	0
November	91	11	6	66	6	0	25	5	6	29	1	0	23	4	0	5	13	0	120	12	6	89	10	0	31	2	6
December	41	6	6	33	2	0	8	4	6	64	1	0	51	4	0	12	13	0	105	7	6	84	6	0	21	1	6
Total...	2,850	12	0	2,271	6	0	579	6	0	748	12	0	599	0	0	149	12	0	3,599	8	0	2,870	6	0	729	2	0

J.

Statement of the number of Native Passengers who have arrived at the under-mentioned Ports during the years 1866 *and* 1867 *under Act XXV. of* 1859.

Districts.	Ports.	Years.	From Ceylon.	From the Coast & Bengal.	From Rangoon, Moulmein, and Ports on the opposite Coasts, &c.	From the Straits.	Total.
Malabar.	Cochin	1866	...	...	...	...	...
		1867	64	...	...	...	64
Tinnevelly.	Tuticorin	1866	15,519	...	...	...	15,519
		1867	5,004	...	...	...	5,004
	Coolasagarapatam ...	1866	1,619	...	...	...	1,619
		1867	1,142	...	...	...	1,142
	Coilpatam	1866	228	...	...	...	228
		1867	220	...	...	...	220
Madura.	Keelakarry	1866	3,319	...	...	...	3,319
		1867	3,984	...	...	...	3,984
	Davepatam	1866	10,065	...	...	499	10,564
		1867	11,511	...	...	534	12,045
	Paumben	1866	3,686	20,447	...	...	24,133
		1867	2,475	14,654	...	...	17,129
	Toady	1866	2,002	...	...	...	2,002
		1867	2,451	...	...	...	2,451
Tanjore.	Trimulvassel	1866	69	3	59	...	131
		1867	50	...	78	...	128
	Tranquebar...	1866	157	...	...	...	157
		1867	154	8	8	...	170
	Nagore...	1866	...	...	...	...	...
		1867	11	45	723	...	779
	Negapatam	1866	3,765	1,099	2,007	919	7,790
		1867	3,516	511	723	303	5,053
	Topetoray	1866	1,233	...	29	...	1,262
		1867	913	354	...	...	1,267
	Muttupetai	1866	413	31	...	...	444
		1867	507	121	...	...	628
	Adrampatam	1866	838	74	...	...	912
		1867	672	62	...	...	734
	Ammapatam	1866	336	30	...	...	366
		1867	276	46	...	...	322
	Cottapatam	1866	358	5	...	...	363
		1867	353	8	...	...	361
	Cuttoomavady	1866	34	...	...	...	34
		1867	1	...	...	...	1
Godavery.	Cocanada	1866	...	...	2,200	...	2,200
		1867	...	46	1,519	...	1,565
	Nursapore	1866	...	...	...	...	...
		1867	...	39	...	...	39
	Total...	1866	43,641	21,689	4,295	1,418	71,043
		1867	33,304	15,894	3,051	837	53,086
	Total for two years...	...	76,945	37,583	7,346	2,255	124,129

K.

Statement of the number of Native Passengers who have left the undermentioned Ports during the years 1866 *and* 1867 *under Act XXV. of* 1859.

Districts.	Ports.	Years.	To Ceylon.	To the Coast and Bengal.	To Rangoon, Moulmein, and Ports on the opposite Coasts, &c.	To the Straits.	Total.
Tinnevelly.	Tuticorin	1866	17,731	...	...	...	17,731
		1867	6,614	...	...	...	6,614
	Coolasagarapatam ...	1866	690	...	..	...	690
		1867	654	...	...	...	654
	Coilpatam	1866	79	...	...	...	79
		1867	113	...	...	...	113
Madura.	Keelakarry	1866	3,515	...	...	...	3,515
		1867	2,938½	...	...	...	2,938½
	Davépatam...	1866	61,664	...	...	...	61,664
		1867	19,396	...	...	...	19,396
	Paumben	1866	4,298	7,835	106	114	12,348
		1867	2,185	4,999	...	378½	7,562½
	Tondy	1866	86	...	...	..	86
		1867	3	...	...	...	3
Tanjore.	Trimulvassel	1866	25	10	...	...	35
		1867	43	21	...	...	64
	Tranquebar...	1866	249	...	...	132	381
		1867	147	15	315	236	713
	Nagore...	1866	...	...	...	...	...
		1867	23	39	53	...	115
	Negapatam...	1866	6,157	613	2,190	2,179½	11,139½
		1867	4,283	186	2,013	1,790½	8,272½
	Topetoray	1866	1,484	10	...	...	1,494
		1867	1,325	102	...	...	1,427
	Muttupetai	1866	569	51	...	...	620
		1867	520	117	...	...	637
	Adrampatam	1866	451	9	...	...	460
		1867	396	24	...	...	420
	Ammapatam	1866	95	7	...	...	102
		1867	86	32	...	...	118
	Cottapatam...	1866	29	16	...	...	45
		1867	53	4	...	...	57
	Kodiyembolayem ...	1866	...	...	...	...	...
		1867	...	2	...	...	2
	Gopaulpatam	1866	...	...	...	...	...
		1867	16	...	...	...	16
Godavery.	Cocanada	1866	...	11	3,860	...	3,871
		1867	...	...	2,641	...	2,641
	Nursapore	1866	...	...	...	...	...
		1867	...	16	422	...	438
Ganjam.	Calingapatam	1866	...	...	...	...	...
		1867	...	...	116	...	116
	Total...	1866	97,067	8,562	6,156	2,425½	114,210½
		1867	38,795½	5,557	5,560	2,405	52,317½
	Total for two years...	...	135,862½	14,119	11,716	4,830½	166,528

L.

Statement shewing the Receipts and Disbursements of Coals at Madras and the Out-ports during the official year 1867-68.

	Tons.	Cwt.	Qrs.	lbs.
Madras.				
Balance on hand on the 31st March 1867.. ...	2,027	7	2	5
Receipts from 1st April 1867 to 31st March 1868	3,303	18	0	0
	5,331	5	2	5
Disbursements from do. to do...	2,012	8	3	20
Balance on hand on the 31st March 1868.. ...	3,318	16	2	13
Cocanada.				
Balance on hand on the 31st March 1867.. ...	376	0	2	22
Receipts from 1st April 1867 to 31st March 1868...	...	...	...	...
	376	0	2	22
Disbursements from do. to do...	50	0	0	0
Balance on hand on the 31st March 1868.. ...	326	0	2	22
Munsoorcottah.				
Balance on hand on the 31st March 1867, unserviceable and unsalable	126	0	0	0
No Receipts and Disbursements	...	...	...	...
Balance on hand on the 31st March 1868, unserviceable and unsalable	126	0	0	0

M.

Statement of

Month and Year.	Aggregate Tonnage.											Pilotage,		
	British.		Foreign.		Steamers		Total.		Pattimars, Dhonies, &c.		Total Tonnage and Fees.			
	No. of vessels.	Tons.	Number.	Tons.	Number.	Tons.	Number.	Tons.	Number.	Tons.	No. of vessels.	Tons.	Fees.
1867.													RS.
April... ...	33	8,236	4	1,218	7	4,102	44	13,556	123	4,634	18	6,223	590
May	6	1,329	3	987	11	5,310	20	7,626	9	517	17	5,466	565
June	2	430	...	...	9	5,070	11	5,550	...	...	1	155	25
July	1	401	...	...	9	5,378	10	5,779	...	...	3	668	90
August ...	1	100	...	...	7	3,968	8	4,068	...	...	6	1,534	165
September...	4	806	...	...	7	3,332	11	4,138	50	2,521	7	2,136	220
October ...	15	2,198	...	...	2	1,612	17	3,810	77	2,588	...	...	...
November...	25	8,307	2	694	3	1,888	30	10,884	241	8,311	5	1,703	155
December...	20	4,854	1	274	2	955	23	6,083	226	6,837	9	3,121	285
1868.													
January ...	22	6,829	1	274	4	1,725	27	8,828	240	6,154	12	4,155	400
February ...	30	6,624		621	3	2,001	35	9,246	200	5,590	8	3,124	270
March ...	31	9,152	3	904	2	1,078	36	11,134	148	3,484	9	2,519	270
Total...	190	49,3[illegible]6	16	4,972	66	36,414	272	90,702	1,309	40,636	95	30,804	3,035

Statement exhibiting the difference between

Years.	Total square rigged Tonnage.		Difference in decrease		Total Tonnage of Pattimars, Dhonies, &c.		Difference in Increase.		Grand Total.		Difference in	
	No. of vessels.	Tons.	Number.	Tons.	Number.	Tons.	Number.	Tons.	Number.	Tons.	Number.	Tons.
											Increase	Decrease
1866-67	308	1,25,399	...	...	1,058	32,644	...	...	1,366	1,58,043	...	...
1867-68	272	90,702	...	...	1,309	4036	...	...	1,581	1,31,338	...	...
			36	34,697			251	7,992			215	26,705

M.—(*Concluded.*)

Port Tonnage.

Tonnage, and Fees.						New Vessels Built.				
Senior Pilot's share.		Junior Pilot's share.		Total Pilots' share 3-5ths.	Government share 2-5ths.	Names.	Tons.	Estimated value.	Wood.	Remarks.
RS.	A.	RS.	A.	RS.	RS			RS.		
199	2	154	14	354	236	Padawa "Ahmoody"...	19	988	Benteak and white Cedar.	Built at Cochin*
190	11	148	5	339	226	Munjee "Salamaty"...	10	500	Do. do ...	Do. at Chowghat*
8	7	6	9	15	10	Dhoney "Cader Bux"...	24	360	Anjelly and Mangoe...	Do. at Panatora*
30	6	23	10	54	36	Brig "Mooyelin Bux".	194	18,000	Do. Teak, Ben teak, & white Cedar... ...	Do. at Cochin*
55	11	43	5	99	66					
74	4	57	12	132	88					
...	...	...	...	...	...					
52	5	40	11	93	62					
96	3	74	13	171	114					*Measured under Act No. X of 1841.
135	0	105	0	240	160					
91	2	70	14	162	108					
91	2	70	14	162	108					
1,024	5	796	11	1,821	1,214		247	19,848		

the official years 1866-67 *and* 1867-68.

Total Pilotage, Tonnage and Fees.		Difference in decrease.		Pilots' share 3-5ths	Difference in decrease	Government share 2-5ths.	Difference in decrease	Total new tonnage and estimated value.				Difference in decrease.			
Tons.	Rupees.	Tons.	Rupees.	Rupees.	Rupees.	Rupees.	Rupees.	Tons.	Rupees.	Annas.	Pice.	Tons.	Rupees.	Annas.	Pice.
43,223	4,170	...	...	2,502	...	1,668	...	1,400	1,01,947	0	0	...	...	...	...
30,804	3,035	...	...	1,821	...	1,214	...	247	19,848	0	0	...	...	...	...
		12,419	1,185		681		454					1,153	82099	0	0

N.

Particulars of the Trade of the Ports in each

Districts.	Names of Ports.	British. Vessels.	British. Tonnage.	British. Dues. RS.	A.	P.
Ganjam.	Ganjam	2	600	61	15	0
	Munsoorcottah	38	23,947	...	...	...
	Calingapatam	42	34,865	1,786	7	0
	Pudi	4	2,175	...	...	...
	Bapanapaudu	2	2,452	...	...	...
	Total...	88	64,039	1,848	6	0
Vizagapatam.	Vizagapatam	85	54,368	1,603	10	9
	Bimlipatam	89	50,848	2,639	5	6
	Pudimadakah	...	...	...	...	...
	Pentacottah	5	4,093	...	...	...
	Total...	179	1,09,309	4,243	0	3
Godavery.	Coringa	...	...	...	...	...
	Cocanada	108	72,462	5,009	3	5
	Narasapore	...	...	...	...	...
	Total...	108	72,462	5,009	3	5
Kistna.	Masulipatam	44	26,988	1,448	10	6
	Nizampatam	...	...	...	...	...
	Kottapollem	...	...	...	...	...
	Epurupollem	...	...	...	...	...
	Motupalli...	...	...	...	...	...
	Total...	44	26,988	1,448	10	6
Nellore.	Kottapatnam	...	...	...	...	...
	Itamukala	1	124½	...	...	...
	Pakala	...	...	...	...	...
	Ramayapatam	41	3,299½	...	...	...
	Chennayapolem	1	189	...	...	...
	Iskapalli	11	979½	...	...	...
	Ponnapudi	9	827	...	...	...
	Tummalapenta	1	119¼	...	...	...
	Joovaladinna	1	119¼	...	...	...
	Kristnapatnam	60	5,055¾	...	...	...
	Mypadu	11	894¾	...	...	...
	Doorgarazapatnam	3	235	...	...	...
	Total...	139	11,843½	...	...	...

N.—*(Continued.)*

District for the official year 1867-68.

Foreign.					Country or Native.				
Vessels.	Tonnage.	Dues.			Vessels.	Tonnage.	Dues.		
		RS.	A.	P.			RS.	A.	P.
...	...	...	...	...	13	1,624	84	0	6
4	1,827	...	...	...	36	6,491½	...	...	...
12	4,814	229	5	0	70	10,848	297	12	0
1	593	...	...	...	53	7,443	...	...	...
...	...	...	...	...	47	6,922	...	...	...
17	7,234	229	5	0	219	33,328½	381	12	6
4	1,697	182	10	0	96	13,500	704	0	11
13	5,867	420	1	3	31	3,464	194	13	0
2	850	...	...	...	19	2,425	...	...	...
2	993	...	...	...	46	5,935	...	...	...
21	9,407	602	11	3	192	25,324	898	1	311
...	...	...	...	...	165	30,518	3,123	9	11
39	17,209	2,566	13	7	90	11,627	967	9	5
...	...	...	...	...	135	5,481	...	...	...
39	17,209	2,566	13	7	390	47,626	4,091	3	4
7	4,074	221	7	0	127	7,010	375	10	0
1	20	...	...	...	107	4,569$\frac{40}{130}$	...	...	...
...	...	...	...	...	105	8,870$\frac{45}{130}$	...	...	...
...	...	...	...	...	99	12,943$\frac{27}{130}$	...	...	...
...	...	...	...	...	35	1,806$\frac{36}{130}$	...	...	...
8	4,094	221	7	0	473	35,199$\frac{18}{130}$	375	10	0
1	69	...	...	...	147	10,665½	...	...	...
...	...	...	...	...	60	6,466	...	...	...
...	...	...	...	...	26	2,782	...	...	...
...	...	...	...	...	...	...	...	...	...
...	...	...	...	...	...	...	...	...	...
...	...	...	...	...	...	...	...	...	...
...	...	...	...	...	...	...	...	...	...
...	...	...	...	...	...	...	...	...	...
...	...	...	...	...	...	...	...	...	...
1	69	...	...	...	6	205	...	...	...
...	...	...	...	...	...	...	...	...	...
...	...	...	...	...	5	383	...	...	...
2	138	...	...	...	244	20,501½	...	...	...

N.—*(Continued.)*

Particulars of the Trade of the Ports in each

Districts.	Names of Ports.	TOTAL. Vessels.	Tonnage.	Dues. RS.	A.	P.
Ganjam.	Ganjam	15	2,224	145	15	6
	Munsoorcottah	78	32,265½	1,672	13	6
	Calingapatam	124	50,527	2,313	8	0
	Pudi	58	10,211	...	...	...
	Bapanapaudu	49	9,374	...	...	...
	Total ...	324	1,04,601½	4,132	5	0
Vizagapatam.	Vizagapatam	185	69,565	2,490	5	8
	Bimlipatam	133	60,179	3,254	3	9
	Pudimadakah	21	3,275	...	...	...
	Pentacottah	53	11,021	...	...	...
	Total ...	392	1,44,040	5,744	9	5
Godavery.	Coringa	165	30,518	3,123	9	11
	Cocanada	237	1,01,298	8,543	10	5
	Narasapore	135	5,481	...	...	...
	Total ...	537	1,37,297	11,667	4	4
Kistna.	Masulipatam	178	38,072	2,045	11	6
	Nizampatam	108	4,589 $\frac{40}{130}$	...	...	...
	Kottapollem	105	8,870 $\frac{45}{130}$	...	...	...
	Epurupollem	99	12,943 $\frac{27}{130}$	...	...	...
	Motupalli	35	1,806 $\frac{36}{130}$	...	...	...
	Total ...	525	66,281 $\frac{18}{130}$	2,045	11	6
Nellore.	Kottapatnam	148	10,734½	...	...	...
	Itamukala	61	6,590½	...	...	...
	Pakala	26	2,782	...	...	...
	Ramayapatam	41	3,299½	...	...	...
	Chennayapolem	1	189	...	...	...
	Iskapalli	11	979½	...	...	...
	Ponnapudi	9	827	...	...	...
	Tummalapenta	1	119¼	...	...	...
	Joovaladinna	1	119¼	...	...	...
	Kristnapatnam	67	5,329¾	...	...	...
	Mypadu	11	894¾	...	...	...
	Doorgarazapatnam	8	618	...	...	...
	Total...	385	32,483	...	...	...

N.—*(Continued.)*

District for the official year 1867-68.—(Continued.)

Value of						Duty on						Sea Custom Revenue.		
Export.			Import.			Export.			Import.					
RS.	A.	P.	RS.	A.	P.	RS	A.	P.	RS.	A.	P.	RS.	A.	P.
63,483	8	9	7,622	4	0	2,093	10	0	...	...	...	2,093	10	0
17,35,289	2	1	6,92,027	0	6	7,761	5	1	83	0	0	7,844	5	1
10,32,452	5	7	1,24,724	2	8	64,617	7	1	849	3	11	65,466	11	0
3,04,719	1	0	1,03,915	8	0	9,231	6	0	57	2	7	9,288	8	7
2,97,439	13	0	2,04,252	8	0	1,265	10	0	...	...	...	1,265	10	0
34,33,383	14	5	11,32,541	7	2	84,969	6	2	989	6	6	85,958	12	8
9,11,199	6	11	13,53,971	12	1	16,918	7	3	562	6	10	17,480	14	1
20,82,210	6	2	9,53,766	7	10	44,286	7	6	3,616	7	8	47,902	15	2
2,20,023	9	11	355	0	0	250	14	8	...	...	...	250	14	8
4,00,504	6	6	24,384	3	3	8,540	5	8	...	...	...	8,540	5	8
36,13,937	13	6	23,32,477	7	2	69,996	3	1	4,178	14	6	74,175	1	7
4,78,543	0	0	3,37,327	0	0	106	14	1	6,393	13	11	6,500	12	0
43,46,059	0	0	11,08,551	0	0	9,963	5	7	61,687	11	7	71,651	1	2
...	...	...	...	...	...	...	...	...	...	...	...	...	...	...
48,24,602	0	0	14,45,878	0	0	10,070	3	8	68,081	9	6	78,151	13	2
33,86,545	0	7	11,81,298	0	6	4,815	6	2	1,202	6	8	6,017	12	10
3,37,655	10	10	81,979	10	8	248	14	3	46	9	2	295	7	5
60,525	14	4	66,225	4	3	...	...	...	...	...	...	...	...	...
3,16,420	3	5	8,06,209	3	11	272	9	3	...	...	...	272	9	3
65,672	13	8	67,938	1	6	...	...	...	...	...	...	...	...	...
41,66,819	10	10	22,03,650	4	10	5,336	13	8	1,248	15	10	6,585	13	6
2,72,880	8	6	4,51,282	13	2	154	0	8	4	7	6	158	8	2
1,44,064	2	3	2,72,392	1	7	54	3	11	...			54	3	11
69,971	12	2	18,952	12	6	...			...			...		
10,893	3	3	10,017	13	10	...			...			...		
...	...	...	2	0	0	...			...			...		
26,179	10	5	819	0	0	...			...			...		
33,449	10	10	8,388	9	10	...			...			...		
171	9	0	...	...	...	...			...			...		
235	5	0	...	...	...	...			...			...		
70,688	7	3	47,580	8	0	...			...			...		
59,441	12	9	3,544	10	0	...			...			...		
9,469	8	9	6,606	12	2	...			...			...		
6,97,445	10	2	8,19,587	1	1	208	4	7	4	7	6	212	12	1

N.—(*Continued.*)

Particulars of the Trade of the Ports in each

Districts.	Names of Ports.	British.				
		Vessels.	Tonnage.	Dues.		
				RS.	A.	P.
South Arcot.	Cuddalore	12	2,325	260	14	6
	Porto Novo	83	14,833½	...	...	...
	Total...	95	17,158½	260	14	6
Tanjore.	Terumalavassal	177	15,688	...	...	...
	Tranquebar	4	1,635	312	0	0
	Nagore	98	16,278	135	5	6
	Negapatam	1,058	1,46,188	4,270	13	10
	Thoputoray	725	21,883	...	...	...
	Muttupettai	654	31,629	...	...	...
	Total...	2,716	2,33,301	4,718	3	4
Madura.	Keelakarry...	22	5,694	...	...	...
	Davepatam...	...	...	...	...	...
	Paumben	...	...	...	...	...
	Tondy	...	...	...	...	...
	Total...	22	5,694	...	...	...
Tinnevelly.	Tuticorin	85	38,528½	4,908	9	0
Malabar.	Cannanore...	78	35,094	1,476	13	0
	Tellicherry...	40	15,148	557	9	11
	Kalay...	...	...	...	...	...
	Bodagara	10	3,137	...	...	...
	Kovilkandy	11	6,645	...	...	...
	Calicut	100	49,576	2,451	2	6
	Beypore	13	6,119	226	11	0
	Tannur	...	...	...	...	...
	Ponany	...	...	...	...	...
	Chowghat	...	...	...	...	...
	Cochin	186	44,981	4,543	5	3
	Total...	438	1,60,700	9,255	9	8

N.—(*Continued.*)

District for the official year 1867-68.—(Continued.)

Foreign					Country or Native				
Vessels.	Tonnage.	Dues.			Vessels.	Tonnage.	Dues.		
		RS.	A.	P.			RS.	A.	P.
1	777	48	9	0	164	9,751	449	0	9
2	152½	...	...	...	408	18,378¾	...	...	...
3	929½	48	9	0	572	28,129¾	449	0	9
...	...	...	...	...	...	...	...	...	...
9	3,616	175	10	0	160	14,895	385	3	6
3	66	...	...	...	32	588	8	0	9
7	2,320	52	15	9	69	3,173	432	2	9
...	...	...	...	...	...	...	...	...	...
...	...	...	...	...	...	...	...	...	...
19	6,002	228	9	9	261	18,656	825	7	0
1	17	...	...	...	933	42,452	...	...	...
...	...	...	...	...	1,591	82,722	...	...	...
...	...	...	...	...	4,424	3,38,584	...	...	...
...	...	...	...	...	686	26,850	...	...	...
1	17	...	...	...	7,634	4,90,608	...	...	...
1	17	1	9	6	373	18,719¾	963	15	7
2	1,724	107	12	0	1,254	28,607	854	9	10
6	2,785	223	4	6	1,135	19,223	584	13	0
...	...	...	...	...	403	5,677	...	...	...
4	3,647	...	...	...	609	14,687	...	...	...
...	...	...	...	...	323	7,832	...	...	...
3	2,309	224	14	0	2,261	73,196	2,648	5	0
...	...	...	...	...	647	23,619	485	12	3
...	...	...	...	...	158	5,843	...	...	...
...	...	...	...	...	543	20,364	...	...	...
...	...	...	...	...	55	2,915	...	...	...
7	2,047	298	1	0	1,449	44,841	2,591	3	9
22	12,512	853	15	6	8,837	2,46,804	7,164	11	10

N.—(*Continued.*)

Particulars of the Trade of the Ports in each

Districts.	Names of Ports.	TOTAL				
		Vessels	Tonnage.	Dues.		
				RS.	A.	P.
South Arcot.	Cuddalore...	177	12,853	758	8	3
	Porto Novo	493	33,364¾	...	...	...
	Total...	670	46,217¾	758	8	3
Tanjore.	Terumalavassal	177	15,688	...	...	...
	Tranquebar	173	20,146	872	13	6
	Nagore	133	16,932	143	6	3
	Negapatam	1,134	1,51,681	4,756	0	4
	Thoputoray	725	21,883	...	...	...
	Muttupettai	654	31,629	...	...	...
	Total...	2,996	2,57,959	5,772	4	1
Madura.	Keelakarry	956	48,163	...	...	...
	Davepatam	1,591	82,722	...	...	...
	Paumben	4,424	3,38,584	...	...	...
	Tondy	686	26,850	...	...	...
	Total...	7,657	4,96,319	...	...	...
Tinnevelly...	Tuticorin	459	57,265¼	5,874	2	1
[illegible]	Cannanore	1,334	65,425	2,439	2	10
	Tellicherry	1,181	37,156	1,365	11	5
	Kalay	403	5,677	...	...	...
	Bodagara	623	21,471	...	...	...
	Kovilkandy	334	14,477	...	...	...
	Calicut	2,364	1,25,081	5,324	5	6
	Beypore	660	29,738	712	7	3
	Tannur	158	5,843	...	...	...
	Ponany	543	20,364	...	...	...
	Chowghat	55	2,915	...	...	...
	Cochin	1,642	91,869	7,432	10	0
	Total...	9,297	4,20,016	17,274	5	0

N.—*(Continued.)*

District for the official year 1867-68.—(Coneinurd.)

Value of						Duty on						Sea Custom Revenue.		
Export.			Import.			Export.			Import.					
RS.	A.	P.	RS.	A.	P.	RS.	A.	P.	RS.	A.	P.	RS.	A.	P.
3,14,832	0	0	30,077	0	0	19,890	6	4	221	14	5	20,112	4	9
4,15,757	0	0	1,51,400	0	0	36,493	13	3	11,701	0	7	48,194	13	10
7,30,589	0	0	1,81,477	0	0	56,384	3	7	11,922	15	0	68,307	2	7
6,87,591	0	0	54,135	0	0	42,743	0	4	3,314	1	3	46,057	1	7
5,07,534	0	0	18,746	0	0	26,719	14	1	1,322	3	9	28,042	1	10
94,995	0	0	6,80,454	0	0	3,415	1	8	35,255	6	6	38,670	8	2
32,45,316	0	0	25,12,946	0	0	1,49,480	7	3	98,763	2	6	2,48,243	9	9
1,18,985	0	0	12,689	0	0	6,572	2	11	587	0	2	7,159	3	1
10,58,939	0	0	1,00,647	0	0	58,433	11	8	4,669	5	7	63,103	1	3
57,13,360	0	0	33,79,617	0	0	2,87,364	5	11	1,43,911	3	9	4,31,275	9	8
2,46,998	14	4	6,71,311	12	8	4,468	9	8	17,187	0	10	21,655	10	6
41,492	4	0	2,74,265	15	2	687	9	7	917	15	9	1,605	9	4
2,58,958	15	0	2,43,550	1	10	294	12	3	1,336	4	8	1,631	0	11
18,553	6	0	2,41,767	6	10	667	13	9	1,639	8	7	2,307	6	4
5,66,003	7	4	14,30,895	4	6	6,118	13	3	21,080	13	10	27,199	11	1
56,45,697	0	0	13,89,376	0	0	14,740	12	3	56,086	15	7	70,827	11	10
17,35,889	0	0	25,64,433	0	0	2,311	15	3	3,339	5	9	5,651	5	0
19,82,518	0	0	17,11,703	0	0	2,761	9	10	777	11	8	3,539	5	6
82,767	0	0	2,85,107	0	0	...	...	...	...	...	...	...	...	...
15,95,740	0	0	6,63,770	0	0	470	14	10	212	1	2	683	0	0
2,31,248	0	0	2,01,588	0	0	25	12	8	19	10	4	45	7	0
45,84,533	0	0	35,49,197	0	0	7,168	0	0	9,872	7	9	17,040	7	9
6,69,680	0	0	8,82,974	0	0	104	14	10	675	3	5	780	2	3
2,23,845	0	0	49,426	0	0	0	9	3	...	...	...	0	9	3
5,76,337	0	0	1,95,043	0	0	...	...	...	...	...	...	...	...	...
79,741	0	0	20,889	0	0	...	...	...	...	...	...	...	...	...
73,10,289	0	0	50,92,474	0	0	34,690	10	8	20,518	14	8	55,209	9	4
190,72,587	0	0	152,16,604	0	0	47,534	7	4	35,415	6	9	82,949	14	1

N.—*(Continued.)*

Particulars of the Trade of the Ports in each

Districts.	Names of Ports.	BRITISH				
		Vessels.	Tonnage.	Dues.		
				RS.	A.	P.
South Canara.	Mangalore	110	53,126	950	3	3
	Mulki	...	...	...	...	...
	Munjeshwar	...	...	...	...	...
	Kumbla	...	...	...	...	...
	Cassergode	...	...	...	...	...
	Udipi	...	...	...	...	...
	Barkur	...	...	...	...	...
	Kundapur	...	...	...	...	...
	Baidur	...	...	...	...	...
	Naikinkottah	...	...	...	...	...
	Total...	110	53,126	950	3	3
Madras.	Madras	294	2,28,281	30,473	0	0

N.—*(Continued.)*

District for the official year 1867-68.—(Continued.)

Foreign					Country or Native				
Vessels.	Tonnage.	Dues.			Vessels.	Tonnage.	Dues.		
		Rs.	A.	P.			Rs.	A.	P.
414	35,488	1,759	0	7	2,986	57,431	966	7	7
22	367	...	...	...	667	8,909	...	...	...
29	1,718	...	...	...	192	3,928	...	...	...
44	767	...	...	...	343	5,793	...	...	...
48	842	...	...	...	485	6,651	...	...	...
35	841	...	...	...	834	10,465	...	...	...
202	3,679	...	...	...	1,176	17,619	...	...	...
167	11,355	...	...	...	1,135	19,561	...	...	...
...	...	...	...	...	446	4,382	...	...	...
...	...	...	...	...	114	1,125	...	...	...
961	55,057	1,759	0	7	8,378	1,35,864	966	7	7
53	39,250	3,641	0	0	1,009	1,18,817	9,451	0	0

N.—*(Concluded.)*

Particulars of the Trade of the Ports in each

Districts.	Names of Ports.	TOTAL Vessels	TOTAL Tonnage.	TOTAL Dues. RS.	A.	P.
South Canara.	Mangalore	3,510	1,46,045	3,675	11	5
	Mulki	689	9,276	...	...	...
	Manjeshwar	221	5,646	...	...	...
	Kumbla	387	6,560	...	...	...
	Cassergode	533	7,493	...	...	...
	Udipi	869	11,306	...	...	...
	Barkur	1,378	21,298	...	...	...
	Kundapur	1,302	30,916	...	...	...
	Baidur	446	4,382	...	...	...
	Naikinkottah	114	1,125	...	...	...
	Total...	9,449	2,44,047	3,675	11	5
Madras	Madras	1,356	3,89,614	43,566	0	0

N.—*(Concluded.)*

District for the official year 1867-68.—(Continued.)

Value of						Duty on						Sea Custom Revenue.		
Export.			Import.			Export.			Import.					
RS.	A.	P.	RS.	A.	P.	RS.	A.	P.	RS.	A.	P.	RS.	A.	P.
43,31,173	0	0	24,99,154	0	0	18,153	9	6	10,249	5	6	28,402	15	0
2,25,097	0	0	58,778	0	0	49	14	0	...	...	...	49	14	0
1,19,869	0	0	28,498	0	0	1,314	3	7	...	...	...	1,314	3	7
1,24,701	0	0	15,081	0	0	1,080	12	2	1	3	10	1,082	0	0
75,262	0	0	57,810	0	0	...	...	...	97	0	11	97	0	11
2,54,108	0	0	2,13,131	0	0	250	2	11	54	6	10	304	9	9
7,12,637	0	0	1,81,007	0	0	11,301	3	8	194	7	2	11,495	10	10
6,28,938	0	0	1,30,622	0	0	7,382	4	6	317	14	3	7,700	2	9
92,158	0	0	22,159	0	0	...	...	...	...	...	...	...	...	...
34,591	0	0	2,830	0	0	...	...	...	...	...	...	...	...	...
65,98,534	0	0	32,09,070	0	0	39,532	2	4	10,914	6	6	50,446	8	10
182,80,032	0	0	312,35,823	0	0	1,75,475	0	0	11,78,286	0	0	13,53,761	0	0

APPENDIX VI.

A.

Statement shewing the Territorial Revenues of the Madras Presidency, during the years 1864-65 *to* 1866-67.

Revenues and Receipts.	Actual 1864-65.	Actual 1865-66.	Actual 1866-67, (11 months.)
	RS.	RS.	RS.
I.—Land Revenue	418,46,450	430,65,050	365,20,260
II.—Tributes and Contributions from Native States.	34,46,430	34,46,430	31,51,070
III.—Forest	2,98,510	3,65,880	3,29,780
IV.—Abkaree	39,60,540	41,47,180	42,74,520
V.—License Tax	12,81,600	6,64,190	13,450
VI.—Customs	20,38,780	20,85,530	19,35,390
VII.—Salt	103,60,780	101,27,600	104,75,730
IX.—Stamps	26,94,090	30,64,850	28,25,530
X.—Mint	9,47,340	6,83,630	1,59,490
XIII.—Law and Justice	4,34,510	6,06,440	6,64,760
XIV.—Police	56,300	73,260	1,38,290
XV.—Marine	32,460	31,200	24,540
XVI.—Education	45,850	40,480	49,590
XVII.—Interest	90,920	1,07,580	97,340
XVIII.—Miscellaneous	4,37,560	4,04,980	4,56,780
Total, Civil Dept.	679,72,120	689,14,280	611,16,520
Military Department...	14,61,580	12,20,110	9,13,300
Public Works do. ...	4,03,440	16,00,900	25,97,880
Postal do. ...	5,42,290	5,42,690	5,16,650
Telegraph do. ...	1,97,020	2,86,420	2,53,970
Total ...	705,76,450	725,64,400	653,98,320

A.—(*Continued.*)

Statement shewing the Territorial Expenditure of the Madras Presidency, during the years 1864-65 *to* 1866-67.

	Expenditure.	Actuals 1864-65.	Actuals 1865-66.	Actuals 1866-67, (11 months.)
		RS.	RS.	RS.
3	Interest on Service Funds and other Accounts ...	7,89,380	8,72,320	9,40,240
4	Allowances, Refunds, and Drawbacks	1,29,180	3,03,020	2,86,950
5	Land Revenue	38,12,090	39,84,520	37,03,330
6	Forest	2,18,520	2,56,400	2,17,430
7	Abkaree	1,56,830	2,70,420	1,95,670
8	Assessed Taxes	32,510	17,430	......
9	Customs...	1,69,040	1,65,700	1,50,670
10	Salt	14,25,060	14,87,690	14,43,190
12	Stamps	1,08,460	1,24,110	1,20,410
13	Mint	3,12,160	2,06,780	1,53,170
16	Allowances to District and Village Officers ...	3,60,010	3,58,900	3,41,840
17	Administration and Public Departments	12,54,040	12,81,210	11,74,190
18	Law and Justice	36,74,850	39,72,990	39,25,760
19	Police	35,33,590	38,43,420	36,28,530
20	Marine	93,590	2,27,970	2,55,530
21	Education, Science, and Art	7,37,060	7,90,170	7,82,900
22	Ecclesiastical...	4,06,840	3,97,110	3,61,880
23	Medical Services	4,73,050	4,92,850	4,99,830
24	Stationery and Printing..	2,55,900	3,38,200	3,38,080
25	Political Agencies, &c....	66,740	98,820	91,230
26	Allowances and Assignments, &c.	29,98,710	29,72,730	26,35,910
27	Miscellaneous	7,25,030	7,10,180	9,40,650
28	Superannuation, Retired, and Compassionate Allowances	25,72,000	23,89,850	21,23,870
	Total, Civil Dept...	243,04,640	255,62,790	243,11,260
	Military Department ...	210,92,790	222,19,380	200,16,450
	Public Works Department	82,16,300	80,68,900	102,16,780
	Postal do. ...	6,21,640	5,93,850	5,93,580
	Telegraph do. ...	3,15,200	2,91,870	3,75,280
	Total...	545,50,570	567,36,790	555,13,350

B.

Statement shewing the Receipts and Disbursements at the Bank of Madras, on account of Government, during the official year 1867-68.

RECEIPTS.	RS.
Land Revenue	1,30,360
Forest	260
Abkaree	6,700
License Tax	1,01,490
Stamps	1,01,430
Law and Justice	1,84,800
Police	1,97,790
Marine	10,610
Education	28,970
Interest	79,530
Local Loans	12,69,000
Service Funds	13,04,660
Local Funds	2,89,650
Deposits	7,31,210
Advances Recoverable	18,56,830
Revenue Cash Remittances	208,19,370
Public Works Department	1,76,470
Bills drawn	130,10,200
Military Department—Madras	5,82,340
Do. —Bengal	50
Bills drawn on the Secretary of State in Council for India	1,03,280
Madras Railway Company	53,76,280
Madras Irrigation and Canal Company	4,160
Remittances from other Governments	6,67,610
Postal Department	26,220
Electric Telegraph Department	1,19,330
Miscellaneous	59,960
	472,38,560

DISBURSEMENTS.	
Interest on Service Funds and other Accounts	2,95,420
Allowances, Refunds, and Drawbacks	21,790
Land Revenue	2,14,500
Forest	16,300
Assessed Taxes	8,680
Customs	91,170
Salt	2,180
Stamps	34,400
Mint	1,30,740
Administration and Public Departments	12,61,450
Law and Justice	8,26,000
Police	6,48,130
Marine	2,07,570
Education, Science, and Art	4,62,960
Ecclesiastical	1,57,570
Medical Services	3,37,660
Carried forward...	47,16,520

	RS.
Brought forward...	47,16,520
Stationery and Printing ...	3,13,160
Political Agencies and other Foreign Services ...	14,540
Allowances and Assignments under Treaties and Engagements ...	10,46,740
Superannuation, Retired, and Compassionate Allowances. ...	1,23,700
Local Loans under Liquidation ...	10,08,000
Service Funds ...	11,56,590
Local Funds ...	1,51,120
Deposits ...	7,90,520
Advances Recoverable ...	1,84,920
Revenue Cash Remittances ...	33,02,390
Money Order Department ...	3,22,990
Public Works Department ...	12,85,650
Bills discharged ...	15,49,050
Bullion Certificates ...	1,47,930
Military Department—Madras ...	76,03,730
Do. —Bengal ...	730
Do. —Bombay ...	7,300
Bills drawn by the Secretary of State in Council for India. ...	22,80,100
Madras Railway Company ...	46,02,000
Madras Irrigation and Canal Company ...	1,69,700
Great Southern of India Railway ...	1,15,000
Interest on Imperial Loans ...	35,6[illegible],980
Interest on Special Loans for Public Works ...	23,700
Remittances to other Governments ...	118,13,700
Postal Department ...	1,53,500
Electric Telegraph Department ...	70,760
Miscellaneous ...	3,16,280
	468,39,300
Cash Balance on the 31st March 1867 ...	40,57,710
Receipts during the official year 1867-68 ...	472,38,560
Total...	512,96,270
Disbursements during do. ...	468,39,300
Cash Balance on the 31st March 1868 ...	44,56,970

Abstract of Receipts and Disbursements from 1st May 1865 to 31st March 1868.

	RECEIPTS.	DISBURSEMENTS.
	Amount.	Amount.
	RS.	RS.
Official year 1865-66 ...	515,54,660	513,64,240
„ 1866-67 ...	440,04,410	432,68,730
„ 1867-68 ...	472,38,560	468,39,300

APPENDIX VII.

A.

Dr. *Account Current of Receipts and Disbursements of the Travancore State, for the year* 1042 (1866-67.) Cr.

		RS.	RS.			RS.	RS.
1	Balance as per last year's account	....	31,95,471	1	The Devassoms, or Religious Institutions... ...	5,62,428	
2	Land Revenue	16,77,654		2	The Ootooperahs, or Charitable do.	3,02,337	
3	Miscellaneous Revenue	6,26,046		3	The Palace	5,63,026	
4	Customs	3,07,597		4	Huzzur Cutcherry and other Civil Establishments	4,73,998	
5	Arrack and Opium	83,440		5	Judicial Establishment	1,15,895	
6	Tobacco	7,41,122		6	Police Establishment	1,01,052	
7	Pepper	30,503		7	Nair Troops	1,40,115	
8	Salt	8,06,722		8	Elephant and Horse Establishments	65,351	
9	Cardamoms and other goods	82,158		9	Education, Science, and Art	69,127	
10	Timber	41,677		10	Pensions	1,21,614	
11	Interest on Government Securities	47,519		11	Public Works	5,54,750	
12	Arrears of Revenue collected this year	38,381	44,82,819	12	Cost and Charges of goods sold, &c., &c.	3,22,001	
				13	Contingent Charges	1,57,109	
				14	Subsidy to the British Indian Government ...	8,10,374	
						43,59,177	
					Amount part of inefficient balance how charged to account	994	43,60,171
					Balance to be carried to next year's account ...	....	33,18,119
			76,78,290				76,78,290
					Inefficient balance...	1,48,465	

B.

Dr. *Receipts and Disbursements of the Cochin Sircars during the year* 1042 *M. E.* (1866-67.) *Cr.*

RECEIPTS.	Receipts in 1042 M. E. (1866-67) RS.	A.	P.
Amount of land and garden revenue	5,90,243	8	0
Do. of Customs collections	96,537	12	3
Do. of duty on tobacco	10,177	1	5
Do. of duty on pepper	131	4	0
Do. of arrack farm	22,752	0	3
Do. of fees and fines from the Judicial Department	49,595	12	6
Do. of Cranganore tribute	6,857	2	4
Do. of Pollich Ellot, or fees on the renewal of old Deeds	1,167	12	0
Do. sale of salt	1,50,024	6	4
Do. sale of timber	22,427	4	10
Do. sale of dried teak trees in the Chittoor Forests	15,439	11	8
Do. sale of sundry goods	11,462	0	9
Do. sale of extra revenue	41,438	7	0
Do. of revenue arrears of former years now collected	4,132	2	4
Do. of outstanding balance realized from former public servants	174	11	5
Do. of interest on money vested in the British Government loans	57,150	0	0
Total...	10,79,711	1	1
Balance carried forward from previous year...	4,69,387	15	11
Grand Total...	15,49,099	1	0

DISBURSEMENTS.	Disbursements in 1042 M. E. (1866-67.) RS.	A.	P.
Amount of subsidy to the British Government	2,00,000	0	0
Do. of established allowance to His Highness the Rajah and Establishment	1,74,010	0	0
Do. of Devassoms	51,168	1	1
Do. of Oottooperahs and other Charitable Institutions...	44,058	2	4
Do. of pensions	10,155	13	4
Do. of Pattom Meechawarom or Quit-rent	902	2	11
Do. of Tax paid to the British Government for Sircar land situated in the British dominions	4,001	10	9
Do. of Public Servants' wages, Revenue Dept. ...	1,02,750	5	9
Do. of do. Judicial do. ...	39,134	11	0
Do. of do. Police do. ...	14,580	0	0
Do. of Nair Troops' wages	19,575	5	4
Do. of Salt purchase	194	9	5
Do. of Sundry goods	292	8	0
Do. of carriage of salt	7,913	1	6
Do. of Commercial establishment	1,645	8	0
Do. of Hill expenses and establishment	27,308	1	4
Do. of established extra charges	24,957	15	9
Do. of Waga Neki Cheloovoo (a deduction) or sum paid back on some particular lands... ...	4,548	8	1
Do. of Maramut Department	1,60,283	6	1
Do. of Charges extraordinary	1,40,065	2	1
Total...	10,27,545	11	6
Balance to be carried to next year's account...	5,21,553	5	6
Grand Total...	15,49,099	1	0

APPENDIX VIII.

A.

List of Registered Candidates for the Special Test Examination.

Stations.	I. A. Judicial Test, Civil, Higher Grade.	II. A. Judicial Test, Criminal, Higher Grade.	III. A. Revenue Test, General, Higher Grade.	I. B. Judicial Test, Civil, Lower Grade.	II. B. Judicial Test, Criminal, Lower Grade.					
	English.	English.	English.	English.	English.	Telugu.	Tamil.	Malayalum.	Canarese.	Hindustani
Bangalore ...	5	7	1	1	2	2	1	...	...	...
Bellary	5	15	8	...	11	11	...	...	...	1
Calicut	3	6	2	3	8	...	...	10	...	...
Chetterpore ...	4	5	7	1	6	5	...	...	...	...
Chicacole ...	1	1	...	...	1	4	...	...	...	...
Chittoor	3	7	1	3	14	7	10	...	...	...
Coimbatore ...	1	12	7	1	16	...	30	...	...	...
Combaconum ...	2	6	6	7	14	...	12	...	...	...
Cuddalore ...	2	8	9	2	13	...	21	...	...	...
Cuddapah ...	...	3	1	3	18	17	...	...	...	...
Kurnool	...	1	8	5	8	14	...	...	...	...
Madura	6	25	6	3	13	...	11	...	...	...
Madras	32	74	28	5	33	8	26	1	...	...
Mangalore ...	5	8	2	...	1	...	...	...	4	...
Masulipatam ...	4	5	...	1	9	11	...	...	...	...
Negapatam ...	2	5	7	2	9	12	...	...	...	...
Nellore	6	18	7	2	12	21	...	...	...	...
Ootacamund ...	1	4	1	4	5	...	2	...	...	...
Palamcottah ...	10	27	6	4	10	...	16	...	...	...
Rajahmundry ...	6	18	9	1	27	32	...	...	...	...
Salem	11	19	7	5	18	...	13	...	...	...
Secunderabad ...	...	...	...	...	1	...	...	...	...	...
Tanjore	4	14	5	3	11	...	17	...	...	...
Tellicherry ...	...	7	...	...	3	...	...	4	...	...
Trichinopoly ...	2	10	4	3	17	...	7	...	...	...
Trevandrum ...	2	10	...	...	...	...	...	...	...	...
Vizagapatam ...	3	14	12	1	3	11	...	...	...	...
Total ...	120	329	189	58	278	155	166	15	4	1

A.—(*Continued.*)

List of Registered Candidates for the Special Test Examination.

Stations.	III. B. Revenue Test, General, Lower Grade.					IV. Revenue Test, Salt Department.			V. Rev. Test, Sea Customs Dept.	VI. Account Test.
	English.	Telugu.	Tamil.	Malayalum.	Canarese.	English.	Telugu.	Tamil.	English.	English.
Bangalore	...	...	1	...	...	...	...	...	...	...
Bellary	2	6	...	...	...	...	...	...	...	...
Calicut	...	...	...	7	...	...	...	...	2	...
Chetterpore	1	7	...	...	...	...	...	...	...	2
Chicacole	2	2	...	...	...	...	...	...	...	...
Chittoor	3	2	6	...	...	...	...	...	...	...
Coimbatore	5	...	23	...	...	...	...	...	...	1
Combaconum	6	...	14	...	...	...	...	...	...	...
Cuddalore	6	1	15	...	...	1	...	...	...	...
Cuddapah	6	11	...	...	...	...	...	...	...	...
Kurnool	3	14	...	...	...	...	...	...	...	...
Madura	1	...	6	...	...	...	...	...	...	...
Madras	8	5	12	1	...	...	...	...	2	1
Mangalore	...	...	...	...	5	...	...	...	...	...
Masulipatam	2	7	...	...	...	...	2	.	1	...
Negapatam	2	...	11	...	...	1	...	..	1	...
Nellore	2	21	...	...	...	...	...	...	2	...
Ootacamund	3	...	2	...	...	...	...	...	...	...
Palamcottah	1	...	12	...	...	2	...	2	1	...
Rajahmundry	5	30	...	...	...	...	...	...	...	1
Salem	9	...	8	...	...	...	...	...	...	1
Secunderabad	...	...	...	...	...	...	...	...	...	...
Tanjore	1	...	11	...	...	...	...	1	...	...
Tellicherry	...	...	...	2	...	1	...	...	2	...
Trichinopoly	5	...	6	...	...	...	...	...	...	...
Trevandrum	...	...	...	...	...	...	...	...	...	...
Vizagapatam	1	8	...	...	...	...	1	...	...	...
Total ...	74	114	127	10	5	5	3	3	11	6

A.—*(Concluded.)*

List of Registered Candidates for the Special Test Examination.

Stations.	VII. A. Translation Test, Higher Grade.			VII. B. Translation Test, Lower Grade.				VIII. A. Precis Writing, Higher Grade.	VIII. B. Precis Writing, Lower Grade.			
	Telugu.	Tamil.	Canarese.	Telugu.	Tamil.	Malayalum.	Canarese.	English.	Telugu.	Tamil.	Malayalam.	Canarese.
Bangalore	...	...	...	1	2	...	4	8	...	1	...	...
Bellary	1	...	...	19	...	...	...	24	6	...	...	...
Calicut	...	...	...	...	1	12	...	12	...	...	10	...
Chetterpore ...	...	...	...	8	...	...	...	10	6	...	...	...
Chicacole	...	...	...	3	...	...	...	1	5	...	...	...
Chittoor	1	...	...	2	6	...	...	10	...	5	...	...
Coimbatore ...	...	...	...	...	18	...	...	18	...	22	...	...
Combaconum ...	...	...	...	...	17	...	...	14	...	12	...	...
Cuddalore	...	...	...	...	18	...	...	14	...	16	...	...
Cuddapah	...	...	...	11	1	...	...	13	10	...	...	...
Kurnool	...	...	...	9	2	...	...	13	13	...	...	...
Madura	...	...	...	...	23	...	...	23	...	8	...	...
Madras	...	...	1	28	42	1	...	99	6	12	...	...
Mangalore... ...	...	...	...	...	...	1	5	6	...	...	...	4
Masulipatam ...	...	...	...	10	1	...	...	12	9	...	...	...
Negapatam ...	...	1	...	...	11	...	...	16	...	1	...	...
Nellore	...	...	...	15	4	...	...	22	19	...	...	...
Ootacamund ...	...	...	...	...	6	...	...	2	...	...	...	...
Palamcottah ...	...	...	...	...	19	...	...	22	...	14	...	...
Rajahmundry ...	...	...	...	16	1	...	...	22	19	...	...	...
Salem	...	...	...	1	22	...	...	35	...	8	...	...
Secunderabad ...	...	...	...	...	...	...	...	1	...	...	...	...
Tanjore	...	1	...	...	9	...	...	18	...	11	...	...
Tellicherry ...	...	...	...	1	...	4	...	6	...	...	5	...
Trichinopoly ...	...	...	...	...	19	...	...	18	...	11	...	...
Trevandrum ...	...	...	...	...	...	1	...	...	...	...	...	...
Vizagapatam ...	1	...	...	17	...	...	...	23	15	...	...	...
Total...	3	2	1	141	212	19	9	467	108	121	15	4

B.

Particulars relating to the Special Test Examination.

Station.	I A. Judicial Test, Civil, Higher Grade.				II A. Judicial Test, Criminal, Higher Grade.				III A. Revenue Test, General, Higher Grade.			
	Number registered.	Number examined.	Number passed.	Number failed.	Number registered.	Number examined.	Number passed.	Number failed.	Number registered.	Number examined.	Number passed.	Number failed.
Bangalore ...	5	2	1	1	7	4	3	1	1	1	1	...
Bellary ...	5	5	5	...	15	7	5	2	8	6	2	4
Calicut... ...	3	2	1	1	6	4	...	4	2	2	1	1
Chetterpore...	4	2	1	1	5	4	3	1	7	6	4	2
Chicacole ...	1	...	...	...	1	...	...	...	...	...	...	...
Chittoor ...	3	2	...	2	7	6	5	1	1	1	1	...
Coimbatore ...	1	1	...	1	12	10	7	3	7	4	1	3
Combaconum .	2	2	...	2	6	5	2	3	6	5	1	4
Cuddalore ...	2	2	1	1	8	5	2	3	9	8	3	5
Cuddapah ...	...	...	...	...	3	3	2	1	1	1	1	...
Kurnool ...	...	...	...	...	1	1	...	1	3	...	...	...
Madura ...	6	3	...	3	25	23	3	20	6	6	1	5
Madras ...	32	28	17	11	74	65	26	39	28	22	6	16
Mangalore ...	5	3	...	3	8	7	2	5	2	2	...	2
Masulipatam .	4	4	4	...	5	5	3	2	...	...	...	...
Negapatam ...	2	2	1	1	5	4	1	3	7	7	...	7
Nellore ...	6	5	1	4	18	16	4	12	7	4	1	3
Ootacamund. .	1	1	...	1	4	3	...	3	1	1	...	1
Palamcottah. .	10	8	2	6	27	20	11	9	6	5	3	2
Rajahmundry	6	4	3	1	18	12	5	7	9	6	5	1
Salem ...	11	8	6	2	19	13	10	3	7	5	4	1
Secunderabad	...	...	...	...	...	...	...	...	...	...	...	...
Tanjore ...	4	4	1	3	14	12	4	8	5	4	...	4
Tellicherry ...	...	...	...	...	7	4	2	2	...	...	...	...
Trichinopoly .	2	2	...	2	10	10	5	5	4	4	1	3
Trevandrum .	2	2	1	1	10	7	3	4	...	...	...	...
Vizagapatam..	3	1	...	1	14	9	1	8	12	10	8	2
Total...	120	93	45	48	329	259	109	150	139	110	44	66

B.—*(Continued.)*

Particulars relating to the Special Test Examination.

Station.	I B. Judicial Test, Civil, Lower Grade.				II B. Judicial Test, Criminal, Lower Grade.				III B. Revenue Test, General, Lower Grade.			
	Number registered.	Number examined.	Number passed.	Number failed.	Number registered.	Number examined.	Number passed.	Number failed.	Number registered.	Number examined.	Number passed.	Number failed.
Bangalore ...	1	1	1	...	5	5	2	3	1	1	1	...
Bellary ...	...	...	...	...	23	20	(*b*) 4	17	8	8	(*c*) 6	5
Calicut ...	3	3	2	1	18	16	(*b*) 9	9	7	6	3	3
Chetterpore...	1	1	1	...	11	11	1	10	8	5	(*c*) 4	2
Chicacole ...	...	...	...	...	5	5	...	5	4	4	...	4
Chittoor ...	3	2	(*a*)3	...	31	30	(*b*)13	18	11	11	6	5
Coimbatore ...	1	1	1	...	46	40	(*b*)12	30	28	25	(*c*)16	10
Combaconum.	7	4	(*a*)6	...	26	22	8	14	20	18	11	7
Cuddalore ...	2	2	2	...	34	29	(*b*) 6	24	22	21	(*c*)13	9
Cuddapah ...	3	3	2	1	30	21	8	13	17	13	9	4
Kurnool ...	5	4	3	1	22	16	3	13	17	13	12	1
Madura ...	3	3	(*a*)5	1	24	21	(*b*) 7	16	7	6	(*c*) 5	3
Madras ...	5	2	(*a*)2	2	68	60	(*b*)33	36	26	23	(*c*)20	9
Mangalore ...	...	...	...	...	5	5	(*b*) 2	5	5	5	2	3
Masulipatam .	1	1	...	1	20	19	(*b*) 9	11	9	9	6	3
Negapatam ...	2	2	1	1	21	18	(*b*) 4	15	13	12	(*c*) 9	4
Nellore ...	2	1	(*a*)2	...	33	31	(*b*)10	24	23	21	(*c*) 8	14
Ootacamund .	4	4	3	1	7	6	(*b*) 2	5	5	4	...	4
Palamcottah..	4	4	(*a*)5	...	26	22	(*b*)11	15	13	7	5	2
Rajahmundry.	1	1	1	...	59	53	20	33	35	28	18	10
Salem	5	4	3	1	31	29	(*b*)12	18	17	15	10	5
Secunderabad.	...	...	...	...	1	1	1	...	...	...	...	...
Tanjore ...	3	3	1	2	28	26	(*b*)13	15	12	10	(*c*) 8	3
Tellicherry ...	...	...	...	...	7	7	2	5	2	2	1	1
Trichinopoly .	3	3	(*a*)4	1	24	19	(*b*) 8	13	11	6	5	1
Trevandrum..	...	...	...	...	...	...	(*b*) 2	...	...	...	...	...
Vizagapatam.	1	...	...	...	14	12	(*b*) 3	11	9	9	4	5
Total...	58	49	48	13	619	544	205	378	330	282	182	117

B.—(*Continued.*)

Particulars relating to the Special Test Examination.

IV. Revenue Test, Salt Department.				V. Revenue Test, Sea Customs Department.				Remarks.
Number registered.	Number examined.	Number passed.	Number failed.	Number registered.	Number examined.	Number passed.	Number failed.	
...	...	...	...	...	...	...	...	
...	...	...	...	...	...	...	...	(b) 1 of these went up for the Higher Grade, but was found qualified only for the Lower Grade. (c) 3 do. do. do.
...	...	...	...	2	...	...	2	(b) 2 do. do. do.
...	...	...	...	...	...	...	...	(c) 1 do. do. do.
...	...	...	...	...	...	...	...	
...	...	...	...	...	...	...	...	(a) 1 do. do. do. (b) 1 do. do. do.
...	...	...	...	...	...	...	...	(b) 2 do. do. do. (c) 1 do. do. do.
...	...	...	...	...	...	...	...	(a) 2 do. do. do.
1	...	...	...	...	...	...	...	(b) 1 do. do. do. (c) 1 do. do. do.
...	...	...	...	...	...	...	...	
...	...	...	...	...	...	...	...	
...	...	...	...	...	...	...	...	(a) 3 do. do. do. (b) 2 do. do. do. (c) 2 do. do. do.
...	...	...	...	2	2	...	2	(a) 2 do. do. do. (b) 9 do. do. do. (c) 6 do. do. do.
...	...	...	...	...	...	...	...	(b) 2 do. do. do.
2	2	2	...	1	1	...	1	(b) 1 do. do. do.
1	1	1	...	1	1	1	...	(b) 1 do. do. do. (c) 1 do. do. do.
...	...	...	...	2	2	1	1	(a) 1 do. do. do. (b) 3 do. do. do. (c) 1 do. do. do.
...	...	...	...	...	...	...	...	(b) 1 do. do. do.
4	4	2	2	1	1	...	1	(a) 1 do. do. do. (b) 4 do. do. do.
...	...	...	...	...	...	...	...	
...	...	...	...	...	...	...	...	(b) 1 do. do. do.
...	...	...	...	...	...	...	...	
1	1	1	...	...	...	...	...	(b) 2 do. do. do. (c) 1 do. do. do.
1	1	...	1	2	2	1	1	
...	...	...	...	...	...	...	...	(a) 2 do. do. do. (b) 2 do. do. do.
...	...	...	...	...	...	...	...	(b) 2 do. do. do.
1	1	1	...	...	...	...	...	(b) 2 do. do. do.
11	10	7	3	11	11	3	8	

B.—*(Continued.)*

Particulars relating to the Special Test Examination.

Station.	VI. Account Test.				VII A. Translation Test, Higher Grade.				VII B. Translation Test, Lower Grade.			
	Number registered.	Number examined.	Number passed.	Number failed.	Number registered.	Number examined.	Number passed.	Number failed.	Number registered.	Number examined.	Number passed.	Number failed.
Bangalore ...	...	...	...	...	...	...	...	...	7	6	5	1
Bellary ...	...	...	...	...	1	1	...	1	19	17	(a)10	8
Calicut ...	...	...	...	...	...	...	...	...	13	12	9	3
Chetterpore...	2	2	...	2	...	...	...	...	8	7	4	3
Chicacole ...	...	...	...	...	...	...	...	...	3	2	1	1
Chittoor ...	...	...	...	...	1	1	1	...	8	7	5	2
Coimbatore ...	1	1	1	...	...	...	...	...	13	12	7	5
Combaconum .	...	...	...	...	...	...	...	...	17	15	10	5
Cuddalore ...	...	...	...	...	...	...	...	...	13	11	5	6
Cuddapah ...	...	...	...	...	...	...	...	...	12	10	4	6
Kurnool ...	...	...	...	...	...	...	...	...	11	9	3	6
Madura ...	...	...	...	...	...	...	...	...	23	19	14	5
Madras ...	1	1	1	...	1	1	1	...	71	67	28	39
Mangalore ...	...	...	...	...	...	...	...	...	6	5	3	2
Masulipatam .	...	...	...	...	...	...	...	...	11	10	8	2
Negapatam...	...	...	...	...	1	1	1	...	11	10	2	8
Nellore ...	...	...	...	...	...	...	...	...	19	18	7	11
Ootacamund ..	...	...	...	...	...	...	...	...	6	5	1	4
Palamcottah .	...	...	...	...	...	...	...	...	19	18	8	10
Rajahmundry.	1	1	1	...	...	...	...	...	17	14	4	10
Salem ...	1	1	...	1	...	...	...	...	23	19	9	10
Secunderabad.	...	...	...	...	...	...	...	...	...	...	...	...
Tanjore ...	...	...	...	...	1	1	1	...	9	8	2	6
Tellicherry ...	...	...	...	...	...	...	...	...	5	4	4	...
Trichinopoly .	...	...	...	..	...	...	...	...	19	17	10	7
Trevandrum ..	...	...	...	...	...	...	...	...	1	1	1	...
Vizagapatam .	..	...	...	...	1	1	...	1	17	15	12	3
Total...	6	6	3	3	6	6	4	2	381	338	176	163

B.—(*Concluded.*)

Particulars relating to the Special Test Examination.

VIII A. PRECIS-WRITING, HIGHER GRADE.				VIII B. PRECIS-WRITING LOWER GRADE.				REMARKS.
Number registered.	Number examined.	Number passed.	Number failed.	Number registered.	Number examined.	Number passed.	Number failed.	
8	7	3	4	1	1	1	...	
14	19	1	18	6	6	6	...	(*a*) 1 of these went up for the Higher Grade, but was found qualified only for the Lower Grade.
12	11	4	7	10	10	10	...	
10	6	4	2	6	6	6	...	
1	1	...	1	5	4	...	4	
10	9	2	7	5	5	3	2	
18	15	10	5	22	21	13	8	
14	12	1	11	12	12	6	6	
14	12	6	6	16	16	11	5	
13	13	2	11	10	7	4	3	
13	12	2	10	13	9	6	3	
28	26	5	21	8	7	5	2	
99	93	35	58	18	15	10	5	
6	6	...	6	4	4	4	...	
12	10	4	6	9	9	5	4	
16	16	3	13	1	1	...	1	
22	21	7	14	19	16	9	7	
2	...	...	...	...	...	...	...	
22	20	3	17	14	9	6	3	
22	18	3	15	19	15	9	6	
35	30	7	23	8	8	3	5	
1	1	...	1	...	...	...	...	
18	13	4	9	11	10	9	1	
6	5	1	4	5	3	3	...	
18	17	3	14	11	8	6	2	
...	...	...	...	...	...	...	...	
23	20	9	11	15	14	8	6	
467	412	119	293	248	216	143	73	

C.

Statement shewing the number of Candidates who registered their names for the number

Station.	Number of registered Candidates.				Number of Candidates examined.			
	Anglo-Vernacular Branch.	English Branch.	Vernacular Branch.	Total.	Anglo-Vernacular Branch.	English Branch.	Vernacular Branch.	Total.
Bangalore	19	20	18	57	17	17	16	50
Bellary	65	9	7	81	64	7	7	78
Chetterpore	27	9	4	40	25	7	4	36
Chicacole	17	1	21	39	17	1	20	38
Cuddapah	59	6	41	106	51	4	36	91
Chittoor	51	17	24	92	46	16	22	84
Cuddalore	69	5	18	92	68	4	16	88
Coimbatore	72	21	41	134	70	20	38	128
Combaconum	37	...	15	52	37	...	15	52
Calicut	38	10	26	74	35	9	25	69
Cannanore	23	4	16	43	22	3	16	41
Cochin	10	8	...	18	10	7	...	17
Kurnool	19	2	13	34	16	2	10	28
Masulipatam	68	14	23	105	59	14	19	92
Madras	360	283	20	663	347	267	18	632
Madura	79	7	57	143	78	7	56	141
Mangalore	28	3	29	60	26	3	27	56
Nellore	40	6	14	60	39	4	13	56
Ootacamund	...	3	...	3	...	3	...	3
Palamcottah	91	6	84	181	85	5	80	170
Penang	...	1	...	1	...	1	...	1
Rajahmundry	137	3	49	189	131	2	48	181
Salem	62	12	41	115	57	10	37	104
Secunderabad	...	5	...	5	...	5	...	5
Singapore	...	1	...	1	...	...	...	...
Tranquebar	39	2	7	48	35	2	7	44
Tanjore	60	13	17	90	56	9	14	79
Trichinopoly	59	8	24	91	55	7	18	80
Trevandrum	16	23	...	39	13	20	...	33
Vizagapatam	84	9	27	120	78	8	25	III
Total ...	1,629	511	636	2,776	1,537	464	587	2,588

C.—*(Concluded.)*

General Test Examination in each district, the number who attended, and the who passed.

Number of Candidates passed.				Remarks.
Anglo-Vernacular Branch.	English Branch.	Vernacular Branch.	Total.	
4	(a)4	5	13	(a) 2 of these went up for the *Anglo-Vernacular Branch,* but have been successful only in *English.*
5	(a)21	(b)1	27	(a) 19 do. do. in English. (b) 1 do. do. in Vernacular.
1	(a)11	...	12	(a) 8 do. do. in English.
...	(a)4	(b)4	8	(a) These do. do. in English. (b) 3 of these do. do. in Vernacular.
10	(a)10	(b)4	24	(a) These do. do. in English. (b) 3 of these do. do. in Vernacular.
13	(a)14	(b)10	37	(a) 7 of these do. do. in English. (b) 2 of these do. do. in Vernacular.
20	(a)6	(b)19	45	(a) 5 of these do. do. in English. (b) 14 of these do. do. in Vernacular.
18	(a)8	(b)26	52	(a) 2 of these do. do. in English. (b) 13 of these do. do. in Vernacular.
9	(a)4	(b)4	17	(a) These do. do. in English. (b) 3 of these do. do. in Vernacular.
10	(a)8	(b)3	21	(a) 5 of these do. do. in English. (b) 2 of these do. do. in Vernacular.
3	2	(b)5	10	(b) 2 of these do. do. in Vernacular.
2	3	...	5	
3	(a)3	2	8	(a) These do. do. in English.
13	(a)20	1	34	(a) 16 of these do. do. in English.
53	(a)149	(b)20	222	(a) 67 of these do. do. in English. (b) 14 of these do. do. in Vernacular.
17	(a)1	(b)29	47	(a) This do. do. in English. (b) 14 of these do. do. in Vernacular.
10	1	(b)13	24	(b) 2 of these do. do. in Vernacular.
12	(a)9	3	24	(a) These do. do. in English.
...	2	...	2	
18	(a)11	(b)21	50	(a) 9 of these do. do. in English. (b) 12 of these do. do. in Vernacular.
...	...	...	...	
15	(a)25	(b)15	55	(a) These do. do. in English. (b) 8 of these do. do. in Vernacular.
17	(a)10	(b)15	42	(a) 3 of these do. do. in English. (b) 7 of these do. do. in Vernacular.
...	3	...	3	
...	...	...	...	
3	(a)2	(b)2	7	(a) These do. do. in English. (b) These do. do. in Vernacular.
15	(a)6	(b)11	32	(a) 4 of these do. do. in English. (b) 5 of these do. do. in Vernacular.
2	(a)5	(b)12	33	(a) 2 of these do. do. in English. (b) 11 of these do. do. in Vernacular.
...	(a)10	...	10	(a) 2 of these do. do. in English.
9	(a)13	(b)5	27	(a) 10 of these do. do. in English. (b) 2 of these do. do. in Vernacular.
289	365	237	891	

D.

Statement of Account in connection with the Commission during the official year 1866-67.

RECEIPTS.	RS.	A.	P.	RS.	A.	P.	DISBURSEMENTS.	RS.	A.	P.	RS.	A.	P.
To amount of fees collected from Candidates for the Special Test Examination held in Aug. 1866	7,686	0	0				Salary of Secretary	2,700	0	0			
							Cost of Office Establishment	2,236	11	5			
							Office Contingencies	623	2	11			
											5,559	14	4
To do. collected from Candidates for the General Test Examination held in February 1867..	13,575	0	0				To the undermentioned stipends of Examiners connected with the Special Test Examination held in August 1866, as sanctioned in Proceedings of Government, Educational Department, of 21st December 1866, No. 381 of 18th February 1867, No. 45 :—						
							One Examiner in Kindersley's Law of Evidence, Goldsmith's Equity, Code of Civil Procedure, Higher and Lower Grades	1,350	0	0			
							One do. in Norton's Law of Evidence and Code of Criminal Procedure, Higher and Lower Grades	1,800	0	0			
							One do. in Mayne's Penal Code, Indian Penal Code, Law of Contracts, Law of Torts, and Civil Rules of Practice, Higher and Lower Grades	1,750	0	0			
							One do. Criminal Rules of Practice, Higher and Lower Grades, Hindu Law, and Mahomedan Law...	900	0	0			
							One do. in Taluq and Village Accounts, Higher and Lower Grades, Stamp Law, Stamp Rules, Salt Manual, Budget Manual, and Book-keeping	550	0	0			
							One do. in Precis-Writing, Higher and Lower Grades, Limitation Act, and Revenue Regulations and Acts, Higher and Lower Grades	800	0	0			
							One do. in Circular Orders, Board of Revenue, Higher and Lower Grades, and Salt Law.	850	0	0			
							One do. in Law relating to Sea Customs and Sea Customs Manual...	50	0	0			
							One do. in Telugu	300	0	0			
							One do. in Tamil	400	0	0			
							One do. in Malayalum	120	0	0			
							One do. in Canarese	120	0	0			
											8,490	0	0
							To Contingent charges incurred in connection with the above Examination in the purchase of Stationery, &c., as sanctioned in Proceedings of Government, Educational Department, of 5th December 1866, No. 363	1,305	15	1			
											1,305	15	1
							To Contingent charges incurred in connection with the General Test Examination, held in February 1867, sanctioned in Proceedings of Government, Educational Department, of 29th March and 29th May 1867, Nos. 100 and 176	2,583	0	7			
											2,583	0	7
Total ...				21,261	0	0	Total ...				17,938	14	0

APPENDIX IX.

A.

MEDICAL.

Table shewing the number of Vaccinations performed during the official year 1867-68.

	1866-67.				1867-68.				Increase.	Decrease.
	Number Vaccinated.	Successful.	Failures.	Ratio per 1,000 of failures.	Number Vaccinated.	Successful.	Failures.	Ratio per 1,000 of failures.		
Eleven Vaccine Circles	1,68,783	1,48,560	20,223	119·8	2,12,115	1,92,309	19,806	93·3	43,332	......
Vaccine Depôt	5,661	5,117	544	96·09	5,076	4,785	291	57·3	......	585
Three Military Cantonments	10,050	8,334	1,716	170·7	7,446	6,067	1,379	185·2	......	2,604
Divisions and Forces	12,062	9,376	2,686	222·6	14,636	11,847	2,789	190·5	2,574	......
Volunteer Vaccinators	539	516	23	42·6	259	249	10	38·6	......	280
Zemindaries...	15,619	14,529	1,090	69·7	24,928	22,700	2,228	89·3	9,309	......
Railway	322	197	125	388·1	340	268	72	211·7	18	......
Civil Dispensaries	1,950	1,660	290	148·7	4,372	3,865	507	115·9	2,422	......
Municipalities	1,398	1,183	215	153·8	5,410	4,484	926	171·1	4,012	......
Total ...	2,16,384	1,89,472	26,912	124·3	2,74,582	2,46,574	28,008	102·002	61,667	3,469
								Net Increase...	58,198	

A.

PRESIDENCY MUNICIPALITY.

Statement shewing the details of Income and Expenditure of the

District.	Municipality.	Income. Rate on Houses, Buildings, and Lands.			Income. Tax on Arts, Trades, and Professions.		
		RS.	A.	P.	RS.	A.	P.
Bellary	Adoni ... ... about	3,200	0	0	...	...	...
	Bellary	10,027	0	4	...	...	...
Coimbatore ...	Coimbatore	6,104	7	4	...	...	...
	Coonoor	2,064	11	8	1,033	9	0
	Ootacamund	12,622	1	10	3,841	0	0
Cuddapah ...	Cuddapah	5,689	15	0	5,629	0	0
Ganjam	Berhampore	1,601	14	10	2,443	0	0
	Chicacole	3,045	10	1	...	...	...
Godavery... ...	Cocanada	4,030	13	6	4,670	8	0
	Ellore	2,125	9	1	3,027	0	0
	Rajahmundry ...	2,772	8	11	3,055	0	0
Kistna	Guntoor...	1,652	2	9	4,710	0	0
	Masulipatam... ...	3,080	1	5	6,769	15	0
Kurnool	Cumbum	1,062	9	7	1,114	8	0
	Kurnool	6,784	5	9	...	...	...
Madras	Conjeveram	8,623	3	0	3,211	0	0
Madura	Dindigul	700	0	0	1,182	0	0
	Madura	4,000	0	0	10,000	0	0
Malabar	Calicut	14,237	3	0	8,859	8	0
	Cannanore	1,060	4	6	1,343	8	0
	Cochin	4,626	5	5	3,010	8	0
	Paulghat	3,143	4	9	1,709	6	0
	Tellicherry	1,750	3	0	1,590	0	0
Nellore	Nellore	4,608	11	7	3,730	3	4
North Arcot ...	Vellore	...	...	...	...	...	...
	Wallajahpett... ...	1,133	8	9	3,649	8	0
Salem	Salem	11,759	5	1	6,932	0	0
South Arcot ...	Cuddalore	6,866	6	1	5,494	0	0
South Canara ...	Mangalore	6,198	0	3	4,273	9	0
Tanjore	Combaconum ...	5,912	0	7	12,388	0	0
	Mayaveram	3,871	7	6	4,508	0	0
	Munnargoody ...	...	...	...	6,428	9	4
	Negapatam	9,172	12	5	13,987	0	0
	Tanjore	6,657	14	0	20,821	10	4
Tinnevelly ...	Palamcottah	...	...	...	...	...	...
	Tinnevelly	...	...	...	...	...	...
	Tuticorin	3,130	5	2	2,177	8	0
Trichinopoly ...	Trichinopoly	7,689	12	10	7,791	0	0
Vizagapatam ...	Bimlipatam	...	...	...	2,213	9	0
	Vizagapatam... ...	...	...	...	9,903	0	0
	Vizianagram	618	7	0	2,075	6	0
	Total...	1,71,623	3	0	1,73,572	5	0

A.—(*Continued.*)

various Municipalities in the Districts of the Madras Presidency.

INCOME.											
Tolls.			Tax on Vehicles and Animals.			Registration of Carts.			Miscellaneous Receipts.		
RS.	A.	P.	RS.	A.	P.	RS.	A.	P.	RS.	A.	P.
800	0	0	944	0	0	400	0	0	1,005	0	0
4,133	5	0	7,161	14	8	774	8	0	1,382	11	3
10,146	7	0	1,315	8	0	611	0	0	2,215	11	5
1,728	6	9	659	12	0	55	0	0	744	3	0
3,741	10	9	1,896	8	0	329	6	0	398	2	6
8,117	7	6	1,335	8	0	558	0	0	1,487	1	4
5,500	0	0	914	0	0	509	0	0	115	9	0
2,120	0	0	427	12	0	260	0	0	542	12	6
1,954	0	0	328	0	0	...	...	...	3,229	2	7
3,000	0	0	714	12	0	418	0	0	87	10	6
1,610	0	0	322	0	0	160	0	0	405	9	8
6,400	0	0	1,119	4	0	631	0	0	1,756	14	7
4,517	11	6	1,149	0	0	202	8	0	1,215	5	7
1,558	13	6	467	12	0	280	0	0	182	13	6
8,909	10	2	2,065	4	0	460	0	0	2,941	13	7
...	...	...	1,447	0	0	485	4	0	289	5	6
...	...	...	1,000	0	0	250	0	0	...	...	...
20,000	0	0	1,000	0	0	900	0	0	100	0	0
...	...	...	906	0	0	397	8	0	439	0	3
...	...	...	2,200	0	0	142	8	0	81	8	0
...	...	...	93	8	0	39	8	0	70	0	0
5,211	10	8	...	...	...	...	...	...	197	0	9
...	...	...	238	0	0	8	0	0	150	0	3
2,560	2	8	1,531	8	0	699	0	0	803	15	5
3,223	13	6	271	0	0	494	0	0	23	12	0
5,225	3	8	15	8	0	421	8	6	73	11	1
8,755	12	6	1,936	8	0	670	12	0	2,513	6	5
9,489	9	6	3,355	12	0	852	12	0	1,043	4	3
680	15	6	...	...	...	193	12	0	1,198	14	3
13,346	2	6	1,207	4	0	561	0	0	3,809	11	5
...	...	...	569	12	0	188	0	0	624	2	4
8,153	12	0	...	...	...	...	...	...	847	13	1
9,857	6	9	1,956	0	0	702	4	0	7,844	4	5
13,501	0	4	3,030	8	0	549	4	0	7,486	13	7
10,579	14	10	...	...	...	...	...	...	318	15	8
16,669	4	0	...	...	...	...	...	...	255	15	7
5,871	8	0	...	...	...	253	0	0	19	2	0
20,702	8	6	6,150	8	0	1,587	0	0	2,602	9	1
...	...	...	308	8	0	5,940	9	3	115	9	0
9,242	2	10	2,522	0	0	159	0	0	1,770	1	5
4,226	7	9	2,392	0	0	...	...	...	113	11	1
2,31,534	15	8	52,952	2	8	21,142	15	9	50,503	3	10

A.—*(Continued.)*

Statement shewing the details of Income and Expenditure of the various

District.	Municipality.	Income.								
		Government Contribution.			Balance from last year.			Total.		
		RS.	A.	P.	RS.	A.	P.	RS.	A.	P.
Bellary ...	Adoni, about	1,587	4	0	2,871	11	6	10,807	15	6
	Bellary ...	3,609	0	0	1,735	4	10	28,823	12	1
Coimbatore	Coimbatore..	6,450	7	7	3,033	11	7	29,877	4	11
	Coonoor ...	74	3	6	1,008	3	4	7,368	1	3
	Ootacamund.	5,188	2	4	2,886	14	8	30,903	14	1
Cuddapah	Cuddapah ...	7,062	8	0	1,840	4	6	31,719	12	4
Ganjam ...	Berhampore.	1,646	8	0	......			12,729	15	10
	Chicacole ...	911	12	0	270	1	5	7,578	0	0
Godavery ...	Cocanada ...	3,658	8	6	2,981	10	6	20,852	11	1
	Ellore ...	1,360	0	0	1,864	8	1	12,597	7	8
	Rajahmundry	2,000	0	0	416	12	6	10,741	15	1
Kistna ...	Guntoor ...	1,813	10	10	6,412	5	4	24,495	5	6
	Masulipatam	4,396	14	2	1,124	15	4	22,456	7	0
Kurnool ...	Cumbum ...	1,518	14	5	1,540	4	8	7,725	11	8
	Kurnool ...	3,732	1	5	7,488	13	4	32,382	0	3
Madras ...	Conjeveram .	810	13	0	...	...	...	14,866	9	6
Madura ...	Dindigul ...	744	0	0	...	...	...	3,876	0	0
	Madura ...	11,540	0	0	...	...	...	47,540	0	0
Malabar ...	Calicut ...	8,378	2	6	2,700	5	1	35,917	10	10
	Cannanore...	2,075	0	0	...	...	...	6,902	12	6
	Cochin ...	1,375	6	1	1,485	7	6	10,700	11	0
	Paulghat ...	555	2	4	530	10	8	11,347	3	2
	Tellicherry...	...	...	...	1,202	4	3	4,938	7	6
Nellore ...	Nellore ...	5,747	4	1	5,432	13	1	25,113	10	2
North Arcot	Vellore ...	482	10	2	...	...	...	4,495	3	8
	Wallajahpett	1,935	0	0	1	14	0	12,455	14	0
Salem ...	Salem ...	5,704	15	1	1,134	8	10	39,407	3	11
South Arcot	Cuddalore ...	4,000	0	0	1,458	4	4	32,560	0	2
South Canara.	Mangalore ...	1,574	5	4	432	5	10	14,551	14	2
Tanjore ...	Combaconum	4,766	8	1	7,083	14	4	49,074	8	11
	Mayaveram .	3,544	11	7	1,433	4	10	14,739	6	3
	Munnargoody	4,745	1	7	2,999	9	9	23,174	13	9
	Negapatam .	8,044	12	7	905	14	9	52,470	6	11
	Tanjore ...	12,251	12	5	6,844	5	10	71,143	4	6
Tinnevelly	Palamcottah	2,812	8	0	2,276	9	9	15,988	0	3
	Tinnevelly .	3,750	0	0	4,008	8	11	24,683	12	6
	Tuticorin ...	3,024	14	7	183	13	11	14,660	3	8
Trichinopoly	Trichinopoly	11,244	12	4	5,594	15	1	63,363	1	10
Vizagapatam	Bimlipatam .	2,910	0	0	798	0	8	12,286	3	11
	Vizagapatam	8,036	0	0	1,935	7	5	33,567	11	8
	Vizianagram.	3,281	0	0	1,554	2	4	14,261	2	2
	Total...	1,58,344	10	6	85,472	14	9	9,45,146	7	2

A.—*(Continued.)*

Municipalities in the Districts of the Madras Presidency.—(Continued.)

Expenditure.											
New Works, &c.			Repairs.			Conservancy.			Police.		
RS.	A.	P.	RS.	A.	P.	RS.	A.	P.	RS.	A.	P.
500	0	0	1,000	0	0	3,120	0	0	1,877	1	6
...	...	...	1,884	1	4	7,447	8	8	5,596	8	0
1,353	13	2	5,438	11	1	4,558	8	8	7,236	5	1
1,162	4	1	...	...	...	594	2	0	1,133	0	0
6,668	2	9	6,250	13	9	2,714	5	10	9,809	1	8
5,557	7	8	9,774	0	5	2,687	12	9	8,245	12	0
587	12	1	...	...	...	3,152	13	9	4,718	1	4
639	10	9	232	1	3	1,099	14	0	3,619	0	0
6,092	14	8	1,543	10	11	1,931	7	10	5,300	0	0
2,918	3	0	208	8	11	3,734	7	2	3,568	0	0
1,169	7	0	105	15	6	3,773	14	0	3,873	0	0
4,973	9	9	1,867	2	2	4,161	12	10	4,641	4	11
1,145	6	0	102	9	0	3,520	2	8	7,248	11	6
54	5	0	288	1	2	456	3	2	4,689	14	4
5,591	8	3	1,438	1	6	3,526	3	4	6,620	0	0
...	...	...	20	0	6	5,375	4	2	5,401	2	8
...	...	...	...	...	...	...	...	...	1,846	0	0
...	...	...	...	...	...	24,104	0	0	17,456	5	0
4,073	4	5	12,888	9	0	1,764	9	8	10,641	7	8
150	0	0	783	8	8	566	14	0	...	...	...
1,813	12	8	1,112	13	2	1,188	0	4	...	...	...
663	7	0	1,256	6	0	2,060	13	6	2,489	7	3
...	...	...	34	6	0	790	0	0	...	...	...
7,625	0	8	4,631	12	4	3,346	7	7	6,624	0	0
24	2	0	...	...	...	974	4	0	80	8	0
483	7	7	845	15	3	2,199	15	0	3,135	1	0
2,520	2	3	485	11	3	5,648	6	8	8,843	7	6
6,050	6	4	1,559	0	0	8,986	11	10	8,624	0	0
65	15	3	2,468	13	6	958	1	0	6,116	3	8
3,267	4	0	5,300	0	0	8,831	11	10	15,226	8	0
1,287	8	5	2,212	0	4	2,620	0	7	5,946	6	8
590	4	6	8,251	8	4	3,126	8	0	4,479	2	1
16,051	0	7	6,815	6	7	8,853	7	5	11,527	12	0
9,864	7	5	12,803	13	4	7,050	3	0	15,387	12	0
4,102	8	7	2,519	11	7	1,850	3	5	3,674	0	0
10,689	10	5	766	5	7	2,074	6	1	4,847	0	0
7,440	4	1	1,081	9	5	1,157	12	3	2,934	0	0
2,183	2	9	12,309	14	10	21,704	4	8	10,851	8	8
...	...	...	5,066	6	3	896	1	0	3,986	10	8
1,400	4	5	6,186	15	10	10,771	12	7	9,695	8	0
2,872	3	10	1,652	2	11	2,501	9	6	5,036	0	0
1,21,832	13	4	1,21,186	11	8	1,75,880	12	9	2,43,025	11	2

A.—(*Concluded.*)

Statement shewing the details of Income and Expenditure of the various

District.	Municipality.	Expenditure. Establishment.		
		RS.	A.	P.
Bellary	Adoni ... ...about	1,272	0	0
	Bellary	4,347	14	6
Coimbatore	Coimbatore	2,668	13	3
	Coonoor...	1,750	5	11
	Ootacamund	2,685	11	9
Cuddapah	Cuddapah	5,177	11	6
Ganjam	Berhampore	1,763	8	8
	Chicacole	1,412	6	0
Godavery	Cocanada	2,218	4	8
	Ellore	2,168	4	7
	Rajahmundry	1,192	8	5
Kistna	Guntoor	2,270	15	2
	Masulipatam...	3,042	12	0
Kurnool	Cumbum	1,317	10	7
	Kurnool...	2,828	2	9
Madras	Conjeveram	1,774	6	9
Madura	Dindigul	780	0	0
	Madura...	4,599	11	0
Malabar	Calicut	4,144	11	2
	Cannanore	1,900	0	0
	Cochin	1,386	14	4
	Paulghat	1,939	5	4
	Tellicherry	1,998	2	6
Nellore	Nellore	2,772	8	10
North Arcot	Vellore	851	10	10
	Wallajahpett...	3,724	4	10
Salem	Salem	3,859	8	2
South Arcot	Cuddalore	3,566	11	5
South Canara ...	Mangalore	3,195	9	2
Tanjore	Combaconum...	6,158	12	4
	Mayaveram	1,625	4	0
	Munnargoody	1,514	4	6
	Negapatam	5,486	14	9
	Tanjore	8,799	15	1
Tinnevelly	Palamcottah	2,939	11	11
	Tinnevelly	3,272	0	10
	Tuticorin	1,735	14	7
Trichinopoly	Trichinopoly	6,060	9	11
Vizagapatam	Bimlipatam	1,992	3	10
	Vizagapatam	3,708	13	10
	Vizianagram	1,964	11	11
	Total...	1,17,869	15	7

A.—(*Concluded.*)

Municipalities in the Districts of the Madras Presidency.—(Continued.)

EXPENDITURE.								
For purposes other than those specified in Section 25.			Miscellaneous.			Total.		
RS.	A.	P.	RS.	A.	P.	RS.	A.	P.
156	0	0	...	...	...	7,925	1	6
1,429	4	8	...	...	...	20,705	5	2
...	...	...	...	...	...	21,256	3	3
...	...	...	...	...	...	4,639	12	0
...	...	...	1,860	14	10	29,989	2	7
...	...	...	...	...	...	31,442	12	4
...	...	...	...	...	...	10,222	3	10
...	...	...	...	...	...	7,003	0	0
1,624	13	2	1,755	4	4	20,466	7	7
...	...	...	...	...	...	12,597	7	8
225	15	9	48	8	2	10,389	4	10
68	14	6	619	3	1	18,602	14	5
...	...	...	45	2	0	15,104	11	2
...	...	...	...	...	...	6,806	2	3
2,166	10	8	...	...	...	22,170	10	6
...	...	...	1,177	14	2	13,748	12	3
...	...	...	350	0	0	2,976	0	0
...	...	...	...	...	...	46,160	0	0
...	...	...	998	7	6	34,511	1	5
...	...	...	...	...	...	3,400	6	8
527	7	6	...	...	...	6,029	0	0
...	...	...	...	...	...	8,409	7	1
663	1	4	...	...	...	3,485	9	10
656	7	6	...	...	...	25,656	4	11
...	...	...	...	...	...	1,930	8	10
175	0	0	...	...	...	10,563	11	8
3,288	8	6	...	...	...	24,645	12	4
...	...	...	2,400	10	0	31,187	7	7
...	...	...	...	...	...	12,804	10	7
...	...	...	2,283	12	11	41,068	1	1
...	...	...	39	6	0	13,730	10	0
...	...	...	477	2	1	18,438	13	6
...	...	...	...	...	...	48,734	9	4
...	...	...	5,953	15	8	59,860	2	6
890	0	4	...	...	...	15,976	3	10
1,702	11	10	...	...	...	23,552	2	9
...	...	...	...	...	...	14,349	8	4
2,291	1	11	...	...	...	55,400	10	9
...	...	...	126	3	10	12,067	9	7
...	...	...	...	...	...	31,763	6	8
125	7	7	...	...	...	14,152	3	9
15,991	9	3	18,136	8	7	8,13,924	2	4

PLAN of THERMOMETER SHED

SHOWING ARRANGEMENT OF INSTRUMENTS.

ENLARGED VIEW OF BOARD.

4' 5"

f h g c e b a d

The instruments to face due North and to be in a line with the centre of the two side screens.

END VIEW

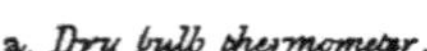

a. *Dry bulb thermometer.*
b. *Wet bulb do.*
c. *Maximum dry bulb.*
d. *Minimum dry bulb.*
e. *Minimum wet bulb.*
f. *Minimum grass thermometer*
g. *Solar black bulb in vacuo*
h. *Solar black bulb freely exposed.*

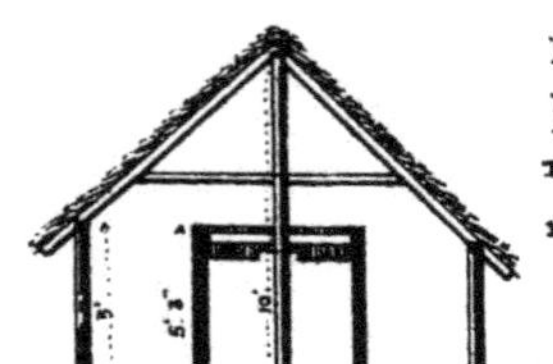

k. *Ozonometer cage, five feet from ground.*
l. *Rain gauge.*
m. *Turnstile.*
n. *Lampshelf 4' 3" from ground*
f g h *Thermometer stand showing positions of thermometers* f g h *when exposed for use.*

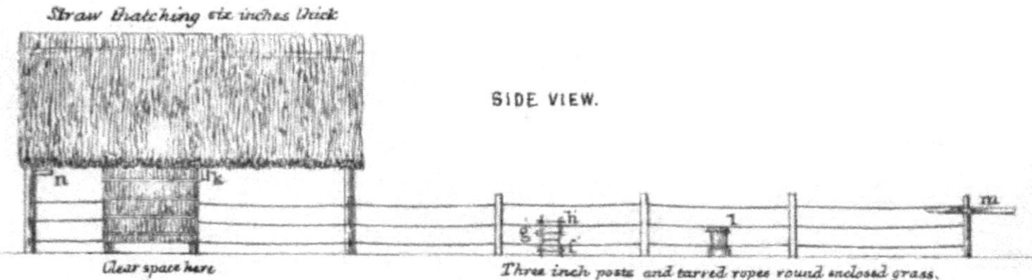

PLAN.

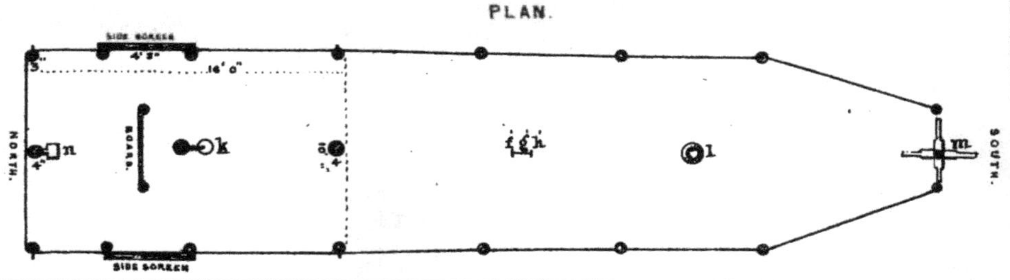

DRAWN BY J SUARES AND T.THAGAROYARAJOO AND LITH BY R.BALDREY. GOVT LITH. PRESS P.W.D. FORT St GEORGE. MADRAS 1868.

CPSIA information can be obtained
at www.ICGtesting.com
Printed in the USA
BVHW082045200622
640215BV00001B/187